Praise for *Sudden Rain*

'I enjoyed *Sudden Rain* very much. It is a novel of integrity, written with truth and a clear vision'   ELIZABETH BUCHAN

'In this fiercely beautiful and exhilaratingly intelligent novel, Maritta Wolff anatomizes her characters with such vivid clarity that it's almost impossible to believe that they aren't still driving the streets of Los Angeles . . . a superb reintroduction to Wolff's work'   MARGOT LIVESEY

'A riveting tale of infidelity, love and divorce. Think *The Corrections* meets *Desperate Housewives*'   *Woman & Home*

'An always compelling work in which so much has unusual liveliness and humanity'   *Literary Review*

'A fascinating time-capsule take on living and loving in late Sixties Los Angeles'   *The Daily Express*

'A remarkable book, made poignant by the ironically false hopes throughout'   *Scotland on Sunday*

'The gripping novel charts the impact of divorce and feminism on a group of woman in their 20s, 30s and 40s'   *YOU magazine*

'Romantic discontent on a muggy weekend in 1970s LA'   *FT magazine*

'Here, opening before us, are the lives of people in a particular place during a particular time – California of the early 70s. With these illuminating portraits comes a picture of American life as it inimitably was. Wolff, with her knack for unexpected events and realistic conversations, energetically and splendidly puts these people on the map'   ELIZABETH STROUT

Acclaim for Maritta Wolff

Sudden
Rain

Also by Maritta Wolff

Sudden Rain

Maritta Wolff

POCKET
BOOKS

London · New York · Sydney · Toronto

First published in Great Britain by Simon & Schuster UK Ltd, 2005
This edition published by Pocket Books, 2006
An imprint of Simon & Schuster UK Ltd
A CBS COMPANY

1 3 5 7 9 10 8 6 4 2

Simon & Schuster UK Ltd
Africa House
64–78 Kingsway
London WC2B 6AH

www.simonsays.co.uk

Simon & Schuster Australia
Sydney

A CIP catalogue record for this book is
available from the British Library

ISBN 0 7434 6877 5
EAN 9780743468770

Printed and bound in Great Britain by
Cox & Wyman Ltd, Reading, Berks

CONTENTS

INTRODUCTION

Maritta Wolff, who died at the age of eighty-three on July 1, 2002, has several claims to fame. She was a child prodigy whose remarkable first novel, *Whistle Stop*, was originally written for a class at the University of Michigan and was published, to rave reviews, when she was twenty-two. In spite of this early success she was that rare being: a person in contemporary life who shuns publicity. But her largest and most valid claim is the book you now hold in your hands, *Sudden Rain*, a novel that still, thirty years after she typed the last page, strikes the reader with all the power and pleasure and freshness of great art.

The reason why we have waited three decades for Wolff's last work is in itself a great story. After her early success, she went on to publish five more successful novels. According to her husband, she finished *Sudden Rain*, her seventh novel, in 1972 (her previous novel, *Buttonwood*, had come out in 1962), but when asked by her publisher to promote the book, Wolff refused. She also refused to approach another publisher. Instead she put the manuscript into the refrigerator—someone had told her this was the safest place for documents—where it remained until her death. She never wrote another novel.

Of course we have questions: What kind of refrigerator? Did she keep it in the freezer or the fridge? Did the fridge last thirty years? Why didn't she write another novel? Perhaps some will be answered by biographers (and seized upon by the manufacturers of fridges) but the real question, which is of course unanswerable, is how Wolff came to write such an excellent novel. We do, however, get glimpses in some of her comments. "My one hobby," she wrote, "was developing as far back as I can remember, an inordinate interest in people and anything and everything happening to them." And in an early interview she said that her characters "have a habit of getting their own ideas. . . . They run away and do as they please."

Both of these remarks point to one of the most striking aspects of *Sudden Rain*: the immense vitality of the characters. It is surely no accident that dialogue plays such a prominent part in the novel. Everyone in this book—and the cast is large—is more than ready to speak for her- or himself. And to speak interestingly, appropriately, passionately on a large range of subjects from marine biology to divorce, from ladies' hosiery to racing automobiles, from trying to get a NASA contract to child care.

Sudden Rain is set in Los Angeles in the autumn of 1972 and concerns a group of mostly middle-class women and men, young and middle-aged, each of whom is in some way, to some degree, struggling with the perplexing questions raised by the prevalence of divorce and by the awkward, barely articulated awareness that women may no longer be entirely satisfied by being wives and mothers. The plot is fierce, surprising, entertaining, and full of unexpected developments and difficult encounters. The novel has one of the most amazing endings I have ever read.

But what makes me want to stop strangers in the street and tell them about *Sudden Rain* is none of the above, not its odd history nor its wonderful characters, not its skillful plot nor its stunning denouement (though any of these might be more than enough). What makes me want to ask people to put aside everything to read this book is the sense I have that these artfully made pages are more real than life itself, and that my own singular life is the larger for having read them.

—MARGOT LIVESEY

Sudden
Rain

1

Thursday

PETE AND KILLIAN WERE DIVORCED ON A THURS-day afternoon early in November. It was an unremarkable enough day on the face of it. The freeways, the vital circulatory system that made it all possible, were clear and streaming throughout the urban sprawl. The beaches were overcast, with sunshine in the mountains and upper deserts. The temperature registered seventy-seven degrees at the Civic Center, and there was smog in the basin.

The big court building beneath the common pall of haze generated its own temperature of course and, for that matter, its own peculiar climate. As it happened, Cynny Holman was there that same Thursday afternoon, engaged upon a similar though unrelated matter. While Killian was making her way up through the subterranean parking levels, Cynny was already in the courtroom, one of a number of identical wood-paneled boxes which lined the corridors of the building, floor upon floor.

The court was momentarily quiet except for the surreptitious rustle of a newspaper from somewhere among the spectators. The judge coughed softly and turned his chair on the swivel, tilting it a little in order to rest his back.

"You say he was frequently absent from home for several days at a time?"

Cynny was in the witness chair on his right, her hands folded over her purse. She was feeling more nervous than she had expected and kept her eyes fixed upon the well-shaven face above the black robe, avoiding the rows of spectators below. Most of all, she did not want to look at Janet in her chic black-

and-white dress, seated erect and alert between the lawyers at the counsel table in front of the bench.

"Yes, that's correct," Cynny said. "It was very upsetting to Mrs. Anderson, naturally. And very difficult and embarrassing for her to try to carry on their normal social life. I remember one occasion, my husband and I attended a dinner party at their home and Mr. Anderson simply didn't appear at all. Mrs. Anderson held up dinner as long as she could, she obviously was upset and under great strain. Finally she made some very feeble sort of explanation that she had reached him by phone and he was detained on business, and she served without him. All through dinner she seemed to be trying not to burst into tears."

Someone departed through the doors at the rear, and there was the sudden sound of intermingled voices and footsteps from the corridor outside, a brief thrust of life into the air-conditioned insularity of the courtroom. The doors swung shut again, and the room hushed. Among the rows of spectators (most of whom were pairs of women bound on a similar errand), a woman murmured to her attorney, and the bailiff stared at her warningly.

"And on occasions when he did appear with her at social gatherings, what was Mr. Anderson's behavior toward his wife?" the judge asked, teetering his chair comfortably.

Cynny looked into his plump face and wondered if this man really could have the least possible interest in learning that. It seemed more likely that through the years he had trained himself not to listen to a single word of this, one more dreary recital of the same clichés and half-truths that he must hear repeated every day that he sat on this bench.

"He behaved very badly," she said in her clear, unhurried voice. "It was really terribly embarrassing. Either he would make a point of ignoring Mrs. Anderson in a cruel, obvious way, or he would say the most cutting and unkind things to her in a humorous—well, in the guise of humor but it wasn't in the least funny. His attitude in every way, he seemed to be constantly belittling her."

"Belittling," the judge murmured. "Yes."

Have I said the magic word, Cynny wondered. And within her mind the stolid man on the bench was transformed into an IBM card-sorting machine, chastely draped in a black robe and sifting through punch cards with tremendous speed and efficiency for the right combination of clichés to fit the formula. What could the formula be, three *cruel*s plus two *tears*es, four *humiliating*s, and one *belittle*, all equal to one blow struck before witnesses? All the cards flashing back and forth until finally, triumphantly, the last card fell into the last slot, bingo, decree granted! Cynny studied the handles of her black leather purse to refocus.

"I recall one very typical incident that happened at a cocktail party last summer," she said. "Janet, Mrs. Anderson, was standing with four or five other people, she was telling a story, just something amusing that had happened to her that day. She tells such stories very well, she's very witty and entertaining. Mr. Anderson came up behind her all at once while she was talking, she had no idea that he was there. And he began to—well, to mimic her, a sort of pantomime without any sound, very exaggerated and terribly unkind, waving his hands and tipping his head from side to side, raising and lowering his eyebrows, pretending to be talking very rapidly. Mrs. Anderson finally sensed that something was wrong. She stopped and turned round. Mr. Anderson laughed then in a very sarcastic way and walked off. There were things like that that were very humiliating for her."

Poor Fred, Cynny thought with faint disgust, what a shabby story to repeat to anyone. I like Fred Anderson, I always have. In many ways, he is a much kinder human being than Janet is.

The judge turned back to his desk suddenly, stacking together several papers with an air of finality. "I assume this had a detrimental effect upon Mrs. Anderson's health," he said neutrally. "She cried a great deal and—"

"Oh, yes," Cynny rushed, with the guilty feeling that she had been cued back to her lines. She was nervous no longer, only a little tired now, the beginnings of a headache behind her eyes, and anxious to be done.

"Mrs. Anderson lost a great deal of weight, she was under a doctor's care. I remember one particular occasion when she telephoned me early this fall, it was the night before her son's birthday actually. Both children were arriving from school the next day, and Mr. Anderson hadn't come home. She was worn out and really quite hysterical. It was very late but I reached her doctor finally, and he came over and gave her sedatives so that she was able to sleep. I would say all this had a very detrimental effect upon her health."

"Yes," the judge murmured. And then he added, with a glance at the counsel table, "If there are no questions, you may step down, Mrs. Holman."

"Thank you."

"Thank you, Mrs. Holman."

The uniformed bailiff opened the little swinging gate, and Cynny descended the steps. The younger of Janet's pair of lawyers was on his feet, pulling out the chair for her at the counsel table, and she whispered her thanks, smiling. As she sat down, Janet was just rising in answer to her own summons to the witness stand. The two women exchanged swift looks of commiseration and encouragement. Cynny settled herself in the chair, relieved to be, once more, rejoined with the anonymous aggregate of spectators in the courtroom.

Janet was sworn in and turned expectantly toward the judge, composed and elegant. Cynny listened only long enough to note that Janet was carrying it all off with great style, just the proper mixture of indignation, wry humor, hurt pride, and grief. And then, with a little twinge of distaste, Cynny closed her ears. She sat erect and motionless, hands folded, a small, slim woman in a tweed suit, hatless, smooth, dark hair and a quiet face with traces of humor at the mouth and eyes.

For a time, she watched the court stenographer, a young woman with glasses and elaborately coiffed blond hair, whose fingers flew over her silent little machine. And then her gaze wandered back to the judge in his black robe, seated behind his high desk flanked on either side by the American and California State flags, hanging limp. Had he indeed mastered the trick of listening with one ear so that his mind now roamed over golf scores and stock quotations? Did he long for nothing more complicated at this moment than an Alka-Seltzer and an unhurried trip to the bathroom, or did he ever fall prey to flashes of human curiosity, the nagging desire to cut through all the idiotic verbiage and learn what actually had happened between Fred and Janet or any of the countless other Freds and Janets who appeared before him? How absurd and ridiculous it really was, she thought. Why was it not possible to come here and tell the simple truth of the matter? The simple, unextraordinary truth, that Fred and Janet had—what? She puzzled over it briefly. Had outlived their period of strong sexual attraction, she supposed, as most married couples did, had substituted other shared interests for it, primarily the rearing of their children. But years pass and children grow older. Married people live separate enough lives at best these days, the points of real contact can become fewer and fewer. If people have not developed a strong need for each other somewhere along the line, what is there finally left to hold them together?

And once that point was reached, she thought wryly, it all became a matter of time and opportunity and individual temperament, didn't it? After all, there were always new sexual attractions, and people never outlive their need to feel important, to love and be loved. Either they limped along together, taking out on each other their resentments at their deprivation, or they found opportunities to satisfy their needs elsewhere, through lovers, children, friends. In this case, it was Fred who, a year or so ago, started an affair with a girl from his office who was fifteen years younger than Janet, a divorcée with two young children. And now they were all here today, primarily because Fred had decided that it was worth the property settlement to him to obtain the divorce and marry this girl. And worth a certain extra generosity in the settlement agreement if Janet would refrain from bringing up her name in court. And there it was. No one's fault really, not Fred's, not Janet's, just the way things happened.

Janet's testimony came to an end just then, and she returned to her place at the table. The judge began examining the documents pertaining to the property settlement, and there was a noticeable sharpening of attention throughout the courtroom. At some point he raised a question that brought both sets of lawyers to their feet, and Janet leaned forward, her face strained, reaching out to Cynny's hand beside her, pointed nails digging hard into Cynny's flesh.

And then it was over. Janet's lawyer turned away from the bench, smiling. He lifted Janet from her chair with a hand beneath her elbow, and Cynny too, propelling them both with him to the doors, while the younger member of the firm packed away papers behind them.

Outside, they were engulfed by the noise and confusion of the wide marble corridor, and the lawyer was saying, "There now, that wasn't so bad, was it?"

"You speak for yourself, Ed Hines," Janet said. "It was perfectly ghastly. For a minute there I thought that miserable judge was going to throw out the entire property settlement. I nearly died!"

"Well, I warned you about the judge," the lawyer said genially. "Didn't I tell you that for some reason he's had it in for you girls lately? If your settlement hadn't been nailed down to the last detail, I'd have wrangled a change of calendar, you can be damn sure of that."

"Absolutely ghastly," Janet said again. "Cynny, you were wonderful, darling. The perfect witness."

"She's right, Mrs. Holman," the lawyer said. "You looked damn good. You stayed right to your points, and so did you, Janet. I was proud of you both."

Cynny murmured deprecatingly, her eyes on Janet. She was

talking too rapidly, Cynny thought, her eyes too bright, hands moving too quickly as she fumbled inside her purse.

"Here, have one of mine." The lawyer held out the cigarette package to them both.

"Well, thank God it's over, that's all I can say," Janet was saying. "Are there telephones? I promised Mollie I'd phone her the instant this was finished."

The lawyer held the lighter for each of them in turn. "Look, you girls have phone calls to make, and powder your noses and all that. There is an errand I could do upstairs since I'm here anyway. Suppose I meet you in a half hour or so? Then we'll go back to the Pavilion for a drink before we leave for the airport, all right?"

"Marvelous," Janet said. "You don't have to dash off right this minute, do you, Cynny? Please don't."

"No, of course not," Cynny said.

"Do you have change for the telephones?" The lawyer scooped a handful of coins from his trousers pocket as he spoke.

"My God, at this moment I don't know what I've got," Janet said, picking silver from his palm. "I'm so happy this is over that I could dance a fandango right down the hallway!"

"I told you it would be all right, didn't I? Be good now. See you girls in a few minutes." He moved off toward the bank of elevators.

Cynny reached out to Janet's arm. "The phone booths are down here at the end, love. Right outside the ladies'."

"Good." Janet set off so fast that Cynny hurried to keep up with her. "I must call Joan, too, I promised. I'm sorry, darling. Do you mind waiting?"

"Don't be silly! What about the children?"

"No. They know today is the day, but they'll be off at classes and all that. Anyway, I'd rather wait and phone them both from Palm Springs tonight."

"Much better. Look, don't hurry. I don't mind waiting at all."

"Bless you! I mean that, Cynny. I can't tell you how I appreciate all this. I was about to say I'd do the same for you one day, but obviously that's not exactly what I mean, is it? Thank your stars, darling, you have the last happy marriage left in town."

She closed the sectioned glass door of the telephone booth, and Cynny moved away a few steps, out of the flow of traffic. She stood near the wall and smoked her cigarette, watching the comings and goings along the corridor. Relatively few men had business on this floor of the building, aside from the lawyers with their attaché cases who greeted one another jovially. But there was a ceaseless flow of women, women of all sorts and descriptions. Our one true meeting ground, Cynny thought ruefully, we all come here sooner or later, for the one reason or the other. She watched what was obviously a young Hollywood starlet, chic in an expensive suede pantsuit, gliding by on the arm of her handsome, silver-haired attorney. And just behind her, a woman in an ill-fitting pink dress lugging a dirty-faced infant, a gaggle of small children clinging to her skirts. All kinds of women but with one common denominator.

Just then a tall, florid woman in a tight, dark suit moved past Cynny to stand beside her. The woman was accompanied by a lawyer, a small, balding, youngish man who propped one foot against the end of a wooden bench, balancing a legal tablet on his knee.

"Look," he said to the woman softly, "my advice to you is to agree to this."

"But he's taking my daughter away from me," the woman said in a hoarse voice. "That's what it really amounts to."

Cynny stole a look and saw tears running down her cheeks; she quickly averted her eyes.

The lawyer was silent, frowning as he doodled a web of precise black-penciled squares on his pad.

"I didn't tell you this," the woman said finally. "There was a while last spring when I was drinking pretty heavy and going around to bars and—all that. He'll bring that up against me, won't he?"

"Yes," the lawyer said drily. "I think you'd better be prepared for that."

Cynny could not resist looking once more into the woman's face. The silent tears were running faster now, huge, shining droplets streaking furrows in her heavy makeup.

The lawyer cleared his throat. "It really isn't such a bad arrangement, you know. Your daughter goes to this boarding school up north at his expense, and you share the school holidays. How old is she, nearly fourteen? Well then, in a couple more years she'll be allowed to choose, and by then—"

"By then it will be too late," the woman said in a flat voice.

"Oh, now—" he began.

"No," the woman said. "Anyway, by then they'll have her poisoned against me. Him and that damn holier-than-God sister of his!"

Cynny snuffed out her half-smoked cigarette and walked back to the telephone booths. Janet, looking out through the glass, caught her eye and waved, smiling brightly over the black receiver. Cynny smiled in return and stabbed her finger twice into the air, indicating the door of the women's lavatory. Janet nodded.

Inside the big, barren room, there was a constant gurgle of plumbing and a babble of voices above it. Five or six women were already lined before the long mirror over the washbowls, and Cynny waited her turn. She moved to the mirror at last, setting her purse on the stainless steel shelf. For no particular reason, she turned on the water in one of the white sinks, speckled with pink face powder, and washed her hands, lathering them thoroughly with institutional soap.

The room gradually emptied. Cynny, already regretting the clinging reek of the soap, rinsed her hands a second time and scrubbed at them with squares of harsh brown paper toweling. She retouched her lipstick and then moved off, lighting a cigarette from a pack in her purse.

A final pair of women left the room, and Cynny was suddenly

aware that she had the lavatory to herself. The noise from the corridor was muffled here, and she welcomed the respite. Her headache had now materialized into a small, dull pain behind her eyes. She wished there were some tactful way to avoid having drinks with Janet and her lawyer, but she could not think of one. The final duty of a conscientious witness. It likely would mean that she would be caught in the thick of the going-home freeway traffic, but there it was. Obviously she could not abandon poor Janet until she was safely on her way to the airport.

Then, in the silence of the lavatory, there came the unmistakable sound of someone vomiting. Cynny looked up, startled, and saw what she had failed to notice before, that one out of the row of gray cubicle doors was closed. The sound of retching came again. So much for the sense of privacy and refuge. A new duty now confronted her.

Oh, hell, she said to herself.

Cynny listened, but there was no further sound. She slowly burrowed her cigarette into the sand in the urn beside her, hoping for some last reprieve. None came, and she moved indecisively toward the cubicle. Just outside the closed door, she listened again and heard a faint gagging, to which her own stomach made a queasy response. Then she heard another sound, a strangulated whispering, a dry, smothered sobbing, but the words distinct, "Oh, Pete, I can't! I can't, I can't! Oh, Pete, Pete!"

After that it was still. Cynny waited for several seconds before she said, "Are you all right? Is there anything I can do?"

There was no answer.

"Are you all right?" Cynny asked again, more urgently.

There was only silence.

Then the toilet flushed. The bolt was thrown back with a clatter, and the gray metal door swung open.

The woman who came out from the cubicle was very young, slender in a smart, plain, dark blue pantsuit. A girl, Cynny thought, who at some other time might even be beautiful, with smooth, shining, leaf brown hair hanging below her shoulders and wide, clear eyes of the same warm color. Now she looked green and ill, perspiration glistening in drops over her face.

"I'm sorry, I thought everyone had gone," Killian said. "That must have been disgusting to listen to. My witness gave me a wild new tranquilizer on top of a lot of wine at lunch, and it didn't mix."

She went to the mirror and began to blot at her face with a piece of tissue, her hands shaking.

It came to Cynny with a pang that this girl, whoever she was, was not so many years older than her own daughter. She followed her, reaching out a hand sympathetically to her shoulder. "Why don't you stretch out on that bench for a minute and I'll go fetch your witness, shall I?"

"It's very good of you," Killian said, "but I don't think it's a terribly practical idea. I'm due in court this minute. And my witness is a man."

Her little metal tube of lipstick shot out of her trembling hands, and Cynny bent to retrieve it from the floor.

"Why do all these women bring other women for witnesses? It must be so dull for them," she said as she took the small gold cylinder that Cynny silently held out to her. She turned back to the mirror and went on talking with what struck Cynny as an irritating bravado.

"Anyway, I had to bring this boy. First he was going to be corespondent, and of course he absolutely adored that. Then my mother spoiled everything by insisting that I be the one to get the divorce, and he was so disappointed that I had to promise him he could be my witness. I don't imagine that will be nearly as much fun, though, do you?"

If this were a child of mine, I'd slap her, Cynny thought, and so she could not quite resist.

"Pete?" she said.

"Not Pete, Robbie." Killian was intent upon her lipstick. "Pete's the one I'm divorcing."

Then she went taut and still. She looked up slowly to meet

Cynny's eyes in the mirror. Incredibly, she went still paler, then chalk white, with the pastel lipstick shining upon her mouth like grease.

After a moment, she said harshly, "Leave me alone. I'm all right now. And even if I wasn't, I'd go in there and divorce that son of a bitch if it was the last thing I ever did!"

Cynny opened her mouth to speak again, then thought better of it. She turned away instead and went back into the corridor.

PETE, AT THAT MOMENT, WAS PEACEFULLY ASLEEP, his long frame stretched out on top of a bed in the well-appointed room designated his in his mother's new house in the hills above Bel-Air. Actually, it was Pete's father, Tom Fallon, who was thinking of Killian just then, and of that court building in the smog-enshrouded Civic Center.

Tom had spent all that Thursday in his office in a complex near International Airport. As it happened, it had been a particularly busy day. A short, thickset man with silvery hair cropped above an impatient face, he lunched at his desk, munching on a sandwich provided by his secretary, joyfully immersed in the kind of work that he always found most engrossing and satisfying. But all the same, it was with him throughout the day, continually there at the edge of his consciousness, the stark geometrics of that building, the hive of judicial chambers and hearing rooms it contained, and the errand there upon which Killian was bent.

Sometime past midafternoon, Tom made a final computation, together with a rapid note to himself in his slashing black script. He put down the calculating machine and leaned back in his desk chair, his face keen and concentrating. He mentally sifted through fifty last bits of pertinent data, filing them in his mind. And that was about it, he decided. The presentation was complete. He had everything he would need to answer any and all of the questions that would be fired at him. He had no doubts whatsoever. The conception was brilliant, the gadgetry was good, damn good. It more than met every specification, it would

15

do the job under the required conditions. In addition, it left a wider safety margin than they would have had any right to expect. It simply could not be done better than this.

Tom put the project aside in a mental compartment beyond the reach of any doubts, anxieties, or second thoughts and closed the door on it. He removed the heavy, black-rimmed glasses that he wore for reading and massaged his eyelids. Then, with a sudden unleashing of energy, he bounded up from his chair. Scooping a leather attaché case from the floor, he began to pack it, selecting papers from the littered desktop, stacking and stowing them with swift efficiency. In the midst of his packing, he paused to glance at his watch and reached for the switch of an intercom unit.

"Batesey, I'm all clear, I'll take calls now," he said. "But first ring up my house for me, would you?"

"Right, Mr. Fallon," the feminine voice answered. "Mrs. Fallon has phoned a couple times. I offered to put her through, but she said it wasn't important. I'll get her for you right away."

"Righto."

He continued to pack the attaché case until one of the telephones buzzed softly and he sat down on the end of the desk, lifting the receiver.

"Hello, Nedith?"

"Tom, I've been trying to call you for hours," the faintly aggrieved voice said.

"I had some work to finish. If it was important, you should have let Batesey put you through."

There was total silence.

"Well?" he said. "What is it, what did you want?"

"You're the one who called me, for heaven's sakes! What do you want?"

"Oh, Christ!"

"Well, you'll be home, won't you?" she said. "Or won't you? What time are you leaving?"

"Yes, I'll be home. I have to pack. I have a couple last things to wind up here first." He glanced again at his watch. "Take me five, ten more minutes. I don't know yet exactly when I'm leaving, I still haven't had the confirmation on my flight. Look, is Pete there?"

"That's why I've been calling you," she said, with a thin note of exasperation. "He's been shut up in his room all day long. I don't like it, Tom."

"Yeah. Well, put him on, would you?"

"Why?" she asked flatly.

He hitched about impatiently on the desk corner. "No big deal. I thought I'd ask him to meet me somewhere and we'd have a drink, that's all."

"I thought you said you were ready to leave the office. If you want to have a drink with him, you could just as well do it when you get home, couldn't you?"

"Nedith," Tom said, his face thunderous. "You say he's been shut up in his room all day. I thought it might be good for him to get out and move around and meet me somewhere."

"Well, he may not want to do that," she said dubiously.

"Just put him on the phone, would you, please?"

"All right. Tom? You'll be nice to him, won't you? I think he's terribly upset. You know what today is, don't you?"

He came off the desktop in a bound, rocking on his feet like a boxer. "Nedith, for the love of God! What else have we been talking about for the last two minutes? Yes, I do know what today is!"

"You needn't take my head off. You're not exactly noted for remembering dates that are important to your family these days, are you?"

"Now we're back to last week again. Apparently I'm never going to be allowed to live that down."

"Well, you can't deny it, can you? You did forget Tippy's birthday. Sally was very hurt. She pretended that it didn't matter to her, but it did."

"Oh, Christ! I'm not trying to deny anything. Last week I

forgot that one of my grandchildren was two years old on Tuesday. But I do happen to remember that today my son's wife is in court divorcing him. Nedith, look, I'm in a rush. You can chew me out all you like once I get home. Would you just ask Pete to pick up the phone, please?"

At the other end, the receiver was banged down on a tabletop with an audible crash. Tom waited, sitting down again on the corner of the desk. He riffled through a stack of typed letters in a tray, picked a memo from a spindle, read it, and discarded it in the direction of a wastebasket. Finally he reached out to the gleaming model of a multistage rocket that stood on the desktop, his blunt-fingered hand suddenly delicate and precise.

"Hello, Dad?" The voice in his ear was young and noncommittal.

"Pete," Tom said. "It's good to have you home."

He hesitated, frowning as he turned the rocket a little upon its mountings. "Why, I just had an idea, Pete. I'm knocking off early, I'm flying down to Houston later on today. I thought maybe we could meet somewhere and have a drink. How about it?"

There was a perceptible pause on the other end. "Sure. I guess so. If you'd like."

"I would like," Tom said. "Very much. You don't get home that often anymore. Look, I have to wind up here, and then I'll be in a bit of a rush. Maybe we could meet somewhere halfway. Got any old favorite spot around Santa Monica you'd like to have a drink?"

"No. Anywhere you say, Dad."

Tom absently stroked the little capsule poised upon the top of the rocket booster, his finger moving over it with infinite gentleness. "Okay, how about the Orlatti's on Wilshire?"

"Fine with me."

"Right. I'll finish up here in about ten minutes. Let's say the bar at Orlatti's in twenty minutes, okay?"

For the first time the voice at the other end warmed. "Oh, hey!" Pete said amusedly. "You must be way ahead on speeding tickets this year, Dad. What's the matter with those cops out there on the San Diego Freeway anyway, they losing their touch or what?"

Tom whooped delightedly. "Hell, no, it's me. I'm a reformed character."

"You must be kidding! Better make it Orlatti's in a half hour anyway. I have to shave."

"Right. See you there, Pete."

The voice from the other end altered then, becoming once more guarded and impersonal. "Want me to put Mother back on?"

"No, never mind," Tom said. "I'll see her when we get home."

He slid from the corner of the desk as he put down the phone, walking rapidly around to the chair behind it. For a moment, he gave his complete attention to the attaché case, adding several last papers before he closed it, putting it down upon the thick rug beside him. He reached again for the intercom switch.

"Batesey, I'm in a hell of a rush now. Let's see how fast we can get this show on the road. Are there any other letters I have to sign besides the ones here in the tray? I'll have time for two or three phone calls, use your own judgment. But before we start on those, would you get me Mrs. Christopher over at the store, please?"

"Don't worry, Mr. Fallon, we'll get you out of here in a flash," the feminine voice said. "There's only one other letter, the one to Chemco. It's being typed now, I'll have it in to you in a minute. And I'll get Mrs. Christopher right away."

"Good girl."

Tom cleared another section of desktop with a careless swipe. He donned the reading glasses once more and began on the tray of letters, skimming each one before he added the rapid, illegible scrawl of his signature.

The telephone buzzed softly, and Tom reached for it, flipping off the intercom switch with his other hand, his eyes still fixed upon a letter before him.

"Hello?" a warm, slightly breathless voice said into his ear.

Tom smiled. "Hallie," he said, with a lingering inflection over the word, his voice softened.

"Oh, Mrs. Morgan, how nice, how are you?" the voice said in a delighted rush of words.

"I take it your boss lady is breathing down your neck," Tom said with amusement, scribbling his signature once more and reaching for another typewritten sheet.

"That's right," the voice said with an answering twinkle of humor. "One dozen pair, size ten, Dark Echo."

"Look, Hallie, I'm in a bit of a bind, but I'll be there as soon as I can. I'm just leaving here to have a drink with Pete. He turned up at the house late last night. I don't know what brought him up from San Diego, the divorce hearing today, I assume. I thought we'd have a drink in case he'd like to talk to me. After that I have to stop by the house for a minute to pick up some clean shirts. So I'll be a little late, all right?"

"That's perfectly all right, Mrs. Morgan. Don't worry about it. I'll be in touch with you the minute they come in."

"I thought you could ride out to the airport with me. My flight's at eight-forty, we'll stop for dinner somewhere on the way."

"Yes, I'd be happy to."

Tom scrawled his signature at the bottom of another letter. "So I'll see you in a little while then. Hallie?"

"Yes?"

"I love you, Mrs. C."

"Ah, thank you very much!" the warm, breathless voice said. "I feel exactly the same, you know. Thank you for calling."

Tom put down the phone and reached to the intercom.

"Okay, Batesey. Where the hell's that letter to Chemco? Let's mop it up now. I want to get out of here."

Thirty minutes later, Tom was at the wheel of his dusty blue sports car, off the freeway, and cutting back and forth through the traffic along Wilshire Boulevard. The clouds were low, and in the wan light the architectural forms of the shops and banks, restaurants and bowling alley that lined the street were obscured behind the superstructure of their advertising signs, the gaudy patchwork overlay that floated in the mist on either side. Tom slammed on his brakes, catching a glimpse ahead of rustic brown timbers, an incongruous Swiss chalet perched above the sidewalk with several tall old pine trees clustered behind it. He swung into the left-turn lane, braked a little more, and then, with a snarling roar of power from the engine, shot across before the lines of oncoming traffic and up the precipitous driveway to a head-snapping stop. He was out of the leather bucket seat almost before the brakes engaged. Lifting his hand in brief salute to a uniformed parking attendant, he bounded up the steps to the heavy wooden door.

Inside, the room was dark, and Tom hesitated for an instant until his eyes adjusted and he caught sight of Pete's fair hair gleaming in the subdued blue-green light from behind the bar. He set off along the barstools then with rapid strides.

"Pete! Hey, it's good to see you!"

"How are you, Dad?"

Pete slid from his stool, and they shook hands briefly. He was nearly a head taller than Tom with a big, smooth-muscled body and a contained, intelligent face, deeply suntanned, and surrounded by longish, streaked, dark blond hair.

Tom swung up onto the stool beside him. Smiling, he reached out his hand to Pete's shoulder. "Damn good to see you, kid. Sorry I'm late."

"That's all right. I just got here myself."

"Have you ordered yet?" Tom turned to the hovering bartender. "I'll have Scotch on the rocks, J and B. What'll you have, Pete?"

"A beer, I guess. No, make that Scotch and soda, tall."

Tom pulled a crumpled cigarette package from his jacket pocket. "Christ, I thought I'd never get loose!"

"So you're off to Houston. Got a big deal cooking with NASA?"

Tom laughed. "Any deal with NASA is a big deal these days. We're glad to take anything we can get. This one's in the bag though. Damn it, Pete, I wish you'd come out to the plant this morning. I should have phoned you. You could have taken a look at a couple of the new gadgets we're tinkering with. It's pretty interesting stuff. You'd have gotten a bang out of it."

Pete's eyes were studiously fixed upon a small metal ashtray that he spun in his fingers. "Yeah, I should have done that," he murmured.

Tom glanced at him and then said abruptly, "Well, that's enough shoptalk. So what's new with you, Pete? How's everything down at the waterworks?"

"Great. Just great."

"All the fish well and accounted for?" Tom said lightly. "The forest thriving? Damn, I wish I'd taken up diving myself about ten years ago. I'd really like to see that kelp forest, it must be quite a sight."

"No reason why you can't see it anyway if you'd like to. You're in great shape and a good swimmer. There's not as much of a trick to it as you may think. Come to La Jolla some weekend and I'll take you down."

"Hey! I'd like that."

The bartender put the drinks before them on small, square paper coasters.

"Hold the check, would you?" Tom said. "Well, cheers."

"Cheers."

They touched glasses, and after he drank, Tom snuffed out his cigarette and swung around on the stool, his elbow upon the bar top, fingers locked in front of his chest, eyes fixed on the boy beside him.

Pete shifted and said a little too quickly, "Did you get out to the Rams game Sunday, Dad?"

"No, something came up. I'm sorry I missed it, though. How about you? It was televised in San Diego, wasn't it?"

"Yes, I saw about ten minutes of it. I had a lot of work to get through. For some reason, I've been working my butt off this quarter."

"I don't see how they can run a graduate school on the quarter system," Tom said. "You going back down tonight then, or are you staying in town for a day or two?"

"I'd planned to stay up through the weekend. What I really wanted to do was go out to Malibu for two or three days, but Mother more or less vetoed that. She says the house has been closed up for the winter."

"Damn good idea, why don't you do it? Take you about five minutes to turn on the icebox and all that once you're out there. You might even get some sun, though I doubt it."

"I believe I will. I'll pick up some stuff at the house and go on out later."

"Good deal." Tom swung back to the bar. He took another drink from his glass and then turned it in his hand, his eyes upon it. "Well, Pete," he said, "as of today, I take it you're on your way back to being a single man."

"That's right," Pete said, with no inflection.

Tom rattled ice cubes together vigorously, frowning a little. "I'm damn sorry about this, Pete. I imagine you are, too."

Pete shrugged, the faintest motion of his wide shoulders.

Tom glanced at the boy's even, unsmiling profile in the dim bar light. "All I meant to say, I assume you got married with the same hopes most people do. I'm sorry as hell it went bust for you, that's all."

"Thanks," Pete said. "I knew what you meant. It'll be all right. It's pretty much behind me already."

He smiled suddenly with no particular humor. "I guess this is one we have to chalk up for Mother though. She called it right on the button, didn't she? She said from the beginning that this was how it was going to turn out."

Tom's fingers tightened upon the empty cigarette package, squeezing it into a crumpled ball that, when he dropped it, bounced upon the polished bar top. "With all due respect to your mother," he said drily, "she has been known to be wrong about things, too. Personally, I thought Killian was a wonderful girl."

Pete was silent, staring at the rows of shining bottles before him, his shoulders hunched beneath the thin knit of his sports shirt.

Tom hunted through his pockets for more cigarettes, then abandoned the search and leaned upon his folded arms, his eyes once more on Pete's face.

The bar was beginning to fill up, with a constant swinging of the door at the front, and waitresses in short black skirts moved among the tables. There was an increasing hum of voices and clink of glassware along with the soft music, and blue cigarette smoke drifted in the dim light.

"Pete." Tom's voice was a little wistful over the word.

At last he said, "I don't know what went sour with you kids down there in La Jolla, but that's something that is strictly between you and Killian anyway. You're a pretty mature, level-headed guy, Pete. I thought you knew what you were doing when you married her, you must know what you're doing now, too. I wouldn't think of questioning that. I know it's been a lot rougher for you than you've cared to let on, but—"

Pete stirred upon his stool, and Tom said, "No, let me finish. It may be rough for a while, but one thing is for damn sure in this world. A bad marriage is no asset to a man who's just starting out in life. It may be rough to find it out now, but it's a hell of a lot easier than finding it out a few years from now, when you have children and ties and roots together. Anyway, that's past history, it's only the future that really counts for any of us."

He paused, draining the last whiskey from his glass. "Pete, there are a lot of things that you and I have never talked about. I don't know why we didn't, I wish to hell now we had. Marriage is a damn funny business. I'd give a lot right now to be able to look into your mind and find out what you really think about it. Take—your mother and me, for instance. You probably have your own opinion of what our marriage has been like, and maybe— Or it's not unlikely that—"

Tom floundered and stopped, and beside him Pete's shoulders were tensed and rigid.

"Damn, I know I brought more cigarettes," Tom murmured, beginning another desperate search through his pockets. "The thing is, now you've had a go at it yourself, and it didn't turn out. What I'm trying to say is, don't scrub the whole idea of marriage now, Pete. Hell, I'm no psychiatrist, or sociologist, or cultural anthropologist, or whatever the hell kind of an expert it takes these days to give you the reasons why, but marriage is still the most satisfactory way for a man to live that we've come up with yet. And that goes for the hippie communes and all the other experiments. Except there is an *if* to it, and it's a pretty damn big, important *if. If* you marry the right woman! Maybe this is going to sound corny to you, or square, or whatever you call it, but don't scrub it, keep looking. It's not just raising a family, though that's a pretty satisfying thing, but you find the right girl, that in itself is going to be worth more to you than maybe you can even dream at this stage. A warm, loving, happy woman, oh, Christ! You're lucky enough to have that, Pete, it can make all the difference in your life. Hell, I'm no good at saying these things, you can get along without it, sure. But take my word for it, once you've found it, you—"

Pete slid from the stool. "Hold it a minute, Dad. There's a cigarette machine over by the door." He was gone.

Tom reached for his glass. He found it empty and looked for the bartender, who was engaged over a tray at the far end of the bar. He turned back then to gaze after Pete, his face still intense with concern.

Pete was standing before the large metal cigarette dispenser groping for coins in his trousers pocket, and the outer door swung open again to admit several men in business suits. A shaft of harsh gray daylight streamed through the doorway, and in that brief illumination, Tom saw the curious white line like a scar across Pete's tanned face. He stared, startled, and then recognized it in a flood of memory.

It had been a long time since he had seen that mark, so long a time that he had imagined it was something Pete had outgrown, a part of a tender recollection of his son as a small boy: pale hair, skinned knees, the clear, earnest eyes of childhood, and on occasion, this curious narrow, white ridge that would appear along the boy's upper lip and down to the corners of his mouth, and as suddenly disappear again. Tom remembered it from a dozen times at once: a small boy holding out a cut foot that dripped blood onto the beach sand; the time Pete had sprained his wrist in the sprawled landing from a leap from the garage roof; the time Tom, relief mixed with his anger, had punished the boy for straying off in the early winter darkness, only to learn later that he had been sent upon an errand by the family maid; times when a small boy's pride struggled against his desire to weep.

And later on, when Pete was grown? Tom rummaged through a fund of recollection. Only a few occasions now: the time Bob Rinkler had borrowed Pete's brand-new surfboard without permission and shamefacedly returned it with a great jagged hole in the nose, and Pete had been shaking with an icy, controlled fury; once after a college swim meet when Pete was staggering with exhaustion; one bad night when Tom and Nedith had quarreled bitterly after a party, assuming Pete to be asleep upstairs only to discover him at the kitchen table, silent and miserable before an untouched sandwich and glass of milk. And now.

Tom abruptly turned away. He listened to the metallic clanking of the cigarette machine through the murmur of voices and the insipid canned music, and studied his hands, clasped and momentarily still.

But what did I say to him that was wrong, Tom asked himself. What did I say? I love this kid!

For an instant, he felt a bereavement as acute as a physical pain, the sense of a yawning space that separated him from his son, one that he was powerless to traverse.

Christ, I should have known better than to try, he told himself. With all the affection in the world on both sides, there is still no way it can be done.

Pete slid back onto the stool beside him. "Here you go, Dad."

"Thanks." Reaching for the cigarettes, Tom stole a glance at Pete's face and found it once more tanned and impassive. The puckered white mark was gone without a trace.

"So you were saying, Dad?"

"No," Tom said. "No more lectures. I mean it, Pete."

"Go ahead," Pete said pleasantly. "Be my guest. Considering the amount of time and money this matrimonial venture of mine has cost you, I assume you feel you're entitled."

"Entitled?" Tom said, the hurt in his voice. "I never felt I was entitled. What the hell would entitle me?"

They sat in silence for a moment until Pete said, "Sorry about that, Dad. I know it isn't true. How do you computer guys say it? Let's dump all this and start a new run, okay?"

Tom, smiling, reached out to his shoulder. "Hell, yes. Let's talk about something else. I don't see you that often anymore."

And then he hesitated. "There is one last thing, Pete. No lecture, I promise you. Just a sort of loose end to all this that I think we should discuss, all right?"

Pete turned to look at him warily. "Of course."

"It's about the financial end of things. In the beginning, Killian's demands were way out of line, obviously. But that's still a long way from no cash settlement or alimony at all. I wondered how you felt about that by now."

"She signed the agreement and it's done," Pete said, his voice colorless. "I don't see what there is to discuss, frankly."

"I know she signed the agreement. I imagine she got a certain amount of pressure from her family, they couldn't have been anxious to have you cross-file. And then you can bet the lawyers were pretty damn hard on her, too. Which it's their business to be in these financial settlements, it's why we hire them. I'm sorry about that, Pete, but I felt I had a responsibility to you. I hated to see you start out in life with a financial liability tied to your neck because of a school-day marriage that lasted, what—eight or nine months. The point is, Killian has no legal claim on you now whatsoever, but I don't see what's to prevent me sending her a little something every month for a while, if you'd like to feel that she is provided for until she has a chance to get herself settled again. It's up to you, Pete."

"No," Pete said quietly. "Leave it the way it is."

Tom glanced at him. "I know your mother had some pretty definite opinions on all this," he said carefully. "That's only natural, I suppose. But I think what it really comes down to is whatever would make you feel the most comfortable in your own mind right now."

"I'm perfectly comfortable," Pete said. "When Killian married me, my income was minimum to zero and she knew it. It's still the same. That would seem to answer the whole question."

"Well, I wasn't thinking about this strictly as a matter of economics," Tom said mildly. "Or even ethically or morally, or however you want to put it. It comes down to a very personal thing. Killian was your wife, you might like to feel that she was looked after for a while, that's all. In case you did, I wanted you to know that, in spite of all the damn lawyers and their signed agreements, I'd be happy to stand behind you."

"I appreciate that, Dad. But Killian can look after herself just great. None of us has to worry about that."

"All right, fine. It's entirely up to you, Pete. So far as I'm concerned, the subject is now closed. Let's have another drink, should we? Hey, bar!"

"I'll stay with this one, Dad."

"Sure? Then just one more here, that's J and B on the rocks."

Out of a momentary awkwardness, Tom hitched about to a more comfortable position on the stool, the flame from his chrome lighter flaring in the dim light. "Damn, it's good to see you, Pete. It seems like it's been a year since we've had a chance to sit down like this and talk together. So tell me, what about that grant for the work in Europe, what did you finally decide about it?"

"Actually, I still haven't decided," Pete said. "It wouldn't interfere with my deal with the Navy, so it's strictly a matter of which direction I want to take now. I'll have to make up my mind about it in the next couple weeks though."

"Well, give yourself some time. You've had other things on your mind just now, obviously."

"No, it's not that. I'm carrying quite a load of work this year, I've been busy as hell. That's one reason I wanted to get away and go up to Malibu this weekend, just poke around on the beach for a couple days and do some thinking about the whole thing."

"Yeah, I know what you mean," Tom said sympathetically. "It's the hardest thing in this world to come by, just a little time to yourself to think about something."

The bartender brought the drink just then, and they were silent for a moment while he wiped off the bar top, collected soaked paper coasters, exchanged Tom's untidy ashtray for a clean one, and departed toward the cash register.

"Cheers," Tom said, saluting with his glass. "You know, Pete, I was thinking just now. I hadn't intended to mention this until you'd made up your mind one way or the other about the European thing. But since you're still mulling over plans, maybe this is something you'd like to bear in mind. You needn't say anything about it to your mother just yet, by the way, it's still strictly in the thinking stage, but I've been considering selling out the business."

Pete turned to stare at him, his face for the first time unguarded in his astonishment. "Dad, you must be kidding!"

"You seem surprised," Tom said cheerfully. "Why should you be? It's done every day."

"Well, it's just that— Well, I can't imagine you, Dad, of all people, without the plant and your work. What would you do with yourself?"

"There are lots of things," Tom said. "I'd like to travel a little, for one. Something besides business trips. All airline terminals and all business offices all over the world look exactly the same, did you know that? What I'd really like is just to take it a little easier, enjoy everyday living a little more. This seems to surprise you. It's reasonable, isn't it? Of course, I'd do consulting jobs, I'd never want to get out of the field entirely. That's not a bad deal either. It's a chance to do the work I like best with less of the overall headaches and red tape, and at the same time pace myself so that I'd have a little more time for some other things."

Pete's face was still incredulous. "I suppose that's true," he said dubiously. "It might work out very well for you."

"Actually, it's something I've been thinking about off and on all this past year. But naturally I'll file it now till you've made up your mind about this European thing and all."

Pete put down his glass very carefully in the center of the paper coaster. "I don't think I exactly follow that," he said quietly. "Whether I go to Europe or not, what's that got to do with you selling the business?"

"Well, Christ," Tom said, snuffing out his cigarette, "you certainly don't think I'd sell out the business while there was the least chance that you'd ever want it!"

Pete's face was rigid. "Dad, I know what you're thinking, but you're wrong. If I've been slow to make up my mind about this European thing, it's only because it's a question of which direction I want to take. Marine biology is my field from here on in. I've known that ever since I was a kid."

"In other words," Tom said shortly, "you still don't want any part of the damn business. Well, that answers my question, doesn't it? I may as well sell it."

"Why?" Pete said, anguish in his voice. "It's yours. It's your life and the work you love and—"

"Yeah," Tom said. "But let's face it, I'm not going to be around forever, am I? I should spend the last good years of my life breaking my back to keep building the business for who? Christ. You tell me!"

"For yourself, the same as always. For the satisfaction you get out of it yourself."

Tom snorted, a sound of impatience and disgust, and hitched about on the stool, facing toward the bar once more.

They sat in a strained and miserable silence until Pete said finally, "I'm sorry, Dad. I thought this was something we'd settled between us, three or four years ago."

Tom swung around again, leaning over his arm, his face earnest and intent. "Pete, think it all over again! You're older now, what, twenty-three? Think about it. This whole field of aerospace, it's a hell of an exciting field, the most exciting. And it's just at the beginning now. The next fifty years, Christ! It's where all the action is going to be! I know they're cutting back on the money now and it looks sour, but that's only a temporary thing. It's the big frontier, the one it's taken us centuries to reach. And you're just the right age for it, Pete, you're just starting out, you could have it all. Think about it!"

Pete shook his head, a slow, rhythmic rolling of the muscles in his neck. "Dad, we've been through all of this a hundred times. It's not for me. I don't have any feeling for it. The gadgets, computers, machines, it's not my bag."

"All right! All right, but that's only part of it," Tom interrupted. "Just listen to me for a minute, Pete. All that's only a springboard. If I could only make you see this! Oh, Christ, what I wouldn't give to be in your shoes today. You're twenty-three years old, you're healthy as a horse, you've got an IQ way up in the genius range. Pete, these moon shots, they're nothing. Another few years, they'll be putting together teams for the Mars shoot, Venus, Christ knows where. Think about it! You could be on the Mars shoot! This background you have now in biology, that could be a great asset to you, coupled with—"

"We all make our own choices, Dad. I don't want to go to Mars. If you could guarantee me, right today, a place on the Mars team ten or however many years from now, I'd turn it down. It doesn't interest me."

Tom stared at him, anger and incredulity mingled in his face. "I just don't understand you," he said softly. "The challenge of this century and the next, the project that is going to involve the best brains of your whole generation, the chance to get off this planet and contribute to the first significant knowledge mankind has ever been able to acquire about the universe we live in, and you tell me that doesn't interest you!"

"Let's put it this way. It doesn't interest me enough."

"Then tell me what does. Spending a lifetime in a rubber suit and a pair of swim fins in order to add one more classification of seashells or cuttlefish or some damn thing to the sum total of human knowledge? Christ's sake, Pete, use your head! That's kids' stuff!"

"Kids' stuff?" Pete's voice was very controlled. "Dad, at least be fair. The sea is a frontier just as much as space. But the ability to live in the sea and utilize its resources is going to have more effect in the long run on the future and perhaps the final fate of mankind than a dozen trips to Mars and Venus and every other planet in the solar system!"

"Balls!" Tom said. "The end result of all your sea exploration is going to be a major increase in underwater mining and oil-drilling projects, that's all. The fishing industry may take a spurt, they'll dredge up a few more archaeological objects for the museums, a couple more men will get rich selling kelp fertilizers, and the Japanese will invent a way to make plankton palatable. If this is what you really want to invest your life and your talents in promoting, fine. But let's be realistic about it and skip all this highly significant 'romance of the deep' crap!"

"And you rocket guys and your romance with space?" Pete said softly. "You know, you're very large on the philosophical aspects of adding to man's knowledge of the universe. Funny how you neglect to mention your missiles and your bombs. Because they're really what makes the mare go, aren't they? They are what keep the appropriations rolling in and the research going that you like to boast about, and the whole enchilada! The space race! Underneath all the romance, it's a dirty business you have there. It's worse than that, because by the time you space heroes are done with it, the sea may be the last refuge for life left on this planet. That is, if you haven't turned it into a cesspool by then, or there's any planet left at all."

"You sound like one of those wild-eyed kids at an ecology rally. All right, if this all worries you so much, get out there and fight for what you believe in like a man. Don't stay on the sidelines and bellyache, get the hell into the field yourself and take a hand in what happens and the uses the research is put to."

"Thanks all the same," Pete said. "It's a little late for that. Your mare is already a dying horse. You don't seem to realize that. There'll be all the fighting ahead that I can handle, trying to keep any more pollution and weapons out of the sea than are already there. I'll stay where I am."

"You do that," Tom said. "But when the time comes that you regret it, just remember I did my damndest to talk you out of it."

"I will," Pete said. "Be sure of it!"

Tom downed the last of his drink and dug into a trousers pocket as he slid from the stool. "Let's shove," he said, his voice shaken. "I have a plane to catch."

He left the money on the bar top and strode to the door with Pete behind him. They came out abruptly into waning daylight and the cool, damp air. "A Ford convertible, 'sixty-eight," Tom said shortly to the attendant. "And a blue Corvette."

The attendant sped away, and Tom and Pete waited silently together at the bottom of the steps. Pete stared fixedly at building fronts on the far side of the street, and Tom rocked upon his toes impatiently, his face brooding.

A moment later the attendant drove a shabby red convertible into the driveway and stopped.

"Here you go, sir."

"That's his, mine's the 'Vette," Tom said. "Hurry it up, would you? I'll take care of you for them both."

"Thanks for the drink, Dad. See you back at the house."

"Right."

He watched Pete go, walking unhurriedly around the back of the car to the driver's side. All of Tom's anger and frustration flamed suddenly like a white-hot magnesium flare, then slowly died. By the time Pete nosed the car out into the traffic, Tom felt only a grieving tenderness.

Poor damn fool kid, he was thinking. He is so wrong, but how can you make him see it? You can't get to him, it's like talking to a wall. And he's so damn keen, so solid for what he believes. He's great, he really is. He's really one hell of a guy!

TOM ARRIVED HOME FIRST, SWINGING THE BLUE sports car into the driveway at the side of a low, sprawling, stone and stucco house set amid a contrived undergrowth of tropical planting. He brought the car to a stop before the front entrance, climbed out, and strode up a path of smooth pebbles set in concrete winding between lava rock boulders, oversize tree fern, and towering Hawaiian ginger plants. At the door with his key ready, he discovered that the big brass doorknob turned in his hand. Inside, it was cool and quiet, a large foyer with a polished slate floor and ornately carved wooden divider panels at the back. There were more of the large plants massed in outsize pots, a little too green and perfectly pruned to appear real, and on a low pedestal among them a tall, slim Chinese bronze cunningly lighted from the base. Tom crossed the foyer, bearing to the left into a thickly carpeted corridor that led toward the rear of the house. The heavy front door closed after him.

"Pete? Is that you, darling?" a voice called out from somewhere.

"It's me, Nedith."

Tom strode on without pausing, entering a bedroom that opened from the hallway. It was a huge room bearing the unmistakable stamp of a decorator's penchant for matching everything, sparsely furnished and without visible sign of human occupancy. The wide expanse of empty floor was covered by thick gold carpeting; twin beds were draped with woven, fringed, blue and gold spreads, and flanked by lamps with towering cylindrical shades. At the other end of the room draperies in a lighter shade of gold were pulled open along a wall of glass that looked onto a small patio lined with more of the lush planting, and beyond that an enormous swimming pool. Without a glance in any direction, Tom crossed the bedroom into a smaller dressing room, reaching out to a light switch beside the door.

"Tom, where is Pete? Tom?"

"I'm in here, Nedith."

She came to a halt in the middle of a sea of gold carpet, a slender woman in a brown-and-white pantsuit, with the trim, quick-moving figure of a young girl. Her hair was bleached a peculiar shade of silvery beige and back-combed about her face, a pretty face with alert, dark eyes and the smooth skin of an expert face-lift.

"Well, is Pete coming back here or what?"

"I think so," Tom answered. "We left at the same time, he'll probably be along in a minute."

"Where were you, for heaven's sakes?"

"The Orlatti's in Santa Monica." There was the sound of a door sliding along a track from the dressing room.

"Then he should be here. Unless he went someplace else. Do you think he was going someplace else?"

"Christ's sake, Nedith, quit fussing!" Tom said irritably. "Look, where's that little suitcase of mine? I keep it here at the end of the closet. Now what the hell's become of it?"

"What? Oh, the bag you use for business trips. Why, it's right where it always is, in the cupboard over the closets with the rest of the luggage. Honestly!"

"Nedith, will you kindly leave that suitcase alone? I like it here where I can get to it in a hurry. I've told you that a hundred times, and every goddamn time you put it way to hell and gone where I have to climb up on a stool and—"

"You needn't take my head off. You're the one who designed the dressing room, aren't you? If you don't like the luggage storage over the closets, why did you have it built that way?"

There was a muttered cursing from the dressing room and the sound of a piece of furniture being dragged across the floor.

Nedith moved about the bedroom restlessly, twitching at a corner fold of one of the bedspreads until the fringe was aligned more precisely upon the carpeting, pausing finally before a long, low chest of drawers.

"Tom, how did Pete seem to you? Do you think he's all right?"

"He's all right."

"Well, I think he's trying to hide it but that he's terribly upset."

"That's only natural, isn't it? He'll get over it."

"Of course this isn't easy for you to understand," Nedith said. "You've never been an emotional person. But Pete's not like you. He can be very calm and casual on the outside, but underneath he feels things very deeply."

"Look, it's natural for him to be upset. I'd be more worried about him if he wasn't."

There was the sound of drawers being pulled out rapidly and slammed shut again in the dressing room.

"It's just like everything else," Nedith said. "You never really take the time to pay attention to things that are right under your nose. Why do you suppose Pete drove up here from La Jolla in the middle of the week if he wasn't terribly upset, for heaven's sakes!"

Tom appeared suddenly at the dressing room door, a leather shaving kit in his hands. "Nedith, for the love of God! I never said he wasn't upset. I'm sorry about it and you're sorry about it, but what the hell do you propose that we do? He's not exactly a child anymore. Divorces upset people! Besides, you're the one who's always said that he wasn't in love with Killian in the first place. You can't have it both ways, can you?"

"Don't even mention that miserable little bitch to me! Of course love had nothing to do with it. She simply moved into the apartment with him down there in La Jolla and finally talked him into marrying her. Disgusting little hippie! I told you right from the beginning, didn't I, that this was exactly the way it was going to turn out."

"Yeah, you told me."

"Well, you can't deny it, can you? You always took her part, but I told you right from the beginning that she was an absolutely self-centered neurotic conniving little bitch with the morals of a jackrabbit, and that sooner or later she'd come out from under cover and Pete would have to face it that it was money she was after instead of—"

"Nedith." His voice was weary suddenly. "Have a little charity, can't you? She's just a kid. They both are. They made a mistake, it happens every day. Pete seems more bitter about it than I like already. Don't keep harping on all this and make it worse."

"I'm not harping, I—"

She stopped short, and an instant later she was at the dressing room door. "What did Pete say to you? You didn't mention the divorce to him, did you?"

Tom was stuffing rolled pairs of socks into a corner of the overnight case spread open before him on the countertop. "Hell, yes! How could I not mention it to him? It would have been pretty damn unfeeling of me not to, don't you think?"

"Well, what did he say?"

"Actually, not much of anything. He's never been exactly talkative on the subject, you know that."

"He must have said something. You said he felt bitter. What did he say?"

"Oh, Christ! It was just an impression I got. He didn't say anything. I did most of the talking."

She hovered in the doorway, working thin gold bracelets together at her wrist with a sharp metallic tinkle. "Tom, honestly! This was exactly what I was afraid of! I suppose you dragged it all up and probably upset him even more than he already was, and—"

"Nedith, would you kindly be quiet for a minute," Tom said. "I'd like to check over this suitcase and see if I've got what I need. Just give me one minute, and then you can go right on chewing me out about anything you happen to think of."

"Oh, but of course!" she said. "Now it seems I'm not even allowed to speak to you anymore. I phoned you twice at the office, but 'Mr. Fallon isn't taking phone calls unless it's an emergency!' Now you're in the house and out again in ten minutes and off somewhere for days but I'm not allowed to speak to you because you're packing a suitcase."

Tom turned reluctantly away from the bag. "Look, I'm sorry. Batesey should have put you through. I'll see that it never happens again. But I did call you back. What else did you phone about?"

"Well, I've had a rotten day," she said. "Not that I expect you're really that interested."

"What happened?"

"Well, first it was Pete. He's trying to hide it, but I think he's terribly upset and—"

"Yes, I know. You've already told me that."

"You know it was very late when he got in last night and he went straight to bed. I was planning to meet Sally at Saks this morning, we were going from there to Sloane's to look for the divan she needs for Jack's study. Of course I phoned her that with Pete coming home like this and under the circumstances, I didn't feel I ought to leave. Then Pete slept till nearly ten, and he didn't say two words over breakfast and went straight back to his room and closed the door. I waited awhile, and then I got thinking I might just as well meet Sally, for heaven's sakes. She's terribly anxious to order the divan, you know she's having that big party next month. I must have told you about it, it's—"

Tom cleared his throat and glanced meaningfully at his watch.

"Anyway, by the time I phoned her back, she'd already left the house. I tried to reach her at Sloane's, but she wasn't there nor had she been in earlier. It was absolutely maddening. I didn't know whether to drive on in to Sloane's or whether she might have gone to lunch with Sue Reynolds. Sue came in from Dallas for the week, she—"

"Nedith," he said. "I have a plane to catch."

"Well, I know that! Anyway, I knocked on the door finally and asked Pete if he wouldn't like to go out somewhere to lunch, but he said he didn't want any lunch, he'd just had breakfast. I don't know what he was doing in his room, it was absolutely quiet in there, he didn't have the television on or anything. Then I phoned Jean, but she'd already left for her dental appointment. Did I tell you, she's started with Dr. Hogle, she has this—"

"Nedith!"

"Why won't you ever listen to me?" she said, staring at him for an instant, her face baffled and, briefly, wistful. "You wanted to know why I phoned you, didn't you? Well, I'm trying to explain, if you'd take the time to listen to me for just one minute. Anyway, while I was still dithering around the house, I got this phone call. Honestly!"

"What phone call?"

"Shady Glade. It makes me so furious."

"How is your mother?" Tom's attention was straying, and he slid back a panel of mirrored glass that concealed a medicine cabinet, dropping a bottle of aspirin from it into the open suitcase.

"Oh, she's all right. I mean, she's just the same. It was the same thing that has happened before. Apparently, she'd gotten out one of the side doors somehow, but luckily someone found her while she was still on the grounds. But she was definitely trying to run away again. They said she had her purse with her, and then her tooth powder and some photographs and junk in a pillow slip. It's sickening, I can't bear to think of it. Tom, suppose she'd gotten out onto the highway, she could have been struck by a car or anything."

Tom rummaged further through the cabinet shelves and added a bottle of Alka-Seltzer to the suitcase. "So did you go out there then or what?" he asked absently.

"Of course! I had to, that Watson woman who runs the place insisted. It's ridiculous, it isn't as though there were anything I could do. They had her in bed by the time I got there. They're supposed to keep her on tranquilizers anyway, but they'd given her something stronger, a sedative or something. It was just the same old thing, she was crying and completely confused and kept saying she wanted to go home."

"Maybe it would have been better to have left her in the apartment," Tom said mildly. "At least there she had her furniture and familiar things around her."

"Tom, you know that got to be impossible." Her voice was both exasperated and complaining. "Where was I supposed to get someone reliable to look after her. You simply can't find those kind of people anymore. I had to put her into a nursing home, I hadn't any choice."

Tom made a small sound of agreement in his throat and shuffled through the contents of the suitcase.

"There's another box of shirts just in from the laundry if you need them. No, it's the principle of the thing, it makes me absolutely furious. Shady Glade is supposed to be the very best geriatrics place in this whole area, and God knows, they ask enough money. So you'd think they could at least cope, that's what you're paying them for, isn't it? At their prices, you'd think you were at least entitled to a little peace of mind. Instead of that they let her wander off onto the highway, where she could get herself killed. And then because she's crying and upset, they telephone me every five minutes. It's their job to make her happy out there, isn't it? I wouldn't mind if there was anything I could do once I get there. It's a miserable drive besides. Do you realize that even with the freeway it takes over an hour? And today of all days, when Pete was home and—"

"Why didn't you take him along? He could have done the driving at least. It's been a long time since your mother has seen him, she'd have enjoyed that."

"Tom, honestly!" There was a shadow of petulance and irritability upon her face. "That is just what Pete needed today of all days, isn't it, a nice depressing trip out to Shady Glade. You wouldn't know, of course, because you never go out there like I have to, those creepy senile old things in the lounges and corridors, and—" She stopped suddenly, spinning about and out the door. "Ah, there's Pete!"

Once she was gone, Tom added a last item or two to the suitcase before he closed it. He removed his tweed jacket then, dropping it carelessly over the case, and rolled back his shirtsleeves as he moved down the marble countertop. At a washbowl, he turned on faucets cast in the shapes of leaping dolphins and began to splash water vigorously over his face. He was just groping for a towel, when Nedith spun back through the doorway, her eyes grim with anger.

"Tom! Pete's packing things to go to Malibu. He says you told him it wouldn't be any trouble to open the house!"

"Nedith—" Tom began, his face muffled in the folds of the towel.

"Tom, I'm sick and tired of this," she said in a low, furious voice. "Years and years of it, I'm sick and tired! I do all the worrying, I take all the responsibility, and all I ever get from you is this kind of stupid interference that only makes everything a thousand times harder for me. Why do you suppose I told Pete the house was closed for the winter? Because when he's upset like this, it's not good for him to be up there all by himself. But of course you never thought of that, did you, you were too busy thinking about something else!"

Tom lowered the towel. "Nedith, Pete's a grown man. He got divorced today. He's going to be upset whether he's here or in Malibu. Did it ever occur to you that he might want to be by himself for a couple days?"

"If he wants to be by himself, he can do it right here at home. He was alone in his room all day today, I never went near him. But that's different than being all by himself out at that depressing, gloomy old beach house. At least here he's at home, where—"

"Oh, come off it!" Tom said roughly. "What makes you think this place is home to Pete? You never built it till he was away at school. I should think this place seems about as much like home to him as the American Airlines terminal at International Airport. I should think the old beach house in Malibu, where he's spent half his life, is the one place left on earth that seems like home to Pete."

"This place!" she said bitterly. "I know perfectly well by now how little this place means to you. You've made it perfectly clear. If 'this place,' as you call it, isn't a home to Pete, it's because it takes two people to make it one. I've done my best, but it's something I can't do alone."

Tom flung down the towel and began to struggle back into his jacket. "Well, it was your own idea. You nagged the hell out of me to build this house, and now you've got it. It doesn't seem to have done that much for you, either. Why don't you leave Pete be? Let the poor kid go on up to Malibu and have a little peace, for Christ's sake! It'll be good for him."

"How would you know that! You don't know the first thing about Pete. He might as well be a stranger to you. You're not a father to him, you never have been."

"If I'm not," Tom said, "it is because you've built a wall between us it will take me the rest of my life to climb over. If I'm ever lucky enough to get over it at all. I found that out again today. Christ, he'd be out there at the plant with me right now if you hadn't systematically turned him against me ever since he was a baby!"

"So that's it!" Nedith hissed at him, triumphant in her fury. "I might have known! You were so worried about Pete today, you were going to take him out and have a drink with him. Isn't that sweet! You were just looking for a chance to get him off by yourself so you could beat him over the head again about the damn business. You needn't try to deny it. I know you, Tom Fallon! You haven't one ounce of consideration for one other human being in this entire world. You are the most absolutely, completely selfish, self-centered person I ever knew. Well, you may as well give up. You'll never get Pete to quit his career to go into your business. You might just as well face it."

"You are probably right. After a lifetime of him listening to you throw down on me and what I do, you are probably right. And with you to back him up, he'll probably spend the rest of his life, too, doing just what he is now, puttering around in a school somewhere in a backpack and a pair of swim fins. Christ, what a waste!"

"That's right, I do back him up, and I'm proud to admit it. One day you'll see, one day Pete will make a great name for himself in spite of you, because he's a fantastically brilliant boy. He's twice as smart as you ever were, and that really bothers you, doesn't it?"

"At least I'm smart enough to see what apparently has escaped you entirely, Nedith. That an IQ, even one way up in the rafters, is nothing but a potential. By the time I was Pete's age, I was—"

"Oh, spare me that, I've heard it a thousand times! It's a different world today. Pete knows exactly what he's doing, you needn't worry about that. And if he decides to spend the next five years in school, or ten, I intend to stand right behind him."

"I'm sure you will," Tom said. "And you know what else I think? I think you encouraged him right from the beginning in this whole damn fool marine biology thing, too, out of nothing more or less than pure spite."

Nedith laughed. "Oh, that's funny, it really is! Naturally you'd try to blame it on me. Well, it's all your own fault if you want to know, and you may as well face that, too. Where were you all the years Pete was growing up? You know where as well as I do. It was bad enough with Sally, but with Pete is where it's finally come home to roost. You were too busy with other things, you never spent any time with him, he grew up by himself on the beach. You never really paid any attention to him till he was fifteen years old and it finally dawned on you how really bright he was. Then you were all ready to start making an engineer out of him, but it was too late. And I'm glad. It serves you right. Ah, how it serves you right!"

Tom scooped up his bag and strode past her without a look. He crossed the bedroom and turned down the corridor with angry strides. He passed a door into an immaculate kitchen, cut through a small dining area, walked the length of a large long room walled in glass, a lanai overlooking the placid blue swimming pool, and entered a wing at the opposite end of the house. He stopped outside the doorway to another bedroom, where Pete was sitting on his heels before a chest, rummaging faded sweatshirts out of an open drawer.

Tom stood silently for several seconds, not speaking until the anger had cleared from his face. Then he said, "So, you're off to Malibu."

Pete turned his head and rose to his feet in one easy, fluid motion. "Oh, hi, Dad. I didn't hear you come. Yes, I want to get up there before dark."

"Will you stay the weekend? I might see you when I get back."

"I don't know. Actually, I should go back down on Saturday."

"I'll probably miss you then." Tom was silent, then he added, a little awkwardly, "Well, it was damn good to see you, Pete."

"Good to see you, too, Dad."

"I'll try to get down to La Jolla the first weekend I have that's free and clear. I'd like to take you up on that offer to show me the kelp forest. I'd really enjoy that."

"Great. Any time at all. Phone me, and I'll make the hotel reservations for you." Pete came across the room and held out his hand. "Have a good trip. I hope your deal with NASA cooks up all right."

"Thanks. It will."

They shook hands and Tom said, "Well, take care of yourself."

"You, too. Watch out for radar traps back east."

Tom grinned. "Damn right."

He still lingered, and suddenly he reached out to Pete's shoulder. But he merely said, offhandedly, "So long, Pete. Don't let the fish bite, will you."

"Yeah, I'll watch out for that," Pete said with an answering grin. "Good-bye, Dad. Have a good flight."

Tom turned and walked quickly away.

Nedith met him in the foyer at the front of the house, her face as remote as the Chinese bronze behind her. "When will you be back?" she asked. "You didn't say."

"Sunday night, I should think. It will probably be late."

"Well, where will you be?"

"Houston and the Cape. Batesey's got the schedule if you should need it." He was already at the door.

"You didn't kiss me good-bye," she said.

"That's right, I didn't."

He hesitated just perceptibly before he turned. She came to meet him, but when he leaned forward she suddenly turned her face away. His lips barely brushed her cheek.

"Good-bye, Nedith."

The heavy front door boomed shut behind him.

Nedith stood quietly, turning the gold bangles over her slender wrist. From outside there was the roar of the engine and scream of tires as the car leapt away. Nedith's shoulders sagged and her face crumpled, but then she caught her breath and lifted her chin. She spun about abruptly, heels clattering against the stone, and set off for the guest wing.

She came through the doorway just as Pete was stuffing a pair of swim trunks into the top of a canvas bag on the bed.

"Oh, Pete! Are you really going up to Malibu? I wish you wouldn't, darling."

"I haven't been there in ages, Mum. It'll be great. Just loaf around for a couple days and hunt up some of the old beach crowd."

"It doesn't sound like much fun to me. There won't be anybody up there, and the weather's terrible. That house is so gloomy this time of year."

"I don't mind. Every once in a while I really get homesick for the old place, fog and all."

Nedith piled cushions against the headboard and sat down on the bed. "Just the same, I wish you wouldn't go. I guess I'm lonesome or something tonight. Your father off somewhere as usual."

Pete glanced at her, the slender, girlish figure propped against the pillows, the pretty, downcast face. "Poor Mum!" he said lightly. "Why don't you round up a girlfriend and go down to Palm Springs this weekend and get some sun? Or go crash at Sally's till Dad gets back?"

Nedith sighed. "Oh, it's not that bad. By now I should be used to being alone, shouldn't I? I really am, too, it's just that sometimes I get lonesome. Anyway, I've a million things to do this weekend, I'll be all right."

Pete leaned on his hand, cramming the contents of the bag together to make additional room. He moved off to a bookshelf in the corner, bending down to run his finger along a row of textbooks.

Nedith watched him, her face tender, dark eyes alert. "Pete, how would you like me to come with you to Malibu?" she said suddenly. "I've nothing to do this weekend that's really so important it couldn't be postponed. It might be fun."

"You must be kidding," Pete said absently, his attention upon the books. "What would you do up there? You've always hated the beach house this time of year. I don't mind being by myself, don't worry about it."

"At least wait till tomorrow morning," she coaxed. "We could go out to dinner somewhere and then see a movie, if you like. Or just come back here and talk, darling. I haven't seen you in weeks."

"I'd better not. Actually, I've got a pile of reading I want to get through tonight. Hey, while I think of it, is there firewood up there or should I take some from here?"

"I ordered a half cord just last spring," she said in a faintly injured voice. "Pete, I get the feeling you don't want to talk to me, and I don't understand that. You've always felt free to talk to me about everything before. Now it seems you can confide in your father but for some reason you don't want to talk to me."

Pete paused, a book spread open in his hands. "I don't think

I exactly follow you, Mum. What am I supposed to have confided to Dad?"

She moved her shoulders petulantly against the pillows. "Well, you go off and have drinks with your father and talk to him about—things. And it seems I'm not allowed to even mention it to you. Anyway, that's the feeling I get."

"If it's the divorce and Killian and all that that you're referring to," Pete said evenly, "I don't see much point in talking about it any longer. Not to anyone."

"Oh, darling, I wish you wouldn't feel so badly about all this. You couldn't see it, but she was never worth your one little finger, right from the start. Now you know the truth, can't you simply put it out of your mind? The world is absolutely full of lovely girls who aren't crazy hippies or—"

"Mother, let's not go all the hell over all this again, do you mind?"

"Pete, don't yell at me," she said. "I get enough of that from your father. Everything I say to him, he takes my head off."

"I'm sorry. If I yelled at you, I didn't mean to. I just don't see the point to hashing it all over again, that's all."

"All right. If that's what you want, I have enough respect for your feelings, I won't say another word. I promise." She smiled at him suddenly, a smile that lighted her whole face. "Friends and buddies?"

"Sure."

"Darling, get me a cigarette, would you, please? I think there are some just outside the door, on the table by the phone."

"Right."

He went obediently, dropping several books into the top of the bag as he passed by the bed. The light was fading from the room, and Nedith reached out to the switch of a lamp on the table beside her. She settled herself against the pillows again, chewing at her lower lip reflectively.

"Here you go," he said as he returned. "And an ashtray." He leaned down briefly to strike the match for her.

"Thanks, darling. Ah, I'm really beat tonight. That miserable trip out to the nursing home and all that."

"I can imagine. Poor Gran, no wonder she hates it out there. There ought to be a better way." Pete crammed the books down into the canvas bag, the sides bulging as he closed the heavy zipper.

"Here, sit down," Nedith said, moving her feet.

"I'd better keep moving. I'd like to get up to the house before dark."

"Five minutes. Now it couldn't make that much difference, could it?"

"Okay, five minutes." He dropped the bag onto the floor and draped himself across the foot of the bed, leaning back on his elbows. "So. How's Sally?"

"She's fine. The babies are so marvelous. Pete, you really should drop by before you leave. Those children absolutely adore you."

"Next time I come up. Tell Sal that's a promise."

"Oh, Pete, I forgot to tell you. Bob Rinkler's got another job. He's in his uncle's brokerage office now in Beverly Hills. Can you imagine?"

"Old Bob, the perennial goof-off," Pete said fondly. "Can't you just see him muddling up the customer accounts!"

They laughed together and then were silent for a moment in the golden pool of light.

"So what else is new?" Pete said. "What have you been doing lately?"

"Well, it's absolutely mad. I no more than finish getting this house decorated than Sally decides she wants to redo hers. If I have to look at one more swatch of drapery fabric, I'll throw up! Oh, Pete, guess what! Last week Jean and I went to see *Last Tango in Paris*. I can't imagine why everybody's been talking about it. It's an absolutely nothing film, and it's really dirty, it's—"

Pete watched her animated face as she talked on, and then he interrupted her. "Mum, whatever happened to your plans for a round-the-world cruise? I haven't heard you mention it in a long time."

"Darling, whatever made you think of that? What do you suppose happened? I've never been able to pin down your father to a date, that's all."

"Why don't you try again? It's just getting him started, you know. Actually, I think he'd love it."

"Well, I really don't care at this point whether he'd love it or not. This is something he promised me. Do you realize, it's over two years now that he's kept stalling on this?"

"You know Dad. It always takes something just this side of a nuclear blast to get him loose from the plant."

"You needn't tell me. This is what I've had to live with all these years."

He reached out suddenly to her ankle. "Mum, I'm serious about this. Go after him again. I think this cruise would be great for you both."

Nedith's dark eyes were instantly calculating. "Pete, why are you making such a point of this all of a sudden? Did your father say something to you this afternoon? What did he say?"

"He didn't say anything," Pete said quickly. "It was just a feeling I had. I get the feeling Dad's in the mood now to take it a little easier and enjoy life a little more."

Nedith sniffed audibly.

"There's nothing so unusual about that, is there? After all, Dad's not getting any younger. Maybe—he gets lonesome, too."

"Your father lonesome?" Nedith said. "Oh, now don't make me laugh, please! Have you any idea just how funny that is!"

He patted her slender, nylon-clad ankle before he moved his hand away. "You know, you do keep pretty busy yourself, Mum," he said mildly. "You've always got a million things going, your shopping and your girlfriends and Sally and the kids and all that. I think Dad might really appreciate spending some time with you when you didn't have much of anything else on your mind except him."

Nedith sat bolt upright on the bed. "Pete, you sound like something was my fault, for heaven's sakes, and you certainly know better than that. I'd like to know what's going on here. Why are you trying to stick up for your father all of a sudden?"

"Nothing's going on, I'm not sticking up for anybody. I'm just saying I think this cruise would be a good change for you both, that it would be great for both of you to get away and spend a little time together."

"Well, we don't have to go off on any cruise to do that, do we?" she said angrily. "Any time your father happens to want to spend time with me, I'm right here, aren't I, right where I've always been. Pete, you know perfectly well by now just how much time your father is ever interested in spending with me. The last couple years it hasn't gotten any better either, I can tell you that. No, we are going to take this cruise because your father made a promise to me. Once we're on that damn boat I don't care if he doesn't say two words to me! I'm used to that, too."

"Don't lose your cool, Mum. I wasn't saying that anything was your fault."

"Well, I should certainly think you'd know that by now. All the years that— I just don't want to talk about it anymore. I told you, your father promised me this trip and I intend to see that he keeps his word, don't worry. Now let's talk about something else."

After a moment of silence, Pete grinned at her. "Friends and buddies?"

Nedith smiled in return, her delightful and disarming smile. "Of course," she said, leaning back again. "So tell me about you, darling. What are you doing with yourself down there in La Jolla these days?"

"Would you believe working my butt off?" Pete stretched out, looking down the length of his legs to examine the state of his tattered sneakers. "Hey, I'd better buy a pair of shoes tomorrow."

"I should think it's about time! No, I didn't mean school. What are you doing with yourself, darling? Is there anyone special that you're dating now?"

Pete laughed. "Mum, I've no time. I'm up to my ears in work. I haven't even seen a movie since the quarter started. You know what's a big deal for me these days? Grab an hour or two late at night once in a while and put on a few records and drink a couple cans of beer."

Nedith stared at him dubiously. "Well, nobody can work twenty-four hours a day, for heaven's sakes. It isn't good for you. Pete, you're not avoiding girls, are you? I think that would be a terrible mistake. Right now you should be dating a lot of different girls and—"

He turned his head to look at her. "Mum, if you're worrying that I've gone into some kind of celibate monk bag since Killian left, the answer is, hell no. I'm honestly working my tail off just now, that's all."

"How is school?" she said tentatively. "Is everything going all right?"

"Couldn't be better. I'm into the work now that I want to do."

"Marvelous. And what about the grant to go to Europe?"

"I still haven't decided, it's getting embarrassing. I'll have to make up my mind in the next couple weeks."

"Do you want to know what I think about it?"

"Sure."

"Don't do it," she said.

He looked up quickly, his face interested. "Why not?"

Nedith studiously removed a tiny bit of ash from her cigarette against the edge of the ashtray. "Well, darling, you can't keep on going to school forever, can you?"

"Oh, hey!" Pete sat up abruptly on the edge of the bed. "Whoever said I intended to? Another year, I'll have what I need and then—"

"Oh, Pete! That's what you said last year. It's what you'll say next year, too!"

"Mother, be fair," he said, a flush of color in his face. "I couldn't very well have said that last year, because last year I knew damn well that—"

Nedith sat upright herself suddenly. "Pete, listen to me. In a couple months you'll be twenty-four years old. How many years can you stay in school anyway? It isn't as though you were studying medicine or law. People do get along without Ph.D.s. You've always said yourself that you didn't particularly want one, so—"

"Mum, I had no idea you felt this way. You've never talked like this before. This is something I'd certainly be happy to explain to you if you like, you've never seemed that interested before in the details of—"

"I'll tell you what I'm interested in," she said. "You have an absolutely fantastic potential. I can't stand to see you wasting yourself puttering around in schools somewhere, year in and year out. Is that the kind of life you really want?"

"Look, Mum, I can see that this might be difficult for you to understand, but—"

"Don't say I don't understand! I'm not like your father. Did I ever once try to pressure you into doing something else the way he has? No, for years I've fought your father tooth and nail for your right to do what you wanted to with your own life. You can't ever deny that. It's just that you're a fantastically brilliant boy and it's time you were out of school and beginning to make a name for yourself."

"Mother, I don't get it. Last year when I married and talked of leaving school, you were the one who kept insisting how important it was for me to finish this program I'd set for myself. It's possible you don't understand that, in school or out, I'm already into the work I want to do. It doesn't make that much difference. I may never 'make a name for myself' as you put it, but—"

"Why not?" Nedith said baldly. "You certainly could if you wanted to. What's wrong with that? It's what I want for you. I want that more than anything in this world!"

For a space of seconds, Pete stared at her, and then he shot off the bed. "You want!" he said softly. "Everybody wants! Well, I *need*!"

"What's that supposed to mean?" she said. "Darling, I'm your mother, for heaven's sakes! Naturally I want you to be successful and famous, what's wrong with that? It's not just money, I've never been a materialistic person, you know that, although as you grow older you'll find out that money is a very important thing to have. What I really want is for you to be absolutely top of the heap in whatever you do, so nobody can ever criticize or throw down on you as long as you live! That's what I want for you, Pete. I'm not ashamed to admit it."

Pete scooped up his bag. "Look, I really have to get moving," he said, his voice not quite steady. "I'll see you before I go back to La Jolla or I'll phone. I'll probably go back down on Saturday."

Nedith swung her legs over the edge of the bed and came to her feet. "Oh, Pete, at least stay for dinner. Then after that if you really want to go up to Malibu, why—"

"I'm sorry. I'd love to, but I've got a hell of a lot of work to do. I'll have a hamburger or something up there."

"And that's another thing. I don't think you eat properly half the time. Hamburgers are not a proper dinner, especially not on a day when you've skipped lunch."

"Yes, ma'am," he said lightly, his voice under control again. "That's probably why I'm wasting away. I'm nothing but skin and bones, you may have noticed that."

"Oh, Pete! Besides, I really think you have lost weight."

She slipped her arm about his waist, and he put his arm around her shoulders as they walked together down the long lanai.

"Pete," she said, her voice suddenly tender, "friends and buddies?"

"Of course."

"Good," she said. "That's really what's more important to me than anything else on earth, you know. Times like tonight, when I'm feeling lonesome, I feel like you and Sally are all I've got in the whole world."

He pulled her more tightly against him for an instant. "You

cheer up, Mum. I'm sorry to go off and leave you all alone in this big empty shack of yours. Get hold of Jean, why don't you, and go out somewhere, okay?"

"Oh, I usually have dinner with Sally on Thursday anyway. Jack's always out on Thursday, some Realtors' meeting he goes to every week."

They stopped at the door.

"Darling, this has been a terribly short visit," Nedith said, reaching up to straighten the collar of his knit shirt. "I wish you'd come up oftener." And then she smiled. "Pete? Think about what I said, will you, darling? Don't go to Europe. I mean it, I really think it's terribly important that you get out of school now, and—"

"Sure, Mum. I'll think about it." He opened the sliding glass door into the misty twilight. "Hey, I smell rain! So. I'll see you before I go back or I'll telephone."

"Good-bye, darling. Drive carefully, won't you?" She circled her arms about his neck, stretching her slim body against his as they kissed.

"Look, get cracking on those cruise plans, will you?" Pete said. "I mean it, Mum. Get Dad pinned down next week."

"Well, I might just do that."

He stepped out onto the wide terrace between the house and the pool, and Nedith lingered in the doorway, hugging herself in the chill air.

"I don't know," she said. "Today everybody packs suitcases and goes off and leaves me."

He looked back over his shoulder, smiling. "Poor Mum! We always come back, though, don't we?"

"That's right," Nedith said. "You better had, too, both of you. And don't you ever forget it!"

AFTER TOM LEFT THE HOUSE, HIS ANGER LASTED no farther than the nearest street corner. By then he had put aside the image of Nedith and her meticulously decorated house. Actually, by the time he was out the door, his mind was already computing the quickest route through the rush-hour traffic.

A few moments later his Corvette shot up the long arc of a freeway on-ramp only for him to discover, too late, a congestion of traffic at the top. He was instantly trapped in the turgid stream of cars. Tom swore aloud. He hitched forward in the leather bucket seat, peering through the mist at the undulating ribbon of taillights that stretched as far as he could see before him. After that he could only sit helplessly as the headlights from the other side of the freeway strobed in his face.

The traffic trickled forward in maddening starts and stops. Tom lighted a cigarette and impatiently punched at the radio buttons. At last, just when the time-wasting had become unbearable, he caught sight of an exit sign and without hesitation twitched his wheels into a quarter-car length of space in an adjoining lane. Several minutes later, with his fenders somehow still intact, he zoomed down an off-ramp in an exultant burst of speed.

From there on, he charted his own course, zigzagging through a maze of surface streets. Just after darkness fell, he reached his destination, an old, gray stucco apartment house on a street of similar dwellings, closer to the urban center. He found a parking space along the curb and paused to lock his car. The street was lined with trees of a deciduous type less common to Southern

California and now half bare, large, yellowed leaves pasted to the damp sidewalk, strewn across the cropped green lawns, and caught on top of the low clipped hedge that bordered the walk up which he strode. The dark building loomed ahead and, over the rooftop, a row of tall, neatly pared palm trees from the street beyond, stark as a comb's teeth against the luminous sky.

He passed a bank of mailboxes in a tiny vestibule and entered an inner foyer, where he waited restlessly for the elevator, the blue smoke from his cigarette caught in a mirror on the wall behind him, where a bouquet of red and purple wax anemones stood on a fake Spanish colonial table. The ancient elevator arrived at last, creaking to a jerky halt and the doors slowly rattling apart. He stepped in and jabbed at one of the buttons.

The upper hallway had given up any pretensions it ever had. There was an undefinable musty odor in the air, a bulb in the chandelier overhead was burned out, spots on the carpeting. Tom walked rapidly past a burst of canned laughter and applause from an unseen TV set and, further on, a gurgle of pipes and the flat voice of a radio newscaster. He stopped before one of the drab doors, rang perfunctorily, then unlocked it with a key from his ring.

The room was empty, though warm and bright, drapes pulled against the damp night. It was a pleasant room, a little disordered and shabby, a jumble of color and bric-a-brac, fresh flowers in bowls, framed prints on the walls, a Mexican folk art candelabra on top of the television set, a collection of wooden Japanese kokeshi dolls next to the books on a shelf. But here and there amid the comfortable clutter were a few good pieces: the thin, frayed Oriental rugs upon the floor were vibrant with color; the exquisite thin-legged desk and chair in the corner gleamed with the patina of old wood, and a good watercolor hung on the wall above them.

"Hallie?" Tom called out as he closed the door after him. He received no answer, but from nearby there was the sound of a shower running.

With the air of a man arrived home at last, Tom removed his tweed jacket and loosened his tie. He leaned over the back of the sagging, comfortable divan, groping behind a curtain for the handle to open the casement window a little against the warmth of the room. On the coffee table there was a silver tray with an ice bucket, bottles, and glasses. He bent over it, absently stuffing peanuts into his mouth from a bowl before he dropped ice cubes into a glass and added a splash of whiskey. He sat down on a corner of the divan then, settling against the cushions, kicking off his black shoes to rest his feet upon the coffee table.

There was a square of unfinished needlepoint embroidery on the cushion next to him, a bright string of yarn and a needle dangling from it. Tom picked it up idly, munching at more peanuts, and reached behind him to fumble inside his coat for his black-rimmed reading glasses. Once he had donned the glasses, he studied the needlework momentarily, a modern design of colorful, abstract flowers. He searched for and found the needle, pulled the string of yarn taut, turned the square to a slightly different angle, and fell to work, placing the minute stitches with surprising speed and exactitude.

Minutes passed while the water continued to splash from the other side of the thin wall. The needle twinkled in the light, and Tom hummed softly, a tuneless, contented bumblebee of sound in his throat. He worked until he had completed that color segment, set the last stitch accurately, secured the needle, and then held the square away for an instant to survey his handiwork approvingly.

He dropped the needlepoint where he had found it, shoved the glasses into his shirt pocket, and bounded up from the divan. He picked up his drink, pausing to scoop another handful of peanuts from the bowl, and set off toward a doorway in the opposite wall.

The inner room was a small bedroom with the same comfortable clutter and disarray, softly lighted, and a delicate scent of perfume in the air. The sound of the running shower was louder there, from just beyond a flimsy door standing slightly ajar. Tom made room for his glass beside a stack of books on a table next to a double bed covered with a blue-and-white woven spread and strewn with sections of a newspaper and several magazines. His attention was suddenly caught by a newspaper cutting pinned to the drape behind the lamp, and he bent down momentarily to grin at a photograph of a disgruntled looking lion seated incongruously on his haunches upon a sidewalk bus bench.

Just then the splash of water stopped and he heard the shower door open and close.

Tom went to the bathroom door and rapped on it twice. "Hallie?"

"Tom!" The door opened wider immediately, and a delighted moist, pink face surmounted by a dripping plastic shower cap peeped out around the doorjamb. "Darling, why didn't you tell me you were here? I needn't have stayed in the shower so long."

"I've only been here a minute. There was a tie-up on the damn freeway."

They kissed, and she said, "Just let me dry myself, I'll be right out."

"How do you feel, Hallie? Are you tired?"

"No, I'm fine. How about you?"

"Great."

He returned to the bed in the corner, this time sitting down and swinging his feet up over the edge to lean against the stacked pillows. "Hey, did you see these Caribbean pictures in *Holiday*?"

"Oh, yes, aren't they beautiful?" she called back amid a flurry of violet bath-toweling. "Tom, read just the first paragraph of the article, it does sound so marvelous."

"I already did. I think that may be for us. How would you like to live in Jamaica?" Then he added, through a mouthful of peanuts, "So tell me, have a busy day today in that elegant clip joint of yours?"

"No, very slow actually. More telephone orders than live customers."

He reached for his glass and idly picked up an opened book

of crossword puzzles from the bed table instead. "Did you go out for lunch or anything?"

"Just a quick sandwich, then I went to see Miss Runkleman. She's that poor woman I told you about, who's been in handbags for thirty-two years and just retired week before last. We've all been taking turns dropping by to see her at lunchtime. The old thing had no life at all outside the store. Everyone keeps telling her now that she should buy a place in one of those retirement villages, but I'm not sure she has the money for that, something about her mother having a long, expensive illness before she died, and no insurance. And those retirement villages are terribly expensive, aren't they, Tom?"

"Depends upon the facility," he said absently, his eyes on the squares of the puzzle. "Fifty thousand and up, I should think. Some of them make rental arrangements, of course."

"There, you see! I'm sure Miss Runkleman couldn't afford that. Besides, I can't see her folk dancing or sculpting or taking up golf once she got there. She's not exactly the type."

"I had some business a year or two ago with a man who was living in a very plush retirement colony down the coast, and I never forgot it. It struck me as being the loneliest, most desolate place I'd ever seen in my life." He erased a word from the puzzle suddenly and began to add a new one in rapid block lettering. "*Hierophant.* That's 'Priest of the Eleusinian mysteries' beginning with an *h.* Then that six-letter word going across would be *plural* instead of *double.*"

"Aren't you clever! But I always thought *hierophant* was feminine gender. Are you sure?"

"Uh-hum. Get your Volks out of the garage tonight? How's it running?"

"Perfectly. I told you, Tom, it just needed a little overhaul."

"Balls! That damn machine isn't safe to drive any longer. Why won't you let me get you a decent automobile?"

"Oh, Tom, my Bug's a perfectly decent automobile! Besides, I love it and it suits me."

"Neither of which alters the fact that it isn't safe to drive. If you're determined, at least let me get you a new model. I mean it, Hallie."

"No, Thomas. N-O, no! I won't have it."

"You know, it's very interesting," he said conversationally. "You definitely have some idiot block of some kind about letting me give you things. You behave as though I'm trying to shower you with sables and Lincoln Continentals. All I want to do is buy you a new Volkswagen, for Christ's sake, for the most purely selfish reason on earth. I'd prefer not to have you get squashed on the freeway one day. At least a new model would reduce the risk, they're better engineered."

"Tom, that's ridiculous! You're always giving me things. Constantly! I just don't want another car."

"All right, Mrs. C., you're a very stubborn woman. But if you're going to keep that Bug, you're going to stay on the surface streets with it. If I ever hear of you setting wheel to a freeway again, I will personally push it over the nearest cliff. You remember that."

"Yes, sir. Tom? It's this compulsory retirement thing, does that make any kind of sense to you? There's simply no reason why she shouldn't still be selling handbags. She's a perfectly healthy, sprightly woman. Now they've scuttled her whole life for her. It seems so unfair."

"What?"

"Miss Runkleman, Tom. It's so sad."

She appeared in the doorway as she spoke, a small woman wrapped in a blue-and-white cotton kimono. Her streaked blond hair was uncombed, her face clean and shining with only a trace of lipstick, an open, lively face that had never been beautiful, her mouth too wide, her nose slightly upturned. Only her eyes were in any way extraordinary, large and clear behind a fringe of lashes, and hazel-brown.

"Hang Miss Runkleman! Come and say hello to me, Mrs. C."

She came pattering in flat slippers to perch upon the edge of the bed beside him. They kissed again tenderly, and Tom pulled her down to rest beside him, rubbing his cheek against her fine, soft hair. She smelled of soap, and he felt the cool dampness of her skin, fresh from her shower, through the thin fabric across her back.

"Ah, Thomas!" she said, nestling to him, her voice richly content.

And then she sat abruptly upright, pushing hair from her eyes, her face sober and concerned. "Now tell me about your poor Pete. How is he?"

"Oh, Christ!" Tom hitched himself higher against the pillows and reached for a cigarette. "What did somebody say once, that dealing with kids was like wrestling string? Well, that describes it as well as anything. As usual, he wouldn't let me within a hundred miles of him."

"Tom, you always take it so personally. Maybe he simply doesn't feel like talking to anyone just now. Everyone has the right to lick their wounds in private if that's how they feel about it."

"I realize that. He doesn't seem to have done that much talking to Nedith either. I suppose it's mostly damn ego, isn't it? You'd like to think that you're the one your son would feel like confiding in when he's in trouble."

She took his hand between both of hers.

"Frankly, it beats me," Tom said. "All along, I had this hunch that he and Killian would make it back together before it came up in court."

"Are you sure the hearing really did take place today? Maybe—"

"No, I had a phone call from my attorneys before I left the office. Killian appeared and it went through. So that seems to be that."

"Tom, what's there to say? Perhaps it's all for the best. They're both so young; if they made a mistake perhaps it's better that—"

"I know," Tom said. "The trouble is, I liked that girl. You

know, Hallie, I think I made a mistake. I think it might have been a hell of a lot better for Pete in the long run if I'd played the heavy father right at the beginning, raised some hell and insisted on having the whole story out in the open. It would have been the normal thing to do, wouldn't it? Instead I shied away. Pete wasn't anxious to talk about it, obviously, and I didn't press him, and by the time the lawyers pried it out of him that Killian had been sleeping with this character, it was too late. I never quite saw myself walking up to him after that and saying, 'Look here, how did your wife happen to start sleeping around anyway?' That's a pretty damn sensitive area, for Christ's sake!"

"Oh, Tom, don't blame yourself. Your instinct was perfectly right. You couldn't have done that."

"The point is, I shied away from the whole thing." Tom moved restlessly, his face brooding behind a haze of cigarette smoke. "I backed off as usual and left Nedith to do all the screaming and the arm waving. And she did quite a bit of it; she wasn't exactly hell-bent on trying to save this marriage. But then you might say that's been the story of my life where Pete's concerned, backing off and leaving things to Nedith."

Hallie listened sympathetically and reached out her hand to his cheek. "Darling, I think you've always backed off, as you call it, at times like this because you're an intuitively sensitive man with a decent respect for Pete's most private feelings. I'd imagine that through the years Pete's come to appreciate that."

Tom kissed her small, moist palm. "Balls! I've backed off primarily because Nedith's always kept me brainwashed that I never spent enough time with them to know what was good for my own children. Damn it, I wish now I'd talked to Killian, at least offered to listen to her side of the story. Actually, I did phone her a couple times at the beginning, and both times the little devil hung up on me. I called once more later on and got her mother. The woman's a fool, she knew even less about what was going on than I did. Well, there's no point in second-guessing it, I doubt if anything I did would have made that much difference anyway. I'm sorry as hell about it, but as you said, it may be the best thing for Pete. A divorce these days— Christ, I'm probably making too big a deal of it."

He fell silent, but his face was still brooding, and she waited with a warm, attentive gaze.

"Hallie, you know it's a funny thing," he said at last. "I was thinking about this today. I think this marriage is the first thing that has ever gone sour for Pete. All his life, everything he's ever wanted seems to have come his way. Starting from the time he was a little fellow and the school had him tested and he turned out to be some kind of wunderkind, he's had it all. Top scholastic honors without particularly trying, and he's a natural athlete, he could have made the Olympic swimming team easily if he'd cared to spend that much time. Plenty of friends always, clubs, class offices, girls have always liked him and he's liked them. When he finished high school, the universities came looking for him. He knew the field he wanted, he got the school he wanted, dean's list, Phi Bete, the whole package. Where most kids have had to hassle the draft, he's had this Naval Reserve deal, doing work for the Navy periodically right in his own field. He's had it made! And then he married Killian and it looked like more of the same. Maybe she was a little offbeat, but I thought she was one hell of a girl, pretty and bright and full of fire and head over heels in love with Pete. And then inside of a year, Pete comes home one day and finds her in their bed with some other guy! I don't know, I think I'd feel easier about this if he'd had to take a few other lumps through the years. Then he'd be a little better prepared to handle this, wouldn't he?"

"Darling, I think it works exactly the other way," Hallie said. "I think it's the one more thing in a whole string of disappointments that is too much sometimes for people to bear. Try not to worry, he'll be all right. He sounds like a very wonderful boy. Besides, he has you for a father, hasn't he?"

"Oh, yes," Tom said drily, "but there are at least two schools of thought on how much of an asset that turned out to be. I don't pretend I'm any great prize as a parent. As a matter of fact, I blew it again just today. Pete and I ended up having a minor-size row there in the bar, the very last thing I intended to happen. It was my fault, too. I put the screws to him again about chucking marine biology."

"Oh, Tom!"

"Yes, I know. I gave myself hell afterwards. I couldn't very well have picked a worse time, could I? You know, it's a funny thing, when Pete's down there in La Jolla, I can be just as damn objective and sensible as you please. I know it doesn't do any good to argue with him about it, and I promise myself never to mention the subject again. But just let me spend anything over a half hour with that kid, face-to-face, and I get so damn irritated about it that I could slug him, and before I know it, I'm at him again. Now how do you explain that!"

Before she could speak, he sat up, smiling. "Anyway, that's enough about all that. Hey, I never fixed you a drink, Mrs. C. Why the hell didn't you remind me? Hold on, I'll get you one." He picked up his own glass and rolled off the edge of the bed as he spoke, setting off rapidly for the living room.

"Part-time work at the counter of a neighborhood leather repair shop on a semivolunteer basis," he called back cheerfully over a tinkle of glassware.

"What!" She looked toward the door, her face startled.

"Your Miss Rinklemeyer, or whatever her name is. It gives her something to do in an area where she is knowledgeable, and whatever the proprietor feels like slipping her under the counter is certainly not going to affect her Social Security or her pension plan from the store."

"Why, Tom, what a great idea! Why didn't I think of that? There's a repair shop just a few blocks from where she lives. He's a terribly nice young Italian, and his wife does try to help out in the shop, but they have small children so it's difficult for them. Do you know, this might be perfect for Miss Runkleman and for him, too. Darling, what a clever man you really are!"

"Damn right!" He was grinning as he returned to the bed, carrying a glass in either hand, the silver bowl of nuts balanced in the crook of his arm. "Here, have a peanut," he said as she took the bowl and made room for him once more beside her. "Bet you can't eat just one! And this is for you, by the way." He pulled from his pocket a small, lumpy package wrapped in yellow tissue paper and tied with a crumpled, faded blue ribbon.

"Oh, Tom! Now see, you're always bringing me presents. Why do you want to say silly things like I won't let you give me things? What on earth . . . it feels like . . . Oh, I can't wait to see!"

Tom crammed pillows behind his back, grinning as he watched her glowing face. She picked at the knot in the ribbon and then abandoned it to tear the thin paper at a fold sealed with tape. A long string of glass beads slid out. They were a deep, shining green, each marked with splotches of a brilliant blue.

"Oh, Thomas!" she said, her voice hushed and breathless. "They are beautiful! Oh, look, they're like peacock feathers, the eye of the feather! They're fabulous. Oh, I have to see!"

She pattered across the room to a littered powder table, perching upon the bench as she slipped the necklace over her head. "Tom, I really think these are the most beautiful beads I've ever seen in my life! Do look how they shine in the light, they're alive. Tom, I adore them! Thank you, thank you, thank you!"

"My pleasure. You're a delightful woman, Mrs. C. You get more fun out of Venetian glass than most women do from diamonds."

"Diamonds, poo!" She returned to the bed to sit at his feet, leaning comfortably against his updrawn knees. "Diamonds are easy, but just tell me where on earth you found these gorgeous things. They're very old, but they're absolutely perfect, not a one of them is chipped. Where did you get them, Tom?"

"Would you believe San Pedro? I was down there on a business errand a couple days ago. You have me pretty well trained, you know. I'd never been inside a junk or antiques place in my life till I met you. Now every damn one I see, I have to take a look."

"But you have an absolute talent for it, you find such treasures. Tom, I can't stop looking at them," she said contentedly. "It's like foil inside the glass, isn't it? Did you ever see anything so shining?"

He reached out to brush back the fringe of hair on her forehead. "Nothing like as shining as your eyes, Mrs. C."

She rubbed her cheek against his hand. "Thomas, I'm a very lucky woman," she said softly. "On top of everything else, you spoil me. You find me marvelous, beautiful, extraordinary things like this."

He laughed. "Beads and gimcracks! Which reminds me, what do you want for Christmas this year, Hallie?"

"Don't say that word! Since I've worked at the store, I cringe at the thought of it. What do you want for Christmas, darling? Never mind, I have something absolutely marvelous hid away for you already. Oh, Tom, I know! Do you want to give me something madly expensive? I've been dying to make one of those rya rugs, you know, the ones from Finland. I've looked at them in shops, but the pattern and the wool to go with it costs an absolute fortune. I'd love one for Christmas."

"Oh, Christ!" he said. "I'd be happy to give you a dozen rugs anytime, don't you know that! If you want one so badly, go get it tomorrow. Why didn't you tell me you wanted one?"

"Tom, stop it! I just said it would make a wonderful Christmas gift. As soon as I have time, I'll leave a list of ones I like at the shop and then you can choose. Just a smallish one for here beside the bed, don't you think?"

She reached toward the bed table suddenly, and anticipating her, he handed her the glass. Then he lifted his own and clinked the edge of it gently against hers. "To you, my darling," he said. "The best is yet to be."

Her eyes went wide and round with pleasure. "Why, Thomas, that's our old toast!"

"You know, come January, we'll have another day to celebrate. An anniversary, a big one. Two years!"

"Tom, it can't be. It seems like yesterday or it seems like forever. Two years! Are you sure?"

"Of course. Two years on the fourteenth of January. You were wearing a blue suit and a white blouse with some sort of lace dojigger at the collar. You had a cold. Your nose was red."

She laughed, an infectious chortle of delight. "Fantastic! I wish I could remember what you were wearing, but I never noticed. You came striding up to that counter, I thought you were the most vital, exciting man I'd ever seen in my life. Even though you were in a roaring temper! You wanted two dozen pairs of hose right that instant, except you hadn't the least idea what size or length or texture or color."

"Well, how was I to know? Batesey always bought the stockings, but she was home that day with flu. I'd been at a business lunch in town, I was running late and busy as hell and it was Nedith's birthday and I needed the damn stockings to take home with me that night. Did I really take your head off? I don't believe it!"

"As a matter of fact, you were absolutely fierce. I suggested you take nine and a halfs in neutral and let her exchange them later, and you said that was a hell of a thing. And then you tipped over the display rack on the counter and the stockings went flying in all directions."

"I don't remember that," Tom said fondly. "I think you made it up. Do you know what I remember, Mrs. C.? The cute way you peeked over your shoulder to make sure your boss lady couldn't hear you and then blew your whole sale. 'Don't buy your wife stockings for her birthday,' you said. 'Buy her perfume or a bit of jewelry, something silly and extravagant that she'd really love to have.' You were so damn cute and earnest, Hallie. Why did you do it anyway?"

"Because you were so exciting and marvelous," she said promptly, "and hose is such a dull gift for a woman who can afford to buy her own. I wanted you to do better than that."

"So I went over into the jewelry department and bought an

old French enamel pin with pearls and Nedith hated it. She said it was exactly the tacky sort of thing she'd expect Batesey to choose, and in the future to tell her to kindly stick to stockings."

They laughed together. Hallie held his one hand cradled against her breasts, and with the other he stroked tenderly at her fine, downy hair.

"Oh, Tom, life really is so extraordinary," she said. "One day when you least expect it, a miracle happens. After bad years and dull years, life suddenly pays you a marvelous dividend. One must always believe in life. Why did you come back, Tom?"

"Hell if I know! The most utterly sound and sensible thing I ever did in my life, and I haven't the least idea why. Because your funny little face haunted me for some reason. Because you were honest and that's a rare thing, because you looked at me as though you cared about me. The way you laughed. Because your eyes are ten feet deep."

They were silent for a moment, eyes clinging together, and then he said, "Hallie, come to bed with me."

"Why, Thomas!" she said. "I would love to!"

They moved at the same time, both sliding from the bed. He opened the belt of his gray trousers and left them in a heap on the floor, standing braced on short, powerfully muscled legs, his fingers fumbling at the small shirt buttons. She moved around to the other side, dropping the sash of her kimono as she slid under the covers. They made love amid a drift of cigarette smoke, in the clutter of papers and books and peanuts and whiskey glasses. Their lovemaking was practiced and passionately economic, a short, strenuous, shared plunge to a common climax, a falling away to languorous, tender love play once more, an intertwining of arms and legs and hands and lips. They rested at last, bathed in perspiration, her soft, heavy breasts against him, her fine hair damp and feathery beneath his chin.

"Ah, Thomas!" she said, the merest breath of sound. "Good, good, good!"

"Damn good!" He moved his hand, his fingers tracing the small hollow just above the generous curve of her buttocks. "Speaking of life's extra dividends! I love you, Hallie. Christ, when I think of the years we've wasted. Why couldn't I have found you thirty years ago!"

"That's silly! We met at exactly the perfect time. The fifties are the time of life for love, Tom, didn't you know that?"

He chuckled. "You don't say! And here the going opinion is that we're a little too long in the tooth at this stage, and a little too short in the clutch. I submit it's a subject you can't approach on a purely academic level. If I could have had you between the sheets just once when I was eighteen that might have presented quite an argument."

"Eighteen!" she said with delicate scorn. "You make me far happier between the sheets right now than you could possibly have when you were eighteen. What do any of us know about love and sex when we're in our teens? At that age it's all just rubbing bodies together, like puppies, because it feels so good."

"All right, the twenties, then."

"If we'd met when we were in our twenties, we'd probably have hated each other. Those are such ego years, people really never stop being preoccupied with themselves, searching for their identities and all that. We're too self-centered then for love, and in the thirties we're too busy. At that age most of a man's energies go into his career, and a woman's into child rearing."

"So what's wrong with the forties then?" he said, amused. "Why couldn't I have met you when I was forty? There's ten good years gone to waste."

"Nonsense!" She propped herself up on her elbow, her face close to his, her other hand beneath his short, strong neck. "The forties are terrible years. Think about it. We turn in on ourselves again. That's when we first come face-to-face with our own mortality. Old age and death! That's when we all go into panics over things we wanted out of life and haven't got. The trauma years! We all go a little mad in our forties."

"And it's any different in the fifties?"

"Oh, Tom, of course it is! These really are the golden years. We've come out the far side of the forties with the wisdom to know that just life itself is the greatest gift of all. That every day is something extraordinary, not yesterday or tomorrow but today, to be lived from morning till night, to be savored and enjoyed. Now this, this is the real right time for one's real right love! Oh, darling, how can you doubt it! Look at us!"

He pulled her down upon his broad, bare chest and held her tightly for a moment. "These may be the golden years, according to your theories," he said, "but they don't come with a guarantee, you know. Do you really have any idea just how damn precious you are to me, Mrs. C.?"

"Why, I must be," she said, "because you make me feel so valuable." She burrowed her hands beneath him until she held him tightly in her arms, nuzzling her face into the grizzled, wiry hair of his chest. "Oh, Thomas, imagine! I am fifty-three years old, middle-aged spread and bad veins and a ticky heart, and I've never been so happy in all my life. I wake up every morning and go zing, like a fiddle string. How do I thank you? I'm all yours, my darling, inside and outside, all of me entire and total, and I love you with every atom and molecule, little gray brain cells and the cuticles of my fingernails and—"

They kissed fiercely and then were silent together for a long time.

"Darling, I hate to bring this up," she said at last. "But you do have a plane to catch."

"Uhmm."

"You never told me about your day. Are you ready to explain that fantastic thingamabob to the NASA people tomorrow?"

"All squared away. As a matter of fact, I worked like hell today. Batesey cut off the phone and kept everybody out. She's a tiger, that Batesey." He lifted his arm and glanced reluctantly at his watch. "Damn, you're right. Do you know we'll have to be out of here in a half hour if we don't want to rush dinner?"

"Darling, why don't I just cook something here? I have some chops."

"Because you've had a long day and I won't hear of it. We'll eat on the way to the airport. Then I'll send you back in a cab unless I can talk you into driving my car back and using it over the weekend."

"Tom, you know I'm terrified of that car of yours. But we could put it in the garage and go out in the Volks."

"What did you say!"

"Oh, all right, I'll come back in a cab."

They were silent once more, relaxed and loath to leave the bed.

"Hallie," he said suddenly, his voice moved. "Do you know what really bugged the hell out of me, seeing Pete today? Christ, I didn't actually expect him to break down and confide in me, he's always been a reticent sort of guy, at least where I'm concerned. I haven't the patience or the tact or whatever the hell it takes to be a good amateur psychiatrist anyway. No, I sat there in that dreary damn bar with the poor kid, Hallie, and what I really ached to do was just load him into the car and bring him over here. No lectures, no advice, no soul-searching, just bring him here. Maybe the poor devil could have—warmed himself a little, it's what he needs most in the world just now. No big deal at all, we'd have fussed over him, poured a few drinks into him, taken him out to dinner with us and— Oh, Christ!"

Her body suddenly tensed, stiff and rigid against him. "Tom—" she began, her voice distressed.

he stopped her with his hand upon her lips. "Sssh, Hallie, don't. There is nothing you can say, and I don't want you to have to try. It's my own fault, isn't it, for not having tidied up my life a long time before this. Hey, look what time it is! We have to get this show on the road." He flung back the covers. "How's the hot water situation? If I run out in the middle of my shower again tonight I'm going down in a bath towel and have a word with your landlady myself."

"I wouldn't advise it. One glimpse of a man in a bath towel

and poor Miss Siddester would expire on the spot. Once that shifty-eyed nephew of hers inherits this place, we'll be lucky if we ever get a drop of hot water again."

Tom leaned over the bed, cupping her chin in his hand for an instant, looking intently into her face. She was smiling, but a shadow of hurt still lingered in her clear eyes. "Maybe I really am a selfish bastard," he said soberly. "But trust me, Hallie."

"Selfish! Oh, darling, you're the most—"

"No, I'll make it up to you one day, Hallie. And that's a promise."

"Thomas—"

He was already gone.

IT WAS ALL BUT DARK THAT THURSDAY AFTERNOON by the time Cynny Holman arrived home. She gratefully turned the long, heavy car into the driveway of a large house from which, she noticed, light already shone invitingly from the windows. It was an older house by local standards, of indeterminate architecture, built on two floors and painted white, with a smooth, green lawn and big, old trees, sycamores and eucalyptus, leaning together at the eaves.

She stopped the car on a concrete apron at the rear of the house, and as she turned off the headlights she caught a glimpse of Joby's blue Volkswagen gleaming through the mist in front of the garage doors. Oh, good, she thought, Joby was home, then perhaps he could be prevailed upon to fetch Susan, since this was GAA day at junior high when Susan finished too late to ride the school bus. But no, that wouldn't work either, today was also Joby's day for algebra tutoring.

She scrabbled up her purse and slid wearily from the car seat, preoccupied now with the domestic logistics of her evening. No help for it, she would have to fetch Susan herself. And it was more than likely that Susan had gone home with Laurie, which would mean driving all the way to the Palisades. Then dinner to be organized and Jim driven to the airport, all presumably before that wretched PTA meeting.

Cynny was gathering up a collection of brown paper sacks from the trunk, juggling them in an attempt to free one hand to close the trunk lid, when a door opened at the back of the house and there appeared a tall, dark-skinned woman in a white dress with a large dog beside her.

"Hi!" she called out. "Let me help with that. What you been doing, buying out the stores?"

The dog darted ahead of her, his stump of tail wagging eagerly as he descended the wooden steps with long-legged grace.

"Thanks, Merna," Cynny said. "It's that damn Grand Central Produce Market downtown, I always lose my head in that place. Janet and I rushed over for a minute after we finished in court. Do you know, her lawyer says at least half of his clients, if he lets them out of his sight, end up at that market, isn't that a riot? Janet told him it's because none of us ever come downtown in the daytime anymore except when we're getting divorces. There, if you can manage these, I'll take this big one." She paused to greet the dog, who nuzzled at her wrists affectionately. "Hello, puppy. He's such a good fellow!"

He was a Weimaraner, short haired and sleek, the color of ashes, with soft, earnest, yellow-brown eyes.

"You mean you ladies lugged all this stuff back up that hill to the courthouse?" Merna's voice was rich with amusement.

"Plus two huge bundles of cheese and sausages that Janet decided to take to her friends in Palm Springs. Her lawyer was so funny, he pretended to make a joke of it, but I think he really didn't like it. Merna, you'll love this, he said this was the kind of thing women did that was enough to scare the hell out of any man—one minute we're in court cutting the knot and the next minute we're tripping off to shop for dinner!"

Merna whooped with laughter as they mounted the steps together, the dog bounding ahead of them.

"So how was your trip to court anyway? You look kind of beat."

"Awful," Cynny said. "I really hate that place. Remind me of that the next time anyone asks me to be a witness."

"Yeah, I'll do that. Here, give me that other sack."

They walked through a laundry room into a large kitchen. It was warm and bright with light and color, pottery jugs and plates and cookbooks on open shelves, and the gleam of copper pots hanging near the stove. Merna carried the armload of sacks to a big butcher's block at one end of the room.

Cynny dropped her purse on a round wooden table. For a moment she stretched, arms lifted, rolling her head slowly to loosen the muscles between her shoulders. "Ooof, it's good to be home! The traffic was terrible and there was a smash at Barrington and cars backed up for blocks. Oh, Putzi, what is it?" she finished to the dog, who leaned his head against her. "I'm not paying enough attention to you, is that it?" She bent down for a moment, her cheek against the dog's sleek head, patting him affectionately. "Merna, what about the drapery man, did he finally get here?"

"Yeah, about two o'clock," Merna said over the rustle of sacks. "While he was at it, I told him he better check all the rods, so he put new cord in that one in Mr. Holman's bedroom, too. Listen, the kettle's boiling, how about a cup of tea or a drink or something? You really look kind of beat, baby."

"It's just a headache, probably from the smog. Anyway, what about Susan? Did she go home with Laurie, did she phone? I may as well fetch her right now and get it over with."

"Don't worry about fetching Susan. She got herself home. She come in style. A boy drove her."

"Really? The Dickson boy, or who?"

"Uh-uh. A stranger boy we never had before. He was driving one of those little bitty open sports cars, an MG or something." For an instant the two women looked at each other in unspoken communication. "These beans are really nice, you know? They're fresh as they can be."

"Have some of them, I bought pounds. Well, I do think it's the limit. This makes the second time now in a week. This time I think I should really crack down on her."

"How?" Merna asked from behind the open refrigerator

door. "You planning to lock her up in her bedroom till she's eighteen or what?"

"Merna, she's barely fourteen! I don't care what she says other girls do, there have to be some sorts of rules, and she has to learn to keep them."

"Did I say there shouldn't? The trouble is, Susan's got your number. She's going to give you a long story now, and she's going to talk so fast and be so reasonable you could die. When she's all through, there won't be nothing left to crack down on. Wait and see."

"Not this time. *You* wait and see!"

"Want to bet a dollar?" Merna's voice was rich with merriment.

Cynny laughed. "It's a bet!"

The dog rose from the floor and padded away, bound on some sudden errand of his own.

Cynny slipped off her loose suit jacket, a nubby woven woolen in tones of black and brown, and reached for a cigarette package. "Well, at least I don't have to go out in the traffic again. I admit I'm not exactly mad about that. Merna, I would love a cup of tea. Were there phone calls?"

"I wrote them down. Nothing that can't wait. Why don't you sit and rest a minute? You want some aspirin?"

"No, thanks, the tea should do it. You have some, Merna. Sit down and relax for a minute yourself."

"Wait'll I finish clearing away around here. Then maybe I'll sit down and take off my shoes and have a little old shot of bourbon before I head for home." She swished a perforated double silver spoon back and forth in a china cup of boiling water. "Listen, why don't I put some potatoes in the oven for you? You're planning to have those lamb chops for dinner tonight, aren't you?"

"Oh, Lord, I forgot! Has Jim phoned yet? Did he leave a message?"

"Why? Was you expecting Mr. Holman to call home around now?"

"Yes, he was to let me know about dinner. He's leaving on

that business trip tonight, Florida and Texas. He wasn't sure about getting on the flight he wanted, so he said he'd phone between four and five."

"Well, he's sure steaming then," Merna said resignedly. "You didn't tell me he was going to call. Susan had a set-to with Joby over their telephone. She's been on your phone for the last forty-five minutes, hashing it all over with Laurie about that boy in the sports car. She's up there on your bed."

"Oh, damn! It's not your fault, Merna, I forgot to tell you." Cynny hastily gathered up her purse, jacket, and cup of tea. "We'd better hold off on the potatoes. If there isn't time I'll make a rice."

She passed through the shadowy dining room into a central hallway lighted by a chandelier, the spicy scent of chrysanthemums from a tabletop vase mingling with the lemon smell of floor wax. She climbed the broad, carpeted stairway, gingerly balancing the teacup as she went. At the top of the stairs, there was a sound of loud rock music, but she turned and walked the corridor to a white painted door that stood ajar.

"Hello, darling."

The girl in the middle of the blue-and-white flowered bedspread was lying on her belly, her legs in jeans waving in the air, her face and the telephone receiver both hidden behind a cascade of long, shining blond hair.

At the sound of Cynny's voice, she raised one small hand, lifting a handful of hair aside. "Oh, hello, Mama," she said and dropped the hair again. "Laurie, play the last part of the record over," she continued into the telephone. "I still say it sounds exactly like Paul McCartney."

Cynny put her teacup on a chest beside the bed. "Susan, your father's been trying to get a call through for the past hour! Now get off that phone this instant!"

"Just a minute, Laurie. Mama, just one last thing, I wanted to know if—"

"Right now, Susan," Cynny said grimly.

"Laurie, I'll have to call you back," she said. "My mother wants to use the phone."

Cynny perched on the foot of the bed and reached for the telephone. "Susan, this is very bad of you," she said, swiftly pushing number buttons. "You promised that if you were allowed to have a phone of your own, you and Joby, you would never use this one again. You know how your father hates it when he can't get through."

Susan bounced up from the bed, hair flying. "Mama, it's not fair! I simply have to have a telephone of my own. That hog, Joby—"

"Oh, be quiet!" Cynny said as the phone began to buzz in her ear. "And, Susan, I'd like you to wait, please. I'm not finished speaking to you. Hello, Karen? Has Mr. Holman been trying to reach me?"

"Oh, hello, Mrs. Holman. Yes, he certainly has. He's on another line just now. Do you want to hold or shall we call you back?"

"Call me back if you don't mind. The line will be open, I promise. Thanks very much."

Before Cynny could put down the phone, Susan erupted in a flood of rapid speech. "And another thing, Mama, Joby calls that stupid Redondo Surf Report about every ten minutes, and that's message units. And when Daddy goes over the phone bill, I'm the one who gets screamed at. It's not fair, practically every girl I know has a telephone!"

"The point right now is that you promised your father—"

"We were to take turns using the phone, ask Daddy, and today Joby wouldn't let me use it at all. Laurie was waiting for me to call, so I had to use this phone. Mama, I was desperate!"

"All right, but when you're using someone else's phone, isn't it a matter of simple courtesy to observe the three-minute rule and—"

"Why doesn't somebody tell that hog, Joby, about the three-minute rule!"

"Susan," Cynny said helplessly, "there must be some other way you can refer to your brother. *Hog* is a very unattractive word—"

"Mama, I'm sorry," Susan said, suddenly penitent. "You weren't home and I didn't know Daddy was going to call. I didn't mean to talk so long, I just forgot. I won't do it again. I promise."

"All right, darling, let's see that you don't."

Susan was seated at the powder table, holding her hair on the top of her head, studying her reflection in the mirror, her pretty face intent and her perfectly shaped breasts all too apparent beneath a tight, plum shirt.

Cynny looked at her and felt tenderness mixed with a certain incredulity. Perhaps that was the difficulty in dealing with children, she was thinking, they kept one a little off balance in the perpetual attempt to get used to their astonishing metamorphoses. It could not have been more than a year ago that Susan's major problem had been finding adequate shelf space for what was surely the largest collection of plastic horse figurines in Brentwood and Santa Monica combined. Sometime in the past year a plump, bouncy child with an alarmingly high-pitched giggle, a colorless bang of hair, and a mouth full of metal bands and braces had been transformed into this delightful female creature. Fantastic!

"There is something else we have to talk about, Susan," Cynny said with a conscious hardening of her heart. "About two weeks ago, you and I had a very thorough discussion about boys and automobiles after school. Do you remember that?"

"Of course I do, Mama. You said I wasn't to ride in cars with boys you didn't know. I promised, but I still don't think it's fair. All the other girls—"

"Then what about today, Susan?"

"Mama!" Her eyes went wide in wounded surprise. "But it was Ricky Kline who drove me home today. You know Ricky!"

"Come on, Susan, I never heard of him in my life!"

Cynny's head was suddenly aching harder, and she reached

for the cup of tepid tea. But the telephone rang just then, and she scooped it up instead. "Hello?"

"Cynny, is this a bad time, are you cooking?"

"Nancy," Cynny said, her face warming. "Can I call you back, love? I'm waiting for a call from Jim."

"Of course." The connection broke immediately.

"Mama, it's really not fair! If you knew the times I say no when people offer to drive me home and how the other girls make fun of me! And then a boy you know perfectly well does drive me home and you say you never heard of him. Mama, you *do* know Ricky. He came to my birthday party, well, I think he had a cold but I did invite him. Anyway, he's been here at the house I'm absolutely positive, and he was in two of my classes last—"

She talked on, and Cynny listened helplessly and with a certain admiration, not to the words but to the ceaseless, fluent, and self-assured speech that flowed out of her daughter. And suddenly Cynny was bubbling with inner laughter, reminded by contrast of herself at Susan's age, the shy, dark, bony child she had been, entirely without poise or confidence not to mention any visible charm. Now really, children were astonishing!

"All right, Susan, I give up," she said, smiling. "But from now on, please remember that when I say 'boys I know,' I mean the boys from here around the neighborhood."

Susan was dipping, magpielike, into one of the powder table drawers. "Well, I still don't think it's fair— Oh, Mama, look! These beads are so neat, may I borrow them?"

"Have them. I bought them at a rummage sale, just for the color."

"Oh, neat! Mama, I have to call Laurie back. Her mother wants to know if I can stay over on Saturday night, they're going out to a dinner party. May I, Mama?"

"Saturday night— Yes, darling, if you like."

"I'll go phone her right away."

Susan whisked out the door, but before Cynny had risen

from the bed the girl had whirled back into the room, her cheeks bright red with anger. "Mama, that hog, Joby—"

"Susan, that's enough. I'll speak to Joby myself."

Cynny went back down the corridor in the direction of the loud rock music.

"Hello, darling." She paused in the doorway, Susan at her heels.

Joby was a lanky boy with long, unkempt, dark hair and a mild case of acne. He was seated at the edge of the bed, the telephone on his knee, and about him a welter of notebooks, papers, and various items of apparel. The room was papered with bright-colored surfing and hot rod posters surrounding a vast and total disorder which overflowed the tops of furniture and spilled across the floor: plastic automobile models fallen into dust and disrepair, bits and pieces of crystal and walkie-talkie radio sets, dozens of ancient and frayed copies of *Mad* magazine, *Surfer*, and *Hot Rod*, music sheets, dirty squares of paraffin for waxing surfboards, yellow boxes containing color slides and negatives, a *Playboy* calendar with a picture of a crouched, nude young woman of extraordinary mammarian proportions, skis and poles, a set of weights, phonograph records, record player and twin speakers, radio, tape deck, cameras, tripod, and a gleaming electric guitar leaned against a large box amplifier.

The Weimaraner slept peacefully at his feet upon a bed of scattered magazines and a sleeveless surfer's version of a black rubber wet suit. He opened his eyes alertly at the sound of Cynny's voice.

"This is true," Joby was saying into the phone. "Oh, hi, Mom. You wanted something?"

"Off the phone, please. Susan wants to use it."

"Sure, Mom," he said agreeably. "Bo, I'll have to call you back. My freaky sister wants to talk to one of her freaky girlfriends for the next hour or two." He broke the connection and immediately began to dial again. "I won't be a minute, Mom. Just let me call the surf report."

Before Cynny could open her mouth, Susan darted around her, plucked the phone unceremoniously away, and hugged it to her breasts. "You don't happen to own this telephone, Joby Holman," she said in a scathing voice. "And you're not going to get your grubby hands on it again for the rest of the night either and see how you like it for a change. Hog!" In a sudden and appalling reversion to the vanished child of the bangs and braces, she stuck out her tongue, crossing her eyes over her nose.

"Mom!" Joby roared.

"Oh, my Lord!" Cynny said softly.

Susan disappeared in a swirl of telephone cord.

"Joby, I am fed up to here with the bickering that goes on over this telephone," Cynny said. "If it doesn't stop, I promise you the phone is going to be disconnected."

"I don't blame you, Mom. That little creep's getting impossible to live with." He dropped to his knees and began to grope beneath the bed, leaning across the resting dog, who lifted his head and looked at him reproachfully. "Shoes," he said vaguely. "Mom, you see my shoes? I have to go see Lovett right away."

"Not till after your algebra lesson, darling. Franklin will be here any second."

"Oh, no!" Joby rocked on his knees despairingly. "Not that cruddy algebra again tonight! I get enough of that cruddy algebra in school every day. Two nights a week I have to stay home and do cruddy algebra, I can't go surfing, I can't do anything. Mom, it's ruining my life! Why do I have to tutor algebra?"

"Oh, Joby, be quiet! You are being tutored in algebra because you've brought home two U notices this term already. This math credit is required for you to graduate. If you flunk it this term you'll have to take it over next term, and it is my understanding from what you tell me that if you have to take algebra over next term you won't have room in your schedule for auto shop, and if you aren't able to take auto shop you intend to kill yourself. Now is that a fair statement of fact?"

"This is true," he mumbled.

"And stop saying 'This is true.' It is not a helpful contribution to a conversation."

Then the doorbell chimed from the lower floor, the telephone began to ring in Cynny's bedroom, and from Susan's room there came an unnerving blast of music. Joby, scrambling to his feet, tripped over an electric cord, dislodging an alarm clock, which fell, jangling, to the floor, and the dog, startled, yelped and leapt to his feet, barking wildly.

Cynny fled to her bedroom. She slammed the door upon the pandemonium outside and grabbed the phone.

"Look, what's going on around that house?" a male voice said, taut with irritation. "I've been trying to call you for over an hour."

"I'm sorry, darling. I just got home a few minutes ago."

"That damn Merna! When you're not home she's got nothing better to do apparently than sit around and talk to her boyfriend, and you let her get away with it."

"Oh, Jim, it wasn't Merna. It was my fault, I should have left a message that you were going to phone. Actually, it was Susan. She didn't know you were going to call and Joby was on their phone, so—"

"Oh, my God! Look, when you conned me into letting those kids have a telephone, they agreed to stay off this phone permanently, didn't they?"

Cynny's face was suddenly tired. "This is true," she said softly.

"I was against this idea of giving them a separate phone in the first place, you know," he said bitterly. "My God, I'd like to have seen my father's face when I was their age if I'd come home and told him I wanted my own telephone! I've given up ever expecting them to be grateful for anything I do for them, but at least they ought to be responsible enough to live up to their end of a bargain, shouldn't they?"

"Jim, can't we talk about this later? What about your flight, what about dinner?"

There was a pause, and then he said, "I finally have space confirmed on the eight o'clock flight. I've only been trying to phone you for the past hour to tell you that."

"Good, that's the early flight you wanted, isn't it? I expect there'll be dinner aboard then."

"Well, I'd rather eat first. I have some work to do on the flight down. All right?"

"Of course. How soon will you be home?"

"I'm leaving the office now. Look, why don't we stop off for a quick dinner on the way to the airport. Let the kids feed themselves."

"If you like, darling. It would save time. I have a PTA meeting at Joby's school tonight, too."

"Right. I'll be home in twenty minutes."

When Cynny left the bedroom, the house was once more relatively at peace. The unvarying beat of rock music now emanated from Susan's room. Next door, Cynny caught a glimpse of Joby hunched miserably over a book at his untidy desk, a thin young man in glasses perched on a chair beside him. She descended the stairs hurriedly and walked back to the kitchen.

Merna was seated comfortably at the table, a glass before her and a cigarette in her hand. "You get it ironed out with Mr. Holman?" she asked.

"Yes, everything's fine." Cynny rummaged among liquor bottles in a cupboard. "He's flying at eight o'clock, so we're going to eat on the way to the airport. Thank the Lord!"

"That's great. Now you'll have time to rest a little before you go out again. Listen, why don't I fix something for Susan and Joby before I leave?"

"Merna, you've worked hard today. They can have TV dinners."

"Cheeseburgers and a salad, what trouble is that? It's a lot easier for me to eat a bite with them than bother to cook when I get home. There's buns in the freezer, isn't there?"

"I think so." Cynny tasted her drink judiciously and dropped in another ice cube. "Just don't let them talk you into fussing over them."

"No way! Don't forget I'm not coming in tomorrow. I have that dentist appointment. You sure you don't want me to come in the afternoon?"

"No, do some shopping or something after the dentist, we'll be fine till Monday." She paused to drop a bill beside Merna's elbow on the tabletop. "Here's your dollar. Susan talked her way out of that boy in the sports car with no trouble whatsoever. It wasn't even close."

Merna laughed delightedly. "Baby, didn't I tell you!"

"Of course. Oh, Merna, damn it! Sometimes I get so discouraged. I don't think I was cut out for raising children."

"Oh, Miz Holman! If there's any trouble with you, it's that you love your kids and they know it. What's wrong with that? They're both good, sound kids. There's nothing wrong with either one of them that a little time won't cure."

"That's what you always say, Merna. I'll remind you of it when Joby flunks out of high school and Susan gets pregnant before she's fifteen. Use that melon in the bottom of the refrigerator for dessert, or there's ice cream."

"Okay," Merna said. "And you remind me Monday to tell you about a woman in our church with a daughter who's about eighteen now. That little girl was something else, too, when she was Susan's age, with all the boys hanging around. Her mother did plenty of worrying, I'll tell you."

"I'll remind you. I can't wait to hear. I'll bet the woman's hair's gone snow white and she's out in Camarillo State Hospital by now!"

She left the room and the sound of Merna's laughter, retracing her steps to mount the stairs again, moving more slowly this time. She closed her bedroom door against the blare of music and put down her drink. She unscrewed her earrings, stepped out of her shoes, and maneuvering around the dog asleep on the rug, lay down upon the bed. She rolled over onto her back, twitching her woolen skirt above her knees, lacing her fingers over her flat belly as she closed her eyes. Her face was composed, pale above her brown silk shirt, tiny crow's-feet suddenly visible at the corners of her eyes and mouth.

The rock music was only an insistent pulse beat now. An automobile passed along the street. The children's telephone jangled, the dog whined, dreaming, and then sucked loudly. And Cynny's day began unraveling before her in disconnected bits rising into her consciousness like scraps of lint in the wind.

Why did one always come away from that court building feeling so depressed and wrung out? If one stopped to think of it, there was only a kind of ghastly comedy about everything that went on there. But if there was a sweet smell to success, what was the odor of human failure? Because that was what that building reeked of, the sour smell of failure permeating every marble block and slab. The terrifying lack of love right down to the final inability to grant a shred of mercy, let alone the simplest human kindness. And all of it, apparently, as true a flower of the tree of marriage as unity, loyalty, and affection.

Poor Janet, gallantly flying off to Palm Springs with her bundles of cheese and sausage. But Janet was a survivor, Fred was the more vulnerable of those two by far. Someone said this girl of his was very nice; she hoped that was true. She hoped it was going to be a happy life for him. Or whatever passed for a happy life. What was a happy life anyway? Whatever you had the capacity to make of any life, actually.

That funny, infuriating little girl in the women's toilet, apparently determined to go into court and divorce a boy with whom she was still head over heels in love. And that poor, miserable woman weeping there in the corridor.

I won't think of her, Cynny told herself drowsily. I can't bear to! To find oneself standing helpless in a courthouse corridor one day while everything that you most value is slipping from your hands, oh, no! Please, let it never happen to me! For who of us can ever see around the next corner in our lives?

She drifted down toward sleep. There was the roar of a low-flying jet plane, gone as abruptly as it had come. And Cynny saw again, in a flash of recollection, a fish that had been lying on a bed of cracked ice in the produce market that afternoon, the huge, powerful, shining body, the implacable ferocity of the popping eyes, the wide, cruel mouth.

She screamed without a sound and opened her eyes. For a moment she lay still, staring at the ceiling, and then she reached for the telephone. She lowered it to the bed beside her and, with the receiver propped against her ear, punched out the number.

"Nancy? Now is this a bad time for you, are you cooking?"

"No, perfect, Cynny. I've just finished feeding the children, they're off watching cartoons on TV or Jerry Dunphy or some damn thing. Dave's working late again tonight, so I don't have to start cooking again for another hour."

"Good. It turns out I don't have to cook at all. Jim's off on a business trip and we're going to eat on the way to the airport. So how was your day?"

"Depressing. What about you, how was your court thing?"

"Fairly dreary." Cynny stretched out her hand for her drink. "But tell me about you, what happened today?"

"Nothing that bad, just one of those days that gets off to a rotten start and goes steadily downhill from there. Sambo woke up with sniffles, and it took me six phone calls to find someone else to do the car pool, all before I'd had my coffee. Then the washing machine backed up and absolutely flooded the laundry room. Naturally it was full of sopping wet bath towels at the time— Murphy's law, well, somebody's law. And poor old Mugger's been sick for a couple days, and today I had to face it, I don't think he's going to make it."

"Why, poor Mugger! He's not that old, is he, as cats go?"

"He may be, he was a stray, you know. Anyway, ever since the vet pulled him through pneumonitis last year he's been very feeble. Now he seems to have another pneumonitis-type infection. He hates the vet's so much, this time I think we should just let him go in peace. But it's so sad, once Sambo was asleep, I just sat down and blubbered. In the middle of that, Mary Barnum phoned. Cynny, you've heard me speak of Peg Schiller? Well, Peg's baby fell into the swimming pool this afternoon."

"Oh, my God!"

"Oh, the baby's all right. I just talked to Peg at the hospital. She had a tiny cut on her head, so they're keeping her overnight for observation."

"How old is she? How did it happen?"

"She's two, a sweet baby. Mary was there having coffee, it was the same old story. She was down for her nap. Peg knew she could get out of her crib, she simply never dreamed she could push open one of those heavy glass doors. It was all so fantastically lucky. They heard a noise, not a splash exactly but some sort of sound. Peg ran to check the nursery, and Mary went out onto the patio. She says she'll never know why, but she walked on around to the pool, and there was the baby just off the bottom in the deep end in her little pink nightgown. Can you imagine? But it was this same fantastic luck all the way. Peg's next-door neighbor was at home, and he started mouth-to-mouth resuscitation and then the Fire Department was there in just minutes."

"Peg was very lucky. But what a ghastly experience for her, poor thing."

"I know. Cynny, do you know what Mary told me? She said Peg really was marvelous through it all, absolutely shaking of course but under control. But after the firemen arrived and the baby still hadn't come around, all at once Peg said, 'Does anyone here know how to pray? Please, won't somebody pray for my baby?' And then she just kept repeating it in this agonized, pleading voice, 'Please, please, won't somebody pray for my baby!' "

"Oh, Nan!"

"I know." There was a tremor in her voice suddenly. "I wish Mary hadn't told me that, I can't put it out of my mind. Can you imagine how completely, utterly helpless Peg must have felt? It seems so terrible that she should have to beg like that for someone else to pray for her baby."

"I expect she's like so many of us, with no religious background or experience. She didn't know how to pray. That's understandable, isn't it?"

"Is it? Cynny, if it were your baby who was dying, and if it popped into your head that there was even the tiniest chance that prayer would help, don't you think you'd just do it? Wouldn't you just cry out inside yourself, 'Look, I don't know how to pray, I don't even know whether I believe that You exist, but if You do, whoever or whatever You are, help my baby!' Well, wouldn't you?"

"I don't know, and neither do you, Nan. This is something none of us can know until we're there. Aren't you being a little hard on poor Peg, love?"

"Oh, Cynny, I'm not blaming Peg! I love her, she's a terribly nice girl. What I can't bear is to think of her standing there watching them work over her baby and feeling so completely helpless and without resources. It's not her fault, it's just—it's such a commentary on our culture!"

"Oh, Nan," Cynny said affectionately. "You and your commentaries on our culture!"

"All right, laugh if you want to, but there is something terribly wrong with the way we live these days. That's exactly the point, we don't really live at all, we just look in the yellow pages! If the TV breaks down, call the repairman, or if we'd like to get married, call Computer Match. If a woman's being murdered in the street in front of the house, ring up the police. And if the baby's dying, try to get hold of someone to pray. Oh, Cynny!"

"Well, did anyone?"

"Did anyone what?"

"Pray for Peg's baby?"

"I don't know. Mary didn't say. Ah, now you're teasing me!"

"No, I'm not," Cynny said dolefully. "I just wondered. It's my fate in life. I'm the one, at the end of the story, who's always left wondering what happened next."

"Well, I suppose no one did or Mary would have mentioned it, wouldn't she? Anyway, now I want to hear about your day. How was your trip to court?"

"I'd better save that whole story for next time we talk. Jim will be here any second. Anyway, Janet's divorce went off without any hitches."

"Was she upset?"

"Of course. But she was marvelous. She carried it all off with really great style. She'd even thought to have a little gift for me, can you imagine? She said if it wasn't a tradition, it ought to be one. That, after all, we give gifts to our bridesmaids when we marry, which is a piece of cake compared to being a witness at a divorce proceeding."

"Oh, no! What was it? What on earth's the appropriate gift to give one's divorce witness?"

"I wonder, I haven't looked yet. But trust Janet to choose the exact right thing. Hold on, it's still here in my purse."

She sat up, reaching for the black leather bag at her feet. "Here it is. It's a tiny package, white paper and gold cord. Knot in the cord—there, I've got it. Jeweler's box, very elegant, layers of cotton, here we are."

She was silent for an instant, the little gold disc twinkling in the light as she turned it in her fingers.

"Well, do tell! I'm dying of suspense."

"It's a gold pendant. Or a charm for a bracelet. It has a circlet of pearls around the edge, and in the middle a bell with a ruby clapper. Ah, how clever, it's a marriage bell with a crack in it! Or is it the Liberty Bell? Ah, well, either way it's terribly appropriate, isn't it? And engraved on the back, 'With love from Janet' and the date. It's really very pretty."

"Now, Cynny! I don't care what you say, that is the end!"

"I know. What a commentary on our culture!" Cynny chanted it along with her and laughed. "Oh, Nan, you are funny!"

There was a brief tattoo on the door just then, the dog lifting his head alertly as it swung open.

"Jim," Cynny said. "Hello, darling."

"No, don't stop. I'll go pack."

He walked on down the hallway, a big, sandy-haired man, not particularly muscular, with just a trace of thickening about his middle and the first suggestion of heaviness in the chin of his angular, intelligent face. He paused at the doorway at the end of the corridor and turned on a light switch. It was a large, high-ceilinged room, a combination bedroom and study, neat and uncluttered, with bookshelves along one wall and a large, shining, steel and black Formica–topped desk in front of the windows. He put his attaché case on the desktop and walked to a wall of closet doors, lifting out a small suitcase and carrying it to the bed, each motion sure and economical. But after he had pulled out a drawer stacked with shirts, he paused for a moment, tired.

Incredible, he was thinking, there was no escape from it anywhere in this house, that damn endless racket the kids called music these days. Hadn't he just asked Joby to turn it down? He felt the beginnings of a headache, the skin-stretched tension from a half hour of the nightly freeway traffic, the familiar jagged, gnawing pain of a half-healed ulcer. He was bone tired, he had a plane to catch and a mountain of work to be done once he was aboard. His mind leapt ahead anxiously to the stack of papers in the attaché case and the project they encompassed.

But through the open doorway he heard just then Cynny's joyous laughter and felt instantly a claw of resentment sharper than the ulcer's pain. Ah, women had it rough these days, he thought, sorting bleakly through the shirts. Stretched on a bed with a drink in her hand and the telephone to keep her company while somebody else ran his tail off in a man-eat-man jungle and paid her dressmaker's bills, hired the house kept for her and the food cooked, the lawn mowed, and her pedicures. Yes, women had it rough, you'd better believe it. And if you didn't, all you had to do was take a look at the actuarial tables of any life insurance company!

The thought brought him no pleasure, only a sense of his own injustice. Because when you came down to it, he thought wearily, it was women who had turned out to be the computer marvels of this century. That one in there juggled a hundred services to keep this household in impeccable running order at all times, and another fifty that had to do with the children's health and education. All of this coupled with the inexhaustible patience to put up with the kids' endless guff, and the time and energy left over for a full social life and a dozen community affairs. Incredible!

This thought brought him no pleasure either, and with a sour brass taste in his throat, he strode suddenly to the doorway. "Job!" he yelled. "I asked you when I came in, didn't I? Turn down that damn machine!"

The music continued unabated, but a moment later it ceased. An instant after that Cynny entered the room, crossing the floor in stockinged feet to where he bent over the suitcase.

"Hi, darling," she said. "So how was your day? You look tired, love."

"I am. Today was a bitch."

They kissed briefly.

"Poor you! I'm sorry it was a bad day. Would you like me to finish packing for you?"

"It's all done now. Except the junk from the bathroom."

"I'm sorry about the telephone this afternoon."

"That's all right. I'm sorry I yelled at you."

"Wait a second, I think I hear Joby leaving." She moved to the doorway. "Joby? Darling, if you're going out, please check with Merna. She's getting dinner for you and Susan, and I don't want you to hold her up. And take Putzi with you, would you? He's been in the house all day."

"Okay, Mom."

"Who's the boy who was just leaving on the motor scooter?"

Jim asked as she turned back into the room. "He looked a hell of a lot more intelligent than most of Joby's friends."

"That must have been Franklin. He's the boy from UCLA who's tutoring Joby in math. He's very nice."

"I should have known. Joby's friends run to the long-haired types with the dirty bare feet. How's he coming with the algebra anyway?"

"Franklin says he's doing much better." She hesitated. "There was another U notice last week though."

"Oh, my God! It's just simple high school algebra, is he stupid or what? I've told you, there's only one way to handle this. Make him turn in his car keys until the grades go up, and no arguments about it."

"Jim, do you really think that would help? I'd like to talk it over with you as soon as you have the time. They all take cars so for granted, you know. He's really terribly unhappy these days as it is, and restless and bored with school. I'm honestly very worried about him, Jim."

"Yeah, I bleed for that kid," he called back from the bathroom. "He's got a room full of cameras and skis and hi-fi speakers and tape machines and you name it. And a custom-made surfboard and a car in the garage. When I was his age I had to get out and work for what little I ever had. The trouble with Joby, he's spoiled rotten. You give him a hell of a lot too much leeway, and it's not paying off. He's turning into a surly, bad-mannered kid, some kind of lamebrain whose only interest or ambition in life is to paddle up and down on a surfboard, for God's sakes!"

"Oh, Jim, he'll be bored with surfing in another year! He's going through a difficult period right now. It's a very hard world for children to grow up in these days, especially—"

"Don't give me that! When has it ever been an easy world for any of us to grow up in? There was the Depression and after that World War Two—I suppose that was easy? It's a competitive world, that's all, it always has been and it always will be in some form or another. With his grades, Joby's never going to get into any decent university. He's already blown that. He never studies, he's always off surfing or fooling around, and you let him get away with it. I never should have let you con me into giving him that damn car in the first place!"

The room was still for several seconds, and then Cynny said, "Jim, that's not fair. You're much more indulgent with the children than I am. You love to give them things, and at the same time you seem to begrudge them everything they have. Especially Joby. That car was not all my idea. I always get this feeling you're trying to make me take total responsibility for the children. If Joby's a problem just now, it's our problem, isn't it?"

"My God, isn't child rearing a woman's function either anymore? How much time do I have to spend with them? You're the one, aren't you, who's here at home with them every day?"

He yanked open a medicine cabinet door, reaching first for the bottle of chalky ulcer medication. He took several hurried sips and then tightened the cap before he dropped the bottle into a shaving kit together with a half dozen vials of pills that he swept from the cabinet shelves—sleeping tablets, stomach soporifics, tranquilizers, and painkillers.

He strode rapidly back into the bedroom, anger flaring in him like exploding rocket shells. Cynny was bent over the suitcase on the bed, and he looked at her with animosity. What he saw at that moment was a dumpy woman in a woolen skirt twisted and bunched at her waist, rumpled hair, and a pale, vacuous face with shadowed eyes and lines at her mouth and throat.

Silly bitch, he said to himself, and then repeated it in a gleeful unspoken chant of hostility. Silly bitch! Silly stupid bitch!

"Jim, this necktie you've packed has a spot on it," she said neutrally. "Would this other one do instead?"

"Which one? Yes, thanks." Then he added, his voice strained, "Look, maybe you're right about the car business. We'll have a talk about Joby when I get back. Right now I have a brute of a headache and a hell of a lot of things on my mind, all right?"

"Of course, darling. That finishes the packing, doesn't it? I'd better go put on some lipstick, we really haven't all that much time."

"Right. I'll change my shirt and be right with you."

When Cynny hurried from her bedroom several minutes later, clad in her suit jacket, her purse over her arm, the suitcase and attaché case stood together outside the open door of Susan's room.

She heard Susan saying breathlessly, "Daddy, these satellite pictures are so neat! Thank you for remembering to bring them, they're exactly what I need."

"Well, what you have there is about the whole story. There's a little more fancy hardware around, but it's pretty much classified. Nothing your social studies teacher is likely to know about anyway."

They appeared just then in the doorway, Susan nestled against him, his arm about her waist.

"Good-bye, Daddy. Have a good trip."

He kissed her and then held her close against him for an instant longer, his face buried in her thick, shining hair, while Cynny waited, adjusting the knot of her scarf.

"Good-bye, baby," he said, scooping up the bag and attaché case.

"Good-bye, darling," Cynny added. "I'll go straight from the airport to the PTA meeting. I should be home around ten o'clock, all right?"

"Of course, Mama."

"Be a good girl," Jim called back. "And get to work on that project now. If you get an A on it, we'll talk some more about putting in your own telephone."

"Daddy, you're a love! Don't worry about the project, all I needed was the pictures. It's going to be A-plus-plus, the best in the class."

Jim was chuckling as they reached the bottom of the stairway. "Well, at least we have one A student in the family," he said fondly. "Wouldn't it be a kick if she turned out to be a wizard at math? I wouldn't put it past her, you know."

"Nor I," Cynny said with no particular expression. "Susan is what the school guidance counselors call 'extremely well motivated.'" And then, lifting her voice, "Merna? We're leaving, dear. Good luck with the dentist. See you on Monday, and thanks so much for getting dinner for the children."

"It's okay, Miz Holman," she answered from the kitchen, her voice increasing in volume as she approached the hallway. "I'll see you Monday morning. Mr. Holman, you have a safe trip now."

"Thanks, Merna. Good-bye."

Merna clicked a wall switch that turned on the outside lights at the front of the house. For a moment she lingered in the doorway, watching them with proprietary pride as they descended the steps in the pool of golden light.

They made a nice-looking couple, those two, she was thinking, him big and good-looking and her such a little dainty thing. And for the thousandth time in a lifetime spent cleaning their houses and cooking in their kitchens, she was aware, with a certain amusement, of what seemed to her to be the extraordinary difference between white folks and black. The Holmans were good people, but like all the other white folks she had ever known, in spite of their money and their easy living, they never seemed to know how to really enjoy life or each other. Or maybe that was where the difference actually came in, Merna pondered, maybe white folks got their kicks out of living in other kinds of ways that she couldn't dream of.

I hope that is true, Merna thought as she closed the door. Because I really love that little woman. For Miz Holman's sake, I sure hope that is true.

Jim and Cynny walked together along the drive beneath the tree limbs, the chill mist damp against their faces. It was dark now, except for the lights that twinkled through the leaves.

"Would you rather drive, darling?" she asked as they approached the long, glistening bulk of the car.

"Not unless you're too tired."

"No, I don't mind." She walked on around to the driver's side, reaching into her purse for the keys.

He opened the door on the passenger side and tossed the suitcase and a raincoat into the back before he entered the car. The attaché case he placed carefully between his feet, then fastened the seat belt.

"Where shall we eat, love?" she asked.

"How about that steak place off the freeway? I can't think of the name of it, but you know the one I mean."

"Fine, it shouldn't be too crowded this early. Isn't it funny, I can't remember the name of it either."

He turned to look over his shoulder, pointedly watching for traffic as she backed the car out of the drive, and Cynny's face was momentarily amused. He sat back then, reaching for the attaché case and lifting it onto his knees. His mind turned back to the project it represented, and with an enormous sense of relief he was again immersed in it.

Several minutes later Cynny turned her head, but at the sight of his absorbed face in the dim light she remained silent, giving herself up to her driving instead. It was a full fifteen minutes, when she had turned on the windshield wipers and the sibilant hiss of the swinging blades was suddenly loud in the quiet car, before his concentration was broken.

"I'm sorry," he said quickly. "We're nearly there. I must have been half asleep."

"That's marvelous. It's good for you to rest."

He glanced to where the slender blades cut twin dark swaths across the blurred glass. "Hey, it's raining!"

"Just a drizzle. Wouldn't it be wonderful though if it really would rain?"

"It looks slippery. You'd better slow down."

"It's not that wet. I'm being careful, darling."

He stretched, moving his shoulders against the seat back, and yawned. The few minutes he had spent in a preliminary run-through of his project had been highly satisfying and reassuring. This project had been under his supervision since its inception, and he wanted its approval very badly. However, for the moment at least, he felt a complete confidence. No one else could have come close to it, they could not possibly miss. And with his confidence came a sense of well-being, and a heady relaxation of tension.

The car seemed particularly snug and intimate against the wet night. He discovered that he was looking forward to a well-cooked steak. And he was aware also of the scent of his wife's perfume and Cynny herself beside him, her hands on the wheel, the poise of her smooth, dark head and the clarity of her profile.

"You know, Cynny, you drive a hell of a lot faster than you used to," he said, teasing. "How many traffic tickets are you holding out on me anyway?"

She glanced at him quickly, caught by the sudden shift in his mood, and found his face indeed relaxed and smiling. She laughed. "No tickets, knock wood. I think you've simply gotten used to my poky driving after all these years."

Her smile lingered, and he felt the faintest quickening of an old desire. Cynny in her own way, he thought with a certain mild surprise, was still a damned attractive woman. Never a breath-stopping beauty, but something more subtle and indefinable. Whatever it was about her, it had been there in the turn of her head and the shape of her smile, just as it had been when he'd met her at somebody's dull dinner party a hundred years ago. It came into his mind to wonder with more curiosity than emotion if she had ever had a lover or ever wanted one.

She set the right turn signal blinking. "Good," she said as the car rolled to a stop in the wide driveway. "The parking lot is half empty. We won't have to wait for a table."

The red-jacketed parking attendant offered his hand as she slid from the seat, and Jim came around the front of the car, where fine drops danced in the beams from the headlights. Together, they ducked beneath the overhanging roof. The restaurant was a low, sprawling, nondescript structure with faked timbering over stucco walls and windows of leaded colored glass.

"Jim, I didn't see a sign when we drove in, did you? Do you think it could be that the reason we never remember the name of this place is it hasn't one?"

He laughed with her and reached out his hand to the back of her neck in one of his rare gestures of affection, his fingers moving against the soft, warm skin inside her jacket collar. She looked up at him, her face pleased, and rubbed her cheek against his hand.

He opened the door, and they entered an interior that was considerably darker than the parking lot and pungent with the aroma of smoking charcoal. On the left was a bar, where bottles and glassware twinkled in the gloom, and ahead, a large, half-empty dining room. They were seated immediately at a small table against the wall, and Jim consulted the menu for them both, holding the outsize sheet of glossy cardboard into the candlelight while Cynny hunted in her bag for cigarettes.

After the food was ordered, the point established that they had a plane to catch, and a tall drink delivered to Cynny from the bar, she wriggled in her chair suddenly, her face lighting. "Jim, this is fun! Ye Olde Anonymous Inn seems terribly cozy tonight. It must be the rain. Do you realize this is the first we've had since last April? I hope it absolutely pours! Have some wine, love. Let's get smashed and miss the plane and the hell with the PTA!"

He grinned at her. "Oh, sure! I have to do enough drinking on these trips as it is. Cheers anyway."

"Damn! Then it looks like I'm stuck with the PTA. Cheers, darling. To your trip. Is it something important?"

"Yes, fairly. I've been in on the development of this gadget from the beginning. I'd like to see it go."

"We'll drink to that then. It's NASA, isn't it? Would it be an important contract to get?"

He shrugged. "Any contract these days is important. You

know how it works. NASA was never a big customer necessarily, they buy two of this and a half dozen of that. But this gadget, for instance, could be used in a few other places in a modified version, the Air Force for one, maybe later on even commercial aircraft. If it meets NASA specifications, we're about guaranteed that there'll be some damn big contracts coming along in the next year or two."

"It sounds exciting. Could you tell me about it, or is it terribly classified?"

"Actually, it's pretty technical. I doubt if you'd find it all that interesting anyway."

"I suppose," she said. "Jim? Speaking of the office, something I've been meaning to ask you. Dave Friedman seems to work a lot at night and overtime these days. Must he, or is it his own idea?"

"Why? Has Nancy Friedman been bitching about it to you?"

"Oh, Jim, of course not! I've just gathered, talking to her, that Dave was working rather long hours and was away from home quite a bit. It's my own curiosity. I just wondered if he had to be or whether he chose to be. Actually, it's none of my business, is it?"

"Don't be silly. It's a hard question to answer, that's all. Dave is in on two or three things at the moment, and he's not a clock watcher. Dave's a pretty bright guy, you know. He's liable to do some pretty interesting things one of these days, particularly if he has the kind of wife who won't be nagging him about the hours he keeps or on his back about something else half the time."

"Well, Nancy certainly isn't the nagging type. She adores Dave, she's very proud of him and terribly interested in what he does, as much as she's allowed to be."

"Good. Then what's the problem?"

"No problem," Cynny said mildly. "Just that ever since the summer, Nancy has seemed a little downbeat. It isn't like her. It occurred to me it might be because she is alone too much. But it's certainly nothing important. Nancy is a very bright girl, too. She'll work it out."

"I assume you know that the fact that you're buddy-buddies with Nancy Friedman sows consternation through the whole echelon of younger guys at the office?"

"Oh, Lord, office politics! As bad as the Army. I suppose it's bad form for me to fraternize with the wife of a junior officer. Darling, you don't object, do you?"

"Hell, no. Not if she amuses you. Frankly, I've never found Nancy Friedman all that amusing myself. Too many freckles and a mind like a little steel trap."

Cynny giggled. "Jim, what a thing to say! Well, I like Nancy very much. She always has something else to talk about besides babies and shopping and Dave's career, and that's a switch, I promise you. There, isn't that our food just coming?"

"About time! What do we have on for this weekend, incidentally? I've already canceled my appointment at the barber's and my golf date for Sunday morning."

"Tomorrow night we had that fund-raising thing, cocktails and an art show. I'd love to get out of it anyway, now I have an excuse. Saturday night we have ballet tickets."

"There's a possibility I may stay over Saturday night and have dinner with a guy in Huntsville," he said while the waiter put the hot plates on the table. "You'd better get someone to use the other ticket. What about Sunday?"

"Only the McClures' dinner party."

"I'll be back for that in any case. How is your steak?"

"Just right. Delectable. How is yours?"

"All right."

Conversation dwindled as they ate. The dining room was beginning to fill up now, waiters and busboys hurrying between the tables. Jim's mind turned again, in spite of himself, to the plans in the attaché case. There were admittedly a couple of sticky spots in the presentation, but then he had not yet seen the final figures from the computer; he had reserved those for study on the plane. If they were not what he expected them to be, he was in trouble beyond question. Some of his confidence began to drain away at the thought, and with it the flavor and aroma of his food. Anxiety prickled within him, and for the remainder of the meal he was silent and preoccupied.

The plates were cleared away and steaming cups of coffee placed before them. Cynny reached for her cigarettes. "That was very good," she said contentedly. "Look, there are people waiting in line now for tables, we got here just in time."

He made no answer, and she peered into his tense face.

"Darling, are we running late? We needn't drink the coffee if you need to go."

"No, we have time," he said shortly. He struck a match for her cigarette, and she leaned forward to the small, wavering flame.

"Jim, what is it? If your steak was too rare, you should have sent it back."

"Nothing's wrong, the steak was fine. Waiter! Waiter, could we have some cream here?"

But there was no doubt of it, she was thinking, the good humor with which he had entered the restaurant had unaccountably vanished, and she felt her own spirits begin to fall accordingly.

"I haven't told you about my crazy afternoon," she said finally, her voice deliberately light. "Today was the day I went to court with Janet Anderson."

"God, I forgot. How did it go?"

"Honestly! Do you realize that this makes three or four times I've done this? And every time I swear I'll never do it again. First we had lunch, of course, with everyone being too bright and witty for words. Poor Janet! And it was hot and smoggy downtown, and I had terrible butterflies. The actual court thing wasn't that bad, it's just that that whole place is so fantastic. And depressing. Jim, it was so sad, after it was over I went to the ladies', and I found this girl, she was very young and—"

"What did you say anyway?"

"You mean on the stand? Oh, just the usual. You know. That

we'd been to dinner there when Fred hadn't shown up. That Janet was upset and losing weight and all that. Actually, it was all more or less cut and dried; the lawyers had worked out the property settlement a month ago."

He moved impatiently upon the soft vinyl chair seat. "Fred Anderson is a fool. To uproot his whole life like this! Not to mention the community property. Incredible!"

"Oh, I don't know, I hear that this girl of his is very nice. I expect Fred thinks it's all worth it for a little happiness, don't you imagine?"

"Happiness!" He snorted. "To start over again with a new family at his age? To cripple his business in a property division and then pay Janet a whacking alimony out of his half besides? You call that happiness? Even if this female of his was an angel straight from heaven, he'd have to be crazy. Fred's old enough to know better, for God's sakes!"

She was silent behind a blue drift of cigarette smoke, and what he construed to be the implied criticism in her silence stung him.

"Ah, you girls get very sentimental over happiness, don't you?" he said, more bitterly than he had intended. "But then you can afford to be. California community property laws were made for women. You have it all your way in the courts. A man has to be out of his mind to go that route."

There was a hurt in her face for an instant that he did not altogether understand.

"You make it all sound like a business transaction," she said. "As though that were the only reason for anyone to keep a marriage together anymore."

He stared at her and wondered what precisely she was thinking, and he felt a small, cold trickle down his spine.

"Well, as you say, it's all damn depressing," he replied in an effort at lightness. "Why can't everyone be sensible like you and me? Waiter? I'll have the check now."

A moment later, with his wallet half out of his pocket, he was smiling suddenly. "Well, well," he said. "Look who's here! Our chief competitor, Mr. California Aerospace Electronics himself! Obviously we're not the only ones who've discovered that this is the best place to eat on the way to the airport."

"Where?"

"Over against the other wall. They've just been seated." Jim appeared once more to be in very good spirits indeed.

Cynny looked discreetly along the row of tables, her gaze coming to rest finally upon the thickset, vigorous-looking man with the short, graying hair. "Ah, yes," she said. "Tom Fallon. I didn't see them come in. He really is very striking looking, isn't he?"

"Actually, he's a nice guy," Jim said. "If he weren't such a cocky bastard. The trouble is, he's nearly as good as he thinks he is. But this is once when he could save himself a trip."

"You mean you think he's off tonight on the same errand you are? How funny. Here you are eating in the same restaurant, maybe you'll end up flying on the same plane."

"He's off on the same errand all right, but I doubt if we'll be on the same plane. They'll start him at the other end of the appointment list."

Cynny glanced again across the dark, crowded room. Tom had donned a pair of black-rimmed glasses to read the menu in the candlelight, and his companion, a small woman with streaked, wispy blond hair, was talking to him animatedly.

"I don't think I've ever seen his wife before. She has a very nice face."

Jim was concentrating momentarily over the check. "Who? Oh, Tom Fallon." He looked again in their direction and then laughed. "Well, she may have a nice face," he said cheerfully, "but for your information, she is not Mrs. Fallon. Old Tom's quite a woman chaser, you know. At least it's a switch. Mrs. Fallon happens to be younger and prettier than that female, who-ever she is. Have you finished?"

"Yes. Is there time for the ladies'?"

"Just. I'll meet you in the lobby."

A moment later, when Cynny left the powder room, she caught an unexpected glimpse of the pair back in the dining room. The menus had disappeared; they sat now with drinks before them, englobed in mellow candlelight. She saw Tom snuff out a cigarette and reach across the corner of the table to take the woman's hand in his, making of the commonplace gesture something so touchingly intimate that Cynny halted, rooted for an instant in the dim corridor. The woman looked at Tom, her face shining. He spoke to her briefly; she nodded and placed her other hand over his caressingly. For a moment they were silent, engaged in some private communication, an aura of love and tenderness enveloping them as tangibly as the candle glow. Then the moment was gone, and they both moved at once. Tom reached for cigarettes, and the woman tipped back her head to laugh, bursting into rapid speech and tugging at his coat sleeve teasingly, her face crinkling with merriment.

Cynny came back to herself with a guilty sense of voyeurism. There was an inexplicable lump in her throat, and tears smarting beneath her eyelids. Oh, now really, she mocked herself as she set off again.

Jim waited, squeezed against the wall in the crowded foyer, glancing at his watch just as she approached.

"What were you doing in there anyway?" he asked pleasantly. "Never mind, we're timing out just right." He turned away to push open the heavy wooden door. "My God, is that fog? All I need is that damn bus ride out to Ontario tonight. What's the matter, Cynny? You're very quiet all of a sudden."

"I was hoping for the rain, but now it's stopped. We need rain so badly, everything's so dry and parched and dusty. Sometimes I can't bear it, I find myself absolutely longing for it."

"You should be used to doing without it by now," he said lightly. "You know it never rains in Southern California."

"You always say that," she said. "Ah, but don't forget, when it does, it pours!"

IT WAS UNCOMFORTABLY CLOSE TO THE TIME OF his departure when Tom arrived at the airport that night. Since he never boarded a plane until the last possible moment, he and Hallie had evolved a standard procedure for these occasions. Once the dusty blue sports car reached the terminal area along the loop of crawling traffic, Tom cut over in front of an oncoming bus and a honking yellow cab to pause briefly at a street island where Hallie alighted. He roared off then in search of an empty parking space amid the dark, sprawling acres of automobiles, and Hallie, lugging his attaché case, darted through the traffic to enter the terminal and hold a place for him in the line before the check-in counter.

This time, to Hallie's consternation, the check-in line had dwindled away entirely before Tom appeared, striding along with his raincoat slung over his shoulder. She hovered nervously while he presented his ticket and checked his bag. Tom turned to her then, glancing at his watch, entirely unperturbed. "Well, Mrs. C., we timed this out just right, didn't we?" he said, highly pleased with himself.

Hallie, who was temperamentally unsuited to such last-minute departures, moaned. "Tom, come on! There's still the tunnel and the X-ray and that poky escalator—"

"Plenty of time," he said cheerfully, pulling a fold of bills from his trousers pocket. "No, don't you come. No point you hiking all that way. Here, here's your taxi fare."

He thrust a bill into her hand and then enveloped her in a great bear hug. "Good-bye, Mrs. C. Take care. I'll see you on Sunday."

"Good-bye, darling. You take care. Have a good trip. Oh, Tom, go on! Don't just stand here!"

Tom moved off laughing, and Hallie, unable to witness his leisurely progress for another instant, fled around a corner and leaned against the wall to catch her breath.

While Tom was making this departure, Mick Sanford was just arriving in Los Angeles. As Tom's plane idled in a mist-enshrouded corner at International Airport, awaiting its turn to taxi to the runway for takeoff, Mick's plane started through the cloud layer in an angling descent.

Mick was drowsing just then, and he was awakened by the light touch of a stewardess upon his shoulder, her face smiling down at him between smooth wings of hair. "We're coming in now," she was saying. "Would you fasten your seat belt, please? We'll be down in about six minutes."

"Good deal," Mick mumbled, then cleared his throat. He was aware of a slight buffeting of rougher air and sat upright immediately, stretching his cramped shoulder muscles and looking toward the dark square of window glass beside him.

"I hope you brought your raincoat," the stewardess called back over her shoulder. "It's a rainy night in L.A. Don't forget your belt."

"Thanks."

Mick watched her long, trim legs twinkling away up the aisle beneath her short blue skirt, yawned, and then dutifully fastened the belt across his middle. He was a medium-sized man in a rumpled brown jacket. His shaggy, longish hair was very blond, his eyes blue, and he wore glasses with tinted lenses upon a face that was more weather-beaten than tanned.

The plane had already slowed perceptibly, seeming now to hover in the darkness, and the shadowy cabin was quiet, that particular quiet just before a landing when the movie is finished, earphones put aside, cups and glasses collected, cigarettes snuffed out, books closed, and conversations ended, each passenger alone with his own thoughts.

Mick chewed gum rhythmically, his eyes fixed once more upon the little square of window glass, and clasped his hands, with their curious mottling of ridged scar tissue, together over his seat belt buckle. He was thinking about where he was going to stay in Los Angeles. The Miramar Hotel, he supposed. It was his first homecoming since Theo's death, and it was going to seem damn odd not to put up at the old house in Santa Monica as he always had. He was so accustomed to it, as a matter of fact, that it had never occurred to him to make a hotel reservation. But then, to be honest, he had not really thought a great deal about Theo's death since Trav phoned him in London with the news—when? In August, wasn't it? He had not even missed her letters particularly, he recalled with a twinge of guilt, her faithful weekly letters, thin white sheets covered with her meticulous black typing, each one beginning with the old-fashioned salutation "My dear nephew," those great letters, ordered, a little formal, occasionally vivid, and never dull. Like Theo herself.

He thought of her for a moment with deep affection, the image flashing in his mind of the tall old woman in her old-fashioned mink cape, a giant leather handbag over her arm, and the faint fragrance of jasmine as she sallied forth each morning on her endless rounds of charity luncheons and committee meetings, and the Episcopal church on Sunday. Well, she had been a great woman, no mistake, the last of a breed.

As Mick watched, the clouds thinned, and the lights from below pierced the blackness. The plane turned down a wing, swung smoothly, and drifted on. The tapestry of city lights below rose steadily closer. A few drops of rain spattered across the window glass. In an instant they were near enough to the ground to feel a final, exhilarating sensation of hurtling speed. Then there was a thud of contact and a creaking settling down onto full landing gear.

Tension inside the cabin burst like a bubble. Overhead lights came on, there was an instant rustle of sound and motion, and over a crackling P.A. system, a crew member announced that they had arrived in Los Angeles.

Mick was the first passenger out of his seat and among the first to leave the plane. Inside the terminal he paused long enough to drop his wad of chewing gum into a trash receptacle and light a cigarette before he set off again, in search of his luggage. He moved quickly, zigzagging past other pedestrians, and in his haste, the slight unevenness of his stride became apparent.

At baggage claim he was forced to wait, but the luggage appeared at last, and Mick snatched a brown canvas bag from the belt, then went off in search of a taxi.

He waved one down several minutes later, the driver a pudgy man in a pea jacket with a pale, fat, sour face.

"Where you want to go in Santa Monica?"

"The Miramar, I guess."

Bearing right in the flow of traffic, the cab accelerated, shooting off up a steep, curving concrete ramp, and Mick slid over to look out into the gathering fog. "This is new since the last time I was here," he said. "What have they done, rerouted the approach streets?"

"Aaah, they're always tearing up the streets around here," the driver said without interest.

Honking savagely at a slower-moving car ahead, the driver swerved the cab back into the traffic flow, then rocking to an abrupt stop for a red light.

Once the light turned green, the cab entered a dark, straight stretch of highway that ran along one side of the airport. A bearded young man in jeans with a bedroll beside him was thumbing for a ride at the edge of the road, and grinning into the taxi headlights, he lifted his hand in an obscene gesture as they passed.

"Aaah, you bum!" the driver roared, the cab lurching as he returned the gesture. "Starting next month I'm going on days," he added irrelevantly. "I'm getting too old for this night stuff.

Buddy of mine was hit over the head and robbed just last week. Girls, would you believe that? Couple of them dirty little bums with the long skirts and hair. Boy, I never seen nothing like it. You know what they ought to do? They ought to—" His voice was drowned out by the roar of engines as a huge jet swooped low overhead.

The red taillights ahead began to slow, and Mick caught a glimpse of a cluster of shops on the left, surrounding a multi-storied building with a lighted marquee. He shot to the edge of the seat. "Hey, slow down, would you, driver? Is that a hotel up ahead?"

"The Marina? Yeah, it's a hotel, it's—"

"Look, I think I'll stop here," Mick said. "You can just let me off at the corner."

He piled out as soon as the cab was stopped, paid off the driver, and enormously relieved, plunged away to cross the street with the light.

Ten minutes later he was alone in a tidy, silent room with coral-colored walls hung with reproductions of blurry pastel seascapes. He draped his raincoat carelessly over a hanger in the empty closet and went directly to the telephone, reaching into an inside pocket of his jacket for a small address book. He turned on a table lamp with an oversize cylindrical shade and lighted a cigarette automatically before he dialed. He listened briefly to a repeating electronic buzz in his ear and put down the phone. Actually, he had not expected to find Trav at home; he had placed the call merely out of old habit and tradition, that his first call upon arrival should be to his brother. There would be time enough to reach Trav at his office in the morning.

His second call was to a friend, and this time he was smiling as he dialed. Old Bob was going to be surprised to find him in California. How long had it been since he'd seen Bob? A couple summers ago in Europe; no, that time last fall at the Glen. He was rewarded just then by the metallic voice of a recording that informed him he had dialed a disconnected number.

Mick put down the phone a second time and reached impatiently for the directory on the shelf beneath the tabletop, spreading it open upon the bed. He hunted C for Covern, found only a business number for Bob, and recalled the frustrating Los Angeles penchant for unlisted home telephone numbers. He leafed on, the names of a half dozen old friends coming to mind at once, then suddenly slammed the book shut. Struggling against a jet-lag limbo of disorientation, he stood for a moment, smoking, while a television set in the next room squeaked and vibrated. He considered then the one call to which he did not in the least look forward and decided that there was no point in putting it off, better to have done with it.

He rummaged in his suitcase until he found the thin leather folder beneath a wad of soiled shirts. He unzipped the folder and felt inside for the square airmail envelope addressed in Linda's flowing green-ink script. Carrying it back to the telephone, he unfolded the several thin sheets of the letter and skimmed Linda's girlish handwriting in search of the phone number. Once he'd found the number, he hesitated for a time, his hand upon the telephone, his eyes squinted against the smoke of his cigarette, then picked up the phone.

He dialed and listened through the ringing until a feminine voice spoke.

"Hello?"

"Mrs. Shapiro?"

"This is Mrs. Shapiro."

He did not find the voice familiar and, rattled, he said quickly, "Linda? Mick here." It was a telephone mannerism that he never used and even particularly disliked.

"Yes?" she said, her voice puzzled. Then she gasped, "Micky! Is that you? Where are you?"

"Here. California," he said awkwardly. "I just got in. How are you, Linda?"

"I'm fine, Micky. How are you?"

"Fine."

Now he remembered the voice just as he had the handwriting, the same eerie feeling of complete recognition, recalling it from a time when it had been as familiar to him as the musculature of his own hand. A soft voice, high-pitched and sweet, with a tendency to slur words together when she was nervous or excited.

"You're really here," she was saying. "Micky, I can't believe it. I mean, you really did come."

"Didn't you get my letter? I wrote you that I'd come."

"I know, but I was still afraid you wouldn't. I mean that something might come up or— Micky, I didn't tell Killian. I wanted to wait until I was sure you were really here. Oh, Micky, I wish you'd phoned sooner! Killian went to court this afternoon. Didn't I write you the date? Today was the day of her divorce hearing. I was so hoping you could see her before then. And here it was just this afternoon. Isn't that fierce luck?"

The primary irritation he felt at that moment was twenty years old and surprisingly alive and sharp, merely the name Killian reminding him of Linda's father, Don Killian, whom he had come to dislike thoroughly before he and Linda had been married six months. It was a double prong of memory actually, for the name also evoked the image of Linda herself, stiff backed and flush cheeked in a high, white hospital bed, determined with all the mulish obstinacy of which she was occasionally capable to name the newly born infant in honor of her father, recently deceased.

The bitter quarrel that ensued had been, as it turned out, one of their final ones. She had so persistently overridden his objection that he found Killian peculiar and unsuitable as a given name, particularly for a girl child, that eventually he had lost his temper completely, shouting over her tears that, in truth, Don Killian had been a miserable bastard in addition to one notch above a common thief, a fact glaringly obvious to everyone with the sole exception apparently of herself, and that he refused categorically to be party to the perpetuation of Killian's name through any child of his. Linda, of course, had filled in the name on the birth certificate five minutes after he stormed out of the hospital. Well, that was all a long time ago.

"How is she?" Mick asked.

"Killian? Oh, she's—she's fine. Except— you know, as I wrote you. I'm terribly worried about her. She wouldn't let me go to court with her today, that's typical, and she hasn't even phoned, so I don't know what happened or if— Micky, when can you see her? How long will you be in town?"

"A couple days. Just over the weekend actually."

"Well, when can you see Killian? If I'd only known you were here today, I could have—"

"I wasn't here today, Linda. I told you, I just got in about an hour ago. Look, don't you think we ought to—well, talk this over or something, before you start making plans? I don't know her, she doesn't know me, what makes you think she'd even want to—"

"Micky, I wrote it all in the letter! Killy does want to see you. And I think it's terribly important for her. I've talked to Marv about it, by the way, and he agrees. He thinks that especially at this time it might be terribly important for Killy if—"

"Oh, Christ! You know, I really don't give much of a damn what Marv happens to think."

Mick heard himself, appalled, and through the sudden silence marveled over what could have possessed him to say such a thing.

"I'm sorry, Micky," she said finally. "I didn't think you'd still be bitter after all these years. I just meant—well, after all, Marv is a psychiatrist and—"

"Look, I'm not bitter. Was I ever bitter? All I said was that I thought we ought to talk this over a little before you go ahead and set up any meetings for me with—with Killian. It's a damn awkward situation, for God's sakes. You ought to be able to see that."

"Micky, I don't know what to say. I'm sorry you feel this way about it." The remembered stubbornness was there suddenly in the soft voice. "It seems to me it's such a really tiny little thing to ask of you when it's the welfare of your own child. Your very own child, Micky, whom all these years you've never even once so much as—as— No, I'm sorry! I really can't see that it's asking too much of you."

The line was still once more, and when he spoke finally, his voice was strained, struggling for control. "Linda, you wrote me a letter and asked me to come out here. Well, I'm here. Now what in hell is it that you want me to do?"

"Micky, don't! Please!" the small voice said, the words slurring together. "What I really want is for us not to fight over anything ever again. Maybe we should have a talk before you see Killy. I'd—I'd like to see you anyway. Would you—like to come over tomorrow for lunch if you're going to be here such a short time?"

"I don't think I can make it. I'm having lunch with Trav."

"Oh, yes, of course. How is Trav?"

"He's fine, I guess. I haven't seen him in a couple years, but we talk now and then. He was divorced last winter."

"I'm sorry. He and Janie always seemed so happy. And the children were darling. But of course they must be practically grown up by now."

"Yes, as a matter of fact, Trav's a grandfather. Actually, he and Janie were divorced about ten years ago. He was married again since then. He has another child."

"Oh, I didn't know," the little voice said. "Well, I guess it's just the way the cookie crumbles or something. We're all on other marriages and divorces now, isn't it fierce? What about you, Micky? Are you married?"

"No. How about tomorrow afternoon then?"

"Any time you like. Would you like to come over here around four or five? We could talk, and then maybe you could take Killy out to dinner somewhere, just the two of you—"

"Linda," he said helplessly, "don't you really think we ought to talk about this before you—"

"Micky, I don't understand you." She paused and then laughed shakily. "Now that was a stupid thing for me to say, wasn't it? I guess I never did, did I? But you've come all this way, and now you're here I get the feeling that you don't really want to see Killy at all. Why don't you, Micky? She's your own flesh and blood. I know she's terribly mixed up right now, but she's a beautiful girl. I think you'd like her. She isn't anything like me, she's much brighter and more—"

"All right. If you think she wants to see me, and if it means this much to you, all right. Set it up with her for dinner tomorrow night then."

"But, Micky, don't you want to yourself?" She seemed suddenly at the point of tears. "Don't you want to get acquainted with her and find out what she's like and—"

"I don't know, Linda," he said. "I guess it's something I've never thought about, one way or the other. By the way, Theo died in August. You might like to know." And then he added, "My aunt Theodora. You remember."

"Oh, yes. I'm sorry to hear it, Micky. You always thought a lot of her. But she must have been terribly old, wasn't she?"

"Somewhere in her eighties. What time tomorrow night then?"

"I thought you were going to come between four and five. Then we'll have time to talk a bit first."

"All right, around five," he said, the reluctance still apparent in his voice. "And if she's made other plans for the evening, fine. We can always have dinner another time."

"Oh, she wouldn't have any plans that she wouldn't be glad to change. Micky, I don't think you understand how important this is to Killy. Marv says he really believes a lot of her problems just now are because she's still having her identity crisis and—"

"Oh, for God's sakes!" Mick said softly. "I'll see you tomorrow then. Good-bye."

"Micky, wait! Do you have a number where I could reach you if—"

But he had already put down the phone. He stood motionless in the dim, stuffy room with the persistent squeak of the television set from the other side of the wall. His disorientation was now complete. He regretted the impulse that had led him to check in at this strange hotel in the middle of nowhere instead of continuing on to Santa Monica. He regretted that he had not thought to send a wire to Bob Covern before he left London. He regretted having made the phone call to Linda or, more than that, that he had come back to California. For a nickel, he thought, for one lousy nickel, he would return directly to the airport and take the next flight to New York.

He angrily scrabbled up the door key and a pack of cigarettes, yanked his raincoat from the closet, hangers flying, and bolted out the door. In the lobby below, he strode to the car rental desk he had noted on his way in.

He was in luck, the girl at the counter told him cheerfully, only one car still available. Several minutes later he was confronted by the vehicle of his good fortune, a green Pinto with a slight dent in one fender and a gasoline gauge he was warned never registered below a quarter tank, even when it was empty. He pointedly checked the tires before he slid behind the wheel and then revved the engine for a moment, listening intently. He moved off along the narrow parking area before the row of shopfronts and made the left turn into the flow of traffic.

The drizzle had long since ceased. The streets were dry, he noted, although as he swooped down the steep, dark hill he saw a billowing blanket of white fog below. He switched on the radio and accelerated smoothly into the long downhill curve, assessing the handling and responsiveness of the light car. Suddenly he was relaxed and in the best of spirits, glad to be in California once more, filled with anticipation for whatever the night might bring. The phone call to Linda was forgotten.

IT WAS WELL AFTER DARK BY THE TIME PETE reached the beach house several miles north of Malibu. He had driven into the drizzle and stopped only twice, first to wrestle with the top of the convertible and, farther on, to purchase groceries.

By the time he reached the house, the trace of rain was gone and the wind was freshening from the sea. Only one end of the house was visible from the highway in the darkness, a narrow, elongated, two-story frame dwelling, the last in a row of similar houses, standing a little apart from the others with an expanse of dark, empty beach on either side. Pete unlocked the big brown-and-white painted door by the light of his headlights and drove his car into a clean, cavernous garage with fireplace wood stacked neatly against one wall and a pair of battered surfboards leaned against the opposite beside several pieces of terrace furniture. Unlocking another door at the rear, he carried his bag and grocery sacks through a service area into the kitchen. He moved on along a corridor, turning on lights as he went, and down several steps into a large living room. The far end of that room was walled in glass, looking out upon a wooden deck built on pilings above the sand and, beyond, the wide beach stretching away to the dark, frothing sea.

The house was larger than it appeared from outside, chill, damp, and faintly musty smelling. Pete adjusted a thermostat and doubled back to the garage for an armload of wood. He went about laying a fire on the clean, empty grate in the living room, a hasty arrangement of wadded newspaper, kindling, and logs. He poked gingerly with a sliver of kindling at the sooty damper lever in the depths of the chimney and then struck a match, sitting on his heels while he waited for the fire to catch. In the flickering light, his face was tense and impatient. Once the fire began to burn, he sprang up to the telephone on a table in the corner.

But the phone, he discovered, was dead. He tried an extension phone on the wall in the kitchen with a similar result and muttered in exasperation. In increasing haste, he went about wrestling the heavy green refrigerator from the wall, in order to reinsert the plug behind it. Once the light came on and the motor began to hum, he crammed his grocery sacks onto one of the shelves and slammed the door. Then he returned to the living room hearth, where the fire was burning merrily, added several large logs, and closed the screen. By now he was moving at a dogtrot back through the house, zipping up his jacket as he went.

It was only when he reached the garage that Pete became aware of the fog that had swept in during the few minutes he had spent inside, a glistening white vapor scudding swiftly and silently past the outside lights and blotting out the highway and the hills beyond it. He hesitated for only an instant, then pulled the garage door closed and bolted back into the house.

He remained just long enough to pull a heavy turtleneck sweater over his head, his fair hair left standing on end. He scrambled back into his thin windbreaker then and, as an afterthought, grabbed up a book from the top of his suitcase. This time he moved to the opposite end of the house, where he snapped on lights on the deck and loosed bolts to permit the large glass door to slide on its track. Outside, he closed the heavy door behind him without bothering to lock it and pulled up the hood of his jacket against the wet. Bending down, he quickly untied and removed his sneakers, stowing a shoe in either jacket pocket, and tossed his socks onto the damp floorboards of the deck. Then, barefoot, he leapt down the several wooden steps to the sand and struck off into the fog. Within a few yards the lights on the deck behind him paled and then vanished eerily, the entire house suddenly gone, only the pungent smell of the woodsmoke remaining where it was trapped by the fog above the chimney.

In the darkness, the heavy mist became another element, neither air nor water, impenetrable and engulfing, but Pete moved through it swiftly and surely, jogging toward the smell of the sea and the sound of its stirring, the tide rising with a thunderous crash of breakers against the shore. When he reached the water's edge, he turned left and set off at a run over the packed, wet sand. He ran easily, veering off only when a wash of cold water slid across the sand to lap at his bare feet, and once detouring around a pile of rocks where roosting seagulls twittered alarms in the darkness. A few hundred yards farther, however, he stopped, lifting his head to listen for a moment to the roar of the waves and the faint, melancholy beep of a distant foghorn.

Taking a new bearing, he turned his back on the sea and trotted off again at an abrupt ninety-degree angle. There was a pearly incandescence in the sky ahead from the lights of the highway, and several minutes later Pete reached the steep, sandy bank that was the demarcation between the beach and the highway. He turned right, and after a few steps more, there appeared out of the fog a symmetrical row of pale, rectangular patches, the lighted windows of a building. Pete found the end of a narrow, winding path that angled up the sheer slope and climbed, cautious of sharp rocks and squashed beer cans caught in the clumps of wiry grass. At the top, he bounded up a flight of steps and entered through a wooden door.

In the sudden warmth of the dim hallway, he threw back the hood and opened the zipper of his windbreaker. The building was a rambling, unpretentious restaurant and bar. Pete looked first into the dining room at the rear, where there were only a scattering of diners. He moved on then toward the sound of music and voices from the cocktail lounge at the front. He paused in the doorway, fumbling at the sneakers in his jacket pockets as he looked quickly about the large, dimly lighted room. But this room was nearly deserted as well, only three young men sitting together on stools watching television at the far end of the bar and one solitary couple holding hands across a tabletop near the open fire. Pete thrust his sandy feet into the damp canvas shoes and entered, walking toward the bar, where the bright, staring eye of the television set flickered nervously. A bartender in a gaudy Hawaiian shirt was lounged against a shelf, idly watching the screen, but when he caught sight of Pete, he came down the bar to meet him.

"Yes, sir, what'll it be?" he asked, and then as he drew nearer, "Pete! Oh, for God's sakes! How are you, stranger?"

"Charlie! It's great to see you!"

They shook hands affectionately across the polished bar top. He was a small man with a narrow, impassive face and rimless glasses beneath thinning gray hair. He clapped Pete awkwardly upon the shoulder and then shook his hand again.

"Pete, you look fine! What in hell you doing up here?"

"I took a break and came up for the weekend, Charlie."

"You mean up here to the house?"

"Yes, I just got in a few minutes ago."

"That's great, Pete. It's been a long time. Want to go fishing tomorrow morning?"

Pete grinned and with his jacket sleeve wiped shining drops of moisture from his face, a face quite different from the one he had worn for Tom and Nedith earlier: unguarded, self-confident, open, and engaging. "You know what I really want to do tomorrow morning, Charlie? Rack up about twelve hours of sack time. Man, I've been hopping lately. I feel like I could sleep for a week."

"You walk down, Pete? Better have a drink or some coffee to warm you up. The girls just brought me a fresh pot of coffee from the kitchen, how about it? Anything you want, Pete."

"Coffee would be great."

Pete slid onto a stool, propping his foot upon a rung of the stool next to him and bending down to tie his shoelace.

"You still take it black?"

"Yup, thanks."

"Boy, it's sure good to see you, Pete." Charlie never smiled, but when he was pleased there was a perceptible relaxation of the muscles of his face. "How's your school going?" he asked as he handed Pete a mug of scalding coffee.

"It's fine. They have a couple new projects on this fall that are really interesting. I'll tell you about them later. What about your eye, Charlie, did you have the surgery?"

"Yeah, I went in as soon as business slowed down after Labor Day."

"It must have been rough. Are you all right now?"

"Oh, sure. It was just a cataract, and there's nothing to it, the way they remove them nowadays. It's made a big difference already, Pete. Half the time now I bait up without my glasses."

"That's wonderful, Charlie. And how's the fishing?"

The bartender struck a match to a slender black cigar and puffed on it methodically four or five times before he answered. "Oh, hell, Pete, if I was ten years younger, I'd sell out and go up to Oregon. I still go out, three, four times a week, but I don't know. They keep on spewing oil and detergents and every damn thing they can think of into the ocean, there's not going to be any fishing left off this coast pretty soon. It's not the sport it used to be already. You remember some of those beauties we used to take off here even ten, twelve years ago?"

"I remember." Pete held the coffee mug between his hands, the warm steam rising against his face. "You know, Charlie"—his voice was affectionate—"you taught me things about fish in those days that still haven't showed up in any of the books!"

For an instant Charlie's face relaxed into its suggestion of contained pleasure and then, embarrassed, he puffed quickly upon his cigar. "Well, I never saw a kid take to fishing the way you did, Pete. I never had to tell you anything but just once. Boy, tell you once and that was it! You had the hands and the patience and the feel for it; lots of grown-up people never have that. Listen, Pete, tell me something, I came across something kind of interesting just a couple weeks ago. Did anybody down there at Scripps, or that Frenchman or anybody, ever do a study on— Just a sec."

He deposited the cigar in an ashtray and moved off in answer to a summons from the other end of the bar. He refilled glasses deftly at a beer tap and then went about making martinis for the couple at the table. Pete waited, sipping at the still scalding coffee.

The door at the front of the building opened then, and instantly Pete swiveled on the stool. It was two women in heavy coats and slacks, laughing as they loosened buttons and untied scarves, disappearing into the dining room. After one glance Pete turned back to his coffee, but his face was preoccupied and tense once more. And when the bartender returned, he said quickly, "Seen any of the old crowd, Charlie? Anyone I know been in lately?"

"Naw. You know how it is in the winter, Pete." Charlie leaned comfortably upon his arms on the bar top and began the leisurely business of relighting his cigar. "Bob Rinkler was in here one night a couple weeks ago. He didn't say what he was doing now. Oh, for God's sakes! I forgot to tell you! Did you hear about Jay Osterwald? He got killed last week. Out in the Islands."

"You must be kidding! Where?"

"Waimea. Hit his head on a rock or something. It sure came as a surprise to me, too."

"It's hard to believe. He was as good a surfer as there ever was on this coast."

"Yeah, he was. But that North Shore out there can get pretty rough. Boy, you stop to think about it, it seems like your old surfing crowd is racking themselves up pretty fast. Jay makes two, well, three if you want to count Noley Smith, that's got killed out in the Islands now. And then the Army and automobiles and dope. It's a shame. I remember when you were all a bunch of little kids fooling around with bellyboards."

"Yeah." Pete's voice was noncommittal. They were silent for a moment, and then Pete said abruptly, "Charlie, Killian hasn't been in here, has she? Last night or the last couple days?"

Charlie looked up briefly, then away, but his face remained expressionless, his voice dry. "No, she hasn't been in, Pete."

"Are you sure? Maybe sometime when you weren't here?"

"No, I'd have heard about it, Pete. She hasn't been in." He poked at the end of his cigar with a toothpick. He was about to speak again, then seemed to think better of it. For Pete, all at once, was smiling broadly as he peeled off his jacket. As a matter of fact, he appeared entirely relaxed now for the first time that day and, more than that, enormously pleased. "Charlie, when is Moke coming on? I think you and I ought to sit down and have a couple beers and catch up on the news, don't you? I haven't even had a chance yet to tell you about the job I did for the Navy this summer."

"Hey, I'd sure like that. Moke's supposed to take over in about an hour. How you fixed for time? I could phone him to come in early."

"Up to you, Charlie," Pete said cheerfully. "But I'm not going anywhere. I'll probably just hang around here until you close."

Killian just then was making bread in the small, cluttery kitchen of an apartment in the hills above Westwood, kneading the ball of dough in a large wooden salad bowl with vigor and abandon, her faded jeans dusted with pale wheat flour, her arms as well, and another smudge of it across her cheek and nose. She sang joyously along with the loud rock music that filled the apartment, working the dough to the same rhythm, her hair flying, her face intense and shining bright.

"Born free!" she caroled loudly, out of any context with the music. "That's me! Free, free! That's me!"

H ALLIE ARRIVED HOME FROM THE AIRPORT TO an apartment that always seemed too empty and too quiet when Tom had gone. She busied herself for an hour or so, washed a blouse, changed the polish on her nails, and wrote a birthday letter to a friend. It was only when she was ready for bed, when the television news was over and the set turned off, when she was seated at her powder table wearing the beads that Tom had given her over her nightgown and rubbing moisturizing cream into the soft skin of her face and neck, that she finally allowed herself to think of it, the remark Tom had made that had stayed with her all evening like a small, insoluble lump in her throat. She heard his voice again, gruff and moved, "I sat there in that dreary damn bar with the poor kid, Hallie, and what I really ached to do was just load him into the car and bring him over here."

Hallie's eyes were suddenly wet with tears. She grieved for them both, for Tom whom she loved, and for Pete, the lone and troubled boy whom she did not know or ever hope to know. She turned upon herself suddenly in an agony of self-reproach, then stood her ground valiantly. Oh, come off it, Hallie, she told herself sharply. Stop trying to dramatize this into some ghastly soap opera. Who do you think you are, the Mata Hari of the ladies' hosiery department? Tom's marriage polarized into this way of living years ago, it has nothing to do with you, so get your silly ego back under control.

She sat for several minutes more, downcast and snuffling, counting off her shining beads like a rosary, and then she rose

125

resolutely and turned out the light. In bed, she searched for her place in the book she was reading and wandered off into a world of spies and counterspies, intrigue and violence. Thirty minutes later she was overcome with drowsiness, took off her beads, fumbled at the alarm clock button and the light switch, thought of Tom, a brief awareness of him like a kind of touchstone in her mind and in her flesh, and immediately fell asleep.

Tom's plane, meanwhile, with the coastal fog far behind it, sped through starry Texas skies, thirty minutes from bump down. Tom, in a lounge section, was nodding impatiently while a man beside him droned on and on. Eventually, bored beyond endurance, Tom looked at his watch, murmured something about a report to read, drained his glass, and left the lounge. Back in his seat he rummaged through the maps and folders in the pocket on the seat back in front of him, crossed his knees and uncrossed them, hitched at his trousers, looked at his watch again, and finally, because there was nothing else to do, fell to watching a small boy just across the aisle.

Something in the curve of his cheek above his soft neck reminded Tom of Pete when he was young. The child held a large drawing pad on his outstretched legs, his small face wide awake while his mother drowsed beside him. A red crayon outline at the top of the pad resembling a somewhat bulbous sausage Tom took to be a representation of an airplane flying over a row of crooked squares of houses drawn across the bottom. While Tom watched, the child, face intent, the bit of crayon lost in his little, fat hand, was swiftly adding a television antenna to the rooftop of each lopsided building, all sizes and shapes and manner of antennae, each one drawn with surprisingly meticulous and recognizable detail and exactitude. Grinning, Tom all but turned his head to share the small amusement with Hallie and, in the reminder of her absence, was aware one more time of the integral part of his life she had become. What a ridiculous way to live this was, he thought, and then it came to him, entirely without warning, that his time to act was at hand, no longer at some unspecific future date but now.

Well, I'll be damned, he marveled, more surprised than anything. He reexamined it, tested it and found it firm; his decision was made, his time to take action had indeed arrived. For a moment, he puzzled over where this decision had sprung from so suddenly. Not that the idea of marrying Hallie was exactly new to him, but what had occurred, he wondered, to crystallize his intentions at this particular point in time? What final connection had been made without any conscious volition on his part, what unsuspected impulse had flashed at last to activate the circuitry of change? Tom was not an introspective man. He dimly sensed that it most likely had something to do with seeing Pete today and let it go at that. Characteristically, with kindling enthusiasm, he was far more concerned about the immediacy of translating the decision into action, and it was the effect upon his business that he thought of first.

There certainly had been better times for this to have happened, he reflected ruefully, but then there had been worse ones as well. Luckily, at a time when aerospace spending had all but evaporated, this series of contracts was as good as assured to him, but he would need at least one more fair-size contract in some diversified area to ensure the firm's health before he began negotiations on the merger. It might take a bit of doing, five or six months perhaps, to put it all together, but certainly by the summer he and Hallie should be free and on their way.

And then he thought of Nedith, but only briefly and entirely without emotion. His wife became purely a matter for the lawyers, with the sale of the business to facilitate the property settlement. He could not conceive that a divorce could possibly mean that much to Nedith, not so long as she was assured of the house and her charge accounts at Saks and Sloane's. After all, how could a divorce at this stage of things alter her life in any fundamental way? He dismissed Nedith from his mind, thinking of Hallie once more instead as he snuffed out a cigarette and belted in for landing.

Life, when you stopped to think of it, was a damn queer business. From an affair that had begun like any other, out of mild fancy, curiosity, and boredom, had grown a relationship that had become central to his being. Damn queer. And damn queer that Hallie should have been the one. An unremarkable woman in many ways, he supposed, if it were possible to consider her objectively, separate from the extraordinary facts that he loved her and that she was indispensable to him. He had had a number of women younger than she, many of them more beautiful, several more intelligent, others more skilled in bed, and even one or two who might have cared for him as deeply. What was there about Hallie then? An essential womanliness that never ceased to please him, her indestructible goodness, her all-embracing warmth and concern, her childlike zest for life, her gift for joy. All of these things and none of them. Actually, it didn't matter a wet hole in the snow what it was about her, did it, he concluded, amused. She was the fact of his life.

For an instant, while the big plane settled like a feather toward the ground, Tom perceived his life in total shape and structure. Hard work, only a small part of which was the kind he found satisfying, no ego gratification any longer that began to match the intoxication of those years when the business was still growing in prestige and financial success; an ever-widening gap between himself and his grown children; an empty, rewardless marriage; the casual, pleasant relationships with a variety of women, for sex, for relaxation, for fun, and sometimes merely out of the cheerless compulsion of another form of ego need. Well, perhaps it was time he packed it up and made a change. Hallie offered whole new dimensions in living: love, companionship, endless new interests and enjoyments.

And when it came right down to it, Tom asked himself suddenly with exceptional candor, did it really matter which came first, Hallie or his need for her? The fact of the matter was that even a year ago he could not have believed it possible that he would consider entering into the stale entrapment of marriage again so long as he lived, and now it seemed the most natural, pleasant idea in the world to him. Since he had known Hallie, he had scarcely so much as looked at another woman. He could even contemplate putting aside his business without a twinge, rather with a positive sense of anticipation, all the good years ahead that Hallie would help him to fill and make delightful. Any man would have to be a fool to argue with that, wouldn't he? Certainly, he did not even intend to try.

The plane bumped down and rolled off swiftly along a runway. Monday, Tom made a note to himself as he loosened his seat belt. He would be rushed as hell on Monday, but he would get Batesey to make a clear hour for him somewhere and spend it with his lawyers. It would be wise to get on it immediately; these community property settlements were damn complicated affairs, particularly coming as this one would along with a few tons of paperwork connected with a business merger. Best to get the lawyers started at the preliminaries without delay.

He felt an exhilaration suddenly—it was time for action— and a vast impatience to begin. He considered the notion of telephoning his lawyer in the morning and discarded it; at least he would phone Hallie as soon as he reached the hotel. Waiting in the crowded plane aisle, however, he abandoned that idea as well. After all these months, it would keep until he phoned her tomorrow night. She would be asleep by now, and she got too little sleep as it was, setting off so early to that ridiculous job. Well, the time had come to put an end to that, fortunately. In the light of his decision, he certainly was not going to permit her any further arguments on that score. She was going to hand in her notice immediately, he would not have her exhausting herself at that store through another idiotic Christmas shopping season. He would tell her that, too, when he phoned tomorrow.

Tom stepped from the plane into the clear, windy Texas night. At the top of the steep flight of metal stairs, out of sheer confidence in himself and his future, he threw back his head and delivered himself of a loud and creditable imitation of a rebel yell. And then, amid the cold and curious stares, he descended the steps and strode off, grinning, toward the terminal.

CYNNY DROVE HOME FROM THE PTA MEETING through intermittent patches of fog, tensing at the wheel each time as she reduced speed and strained to see her way through the swirling vapor. By the time she reached home, she was chilled and weary. She garaged her car, let out the dog, and announced her arrival up the stairway to Susan and Joby. She returned to the silent kitchen, where Merna had cleared away all traces of the evening meal and performed her final nightly tasks with automatic efficiency: laid the places around the breakfast table and folded filter paper into the top of a coffeepot. Cynny finally made herself a tall whiskey nightcap, whistled in the dog, checked the door locks, adjusted the thermostat, and turned out the lights before she climbed the stairs.

In the hall above, she paused first at Susan's room, smiling momentarily at the contradiction of its growing collection of stuffed animals and the parade of male rock musicians on the walls. Schoolbooks were stacked on a corner of the tidy desk, one of the twin beds was turned down for the night, clothing for the next morning laid out neatly upon the other one, and Susan herself was in the bathroom beyond, blond hair pinned to the top of her head as she soaked in the tub amid a froth of white bubbles.

Didn't she think she ought to get out of that tub and into bed before she withered like a prune, Cynny asked her cheerfully, dropping a kiss upon the damp, upturned face.

At the room next door, Cynny found Joby hard at work on the hated algebra with the radio to keep him company. She applauded his diligence and moved on. Leaving her purse and glass on the chest beside her bed, she followed the hallway to Jim's bedroom-study, where she turned on lights to close the drapes.

The room had a curious air of unoccupancy, no strewn clothing left behind after Jim's hurried departure, no clutter of turned-out pockets on the dresser top, no book or paper out of place. Cynny surveyed the rather barren room ruefully, reflecting as she often did upon Jim's propensity for prompt disposal of all the trivial bits and pieces of living, which she herself seemed to accumulate more with each passing year. It crossed her mind suddenly that if Jim's plane were to crash tonight, how very little of him would be left here; then she quickly put aside the thought as morbid. She lingered a moment longer, smoothing away the wrinkles his suitcase had left upon the bed, opening a book from the bed table and peering into it wistfully, only to discover it to be a technical study on some area of mathematics incomprehensible to her, and finally clicking off the light and returning to her own room.

She undressed and pattered off, naked, to the shower in the connecting bathroom. She soaped herself, then stood for several minutes, her face remote and dreaming, with the needles of hot water coursing over her pale body, a little too full at the hips and belly but still smooth and youthful, small, dark-nippled breasts still firm. Eventually, wrapped in a voluminous bath towel, she creamed her face, brushed her dark hair, and finally, with her eyes tightly closed, extended her tongue ten times toward the tip of her nose, a nightly ritual she believed would aid in keeping firm the muscles beneath her chin. A moment later she was in bed, wriggling comfortably against the propped pillows, smiling with a small sigh of contentment, arrived at last at one of her favorite hours of the day.

After a time, she sipped from the glass on the chest top beside her and then removed a ring of keys from her purse. She sorted through them until she found one small and ornate iron key and leaned over the edge of the bed to unlock the doors of the large wooden cupboard. The interior was crammed with books. She removed one of them and closed the doors again, dropping the keys back into her purse. Settling once more against the pillows, she turned the pages, found her place, and began to read.

The house was still after that, except for the muted music from Joby's radio. No traffic passed along the street outside; the fog swirled silently about the eaves and sifted through the tree limbs. And Cynny read on, her face intent, sipping occasionally at her tall, weak drink.

Twenty minutes later there was a light tap upon her half-closed door.

"Mom?" Joby said from the hallway.

Cynny closed her book instantly and shoved it, title side down, beneath a fold of coverlet. "Yes, darling. Come in."

He drifted in on bare feet and slouched against the wall inside the doorway.

"How's the algebra?" she asked.

"Aaah, that cruddy algebra!"

"Did you finish it?"

"I guess so."

"Good fellow!" Cynny stretched out her hand for her glass. "The PTA meeting tonight was interesting, love. You might like to read over my notes sometime, all about the different colleges and universities."

Joby snorted. "Oh, sure! All those schools are going to be fighting to get me!"

"Darling, don't sound so hopeless. Some good grades this year could make the difference. Besides, if your scores are good on the SAT test next month, you can still make it to the university, did you know that?"

"Aaah, that stupid test! I'm sick of taking their tests."

"I know. But it's the same for everyone. It's just the system."

"Cruddy system!" He moved against the wall, uncrossed his long legs, lifted one bare foot and held it, squeezing critically at a toe. "Mom? Bo's all set up to go surfing up north this weekend. I thought I'd go along. If it's all right with you."

"Where up north? How far did you have in mind?"

He shrugged. "Rincon. Maybe farther. It depends on the surf. See, Bo's going to drive his dad's camper. We'd just camp out in it wherever we happened to be. No sweat."

"Who's 'we,' love?"

"Bo and me. And Lovett. That's definite. Then this guy who's a friend of Lovett's. His folks are out tonight, so he won't know for sure if he can go till tomorrow morning."

"You'd leave early Saturday, I suppose. Would you be back Sunday before dark?"

"Well, the thing is, we thought we'd leave tomorrow. At lunch hour, so we wouldn't have to hassle the Friday afternoon traffic. Bo'd pick me up here in the morning with my board and stuff, and then we'd leave at noon right from school."

"Oh, Joby! That means cutting school tomorrow afternoon."

"Mom!" he wailed. "All I got tomorrow afternoon is gym. Fifth period on they're having some goddamn stupid assembly. It's going to make a lot of difference if I cut school tomorrow afternoon."

"But couldn't you leave early Saturday morning just as well?"

"Mom, we want to be in the water at Rincon by six-thirty Saturday morning, while the tide's out and it's still glassy. What difference is it going to make, one cruddy gym class? And if we wait till school's over, we'll have to hassle the traffic all the way up the beach."

"That's true." Cynny was wavering. "But what about the Haggartys? Won't they mind if Bo cuts school?"

"It was his mom and dad's idea that we leave at noon, Mom. On account of the traffic."

"Well, I suppose it is sensible. But, Joby, then what about homework, if you're going to be away both nights? There's the algebra, and didn't I hear you say you have a term paper due next week? Have you finished the reading for it?"

Joby squirmed against the wall. "Well. Not exactly."

"Oh, Joby!"

"Mom, it's not my fault. All the cruddy books are out of the library."

"That comes of waiting till the last minute and you know it. Anyway, there's always the public library. Joby, what do you expect me to say? You know that schoolwork has to come first."

"Mom, this is really important," he said desperately. "It may be our last chance, the water's pretty cold already. The surf report says this could be a great weekend, one of the really great ones. I *have* to go, Mom. I'll do the algebra Sunday night when I get back and go to the library on Monday."

"Oh, Joby, you make me feel like an ogre. Does it really mean so much to you?"

He looked at her quickly, his face taut, and then his eyes slid away. "You better believe!" he said awkwardly. "It's really great. Especially with the camper. You just stay with the surf and pretty soon you feel like you're a million miles away from everything, shitty school and the whole goddamn shitty world."

Cynny studied her laced fingers soberly for a moment before she spoke again. "Joby, I wish I could understand why you hate school so much. It's this attitude of yours that makes you do poorly. Isn't there even one class that seems exciting to you, even one teacher who—"

Joby snorted. "What's to get excited? They give you the same old shit, year after year, and all they want you to do is memorize it word for word and give it back to them on the exams. It's a bummer, the whole scene. Nothing but one big hassle over grades and picking a major and where you're going to college."

"Oh, Joby!" And then she smiled at him, her face warm with sympathy. "Never mind, darling. I remember my last year in high school too, it was a terrible bore. But college will be different, I promise you. Something happens there, new ideas and new fields opening up, all at once it seems terribly exciting and you get terribly involved and it's one of the best times of your whole life."

His glum face did not appear in any way convinced. "I guess things have changed a lot since you went to school, Mom. Going to college now is nothing but a hassle. I hear guys talk. I'm sick of going to school."

"You can always take a year or two off before college, Joby. Do you realize how lucky you are, love? Now the draft is over you can afford to do that."

"Yeah, sure!" he said bitterly. "Except by next year, they'll probably be fighting in Cambodia or the Middle East or one of those other creepy places. All this stupid country wants to do is have wars and kill people."

"Job, don't say that. I know Nam was a stupid war, but one has to believe in the future, that nothing like that can ever happen again. It's a matter of faith, not just in our own country but in all people everywhere and—"

"That's shit, you know. Then why do they all keep making bombs and stinking up the environment and having too many babies?"

She was silent. For a moment she studied his bleak face beneath the lank, dark hair, then she looked away to her hands upon the coverlet, her own face somber. She sighed and finally, falling back on a favorite bit of nonsense from his small-boy days, she said in a deep, mock-lugubrious voice, "Why, it's Walter Wart, the freaky frog! Frigit! Frigit!"

He struggled against it, but the grin spread across his face in spite of himself. "Frigit!" he said loudly, his voice breaking in his attempt to deepen it.

All at once they were both laughing together.

"Boy, Mom, you're a real kook. Look, I have to call Bo before he goes to bed. What shall I tell him?"

Cynny wiped at her eyes. "Ah, Joby, tell him you'll go. It sounds like a wonderful weekend, something to remember all your life. Go and have fun."

His face lighted, and he plunged for the doorway. "Hey! Thanks, Mom!"

Halfway into the hall, he added, "And I'll really work hard to make up for it, Mom, I promise. I'll get the term paper in on time and catch up on all the algebra by the end of next week."

"Well, see that you do. You can, love, if you'll just put your mind to it."

He stuck his head back around the doorjamb. "Mom, you want me to take Putzi? You always worry about us sleeping out places. I'll take him if you want me to."

"Joby, would you? He loves the beach so much. It would be a marvelous outing for him, too."

"It's a deal. Good night, Mom."

But her smile vanished as soon as he was gone. She sat motionless for several minutes, her face troubled. She thought of Jim, reaching out through time and space, and then fell back upon herself once more with a familiar chill of disappointment. It was no use, Jim honestly had no conception of what Joby was like these days, what he really thought or felt about anything.

Sighing, she retrieved her book from beneath the coverlet and returned to her reading.

Jim, aboard the plane still in flight, was stacking last papers neatly and returning them to his attaché case. He had been at work for several hours, immersed and concentrated, but now he was finished. He closed the case and deposited it on the empty seat beside him, together with an unread magazine. Glancing at his watch, he switched off the small cone of light above his head and released the catch to push back his seat. He settled himself as comfortably as he was able, searching for room for his long legs, and then, closing his eyes, he turned his face toward the window.

He was bone weary but too keyed up for sleep, his mind still running at peak energy. His presentation was complete at last, and the final computer figures had proved even better than he had dared to hope. All his doubts were now dispelled. It was a superb job, deceptively simple, a beautifully engineered design based on an entirely new concept, so apt and applicable to the function for which it was intended that no design derived from previously accepted, more conventional theory could come close to it. They were home free. For an instant, his mind grasped at a half dozen other directions in which this new concept might be applied. They had something very big here, and momentarily he felt the kindling of an old excitement at the sheer creativity of it, the marvelous new rhythm of logic it encompassed.

But then his mind doubled away, thinking instead of the look he would see on the old man's face on Monday, when he arrived at the office to announce that they had gotten the contract, a shoo-in, just as he had prophesied from the inception of the project. He savored that anticipation with a deep, abiding satisfaction. After all, it was his future he had gambled on this project, put it all on the line, and now he had won. The old man wouldn't say much, but he would know all the same, just as he would know the next step that lay ahead for him. The old man had been wrong before this, an increasing number of times actually in the past year or two, but he had never been wrong about anything of this magnitude, and besides, this time he had been so unwise as to put his opposition to the project on record with the board. The old man was far from a fool, he was on the brink of retirement anyway, and he would be shrewd enough to realize that, however painful, the time had arrived, before the board deprived him of the dignity of choice. And once the old man was out, Jim was going to be where he had sweated and ached to be for the past six years.

There was always Junior, of course, poor, dogged Junior, but he hardly posed a threat. Jim had bypassed Junior years ago; Junior had neither the ability nor the grasp, and no one knew that better by now than the old man, unless it was Junior himself. Certainly the board had no illusions about it. What it all amounted to was he had finally made it. This last gamble had paid off in spades. He was there at last.

The exultation Jim felt was a surge of emotion and energy through his entire body. And in that moment he understood that for him the achievement of this goal, to which he had given himself so totally for so many years, was occurring here and now. The actual events connected with his achievement, when they took place, would be the merest formalities; the reality of it was in this moment, alone in the cabin of a plane flying smoothly through the night. He glimpsed the vista of his new status, power, and decision; the flood of exultation rose through his body one more time, then slowly drained away. Startled, and unwilling that his triumph should end so soon, he tried to recapture it. This is it, he told himself. This is what you sweated for, all these years, out of the second slot and number one at last. This is it, boy! But it was useless, the exultation would not come again.

Suddenly chilled, he shivered and felt lassitude creep over him and, with it, a mild depression. He was tired, that was it, he told himself, this damn bone-deep fatigue that so often engulfed him lately. It was worrying. After his last electrocardiogram just a month ago, the doctor had assured him that his heart was perfectly sound. Probably it was just that once you passed forty-five you had to accept it, you simply did not have the bounce you had when you were a kid.

Still, it might well be that, as the doctor so often told him, he really did drive himself too hard. Well, perhaps now he could afford to take it a little easier, he reflected, and knew within the space of the thought that the pressures and demands that lay ahead for him could only increase. Out of a prickle of anxiety, he quickly assured himself that from now on he would at least schedule a night a week at the gym, no matter how much he disliked the prospect. All doctors agreed these days, didn't they, that exercise became increasingly important at his age; likely weekend golf was no longer enough. The real trick, of course, was to discipline yourself to rest during any free moment that presented itself. Right now, for instance, he should be sleeping. His first appointment was early in the morning.

He willed his body to relax, his mind to quiet, but thirty seconds later he was sitting upright, fumbling a stomach soporific out of a little plastic vial from his pocket and swallowing it with the last milk left in a paper cup on the tray in front of him. Lying back in his seat once more, he made another effort to settle his mind toward sleep and failed, and his depression deepened.

What the hell is the matter with you anyway, he asked himself querulously. You have just reached the place where a hundred thousand men in your field would give their eyeteeth to be. And you're still young enough and healthy enough to enjoy being there. Leaving that out of it, you have a hell of a lot more right now than most men achieve in a lifetime. And Cynny and the kids and a damn pleasant life besides. Oh, admittedly, Job was a deep disappointment to him, but he had given up expecting anything from Joby, and he had some comfort in the knowledge that he was not the only father these days to find himself in such a situation. For some reason, it appeared to be symptomatic of the times. No, on the whole, Cynny was doing a good job with the kids. She was too indulgent with them, of course, but in all fairness, he could not hold her entirely to blame for Joby's failure to turn out. Aside from that, he could not fault her in any area, she was a marvel, and as indispensably a part of him by now as his own right arm.

He had seen enough of other women and certainly listened enough to other men talk of their wives to know just how fortunate he was. If Cynny was no longer so exciting or stimulating to him sexually as she once had been, well, he did not mind admitting, he was reaching a place in his life where he no longer attached such prime importance to that. She was unfailingly tender and loving, a good companion, she never nagged, never demanded. She kept a serene, cheerful, well-run house and functioned as an unobtrusive, uncomplaining buffer between himself and all the everyday tensions and problems connected with its maintenance. She supplied him with a diverse and entertaining social life, in which he was always free to participate as little or as much as he happened to feel like. And a round of golf every weekend with a couple men whose company he enjoyed. A damn good life altogether, who could ask for more than this?

But he took no particular cheer in this recital. All right, so maybe it's time you started to live a little more for yourself, he told himself defensively, you've earned it. By next year you will be able to afford a boat, why not buy one, squander a hell of a lot of money on yourself for a change? He tempted himself with it, conjuring in his mind the image of the beautiful sailing ship that had haunted his dreams since his boyhood in the dry, landlocked Middle West. But the image refused to take on color or substance. In truth, he had no time for a boat, to possess one could mean only another responsibility. A lump of dissatisfaction and self-pity swelled in his throat. My God, I'm worn out, I've got to sleep, he told himself desperately. Tomorrow morning I have to be sharp and on the ball.

He settled once more in his seat, moved his cramped legs to another position, and then, with a twinge of shame, fled to the refuge of his favorite fantasy. The plane flew on, but the whisper of the jet engines became for him the turquoise waves of the Tahitian coast. He smelled sea air laden with the perfume of blossoms and felt the languorous tropical heat upon his naked body. And nestled to him, the coffee-cream girl with the smooth, voluptuous body, lustrous, dark hair to her waist, and a crimson flower tucked behind her ear. She gave herself to him with breathless ardor, with birdlike cries and flowing tears. Her eyes— worshiping, velvet-soft, dark eyes—never left him. She ministered to him with loving hands and lingering pink-petal lips. She adored him beyond life and beyond reason, and spoke not one word of English or any other tongue he could understand. He fell asleep finally just as the plane entered the approach pattern for landing.

The big silver aircraft angled down toward the runway lights in Florida, and back across the continent, in California, Cynny took note of the arrival time as she drowsily set the alarm on the clock beside her bed. She hoped the flight was in on time. Jim never slept on planes, so if the flight was delayed, what with the time change, he would be exhausted in the morning, poor thing. She turned out the light and, steeling herself, threw back the covers, leaving the warmth of the bed just long enough to pull open the drapes. Diving back into bed once more, she turned on her pillow to watch the fog in the streetlights outside her window, but only for a moment. The drowsiness engulfed her and she slept.

The house was dark, only the dog awake and moving along the corridor for some reason of his own, his feet noiseless on the carpeting, the metal tags on his collar clinking softly. He went to the doorway of Jim's room, standing there for a time in the darkness, ears alert, then turned back. Cynny's door was ajar; he pushed it open gently with his nose, padding across to the thick rug beside her bed. He settled himself there, nose on paws, sighed, and fell instantly asleep. Then at last the house was still and dreaming.

PETE SPENT THAT EVENING AT THE RESTAURANT on the beach. He dined with Charlie, and they lingered for another hour or two over coffee, talking of fishing and the sea. Actually, it was Pete who did most of the talking, spurred on by the old man's interest and questions, speaking in enthusiastic detail of projects completed, others under way, and still others only dreamed of. The kitchen closed at ten o'clock, and since the fog showed no sign of lifting, at eleven the bar closed as well. Pete declined Charlie's offer of a ride home, and after they had said their good nights, he returned to the cocktail lounge a final time.

"Moke, you going to be around here a while longer?" he asked the round-faced young Hawaiian who was washing glasses behind the empty bar.

"Just till I finish cleaning up, Pete. Maybe a half hour. Why?"

"Well, look, if anybody I know should happen to stop by, tell them I was here and that I'm staying over at the house, okay?"

"Sure, Pete."

"I'd appreciate it. See you tomorrow, Moke."

"So long, Pete. Take it easy now, it's really socked in out there."

"You too. See you."

Pete disappeared into the corridor, pulling up the hood of his jacket.

But Killian, just then, was twenty miles away, propped against a pile of cushions on a divan in her apartment. She was quiet, her vivid face subdued now in the dim light, only her hand

143

moving occasionally as she smoked from a little twist of paper in deep, sipping inhalations.

The room was sparsely furnished with an air of imperma-nence, as though the occupant might recently have moved in or was about to move out. One wall was covered by shelves, empty except for a dozen or two athletic trophies; on the opposite wall was a large, faded poster, mended here and there with strips of tape, a blown-up reproduction of an FBI wanted poster with twin photographs of the delicate, enigmatic face of Angela Davis beneath her oversize mop of hair. The loud music came from a pair of hi-fi speakers: blues, a hoarse male voice against a rhythm background. A tall, dark-skinned young man with crisp curls of natural hair and a loose, bright African shirt was seated beside a table that bore the remains of a meal and a squat candle gutter-ing in a saucer. He teetered lazily on two legs of his chair, his long, slender, bare feet propped upon the tabletop, eyes closed as he played a wooden recorder along with the record in a reedy, plaintive piping.

The record came to an end a moment later, and the black man unfolded himself from his chair and walked toward the turntable, moving with extraordinary grace for his height and size.

Killian stirred, dropping the last burning bits of cigarette paper into a chipped bowl on the floor beside her.

"Rob, drive me to Beverly Hills, okay?"

"What you want to go to your mama's for?"

He turned the record, holding it carefully by the edges between the palms of his big hands, then adjusted the playing arm and turned the volume down a notch. With the sound of music once more, he crossed the room and sat down beside her. He gazed at her appraisingly for a moment, reaching out to brush hair gently back from her face.

"How do you feel?"

"I'm fine."

Her eyes behind sooty lashes were warm brown, the same shade as her long, smooth hair.

She took his hand suddenly between both of hers. "Robbie, thanks for—you know. Today."

"Big deal!"

"No, I mean it, Rob. You're very good to me. You've always been."

"Hey, cut it out!"

He bent down, they kissed briefly, and she held him for a moment, her hands clasped behind his thick, powerful neck. "Mwene Mutapa!" she said, her voice affectionate.

He laughed. "Yeah, mama, that's me. I'm the king!"

"Of course. From a long line of kings. That's why you're so beautiful."

He reached out to the smooth strip of ivory skin visible above her low-slung jeans, slipping his hand beneath the belt to the curve of her hip.

"What was the name of that city again?"

"Zimbabwe."

"Yeah, that's it, Zimbabwe. I really dig that." He repeated it, rolling the syllables from his tongue. "Zimbabwe."

"Lord of the Mine," Killian said.

"What?"

"Mwene Mutapa meant 'Lord of the Mine.' "

"Gold, huh?"

"Tons of it."

"Hey, very heavy!"

"Really fantastic. A huge, beautiful city with a great temple in the center, all teeming with traders and priests and scribes and warriors, and the caravans coming and going." And then she added, her voice teasing, "Too bad it was segregated. Moslems had to live in the ghetto."

"Hot damn!" he said appreciatively. "Now why didn't I take African history while I was in school!"

They were silent for a time, only the sound of the music in the room, the same pain-filled male voice.

"Rob?" she said suddenly. "I can't stop thinking about that

courtroom today. Wasn't it fantastic? The judge and all those lawyers, and people coming and going and absolutely nothing there. A perfectly meaningless, empty, empty place. Wasn't it frightening?"

"Well, I told you not to go, babe," he said sympathetically.

"But it's so awful for anyone who goes. If they're going to make people do it, there ought to be something there. At least a ritual, you know? Think what a marvelous ritual it could be."

"You mean you'd rather get down on your knees in front of the bench and hand up your wedding ring and the judge would stand up there with a big old hammer, wham! And bust it into a thousand pieces!"

"Why not? It would be marvelous. And have candles and drums and incense and—"

"So what would be so meaningful about that?" he asked practically. "It wouldn't really change anything either, would it?"

She looked up at him for a moment before she said, "No, I guess it wouldn't," and turned away, rolling over onto her belly, her face hidden behind her long, heavy hair.

"Hey, I'm sorry!"

She did not speak or move, and he reached out to her shoulders. They did not speak again for a long time while he massaged the back of her neck gently.

"I hate being such a drag—" she began at last.

"Shit, no," he said soothingly. "It sure beats the way you been carrying on around here all night, dancing and singing and jabbering into the telephone."

"Rob, it's no good," she said, her voice strained and shaken. "I have to go to the beach. Will you drive me?"

"The beach! You mean right now? You must be stoned out of your skull, mama!"

"No, please. Will you, Robbie?"

The phone began to ring. He unfolded himself gracefully, and Killian said from behind her hair, "If that's for me, I don't want to talk to anybody anymore. Tell them I'm dead or I've gone to Biloxi."

"Yeah, I'll do that," he said as he scooped up the phone. "Yeah? Oh, yeah, man. So what's happening? I'm sorry I couldn't make it, I was tied up today."

Killian dropped her head upon her folded arms again, her shining hair spilling over the end of the divan.

"Ah, you must be jiving me!" Rob said at last delightedly. "I wish I'd been there. No, I planned to, but I had to be in court today." He laughed. "No, man, divorce court. Killy got her divorce. Yeah, I'll tell her."

Killian lifted her head. "If that's Abdul Kadim, tell him to go fuck himself," she said venomously.

His face creasing with merriment, he said to her briefly over the top of the phone, "Yeah, baby, Abdul says he loves you, too. So tell me more, man. No shit! Well, I don't know. Hold on a second." He spoke to Killian again. "Want to go over to his place for a while?"

"No, I don't. Let him have the revolution without me."

"No, I better not tonight," he said into the phone. "Killy's had a rough day. I wouldn't like to leave her."

"Look, go if you want to go. I'm perfectly all right."

"That's really great," he said, ignoring her. "Sure. Oh, right on, man. Yeah, sure. Tomorrow morning? Okay, where? What? Ah, you're jiving me! All right, hold on a second." He glanced briefly at Killian, his face apologetic, and walked reluctantly through the doorway, carrying the phone with him, the cord stretching taut behind him out of a tangle of knots and loops. "Just a second, babe," he said to Killian as he closed the door.

She stared after him, incredulous for an instant, then rolled over and off the divan. She plunged toward the closed door, then stopped short, rocking on her bare feet. She walked to the window instead, finally, and stood motionless there, looking down at the city lights, glittering like knives in the darkness, and beyond, the ominous black edge of the fogbank towering above the horizon.

He returned at last and put the phone down upon a chair seat, watching Killian cautiously. "Sorry about that."

She did not answer, and he came to stand behind her. "I mean it, babe. I'm sorry."

He put his arms around her and, although she was tall, bent below the level of his shoulders to kiss the top of her head.

"All right," she said softly. "So what pig outfit does Abdul think I work for anyway? The FBI or the CIA?"

He laughed. "I knew you were going to be sore. Look, just forget it. Sometimes Abdul gets uptight about you, that's all. You know how the brothers are."

"With Abdul it's not hard to get the general idea, is it?"

"I wish you'd lay off Abdul, okay?"

"How can I lay off Abdul? He wants to cut off my head!"

He laughed again, and she struggled against him, turning in his arms. "It's not funny! Abdul's sick, sick, sick! He's got a hang-up on violence. A couple years ago he wanted to burn down Los Angeles, now he wants to go to Palestine and bomb airplanes!"

"You never dug Abdul, that's all. He's a real revolutionary. He straightened out my head on a lot of things. I owe him a lot."

"Oh, shit! You don't owe him, Abdul owes you! He talked you into giving up your job playing pro ball and then used it for absolute tons of publicity. Abdul uses you. Why can't you see that?"

"Maybe I see something you don't," he said with the beginnings of anger in his voice. "There happens to be a war on, baby. If you're not for something now, you're against it."

"I don't believe that!"

"You better believe that."

"Rob, listen, you could get out of this town. We could go to New Mexico next week. We could ski and study Swahili and you could learn to play the flute and I'd learn to weave and—"

"Sure we could! How long you really think it would be before we got busted? Or were you planning to have me saw off my legs and conk my hair and get a job in some pig war factory?"

"All right. Then you could—go to Africa. I'll go with you."

"Now who's talking shit! Zimbabwe was a long time ago, baby. There's nothing left there but some stones."

And then his anger vanished, and he was relaxed and smiling once more. "Okay, time out!" he said, blowing an earsplitting whistle upon his fingers.

"You won't listen to me," Killian said. "Why won't you listen to me?"

She walked back to the divan, dropping down upon it and pulling up her feet to sit cross-legged, her head drooping. He followed her, folding his great length until he sat upon his heels before her in perfect poise and balance.

"You're just feeling bad tonight," he said, his face tender. "Okay, you want to drive to the beach, let's go."

"What?"

"Come on, I'll drive you to the beach."

"The beach?" she said blankly, as though she had heard him from a million miles of inner space.

"First you said you wanted to go to your mama's, then you said you wanted to go to the beach."

"Did I?" she said with a small, white smile. "What a funny idea! Do you want to go to the beach?"

"Oh, boy!"

He rose effortlessly, swooping across the room to the shelves, and returned to sit upon his heels again before the divan.

"Here's your book," he said. "And here's your coins." He extended his hand with the three pennies lying on the palm. "Sometime tonight I'd like to get some sleep around here."

She hugged the thick, tattered copy of the *I Ching* against her for a moment, her face somber, then put it down, stretched, and gathered back her hair.

"Poor Robbie!" she said, her gaze suddenly warm. "I don't need a hexagram to tell me. Tonight there's thunder in the earth. No blame, no praise. It furthers the wise person to go to bed."

"Hey, right on!"

"Except I think I should get over to Beverly Hills by morning."

"Aw, not the shit with the alarm clock!"

"It's my ESP," she said apologetically. "I have a feeling Linda's flapping, wanting to talk to me about something."

"Look, see that dojigger over there on the chair? That's a telephone, babe. You could call your mama right now. How about that?"

"No, I really don't feel like coping with Linda tonight. But you don't have to get up, love. You won't need the car before eleven, will you?"

He hesitated. "Yeah, as a matter of fact I need it early tomorrow," he said reluctantly. "Something's come up."

In an instant their eyes had locked.

"Then I'll hitch," she said. "What's come up?"

"I could drop you off in Beverly at eight o'clock," he said quickly. "How's that?"

"Perfect. As long as I'm there for breakfast with Linda."

"Great."

She dove forward without warning, clutching him fiercely, her head burrowing into his chest. "Oh, Rob, don't do it!" she wailed. "You're a marvelous, loving, beautiful human being. Don't do this!"

"Killy," he said. "Promise me something, okay? Quit bugging Abdul. He doesn't think you're so funny anymore."

"Well, I should certainly hope that—"

"No, listen, Killy. You think this is some kind of game? It's not a game. People get killed."

"I'm perfectly aware of that! Are you?"

"Just lay off Abdul. Promise?"

"All right. I'll promise if you'll promise me."

"I promise," he said soothingly. "Just don't worry. There's nothing to worry about, babe. Sure I promise."

She pushed away, hands against his shoulders, until she was sitting upright again upon her knees. Holding his dark, magnificently planed face between her hands, she looked into his eyes, searching.

"Everything's too complicated," she said at last in a small, sad voice. "In my next incarnation I want to be a cherry tree. Just stand and stand with my feet in the dirt and feel the sun and rain."

"Okay," he said with a purr of amusement in his throat. "You be a cherry tree, I'll be your bumblebee."

Killian shivered, her fingers caressing his cheeks. "Ah, beautiful!" she said, her voice rich. "I'll be a million sweet blossoms for you every spring."

"Beautiful!"

Suddenly there were tears in her eyes, and she shook his head gently in mock exasperation.

"Mwene Mutapa!" she said helplessly.

He looked back at her for a moment longer, his own eyes moist, then unfolded to his feet, swooping her up into his arms as though she had no weight at all.

"Ooga booga!" he roared. "Me Mwene! You Jane! That Tarzan of yours one foolish ape-man!"

With a bloodcurdling whoop, he careened off in dizzying circles toward the bedroom, while Killian clung to him, breathless with laughter.

O N THE HILLTOP WELL ABOVE THE WHITE
coastal fog layer, Nedith was just then letting herself into
her silent, empty house. There were lights on everywhere, and
she switched on still others on her way to the cavernous blue-
and-gold bedroom. She paused beside the bed, sliding open a
door in the carved headboard to twiddle knobs on the front of a
radio concealed there before she moved on to the dressing
room.

She couldn't wait to phone Jean, she was thinking. On top of
everything else, it had turned out to be a fantastic evening,
beginning with her arrival at Sally's in the middle of the flaming
row they'd been having before Jack went out. Actually, Nedith
had half-suspected for a long time that Jack might be up to
something, but thank God, Sally had finally had the wit to confide in her so that Nedith could advise her. Because if there was
any one area of life about which she was uniquely qualified to
give advice, Nedith reflected wryly, this was certainly it.

She deposited her purse and slipped out of her sable jacket,
draping it carefully on a padded hanger, her hands lingering over
the lustrous fur. Now her dear son-in-law was going to be in for
a little surprise. Not that she had anything against Jack personally; actually she adored him, she had always thought that he was
an absolute doll. It was just that he was a man, and like even the
best of them, he had the curious potential to turn into the most
complete bastard given half a chance.

Nedith took a shortcut through her sterile kitchen, admiring
as she always did the expanse of gleaming stainless steel and mel-

low walnut cabinetwork. When she reached the lanai, she turned on other lights, walking directly to the elaborately fitted bar at the far end of the room, her mind returning once more to her evening.

Oh, it was worrying, she would admit, but Sally was going to be all right. It was always the woman, after all, who had to determine the shape and structure of any marriage. When you came down to it, it seemed to be against the nature of any man to maintain a marriage relationship for very long. Every girl had to face the reality of that sooner or later and then begin to fight for herself and her children and the kind of life she wanted to have. There were too many divorces these days simply because girls failed to understand that, or were unwilling to accept it. Girls too often clung to the illusion that one man was fundamentally different from another, and too often allowed emotion to run away with them just when they most needed to be clearheaded and practical. It was the hard truth of this life that no one, not even your nearest and dearest, ever really gave you anything; what you wanted you had to get for yourself.

Behind the bar, Nedith turned on another radio and hesitated, absently tapping a manicured fingernail against a white tooth. To tell the truth, she was starving, dinner at Sally's had been a shambles. For a moment, Nedith allowed her mind to dwell upon a thick ham-and-cheese sandwich slathered in mayonnaise, but it was no use. She had gained five pounds in the past two months, and now she had to be tough on herself, particularly with the holidays just ahead. It was the damn estrogen, she supposed, it might be guaranteed to keep you young forever, but if you didn't watch yourself every instant, it also could make you fat as a pig. She reluctantly selected a glass from a shelf and helped herself to ice cubes from the refrigerator and a bottle of diet cola.

But of course it had been worth a dozen bad dinners, the opportunity finally to talk to Sally as she had tonight. It had been touching really, the way Sally had listened to her every word. But then the poor baby was so miserable and confused, not knowing what to do or which way to turn. She could remember exactly how it was, even after all these years.

Nedith sipped at her drink, her nose wrinkling with distaste, and suddenly, to her amazement, she burst into tears. She wept because she was hungry, but most of all, she wept for the young Nedith, not even as old as Sally was now, Sally herself merely an infant in a crib, when she had first discovered that Tom was sleeping with someone else and the sky of her own private world had fallen in upon her head. She wept silently for a moment or two, her face contorted, then dabbed at her mascara with a bit of paper towel. Now really! Whatever had brought that on? It must have been seeing Sally tonight, so young and vulnerable, it had taken her back in spite of herself. Well, thank God, that was all far behind her now; nothing could hurt her like that again so long as she lived.

Nedith resolutely wiped her nose and walked to a battery of switches on the wall, turning on several of them. Immediately the pale draperies over the long outer wall of the lanai began to part, doubling back slowly with a faint metallic humming. Outside the exposed wall of glass the huge, kidney-shaped swimming pool came into view, a limpid glowing surface of unlikely turquoise in the darkness. There were lava rocks massed at either end and an artful jungle of tropical plants and palms with concealed amber and violet spotlights, all of it like an enormous stage set of an alien landscape on some distant planet. But Nedith surveyed it for several minutes with pleasure, drawing from it some abiding comfort.

Before she called Jean, she'd give Pete a ring, she decided, just make sure that he'd found everything in order at the house. She was already dialing before she remembered that the telephone at the beach had been disconnected.

"Oh, shit!" she said above the soft radio music. And another good reason why Pete had no business being alone in that dreary old beach house at a time like this. All Tom's fault, too. She could kill Tom, she could really kill him.

She dialed again rapidly, then tucked the phone against her shoulder while she lit a cigarette.

"Jean!" she said, her face brightening. "Darling, I didn't wake you, did I? No, I just this minute got home, too. I tried to call you earlier, where were you?" She swung up onto a barstool and sipped from her glass while she listened. After a moment, she said, "Well, it doesn't sound too fascinating. I had an absolutely terrible day too, my God, you won't believe it, just one thing after another, absolutely the whole ghastly day. In the first place, Pete was home . . ."

Nedith launched into her recital with relish. It was ten minutes before she paused for breath and sipped from her glass.

"Oh, you know me, I'm indestructible," she said after a moment. "So what about tomorrow, darling? No, I can't make lunch either. There's still that damn divan of Sally's, so we're meeting at Sloane's, elevenish. After Sloane's, I want her to look at some fox jackets. She's been dying for one, and I told her tonight she'll never have a better chance. I mean, it's divine, Jack's in a position where he simply wouldn't dare to squawk, would he? But I should be all clear by three, how about you? Then maybe we could go on to dinner somewhere, can you get away?"

She listened again, leaning comfortably against the bar, blue cigarette smoke eddying about her shining, bleached hair, her eyes fixed upon the unlikely landscape beyond the window glass.

"Darling, I'm sorry," she said finally. "It's just the way men are, that's all. I had the usual row with Tom, too, before he left. No, he's off for the whole weekend. Well, he says it's a business trip, and for once I believe him. Naturally he was being terribly cute about what time his flight was going out tonight and exactly when he'd be back on Sunday, but sometime in between I think he really is going to Houston."

Nedith listened again, her face amused, and suddenly she laughed. "Darling, I'm not a saint to put up with this at all," she said. "If you want to know the truth, I've just about had it with this one. Oh, I haven't had a chance to tell you! I spent two hours with my lawyers again yesterday afternoon." Nedith smiled her charming smile. "Oh, darling, it really is too divine. It's all set now. When I'm ready, all I have to do is lower the boom. I think after Tom gets over the shock he'll never set foot in another ladies' lingerie department as long as he lives! I'll tell you all about it tomorrow. Where shall we meet? Well, I have to buy shoes too, shall we make it Delman's then at three-thirty?"

And just then, a quarter of a mile away, on a dark, two-lane thoroughfare winding over the spine of the mountain, a bright headlight suddenly veered off to the side, the engine cutting out as the motorcycle coasted to a halt on the hard-packed dirt of a pull-off area. Head- and taillights winked off, and the machine and its rider were lost to view in the deep shadows beneath the trees. Only an occasional gleam of polished chrome and the intermittent glow from the tip of a cigarette gave any indication of its presence through the darkness and fog.

By chance, a scrub oak was beginning to die there, and its withered, leafless branches made a small gap in the dense undergrowth, affording a view down the rugged slope. And there it was, only five hundred yards below, the unexpected vista of Nedith's huge, turquoise swimming pool surrounded by its violet-amber rocks and planting, the long, low sprawl of the house beyond.

It was very quiet there in the darkness, no traffic passed along the road, and after a time, lights began to go out behind the long glass wall of the lanai below. For a moment there was even a glimpse behind the glass of Nedith herself, a tiny, doll-like figure with yellow hair. Not long after that the light in the bedroom was extinguished as well, and the house was dark.

The motorcycle and its invisible rider were still there.

S EVERAL HOURS BEFORE DAWN, MICK SANFORD, still functioning in another time zone and therefore wide awake, was driving the rented green Pinto through a section of dark residential streets in Santa Monica. His evening had turned out to be unexpectedly convivial. After leaving the hotel, he had driven by Vinny's apartment and managed to find him at home, in bed as a matter of fact. But Vinny had been so delighted to see him that he had thrown on some clothes and immediately phoned Bob Covern. And Bob had insisted they come over at once and proceeded to round up as many of the old crowd as he could.

It had turned out to be a long and raucous evening. Oh, it had been a good enough party, Mick reflected. At least there had been a number of interesting younger guys whom he had never met, and a dose of the anecdotes and stories that you expected when a group of this sort came together. There had also been an interminable amount of kidding around about the crazy old days, however, with a new and appreciative audience to egg everyone on. Bob's parties might be legendary, but they were also predictable. He had a knack for organizing an event at the drop of a hat, but it was always the same nucleus of guys, the same ample bar, and virtually the same six or eight pretty little birds about Hollywood: the decorative, starlet-fringe type who came and went through the years but never seemed to change except for the length of their skirts.

The trouble with you, kid, you must be getting old, Mick told himself wryly.

He crossed an intersection just then and all but brought the car to a dead halt before the lighted front of a modern four-story apartment building that had not been there before and did not, in his mind, belong. He drove on along the wide, tree-lined street, apprehensive now, the party forgotten, and all at once turned in at the curb, braking to a full stop. Leaning to look out the car window, he saw at last the reassuring bulk of Theo's old house looming out of the fog and darkness, every familiar contour solid, substantial, and indubitably still there, standing silent amid the trees just as he had come home to it on a thousand other nights such as this.

Mick grinned in his relief. He lighted a cigarette, reminding himself that the house had outlasted its occupant. He had a flash of Theo sitting across the breakfast table, as he had most enjoyed her during his infrequent visits home: her thin bang of reddish gray hair above her angular face, cheeks flushed with pleasure, the meticulous and unhurried flow of speech as she poured steaming coffee from the thin, old silver pot, and behind her, through the window, the unaltering view of her garden. Masses of bright flowers against the sprawling shrubbery, the weathered wooden lacework of the old gazebo where he had climbed in earliest childhood memory, and the flocks of sparrows and finches twittering over the bird feeder in the morning's filtered sunlight.

Mick snapped off the radio, decided now to enter the house. But as he reached for the ignition key, it occurred to him that the electricity had likely been turned off with the house empty. Better to come by tomorrow. He would like to walk through the rooms again, every remembered chair and picture, bookshelf and rug, climb the winding staircase all the way to the attic one final time. At the thought came a swift and vivid recollection of going up the attic stairs, the stifling heat trapped beneath the roof and a certain odor like no other in all the world—cedar, moth crystals and dust, rotting fabric and the drying pages of old *National Geographic* magazines. And with it all, an echo of delightful childhood expectation, the promise of barrels, chests, nooks, and crannies to be explored and unsuspected treasures to be unearthed.

Ah, you really are getting old, Mick mocked himself.

Just then he caught a glimpse of a white police car gliding out of the fog through the lighted intersection up the street, and Mick pulled out from the curb and drove away. They undoubtedly would have come on around the block to check out his car lights, and although he had not had that many drinks at Bob's, it seemed more prudent to avoid the encounter.

He was aware suddenly of his weariness, and for an instant he was tempted to check in at the Miramar close by. But it was not a practical idea, he decided, better to return to the other hotel tonight, turn in the Pinto, and come back to the Miramar tomorrow. He would have wheels by then since Bob had insisted on loaning him a car. As a matter of fact, Bob was picking him up at the hotel in the morning; they were to breakfast together at ten.

He found Lincoln in the fog and made the turn, checking the rearview mirror. There was no sign of the police car or any other traffic. He yawned deeply and switched the radio back on. It looked like a busy couple of days, he was thinking. He had made a dozen commitments already.

Oh, Christ! For the first time all evening, Mick remembered his telephone conversation with Linda and his reluctant promise to take Killian to dinner tomorrow. Now that he thought of it again, the very notion shocked and appalled him. My God, he marveled, what have I let myself in for? Why had he been so quick to phone Linda anyway? Now that he was oriented, the whole idea seemed utterly bizarre.

But then his initial mistake likely had been in answering her letter. The fact was, of course, that at the time, Linda's letter had gotten to him. It had been very appealing, timid and awkward in its phrasing, somehow giving an impression that had she not been desperately troubled she could never have screwed up the courage to write it. And the disarming way she had put it, that she had this most enormous favor to ask of him; no reason for him to grant it, she realized, but she could not help but hope that he might anyway.

Ah, what a liar Linda really was, because after only two minutes on the phone tonight she had made it abundantly clear she did not consider it a favor at all but only an infinitesimal part of a duty that he owed to Killian and in which he had been shockingly derelict for all these years. How could he have been so stupid as to be taken in by the letter?

That whole bit about how meeting him might make an important difference in Killian's life did not hold water. The girl was twenty years old, after all, married and divorced, obviously deeply involved with her own life. What real interest could she possibly have in meeting him? No, it was more likely that all of this had been Linda's devious method of getting at him for some reason of her own, although what that reason might be after all these years he could not imagine. Nor could he care less, to be entirely honest.

And then, driving along, Mick laughed out loud. Because it came to him that this entire debate was wasted time and energy, since when it came down to it, he had no real intention of keeping his date with Linda and actually never had. Their phone conversation had been more than enough for him. Frankly, he could not think of a less attractive prospect than even phoning her one more time, let alone going to see her.

But his relief was only momentary. He was left, he discovered, with a sense of unease—something more pervasive than the discomfort of a promise made and broken—that he found himself unable and unwilling to analyze.

Frowning, Mick slammed his foot down hard on the accelerator, and the small car lurched forward at its top speed in the sparse predawn traffic.

2
Friday

THE FOG WAS GONE BY MORNING, BUT THE SKIES were overcast. Cynny Holman spent an hour in her garden, leisurely raking leaves into piles and cutting back summer planting. By eleven o'clock, however, she had dropped the pruning shears to rub her chilled, reddened hands together. She thought longingly of a cup of freshly brewed hot coffee and set off for the house.

The kitchen phone was ringing as she let herself in at the back door, and she hurried to answer it.

"Hello?" she said, out of breath. "Nancy, how nice! How are you, love?"

"Oh, Cynny, I'm so glad you're home! I let it ring, but I was sure that you were out on Fridays."

"Well, I am usually." Cynny pulled out a chair from a small wooden desk and sank down on it gratefully. "My lunch meeting today was canceled. So how's Sambo's cold?" She unbuttoned her suede jacket as she talked.

"He's fine, would you believe? It must have been an allergy. Anyway, I let him go back to school this morning."

"Nancy! Your voice is shaking, you're upset! What is it?"

"I'm at the vet's. I mean, in the phone booth across the street. They just gave Mugger an injection. I don't care how they like to say it, we did not have Mugger 'put to sleep,' we had him killed."

Cynny smiled involuntarily, but her voice was warm with sympathy. "Nan, I'm terribly sorry. Look, darling, come over, why don't you? You're halfway here already."

"Are you sure, Cynny? You've probably got a thousand things to do."

"Don't be silly. I'm about to make a pot of coffee. Come along."

"I really would like to. If you're sure this isn't a bad time."

"It's a perfect time. Hang up that phone and come on. Come round to the back. I have a last bit of pruning in the garden. I'll finish while you're on the way."

Ten minutes later, a long, dusty, red station wagon with a dented fender and a tattered "Save the Redwoods" bumper sticker swooped into the drive. The young woman at the wheel turned off the engine and squirmed over on the car seat, kneeling there to rummage in a collection of large paper grocery sacks in the back. She sorted out several shiny frozen food bags and carried them with her when she left the car, slamming the door carelessly half-closed behind her. She was a sturdy woman with short, curling, reddish blond hair and earnest blue eyes. Just now her face was pinched and bleak, her wide mouth turned downward, and the myriad freckles to which Jim Holman had jokingly referred a livid brown speckling against her pallor. A softer mottling of them was visible over her tanned bare legs. She walked back along the driveway with an energetic stride, brushing at her windblown hair and at the food crumbs and animal hairs caught in the nap of her pea jacket. She paused to let herself through a latched wooden gate in the hedge bordering the driveway, and into the expanse of lawn ringed by sycamores. The land rose gently into a large, bowl-shaped planting area where Cynny was just turning off a spigot.

"Nancy! I didn't hear your car."

"Cynny, your garden looks beautiful. What's that mass of pink up by the wall? It can't be azaleas already."

"Chrysanthemums, love. Actually, the garden's a bit drab this year. We do need rain. Good to see you, Nan."

"Look out for these stupid sacks, they're drippy. It's ice cream, so I thought I'd better stash them in your freezer while I'm here."

The two women embraced, faces touching briefly.

"I really have to do something about our garden. I'd like more rocks and natural planting like yours. Cynny, you have the most beautiful rocks, where did you ever find them?"

Cynny laughed, her clear joyous laughter. "Something tells me you won't approve of this, Nan. I found most of them at Broussard's, at ten cents a pound and up."

"Awful!" Nancy smiled, her somber face lighting briefly. "See, you have to admit yourself that there is something decadent about buying rocks! Up the beach in some of the canyons there are wonderful rocks. Let's go rock hunting some day next week. I'll drive the wagon, we could carry a lot in that."

"Marvelous. Except I warn you, I went all through this years ago. The really divine ones are too heavy to lift. You can't even budge them out of the dirt."

"Oh, damn, I never thought of that. But smaller ones we could. I know, we'll take some boards, and then if we let down the tailgate, maybe we could sort of—well, roll them up the boards somehow, do you think?"

"Oh, Nan, I can just see us. Anyway, we can try. Maybe there'll be a warm, sunny day. We can take sandwiches and have a picnic."

"Let's do. It would be such fun."

Cynny gathered up a rake and pruning shears from the grass. "Come on, darling, let's go have some coffee before your ice cream melts."

They walked together across the lawn strewn with huge, damp yellow leaves, and Nancy lifted her face to the tall trees, their limbs half bare against the low, gray sky.

"I love your sycamores, Cynny, the way they turn in the fall and shed their leaves. They remind me of home." There was a sudden tremor in her voice. "Sometimes I get so damn homesick for the seasons I really can't stand it."

Cynny glanced quickly at her friend's miserable face. "Well, California has seasons too, you know, they're just more subtle. I expect you haven't lived out here quite long enough to begin to appreciate that."

"I suppose."

They entered the large kitchen, and Cynny clicked a light switch by the door. "Ah, it feels good to be inside," she said. "I was getting cold. Who says there are no seasons in California? Take off your coat, Nan. Here, give me your ice cream. Shall we write a note to ourselves so we won't forget it when you leave?"

She deposited the shiny sacks in the freezer and moved on to take down a pair of brown pottery mugs from a shelf.

Nancy draped her coat obediently over a chairback and tugged ruefully at the skimpy sleeves of the striped turtleneck she wore beneath a denim jumper. "Promise not to look at me, Cynny, I'm a mess. I had Sambo's car pool, so I went rushing off early this morning. What are these seedpods here on the table? They're beautiful, I've never seen any like them."

"Jacaranda. Have them if you like, the tree is loaded this year. You look fine, Nancy, you always do. Wouldn't you like some fruit or an English muffin? You must have had breakfast at the crack of dawn."

"No, I couldn't, thanks. Just coffee."

Cynny brought the steaming mugs and sat down across the table from her friend, stretching her legs luxuriously as she reached for a cigarette package.

"Now tell me about poor Mugger," she said sympathetically. "How did he happen to be at the vet's? I thought you weren't going to take him since he hated it so much."

"Dave took him. I'm really furious about it. Of course I'll admit, when Dave got home last night it was sort of pandemonium. The children were in bed, but Jenny was sobbing into her pillow about Mugger, and Sambo was crying because Jenny was, and Davey was sitting up in bed absolutely white under his freckles and furious with both of them. He is exactly like Dave, you know, he can't bear to see them cry so he just kept shouting at them that they were goofy, that Mugger was not going to die.

Well, Dave just blew his stack, that's all. He said I was acting like some kind of a nut, that I should have taken Mugger to the vet's like anyone else would have done, as soon as I realized how sick he was. And maybe he's right, Cynny. Probably I am some kind of a nut. Do you think I'm some kind of a nut?"

Nancy stopped, her eyes swimming with tears.

Cynny reached across the table quickly to pat her hand. "Oh, Nan, come on! Dave didn't mean that and you know it. He'd worked late, he was tired, he just wanted to come home to a quiet, peaceful house and a cold martini and a good dinner. He hadn't any energy left to cope so he shouted at you."

"Oh, he coped all right," Nancy said, winking back the tears as she sipped at her coffee. "He coped just fine. He loaded Mugger into the cat carrier and drove straight to the vet's. And the children were delighted because Daddy had taken Mugger to the hospital, where they were going to make him all well, and they went right to sleep like angels. So naturally when Daddy got back, he pointed out to me that there needn't have been any fuss at all if I'd used the ordinary amount of common sense and gotten Mugger out of the house before they came home from school. He—he said I was entitled to my crackpot notions any-time so far as he was concerned, but not when it came to upsetting the children."

The tears welled out onto her cheeks in spite of her, and she scrubbed at them impatiently.

"Of course there is one fairly obvious fallacy in Dave's approach to all this," Cynny said mildly. "No matter what he told the children, those nice doctors didn't make Mugger well after all, did they?"

"No, they didn't," Nancy said unsteadily. "They said he was too old. Oh, Cynny, they brought him in and put him in the middle of one of those bare treatment tables that they have. He just lay where they put him, I think they'd already given him something, he was sort of glassy-eyed. But when he heard my voice, he lifted his head and tried to focus on me, poor thing. So

I held him and stroked him, and they gave him the injection in his leg. He didn't even flinch when the needle went in. After a couple minutes, the doctor listened with his stethoscope and said it was over. He felt so still and light and small. I put him down on the table again, and he was just a little heap of bones and ruffled fur."

"Oh, Nan, no wonder you're upset. Now you didn't have to be there when they did it, love!"

"Oh, yes, I had to be there!" Nancy said angrily, her face flushing beneath the tears and freckles. "Once Dave started this, someone had to finish it, didn't they? How could I just call up on the phone and say, 'All right, kill him and send us the bill'! Mugger was a good, faithful little animal. He—forsook his own kind to live with us for all these years, and he put up with the children mauling him when they were babies and learned not to hunt the birds that nested in the garden, and gave us nothing but love and affection. Do you think after all that he deserved to have his life ended for him in a strange place, sick and alone and frightened?" She fished a tissue from a voluminous, scuffed leather bag and blew her nose vigorously, a losing battle against her flowing tears.

"Darling, you're absolutely right. It's just that most of us are such cowards."

"Well, I was enough of a coward as it was. I left him there. I should have taken him home and buried him in the garden. I was too chicken to even ask. I suppose the health department doesn't allow it. Dave would just have accused me of being morbid anyway." She gulped wretchedly from her coffee mug. "Cynny, please don't think I'm a total idiot. I loved Mugger, but I've never been irrational over pets. I grew up on a farm, remember? As soon as it's kitten season again, I'll find a cute giveaway in front of the supermarket and probably love him just as much."

But the tears were still glistening down her cheeks.

"What then, Nan? You're not still upset, are you, over what Dave said last night when he was tired and out of sorts?"

"No," Nancy said. "Yes. Oh, I don't know. Oh, Cynny!" Her

mouth turned down suddenly into a tragicomic clown expression, and her tears rolled faster. She bent over hastily and hunted for tissues again in her purse. "Cynny, I'm sorry," she said, her voice muffled and tremulous. "Now I've let go and started to blubber, I can't seem to stop. I've hit the bottom this morning. I'm so miserable, I can't tell you. I feel like I'm in quicksand, there's no firm place I can plant my feet any longer, there's nothing real I can reach out and take hold of. I'm scared out of my wits. Oh, Cynny, I don't know what to do!"

For a moment she looked at Cynny beseechingly; then her face contorted and she began to weep silently and fiercely into her hand.

"Oh, Nan!" Cynny was up from her chair and around the table.

Nancy clutched at her, burrowing her face in Cynny's shirttails and sobbing out loud, her whole body shaking.

"Nancy! Darling, it's all right. You've had a ghastly morning. It's all right, love, it's all right." Cynny hugged her, stroking her bright hair and crooning comfortingly.

Moments later Nancy said, between sobs, "Cynny, I'm sorry! You must think I'm on a bum trip or that I've gone round the bend completely!"

"Don't be silly, Nan! You're the healthiest, sanest girl I know. There are times when we all have to howl. Go ahead and howl."

"Oh, Cynny, why couldn't that poor old cat die at home, in his basket, or wander off into the bushes the way cats like to do? I know the children were upset, but is that wrong? Isn't it the most natural thing in the world for them to—to know death and to grieve and then in a couple months get some new kittens and learn how life renews itself? Why is that wrong? Why is it we all have this thing about death, as if it were something unmentionable and vile and dirty? Just look at us! We can't even grow old ourselves anymore, we have to stay young no matter what, and when the years finally do catch up with us, we're hurried away to some nursing home and hidden out of sight as if old age was an obscenity. If it had been me that was sick instead of Mugger, Dave would have felt the same way, wouldn't he? He would have wanted to hurry me away to the hospital before the children were upset and told them that—"

"Nan!"

"Oh, I'm not blaming Dave, I mean, I'm not angry with him. It's just the way we all live these days. Oh, Cynny, please, please don't laugh, but it's such a commentary on our culture! Well, isn't it?"

"Nancy, I am not laughing at you. I happen to think you're absolutely right."

"Do you? You don't think I'm some kind of a nut? Ah, Cynny, you're such a good friend to me, you'd put up with me even if you did. If I could have another cup of coffee now, I'll try to pull myself together. Oh, look, I've got tears and lipstick all over your blouse."

"Who cares?" Cynny said affectionately. "One day it will be my turn, and then I'll get tears and lipstick all over you, that's a promise. Let me get the coffeepot."

"Cynny, it isn't just this thing about Mugger, though I suppose that's what set me off this morning. Every day it's something else. Like Peg just standing there yesterday watching those firemen work over her baby and begging for somebody to pray. I know you didn't understand how I felt, but I ached for Peg when I heard that story, I ached for us all. Or those terrible things you're always reading in the paper, people just standing around watching a car settle into the water while a man happens to be drowning inside. It's true, we don't get involved with anything, we really don't. Not with living or with dying. Wait, I'll bring the cups."

She leapt up as she spoke. "Cynny, do you ever get this eerie feeling? I seldom leave the house unless it's in my car. There are times when I feel like I spend the whole day in that damn metal box. It might as well be a coffin. Millions of people live out here, and your only real contact with most of them is glimpses of faces through other car windows. I don't even know most of my neighbors by name. I shuttle back and forth, doing errands, and driving the children here and there. I shop all alone in a supermarket full of packets and tins and frozen lumps. Sometimes you begin to feel like a ghost. You turn on the radio just to hear voices, you go home and phone a friend just to make sure there's somebody there. And at night we sit down and turn on TV and look at pictures!"

She stopped for breath and went on again, the words tumbling out. "And that's another thing, Cynny. I think McLuhan was all wrong, television is not bringing us closer together into any global village. We just sit alone in our houses and look at pictures and none of it is ever quite real. We watch men shoot each other in a cops-and-robbers movie and turn the channel and watch news tapes of people being killed in the Middle East or somewhere, and it's really all the same to us, isn't it? Oh, Cynny, you can't tell me there isn't something wrong with the way we live. Sometimes I really can't bear it!"

"Nan, Nan!" Cynny said helplessly, her face half amused. "Darling, we all have moments of this. 'Stop the world, I want to get off.' How can you help it? You've only to get up in the morning and read the paper, people and races and religions at each other's throats. And bombs and missiles and a polluted planet and dying oceans—"

"I don't worry about bombs and missiles anymore," Nancy said forlornly, spooning at her coffee. "I read Ehrlich's book, and I buy low-phosphate soap and white toilet paper, but I seldom even think about what's happening to ecology either. I suppose the whole idea of it is so monstrous that I can't even comprehend it, let alone feel threatened by it. It's like reading those articles in magazines about alienation and lack of communication and all that, it's just words. It's my daily life that frightens me."

"Nancy, not to change the subject, but may I ask you something?"

"I think I know what's coming, but go ahead."

"All right. Are you happy in your marriage these days, love? Is everything all right between you and Dave?"

"Oh, Cynny, I knew that was what you were thinking, but you're wrong. Dave and our life together and the children, that's the absolute foundation of my life, and it's as solid as the rock. I'm so in love with Dave. I know it sounds corny, but I honestly wouldn't know how to live without him. We balance each other so perfectly. I love Dave, and on top of that, I have such respect and admiration for him. He's so damn brilliant, but he's never stuffy. He's a really good man, the way he feels about people, and very mature in his relationships and—"

"Nan, you don't have to convince me. But you're talking all around the question. Are you satisfied with your marriage these days?"

Nancy lifted her chin. "Not entirely, no. But that's not Dave's fault," she added quickly. "Oh, Cynny, more than anything else I wanted us to be a close-knit family, I think it's so important for children. The family is the first social unit, it's where they discover their roots and who they are. My family is all back east, and Dave's mother, so there's really just us. I've tried to give us traditions, like celebrating holidays and birthdays the same way each year and all that, but more and more I feel it isn't any use. We're split apart. We all live separate lives in separate little compartments. The children are always in school or playing with other children their exact same age and sex, and swim classes and music lessons and Little League and Brownies and all the rest. And Dave's in his own compartment. Half the time the children are in bed when he gets home at night, and weekends he plays tennis and goes to the gym. Dave loves the children, but three quarters of all he knows about them is what he's heard from me. Do you know what Davey said to me the other day? He'd been playing with the children up the street on a Saturday morning when their father came to pick them up. Davey came stomping into the house, really furious, and he said to me, 'I think divorced daddies are the best kind to have. They bring you presents and take you to Disneyland and you get to see them all day on Saturday.' Oh, Cynny, that's so sad! It's such a—all right, it's such a commentary on our culture! Dave loves his work, but it's a separate world, he really isn't able to share it with me and the children. When you stop to think of it, our lives, even Dave's and mine, really overlap in such a few areas that—"

"Nancy, we all live like this. It may not be right, but there isn't anything especially new about it, is there? All the way back through the ages, men and women seem to have lived very different and largely separate lives. Darling, why don't I make us some lunch? Just a salad and some garlic bread, and a good stiff drink to start with, how does that sound?"

"It sounds heavenly if you'll promise not to go to a lot of trouble." Nancy bent down to hunt a comb and lipstick from her oversize purse. "All right, maybe men and women have always lived in separate worlds, but I still think something's gone terribly wrong. Maybe our separate lives aren't rich enough any longer to sustain us. Maybe now we need each other more."

Cynny swiftly unloaded vegetables from a drawer in the refrigerator. "Nan, you know you still haven't answered my question. That old saying about it takes more than four legs in a bed to make a marriage is true only so far as it goes. Are you really happy with Dave these days, love?"

"You mean our sex life?" Nancy blushed beneath her tear streaks and her freckles. "Well, to be absolutely honest, it's not always that perfect for me. I mean, Dave's so bound up in his work. Lots of times he's exhausted, or he's home but most of his mind is still off somewhere else. But it's truly not that big a problem for me, if that's what you're getting at. I mean, it's nothing I can't live with. Oh, damn, that doesn't sound right either. I mean, it's honestly not warping my life or—"

Cynny laughed. "It's all right, Nan. None of us lives by sex alone, it's just that Freud made us feel guilty about admitting it."

"Well, I sound like a ninny, and I hate that," Nancy said. She came across the room to where Cynny was opening a can of garbanzo beans. "Let's put it this way, I may not always have the most pluperfect sex life on earth, but I'd still rather be married to Dave than to any other man in the world. Period. And I know myself well enough to know that if my life doesn't satisfy me these days, it's not the kind of lack that orgies every Tuesday and Thursday night are going to fill. I don't knock it. I mean, I know it's that important to some women, but it's not to me. I've always been a terribly monogamous person. I don't seem to be constituted for having affairs. Anyway, I wouldn't risk jeopardizing the least little part of my relationship with Dave for—for—"

"A great, mad fling with Burt Reynolds?" Cynny rubbed a bit of garlic briskly into a wooden bowl.

"He's not my type. Marcello Mastroianni, I guess." She gathered up plates and silver and swooped across the room to the table. "So along with everything else, I guess I'm an absolute dull and hopeless square. What's to become of me, Cynny? Seriously."

Cynny laughed. "Nancy, I do love you! All right, now do you really want to know what I think? I think that for the past ten years you've been completely involved with being pregnant and raising babies, and all at once Sambo is three and off to nursery school and you've come to the end of one part of your life. Now it's time for you to shift gears and spend a little time and energy on Nancy for a change."

"You mean take extension courses at UCLA," Nancy said sadly. "Or rush off to Every Woman's Village like half the girls I know and take classes in belly dancing and sculpting and Chinese cooking. Oh, Cynny! May I have one of your cigarettes?"

"Help yourself, love."

"Well, I've already tried ceramics and yoga and making batiks. And I do party precinct work and my stint for Head Start and retarded kids and the ERA and the League of Women Voters. I think one trouble is, I've lost faith in politics. And another thing, I don't mean discrimination or decent housing, and certainly no human being today should ever go hungry anywhere in the world or any child ever lack for medical care, but sometimes

I wonder what's the use of the Third World people and the migrant farmworkers here at home and all the rest fighting so hard to get a culture exactly like ours. I mean, they are certainly entitled to it, and if they want it, then they must have it. But it's not working very well for us, is it, so what makes them think it's going to work for them?"

She swooped back across the room, holding the cigarette awkwardly and puffing out a great cloud of smoke. "I guess I'm a disgrace to my sex," she said despondently. "I really envy women who have artistic talents or are genuinely career motivated. I taught school for two years before I married Dave, and one day when the children are older, I'll probably go back to it. But what I always wanted most was just to get married and raise a family. Now there's something else that's wrong with this culture, women somehow aren't allowed to do the things anymore that they were meant to do by instinct, and on the other hand, they're expected to do a lot of other things that don't give them any real satisfaction at all. Cynny, something smells so good, what is it?"

Cynny was just lifting a shallow pan containing several red peppers, wilted now, their brilliant skins split and blackened. "Peppers for our salad. Aren't they heavenly? Come on, Nan, how can you say the world is all wrong when you smell peppers roasting in the fall?"

"Easy! Because it *is* wrong. You've just made another very good point. We don't really live with our senses anymore, just with our nerves. Schizophrenic! That's what our lives are these days, all cut off from emotion and reality and nature. We've lost touch with nature completely, and that's the most awful thing of all. Cynny, you know that's true!"

"Darling, I'm not arguing with you. But this is the only world we have, and so far as we can be sure of, the only time we have to be alive in it. I doubt if you're going to be able to make it over single-handed, so sooner or later you may just have to reconcile yourself to making the best of it. Poor Nan! Does that sound terribly unsympathetic?"

"But how do you reconcile yourself?" Nancy said forlornly. "What's the trick to it? How do people manage, tell me that."

"Oh, Lord! In all sorts of ways. Religion or macrobiotics or backgammon or Transcendental Meditation or kite flying or chanting at Nichiren Shoshu—"

"Or psychotherapy?" Nancy finished. "You must have thought of that. I've even thought of that myself. The trouble is, I don't have much faith in psychiatry, do you? It sounds so snobby to say it, but it's horribly typical middle class. And how is some psychiatrist supposed to convince me that all is right with the world when every instinct I have tells me that it isn't?"

"Then you may just have to go it alone," Cynny said. "What else can I say? Brute courage, girl!" She stirred strips of red pepper and golden garbanzos into the crisp greens redolent of vinegar and garlic and herbs, tasted one of the beans, and nodded approvingly. "Here, love, you take this."

While Nancy carried the salad bowl to the table, Cynny dropped ice cubes into a pair of glasses and poured whiskey generously into each. She added water and presented one glass to Nancy.

"Let's drink to Mugger," she said. "May he rest in peace. He was a happy animal. He caught your mice and gave you joy and lived his life to the hilt. And I'll bet you he never spent a single night walking the kitchen floor worrying over trends in modern culture when he could be out among the neighborhood ladies, casting his vote of confidence in the future!"

Nancy smiled in spite of herself as they touched the glasses.

Then she said soberly, "Cynny, tell me something. You're everything I wish I were, you know. You're also the happiest woman I know who isn't a perfect vacuum between the ears, and you and Jim have the secure, forever kind of relationship that I hope for for Dave and me. You have something very strong and solid inside yourself. What is it?"

Cynny stared at her incredulously, then laughed. "Only sheer terror, love! I've run on it for years."

"Cynny, I'm serious. Don't tease me."

Cynny looked at her searchingly for a moment and then at the glass in her hand. "Nan, what can I tell you?" she said at last. "You know, for years when I was a child, I believed that there must be a sort of magic formula for living that grown-ups kept secret, written on a piece of paper probably and locked away in a box. I honestly believed that when I grew up they'd give me the secret so that ever after I would know how to cope with everything and be a grown-up, too. It was one of the greatest disappointments of my life, discovering that the box was empty."

"But how do you manage? How do you honestly get out of bed in the morning and face another day?"

"I stumble out of bed in the morning to do the things I have to do, like everybody else," Cynny said cheerfully. "Oh, come on, Nan! There are compensations, you have to admit it. Grim dawn or no, first thing you know there's the smell of coffee brewing and the light shining through the trees!"

"You mean the simple pleasures." Nancy chewed reflectively upon a bit of ice. "Yes, but how long can you fool yourself, when you know in your bones that fundamentally it's all gone wrong? I go around all the while feeling like a giant condor. I wonder if they know they're an endangered species, too. Oh, Cynny, there has to be a better way to live than this!"

"Nan, I love you with all my heart," Cynny said lugubriously, "but for pity's sake, come on now and let's have some lunch!"

They went, laughing, to the table, arms about each other's waists.

B Y TEN O'CLOCK THAT MORNING MICK SANFORD
was seated at a table in the hotel coffee shop appearing
totally refreshed, shaven, clear eyed behind his large, dark glasses,
his pale, unruly hair still damp from his shower.

"What about your brother?" Bob Covern was saying. "Have
you seen him yet? Ask him to come over to the house for dinner
tonight, if you'd like to."

"I called him this morning. We're getting together for lunch.
I'll see what he has on tonight."

"Look, anybody else you'd like to see, ask them to come over.
You must have a couple old girlfriends here you'd like to check
out again."

"No chance," Mick said, grinning. "I've been away too long.
Besides, if I did, what makes you think I'd introduce them to
you, old buddy!"

"Ah, you devil! I knew you must have a choice piece or two
stashed away somewhere!"

"Yeah, sure." Mick spread golden marmalade over a piece of
toast. "Oh, hey, speaking of auld lang syne, guess who I had a letter from a month ago? Linda."

"Linda! No kidding," Bob said, his mouth full of eggs. "She
still married to that shrink in Beverly Hills? What did she want
anyway?"

"No, she wrote that she and the doc got divorced five or six
years ago." Mick hesitated. "I don't exactly know what she
wanted. It was a peculiar sort of letter. She said she was worried
about the kid. Seems the kid wants to meet me, and Linda

thought she ought to. As a matter of fact, I'm supposed to go over to her house tonight."

"Oh, for Christ's sake!" Bob said disgustedly. He was a stocky, middle-aged man with a florid, handsome face, a large mustache, and restless, dark eyes. "Tell the little cunt to go jump in the ocean. Better yet, don't tell her anything, just keep the hell away from her."

"You think I shouldn't see her then?" Mick's voice was unconcerned, but his eyes behind the tinted lenses of his glasses were suddenly intent.

"Hell, no, I don't think you should see her," Bob declared, reaching across the stiff white tablecloth for a coffeepot. "All she's after is money, you know."

Mick laughed in genuine delight. "Now you have to be kidding!"

"What else could it be after all these years? She probably thinks you're loaded."

"You're crazy! Even if she did, where would she expect to come in? She hasn't any legal claim."

"She knows that. Why do you think she gave you all the hearts-and-flowers stuff about the kid? They're just waiting to sock it to you, pal, the long-lost daddy routine. Then when they've got you softened up a little, they plan to take you for all they can get."

"Oh, for God's sakes!" There was a look of distaste upon Mick's face, and he moved in his chair uncomfortably.

Bob went on, "You know, pal, you've got the greatest instinct about automobiles of any guy I've ever known. About women, you stink. Look, I've dated too many divorced girls, I know how their minds work. Don't you know that if the kid really did want to see you, the last thing Linda would ever do is give you the satisfaction of telling you about it? Women aren't built that way. How old is the kid now anyway, fourteen, fifteen?"

"She's twenty."

"Oh, Jesus, has it really been that long! Well, then you know all that stuff has to be a lot of crap. She's grown up now; if she was so crazy to meet you, she'd have got in touch with you herself."

"I suppose you're right."

"Damn right I'm right. I've got a nose for it, pal. I should have, I've paid through it often enough! It's that old dough-re-mi."

Mick glumly shoved his plate aside and reached for his cigarettes. "That's hard to believe. Linda never cared about money. Anyway, the doc is a pretty big wheel. She must be well fixed, she has a house in Beverly Hills. Why would she want money from me?"

"Why's water wet?" Bob asked sadly. "Because that's what they all want, baby. None of them ever get enough of it. Hey, wait a minute!" He snapped his fingers. "When did you say she wrote you? When your aunt died this fall there was a big story in the *Times*. She probably thinks you're coming into a family bundle now."

"Aaah, you're crazy! Linda didn't even know Theo was dead until I told her on the phone last night."

"You want to bet?"

Mick was silent for a moment, wreathed in cigarette smoke; then he leaned forward over his folded arms, his face once more relaxed and smiling. "Oh, hey," he said. "Guess who I ran into a couple weeks ago—old Denny."

"That crazy son of a bitch," Bob said fondly. "How is the old bastard anyway?"

"When I saw him, he was on crutches and really pissed. Seems one of the Detroit outfits in Europe hired him to run the tests on their new antiskid gizmo. They wait for a nice wet day to go out, it's a real big deal, the company wheels and the computer boys, a camera crew and a truckload of measuring gadgets. Denny takes it around a few times while they're getting set up. Then he gets the signal finally and hits the brakes, and all that happens is everything comes loose at once and old Denny goes on his head. Right on *Candid Camera!*"

They both roared with laughter, and their conversation moved on to other things.

But several hours later, over lunch with his brother in a restaurant on Wilshire Boulevard, Mick said suddenly, "Trav, tell me something. Your older kids, Janie's kids, do you see much of them now that they're grown up?"

"Well, it's obvious you've never been this route!" Trav said. "Let's have another drink, should we? Which is our waitress, the one with the big boobs?"

"No, I think it's the blonde over there by the table."

Trav hitched about in his chair, hand poised to signal. "I usually keep it down to two drinks at lunchtime," he said in his pleasant, resonant drawl. "But what the hell, you don't get home this often anymore. By the way, speaking of the kids, did I tell you that Trav Junior has decided to go to law school?"

"That's great."

Trav was taller than Mick and big boned, lean and deeply suntanned with an air of impeccable grooming that Mick associated with the clothing models in *Esquire* magazine.

Trav pointed to their glasses suddenly, turning back to the table as the waitress nodded. "Oh, law is a good enough field, I suppose," he was saying. "All the professions are overcrowded these days. But I don't mind admitting I'm not exactly looking forward to picking up the tab for it. I'm still in hock as it is from Moira's property settlement. You're lucky, Mig. You've kept clear of these kinds of obligations."

"I don't know, try building cars sometime. A racing engine with a bug in it can eat up money about as fast as any two wives and a half dozen kids, I should think."

"You can think that one over again, kid!"

"All I know is, if we don't sell a few more cars this winter, we stand a good chance of going broke before the end of the next racing season."

"That's too bad. But then I imagine you haven't sunk much of your own money into this company."

"Wrong," Mick said cheerfully. "There isn't that much sponsor money floating around anymore. Times are tough all over."

Trav nibbled at a toothpick-impaled onion from his glass. "Have you been over to the house yet?" he asked obliquely.

"As a matter of fact, I drove by there last night. I was tempted to go in and take a look around, but I thought the electricity was probably off."

"No, all the utilities are on. The appraisers are still working over there and the real estate people in and out. Stop by the office with me after lunch and I'll give you the keys; sometimes they leave the front door on the chain."

"Well, it's no big deal. I may not have time to get by there again anyway."

"You'd better make a point of going over to the house while you're in town. There must still be things of yours there. Or there may be things of Theo's you'd like to keep—paintings or silver or something."

Mick was suddenly absorbed in the rattling chips of ice in his glass.

"Family things like photographs and papers I'm having boxed up and put in storage," Trav said after a pause. "I know there are a lot of trophies of yours upstairs, things like that. I'll put it all in Bekins, shall I? Sometime you might want to sort through it."

"Fine."

Trav glanced at him quickly. "You know, I feel damn bad about this too, Mig. I really hate to see the old place go. You sure you don't want to keep it?" He laughed. "In case you do, I'll sell you my half dirt cheap."

"Thanks. What about you, don't you want it?"

"God, Mig, what would I do with it? I can't see myself ever living in it, it's a barn of a place to maintain. The only practical thing seems to be to sell it off. After all, that house, or the land it's standing on actually, is about the only real asset left in her estate."

"Grandpa's money couldn't last forever," Mick said drily.

"Actually, it could have lasted forever. Even with taxes. You may not know this, Mig, but Theo gave away some pretty sizable chunks of money, particularly in the last four or five years. There's some wilderness preserve up in Wyoming or Idaho or somewhere that I believe she financed nearly single-handed."

"Christ, Trav, don't be such a shit!" Mick said pleasantly. "It was her money to do whatever she wanted with, wasn't it?"

"Did I say it wasn't? All I'm saying is I'm sorry to see the old place go. I wish to hell I could afford to keep it. After all, Grandfather Sanford built that house. It's been in the family for a long time."

"It was Great-Grandfather Sanford who built it. They used to come out here in the winter even before Grandfather Sanford settled in California."

"I hadn't realized that. Then it must be even older than I'd thought. It really is a damn shame. End of an era and all that."

"Nothing lasts forever."

"That's for sure." Trav sighed, his face wistful. "How long are you going to be in town, Mig?"

"Couple days. Just over the weekend."

"That's a short visit. We don't see much of each other anymore. The years roll by pretty fast." He laughed, his pleasant, mechanical laughter, but suddenly his eyes were moist, his voice husky. "You know what they say, blood is thicker than water and all that. We're all the family that's left now, kid."

Mick glanced up at him, surprised. "There's a chance I may be back out here in a couple months though."

"Great. I'm glad to hear that."

The waitress arrived just then with the tray of drinks, and Trav blew his nose loudly into a handkerchief while she exchanged the glasses.

SHIVERING, CYNNY LINGERED TO WAVE A FINAL time as Nancy's red station wagon backed out of the driveway, then fled to the warmth of the kitchen, where she fell to work clearing the lunch table.

The house seemed very quiet now, and Cynny's thoughts returned to Nancy with half-rueful affection. Certainly her restless energy was a large part of Nancy's charm, making her the vibrant, entertaining girl with whom it was normally a delight to spend an hour or two. But today's visit had been like having a small cyclone in the house. Snatches of Nancy's voice were still swirling about in Cynny's head. How like Nan to want to stir up the entire hornet's nest of the twentieth-century world! But Nancy's unhappiness appeared genuine, and Cynny made a note to herself to spend a little time with her in the coming weeks, this rock-hunting picnic next week definitely, and perhaps a day of rummaging through the junk shops in Venice, or some other outing that Nancy would enjoy.

When the kitchen was restored to order, Cynny paused to light a cigarette, turning over in her mind the half dozen projects she had planned for this day. Actually, half the afternoon was still before her, she reminded herself. It was just this evil gray weather that made it seem as if nightfall was already near. Pulling aside a curtain, she stared out into the colorless day and idly wished once more for rain.

And with that thought she was seized by an unanticipated longing: for the smell and sound of rain, and the feeling of it wet and cold upon her skin, for the sight of great silver sheets pounding at the earth, water sluicing dust from leaves and masonry, and oil and grime from the streets, dark rivers roaring through storm drains, shallow, dimpling puddles standing on the grass, lakes of water and debris at city intersections, and endless lines of automobiles stalled and silent upon the freeways.

It was gone in a flash, and half shaken, half amused, Cynny laughed. She walked swiftly through the dining room and hallway to climb the stairs. In her bedroom, she turned on lights everywhere and a radio, and set about changing her soiled shirt for a bulky, brown turtleneck. She touched up her lipstick before the mirror, combed her hair, and dabbed drops of perfume at her ears.

No use, she was thinking, she was no longer in the mood for chores or errands, better to get out of the house and do something amusing. Hunt for a bracelet for Susan's Christmas, for instance, through the antiques shops in Santa Monica, or rummage fabric stores for material for the dinner dress she needed before the holidays. And if she was going to be in Santa Monica anyway, she might as well pick up Jim's jacket from the tailor's where she had taken it to have the lining resewn; she'd phone first to make sure that it was ready.

She found the number in the phone book in her desk drawer, dialed, and heard a busy signal. And then, merely for want of anything better to do while she waited, Cynny thought of Joby's room. Before his departure that morning on his surfing trip, she had warned him that neither she nor Merna intended to set foot in his room again until he had restored it to some reasonable degree of order. But she might at least make up his bed, she relented. She was halfway down the hall at the thought.

She turned on a light and shook her head despairingly. She gathered up an armload of socks and sweaters, and hung jackets and shirts away in the closet. Then, with the bed unloaded, she hauled at the blankets, and a brown leather shaving kit rolled out onto the rug. She recognized it instantly, a hand-me-down from Jim and currently one of Joby's more cherished possessions.

Poor Joby, she was thinking as she stooped to pick it up, he was certain to forget something in such a disorder, too bad it should be his shaving gear.

On an impulse, Cynny opened the zipper fastener and peeped into the case, curious about just what toiletries Joby considered vital to the maintenance of his appearance and well-being. There was the electric razor, of course, another hand-me-down from Jim, neatly wrapped in its cord, a tube of toothpaste conspicuously the worse for wear, but no sign of a toothbrush. Cynny's smile deepened. A comb, another tube containing a preparation designed to conceal the eruptions of acne, a small bar of hotel soap in a paper wrapper yellowed and brittle with age, a half-filled bottle of Hai Karate cologne, and at the very bottom, three large safety pins neatly joined together.

Cynny dropped the pins back into the little bag and felt a familiar wave of tenderness for the curious, half-formed creatures that boys of Job's age really were. At least no prophylactics, but perhaps in this age of the Pill, they were outmoded. More likely, Joby had not quite arrived at that place. But one never knew with boys. For the millionth time, she sadly wished that Jim and Joby had a closer, more communicative relationship. She bunched the contents of the shaving kit together, inverted it, and whacked upon the bottom to dislodge an accumulation of dust and sand. She wadded a piece of candy bar wrapper in her hand and picked automatically at a scrap of plastic clinging to the side. But the bit of plastic did not come loose, not even when she pulled at it. Briefly puzzled, Cynny recalled that many shaving kits were designed with a separate moisture-proof compartment beneath the bottom. And likely Jim had forgotten to clean out that compartment when he gave Job the case.

She found the crack with her fingernails, and sure enough, a leather-covered false bottom lifted easily, revealing an aperture apparently stuffed with a wad of clear, soft plastic. She removed it, a small plastic bag securely knotted at the top, certainly nothing of Jim's that she recalled. Cynny shook the bag and held it closer to the light. An herb, she decided, how odd, but definitely an herb, a shredded, gray-green, leafy material something like oregano. Oregano? Oh, Lord!

Cynny picked loose the knot, more curious than shocked. Well, you might have expected it, she told herself. By the time you were seventeen, you were experimenting with liquor behind your parents' backs, remember? Isn't this merely the equivalent behavior? Her second thought was that, just the same, it might be considerably better all around if Jim were not to learn of this.

She sniffed at the top of the bag, shook the contents to one side, revealing the little packet of cigarette papers, shook the bag again, and brought to view at the bottom a large handful of stubby, oddly colored capsules interspersed with small bright yellow ones, red ones, and a scattering of white pills.

For several seconds, Cynny stood rigid and unbreathing, and then she clawed the pills and capsules out of the bag, bits of marijuana sticking to her fingers, fled into the bathroom, and without hesitation threw them in the toilet and pulled the handle. Only after they had disappeared in a little whispering whirlpool of water did she breathe once more. She walked slowly back into the bedroom on trembling legs, her face pale, and paused to stare about her, uncomprehending. In that moment it seemed to her Joby had become a stranger, and this familiar, cluttered room an alien place.

She scrabbled up the plastic bag, knotted the top again hastily, hands shaking, crammed it back into the shaving kit, and fumbled at the zipper. She shoved the case back into the welter of bed blankets, then turned off the light and fled the room.

Back in her own bedroom, music tinkled lightheartedly, and Cynny snapped off the radio on her way to the closet. She pulled a capelike tweed coat from a hanger, grabbed up her purse, and last of all, picked up a long blue-and-orange scarf. She left lights turned on and forgot to lock the door behind her. In the garage, she winced at the sight of Joby's blue Volkswagen. A moment later, she sent her own long, heavy car hurtling from the drive-way, tires squealing as she accelerated too fast into the turn.

Later on that Friday afternoon, Mick paid his visit to the old house in Santa Monica. Parking his car at the curb, he climbed the broad wooden steps armed with the ring of keys Trav had insisted on giving him. The chain was not fastened after all; the door opened easily. The interior was as chill and drab as the weather outside and equally strange and familiar. He walked through the silent rooms on the lower floor and found it was neither as depressing as he had feared nor as pleasurable as he had hoped, merely, to tell the truth, rather boring. He climbed the stairs, finally, and entered the room Theo had called her sit-ting room.

This room, like all the others, was dim and cheerless in the waning afternoon light, a film of dust upon the tabletops, the fireplace yawning empty behind the brass screen, and the subtle signs of dislocation that the appraisers had left everywhere: a stopped clock and a pair of Meissen vases, for instance, shoved awkwardly together at one end of the mantel shelf, a heavy brass Chinese lamp set on the floor enwrapped in its cord, a small table standing forlornly out of place beside an identical one to make a pair. He noted, however, that the paisley shawl beneath which Theo had liked to nap remained in a neat folded square at the foot of the Empire sofa by the fireplace. Turning abruptly then, he left the room without a backward look.

He paused to use the bathroom next door, a large room with old-fashioned plumbing fixtures, starched linen towels still hanging from the racks, and a fresh oval of Theo's yellow, lemon-scented soap in the soap dish. He flushed the toilet, the sound abrasive in the silence, and automatically washed his hands at the old faucets as Theo had taught him when he was a small boy. Drying them on a white towel, he thought again of Theo's sitting room. He recalled it fondly as it had been in its earlier life: filled with light and the rich colors of nice rugs and upholstery, fresh flowers, polished wood and brass, and a fire crackling on the hearth. There were the dozen or two old family photographs above the camphorwood chest, Theo's favorite oil of a rainswept Norman landscape, and everywhere her stacked books and papers, magazines and colored yarns.

That remembered room was far more real to him than the silent chamber next door. And what of Theo herself then, moving with her brisk and dignified tread through the corridors of his mind? Flinging down the towel, he left the bathroom and lit a cigarette as he descended to leave.

He decided to exit by a rear door for a final glimpse of the garden and the old gazebo. On his way, he passed the library, where books were already partially sorted into stacks on the floor, and the old glass conservatory at the back of the house. He made certain the night lock was set and gave the heavy door an extra hard pull after him.

The garden was smaller than he had remembered it, and already looked a little neglected in spite of the chrysanthemums blooming along the wall. The shape of the old wooden gazebo was visible beneath the trees, and through the mist, he made out an unexpected figure seated upon a bench—a straight, tweed-covered back and a smooth, dark head. Hearing the door slam, the figure leapt to her feet and turned, and Mick saw a woman with a pale face and a vivid blue-and-orange scarf.

With a prickle of irritation, he strode down the porch steps and along the brick path toward her.

"Hello," he called out. "I'm sorry I scared you. You're from the real estate office, I suppose."

She snatched up her purse from the bench, seemingly poised for flight. "No, I'm not," she said reservedly. "I was about to ask you the same thing."

"Well, I'm not a burglar if that's what you're thinking. I used to live here. Miss Sanford was my aunt."

She smiled then, a wide, warm smile, and leaned down over

the railing to hold out her hand. "I'm sorry, I should have recognized you, but your hair is lighter than it looks in photographs. I'm Cynny Holman. I'm not a burglar either. Just a trespasser, I'm afraid."

"Mick Sanford." Her hand was small and cold in his, and he noted that she was younger than he had first judged her to be, a small woman with cropped, dark hair, untanned skin, and clear, pale eyes behind dark lashes. "Are you a neighbor?"

"Not really. Theodora and I were friends." She hesitated. "I still miss her very much. Sometimes I come and sit in the garden; the service gate is always unlocked. I didn't expect there'd be anybody here. I'm sorry if I disturbed you."

"Hell, no. I'm glad there's somebody who still cares enough to come, for God's sakes."

"This must be difficult for you," she said. "It must be the first time you've realized she's really gone. I mean, when you're away it never seems that real, does it? My father died several years ago in Connecticut, and I'm always catching myself thinking of him as still living back there in the old house just as he always did."

"I know what you mean. Had you known Theo long?"

"In a way. She was a sort of local institution, you know. She scared people off a bit, so I didn't really get acquainted with her until about three years ago. You wouldn't think of her that way naturally, but to strangers she was terribly imposing."

"Yes, she did look pretty fierce, didn't she?"

"She certainly did. One would never guess how really unstuffy she was, and her divine sense of humor. I got to be very fond of her, we had a lot of fun together."

"That's great. Did you see her often?"

"At least every week the last couple years. Finally we had a sort of standing date for every Friday afternoon and—".

He whooped with laughter. "Not the Friday afternoon sherry parties! She always wrote about them in her letters. Don't tell me you're the friend who dropped in for sherry every Friday!"

"Yes, I'm afraid so. Except I happen to hate sherry. Theodora kept a bottle of Scotch on hand for me."

"Look, I'm sorry," he said, his eyes still crinkling with amusement. "The reason this cracks me up, when Theo used to write about it, I just imagined—you know. That the friend was another old dowager type from the Episcopal altar guild or whatever it is. I always had this picture of these two dignified old girls getting a little snockered together over the sherry bottle every Friday afternoon." He laughed again and then stopped. "Oh, hey, I'm sorry! That was a hell of a thing to say to you. It wasn't anything that Theo wrote, you know." He teetered uncomfortably. "It was all my own idea, I just—"

She laughed. "It's all right. Honestly. So. Are you here on a visit, or—"

"Yes. Just over the weekend actually."

"I'm sorry to hear that. I was hoping that maybe—"

Understanding her thought, he looked for an instant at the solid bulk of the old house behind them.

"No, I wish I could. I suppose they'll tear it down and build more damn condominiums or something." His voice was suddenly apologetic. "I realize now that I should have come out here months ago, when Theo first got sick. I was busy as hell all summer, so I kept in pretty close touch with Trav, my brother, you know, and he didn't seem to feel there was any reason for me to come. I was coming over in October anyway, so I put it off."

"Theodora never expected you to come, I'm certain of that. She really had improved so much. She knew how busy you were, and she adored all your phone calls and was looking forward to seeing you in the fall."

"Yes. Except as it turned out, fall was a little late."

"How could you have foreseen that?" she said mildly. "Even her doctors didn't. She might have lived for years and never had another stroke. It's not the sort of thing anyone can predict, you know."

"Yes, I know." He came up the steps into the gazebo, groping for cigarettes beneath his crumpled raincoat. Then he glanced upward to the round, raftered roof. "One of the first things I remember is climbing to the top of this. It seemed a hell of a lot bigger to me in those days, I promise you."

She laughed. "Isn't it marvelous? All those absolutely huge things we remember that turn out to be so small." She took the offered cigarette and bent over the lighter flame, drops of moisture shining on her hair.

"Now I'm the one who's disturbing you," he said with a sudden candid gaze.

"Of course not. I'd always hoped to meet you." She hesitated, then sat down again upon the wooden bench. "I'm sorry you had such bad luck with your car at the Glen."

"That's the way it happens sometimes."

"Do you like living in England? But then you've really lived in Europe for a long time now, haven't you?"

"Yes, I suppose. When you move around a lot, you don't much think of yourself as living anywhere."

He walked off several steps and leaned upon the low railing, staring out into the garden. The light was fading, the fog sifting through the tree limbs.

"Well, I think it was damn nice of you to take the time every week to visit Theo the way you did. It meant a lot to her; she mentioned it in every letter she wrote. I think it was pretty damn nice."

"But I did it because I enjoyed it," she said, embarrassed. "We were friends. I think I came to rely on Theodora more than she did on me."

"Just the same, most people wouldn't have bothered, an old woman like that."

"Don't say that! You never thought of her as old."

"That's true." He sat down on the other end of the bench and studied her again. "So give me the real scoop. What did go on at those sherry parties anyway?"

She laughed. "Nothing half as fascinating as the way you imagined it. We just talked. Or sometimes we played Scrabble."

"Hey, that's right, Theo was a demon Scrabble player."

"Wasn't she though! But mostly we just talked. She was always such good company. She was so madly interested in everything about your life and full of such marvelous stories about her own."

"There was a family legend that Theo never married because her first love got killed in a sailboat accident. Did she ever tell you about that?"

"As a matter of fact, she did. I hate to debunk any family lore, but according to Theodora that boy who drowned was a college roommate of your grandfather's and Theodora was only nine years old at the time."

"Well, scratch one family legend. I wonder why she never married then. I didn't have the nerve to ask her. Probably because she was too busy raising my father and then, later on, Trav and me. Poor Theo! I guess it was her fate in life to be an aunt."

"I don't think that's true. She told me once that when she was a young girl she was really terrified of men. She was very shy and terribly conscious of being a sort of ugly duckling when all her sisters had been great beauties. Then she did have a disastrous first love, except that was about ten years later than the boy in the boat accident. It was the winter she came out in New York."

"Hey, I never heard any of this. Tell me about it."

"Well, it wasn't all that much of a romance. She said that whole winter was a nightmare for her anyway. From the fittings at the dressmaker's right through the parties and the balls, which she dreaded and despised. Poor Theodora! She said in those days she was the proverbial girl whom men danced with once at parties and then ran for their lives!"

"So I suppose the first man who paid a little attention to her, she was so grateful she fell head over heels and he turned out to be a rotter and a cad?"

"No, a perfectly eligible man-about-town type. But the romance apparently was all on her side. Toward the end of the season, some other girl announced her engagement to him.

Theodora was crushed. She caught cold, declined straight into pneumonia, and nearly died. As a matter of fact, that was what brought her to California. They shipped her out here to convalesce, with some elderly cousin for chaperone. Of course your grandfather was already living in California, and your father was a small boy."

"So what happened then? Theo just stayed on in California and nursed her broken heart?"

"Well, she said it was less broken heart actually than wounded pride. She'd got it into her head that she'd made a fool of herself over this man and now everyone was laughing at her. She took long walks alone on the beach, then got your grandfather to buy her a horse and went riding in the hills. And that was the beginning of the real love affair of her life, she said, her one with California."

"Yes, she had more feeling for this part of the country than any native I ever knew."

"You know, I always loved to hear her talk about that time before the First World War. She played tennis and golf and learned to swim in the ocean, and went on pack trips up the Sierra and out into the desert. She said there was a kind of romance about doing such things in those days, a sort of new image for women, to be free and independent in a man's world, to hunt and fish and climb mountains and travel and even learn to drive a car. It's fun to think of Theodora as a New Woman, isn't it? Then the war came and your grandmother died in the flu epidemic, and after that Theodora had your grandfather and your father to look after. She adored your grandfather, you know, he'd always been her favorite brother."

"That's the part I know about. And I remember the pictures of her on horseback and the tennis cups in the attic. But no other romances?"

"Oh, yes. She said that she had several chances to marry, and at least once even thought about it seriously. She was very sweet about it. She said that, if she had it to do over again, she would have married one of them, a man from Denver. But she said she valued her independence too highly at the time, and then, as she put it, she was too much of a homebody. She loved this house and her family. She said what it really came down to, she was just too timid to ever leave home."

He laughed. "That's great. Off the top of your head, *timid* is not exactly the word you'd have picked to describe Theo either, is it?"

"I know. Isn't it divine?"

They sat smiling for a moment in companionable silence, and then he said, "This is really great, you know? I like hearing you talk about Theo. I wish now that I'd gotten to know her better. I mean as a person. She was a great woman."

"Oh, yes. She really was."

Streamers of fog were slipping between the weathered timbers of the gazebo, and Cynny wrapped an end of her bright scarf about her throat and pulled a pair of gloves from her pocket.

"Hey, you're shivering! I shouldn't have kept you sitting out here in this muck. I have an idea. Do you think your Scotch bottle is still there? Let's go in and have a drink. I could light a fire."

She glanced at the large blue watch dial on her wrist and rose to her feet. "Oh, Lord, it's gotten very late! Thank you, but I'm afraid I have to run."

"Are you sure? It's Friday afternoon, you know."

"I'm sorry," she said with apparently genuine regret. "I'd really love to. But I have to get back."

"Do you have a car here?" he asked as they left the summerhouse. "Or can I drop you off?"

"No, I have a car. I'm parked out front."

"So am I." He produced the ring of keys from his raincoat pocket. "The front gate key must be here somewhere. Save us the walk around."

"Marvelous."

They walked together along the damp brick path.

"Look, I didn't think," he said. "Maybe you don't like the

idea of going into the house again now that Theo's gone. We could have a drink somewhere else."

"No, I love this house, it's not that. I really have to get home. My daughter's probably having fits right now. She's depending on me to drive her to a party tonight."

"Hey, you have a daughter! How old is she?" He shook apart the keys on the ring and selected one of them unerringly.

"She's fourteen. We have two children; my son is seventeen."

He pushed open the tall wooden gate, and she stepped through.

"That big piece of Detroit iron under the trees is mine," she said as she hunted in her purse for keys. "That gorgeous little red beast must be yours. Is it a Porsche? Now Theodora was the one, she could have told you the year, make, and model, the moment she saw it."

"This one might have given her a little trouble," he said, amused. "It's not exactly stock. It's a loaner, so I haven't had time to get it sorted out myself."

"Some loaner!" she said reverently. She veered off to the front of the car as they drew nearer and surveyed the elegant flare of the shining hood. "Honestly!" She touched a fender lightly and smiled at him. "It's beautiful. Have you ever driven a Lamborghini?"

"Yes, Miuras, and one pretty exotic one in Italy last summer. Look here," he added. "You're probably going to think I'm some kind of nut, but could I ask you something? You have kids. Would you tell me something, just off the top of your head?"

Her face was mildly astounded. "Of course. I'll be glad to if I can."

He fidgeted from one foot to the other, rattling keys and coins in his pockets. Then he said with a feeble grin, "I'm sorry. That was a stupid idea. When it comes down to it, I don't even know what to ask. Forget it, all right?"

"Are you sure?"

"I'm sure. Come on, let's get you into your car. I shouldn't hold you up when you're in a rush."

They walked in silence to the door of her parked car. She turned to face him, and they both spoke at once.

"This has been so nice—" she began.

"Look, this has really been great—"

They laughed together. The little ring of car keys slid through her fingers just then, and in a lightning-swift motion, he caught them out of the air. When he returned them to her, he bent down and kissed her lightly.

"Thanks," he said. "For being so nice to Theo. And for this afternoon. I've really enjoyed this, you know."

She looked back at him for an instant, her face warm, then reached out impulsively to his sleeve.

"Please," she said. "I have a feeling something is troubling you. There is absolutely nothing you could ask me about children that could sound as stupid as half the things I'm dying to ask you about racing if I only had the nerve. Whatever it is, why don't you just ask?"

"Why should I impose on you just because—"

"Why shouldn't you? People ought to impose on people. Otherwise it all gets to be like the cars that pass on the freeway, doesn't it?"

He hesitated and then said, "All right, but I feel like a damn fool already. When kids get to be twenty years old, a girl I mean, they don't really give much of a damn about their parents any longer, do they? They have lives of their own by then, they—"

"Well, I suppose it all depends," Cynny said uncertainly. "On individuals, and the circumstances, and—"

"Oh, Christ," he said with amused self-disgust. "I never was any good at setting up hypothetical cases or whatever you call them. No, the thing is, I was married years ago," he continued matter-of-factly. "We had a baby, then we divorced and my wife remarried. Now after almost twenty years I've had a letter from her. She says Killian wants to meet me, and she thinks it's important that she should, that if I'd just take Killian out to dinner tonight it would be something that—you know—might change her whole life or some damn thing. Now that has to be a lot of crap, doesn't it? Or maybe I'm wrong about it," he finished. "The truth is, I haven't thought much about it. She was only a few months old when we divorced, and I've never seen her since. Which my ex-wife seems to think makes me some kind of monster, and she may be right, but I can't change that now and—"

"Honestly, I wouldn't be made to feel guilty over that if I were you!" Cynny stopped short, then said ruefully, "Oh, hell! I'm sorry, but Theodora once told me about your wife getting your permission for her new husband to adopt the baby at the time of the divorce. Forgive me. I expect you'd rather Theodora hadn't talked about it."

"Hell, no. What difference does it make?"

"Anyway, I just meant that I don't think you have any reason to feel guilty about staying away all these years. Once you agreed to the adoption, what else could you have done?"

` He weighed it for a moment, then his face relaxed into a grin. "Hey, I really appreciate this! You know, I had a hunch all along that staying away was the right idea. Come on, I've held you up long enough."

He opened the car door, and she slid beneath the wheel, inserting the key into the ignition and depressing a button that lowered the window. He closed the door, locked it, and lingered, his hands braced against the metal frame.

She looked at him for a moment, her upturned face pale in the dim light, the dark ends of her hair curling about her slender neck.

"Oh, Lord," she said, half amused. "But I still haven't answered your question."

"What?"

She slid her hands along the rim of the wheel. "Look, take your daughter to dinner tonight, why don't you?" she said in a quick rush. "Would it really be such a hard thing to do?"

To his confusion, her voice suddenly sounded shaken.

"It really could be very important to her. Twenty is not very old, and this can be a frightening, miserable world for children to grow up in. It's not just crap, fathers are terribly terribly important! At least she ought to have the chance to know you if she wants to. What might seem most important to her is just that you cared enough at this point to want to meet her. It's so awful for children to feel that—"

Her voice broke, and he realized she was weeping. "Oh, my God!" he said. "I'm sorry! I never meant to upset you like this."

"No, I'm sorry." She was struggling for composure. "I feel like a perfect fool."

"Look, I'm the one who should feel like a fool. Ever since we met out there in the garden I've been saying stupid things to you and then trying to apologize for them."

"But that's not true. It's me. For a minute I just—muddled up your problem with a problem of my own. This has nothing to do with what you asked me. Honestly." She was dabbing at her eyes with a handkerchief from her purse.

"I'm really sorry," he said again awkwardly. "Is there anything I can do?"

"Just forgive me for—losing my cool like this. I really feel like an idiot." She turned on the ignition quickly and switched on the headlights.

Over the soft hum of the engine, he said, "Are you all right? Why don't I drive you home and grab a cab back over here? I'd feel a lot better about it, you know."

"Don't be silly, I'm all right." Her smile came through fleetingly. "Stop being so nice to me. And about your dinner date tonight. Please don't let this . . . disgusting performance of mine influence you. I shouldn't have interfered. Your first instinct to stay away was probably the right one. I think we should always trust our first—"

"Don't worry about it. Anyway, I think you're right. Take a girl out to dinner, big deal, something that's over and done in an hour or two."

"All right, if you're sure. Oh, Lord, it is late! I really have to go."

"Okay," he said as she put the car into gear. "Take care. This really has been great."

"I've enjoyed it too." She smiled. "More than I can tell you."

The car rolled quietly away beneath the tall old trees that lined the street, red taillights glimmering in the mist.

Mick watched until it had disappeared from view, and for thirty seconds after that. He cursed softly, then strode off, grim faced, to the red sports car parked at the curb.

KILLIAN WAS ONLY TWO OR THREE MILES AWAY just then, in the bedroom of a small ramshackle house off an alley on the fringes of Venice. Clad in jeans and a bulky pullover sweater, she cradled a wailing, blanket-wrapped infant against her shoulder as she walked. The room was empty except for a mattress in the middle of the floor, covered by a welter of dirty blankets and strewn clothing in the dim light of a single hanging bulb in a paper lantern. The air was cold and damp with a stale, musty odor. Perched on a corner of the mattress was a thin young girl with a box of tissues on her knees. She wore a long, high-necked dress with an old olive drab Army jacket draped about her bony shoulders and wiped repeatedly at her reddened, dripping nose.

"Ah, don't cry like this, Gautam, don't cry, love," Killian crooned, cuddling the infant. "Chris, do you think he could be hungry?"

"Oh, Killy, how could he be?" the girl said, blowing her nose once more. "I just fed him. You were here, it couldn't have been even an hour ago, could it?"

"Do you have plenty of milk? You don't fast anymore, do you?"

"Just once a week for purification. But it's perfectly all right, Mark talked to the Guru about it. Anyway, I have lots. When he stops nursing there's always still milk."

"Maybe he's wet, shall I look?"

"I'll do it."

"Let me. You've got a rotten cold."

201

Killian came over to the mattress, holding the infant against her shoulder while she tugged at one of the blankets, straightening it into some semblance of order. She put down the small bundle gently then and began to disentangle the thin wrappings.

"No, he's barely damp," she said. "It can't be that."

For a moment they were both silent, bending over the wailing infant. He was absurdly small, a bulky diaper pinned about his loins, a thin, short-sleeved shirt with yellow milk spots tied across his chest, sticklike arms and legs flailing courageously, a wizened, red face with eyes screwed shut, and an outraged, toothless mouth.

Killian caught an infinitesimal flying hand and felt the birdlike bones of his arm between her fingers. "Oh, Chris, he's still so tiny," she said softly. "He's not gaining at all."

"I know. He eats all the while but he doesn't gain. I've talked to Mark about it, but he just says that he thinks he looks beautiful, not all fat and blubber like most babies are."

They looked at each other with identical half-frightened faces while from a poster on the wall a gaudy Indian Buddha smiled down upon them.

Killian swiftly wrapped the blankets back about the infant. "Maybe your milk's not rich enough. Do you give him anything else?"

"Orange juice. And I mash up fruit for him, but he mostly spits that out. Killy, do you think rice? Maybe I could cook it into a sort of gruel."

"I don't know."

The girl caught up the infant and clutched him fiercely against her, his small head with its pale fuzz against her throat.

"What about your mother?" Killian asked reluctantly.

The girl shook her head, a brief, vehement jerk. "She refuses to come here, so Mark's asked me not to go home anymore." She turned her face carefully away from the baby to blow her nose while Killian watched them both with anxious eyes.

"Chris, you have to do something. You know that, don't you?"

she said at last. "He's just too tiny, and winter's coming on, and it's so damp and cold here at the beach."

"Maybe it will be better when we go to the commune in New Mexico in January." Her voice lacked conviction. "I know it's colder there, but it's a drier climate."

"Oh, Chris, stop it! You'll have to take him to a pediatrician. I know how you feel about it, but you'll have to do it."

"Killy, how can I? You know what Mark thinks of doctors. He'd kill me first."

"Look," Killian said urgently. "Don't tell Mark. Just take him." She upended her leather shoulder bag over the blankets and began to sort through a collection of keys, eye pencils, scarves, earrings, and bits of paper, pushing coins and several crumpled bills together.

The mound of money was very small. Killian searched a second time, hesitated, then slid a narrow gold bracelet over her hand and dropped it on top of the bills and coins.

"Oh, Killy! That's the bracelet Pete gave you when you—"

"Sssh, it's for Gautam. Lisa Luckman's always had green eyes for this bracelet. Make her give you fifty for it, she can afford it. Just promise me you'll take him."

"All right, I will," the girl said, rocking the child. "I'll go on the bus to Dr. Roberts. Your mother used to take you to Dr. Roberts too, didn't she? Didn't he used to have office hours on Saturday mornings? Anyway, I'll phone first. Oh, hush, my precious, don't cry! It's going to be all right, darling, it's going to be all right!"

And then she said suddenly, "Killy, do you know what Mark says? He says that Gautam cries like this because he's such an advanced soul that he still remembers his past lives. Mark says it's beautiful to hear him cry, he's expiating karmic guilt."

They looked at each other gravely for a moment, and then they were both laughing helplessly.

The girl juggled the baby in order to blow her nose again and wiped at her eyes. "Killy, I'll never forget this," she said soberly. "And I'll pay you back the money as soon as I can."

204 — Maritta Wolff

"Oh, Chrissy, what kind of talk is that!" Killian said, cramming the last of her belongings back into her bag as she rose to her feet. "You'd do the same for me, wouldn't you? Anyway, what is there in this fucked-up world that's as important as a baby?"

She leaned down for an instant to peep under the blankets, her long hair sliding forward, and touched his small, red cheek, her face wistful and infinitely tender. "Good-bye, my little one," she said softly. "Live long and prosper."

And then she was whirling off to the door. "Chris, dear, I'm late. I really have to run."

Pete at that moment was parking his car on a graveled turn-around area in the hills above Malibu. He piled out of the old red convertible, a small paperback in his hand, and walked along a high redwood fence covered with the large leaves and giant golden flowers of a copa de oro vine. At the end of the fence a flight of wooden steps angled up the steep hillside. Pete bounded up until there became visible a large modern house, a shimmering expanse of glass poised on the edge of the cliff like some huge, improbable, angular soap bubble. As Pete climbed he triggered an electronic device at the side of the stairway, and in response a door opened above, where a dark-haired woman in jeans appeared, accompanied by a large dog who set up an immediate yapping.

"Pete, is that you, darling?" she called out. "Oh, Barnaby, be quiet, it's Pete!"

"Myra! It's great to see you. Shut up, Barney!"

At the sound of Pete's voice, the dog plunged down the steps and leapt upon him, wriggling ecstatically and licking at his hands and face. He was a standard black poodle, stylishly clipped but gone gray about his nose and ears.

"There now, that's more like it," Pete said, pausing to hug and pat the dog affectionately. "You wouldn't forget me, would you, Barney?"

"What a thing to say! It's just his eyesight that's failing. He still goes to your old room to look for you every day of his life."

"Well, I miss you, too, Barney." Pete gave him a final hug and came up the last of the steps, the dog at his heels. "Hey, you're letting your hair grow, it looks great."

"Oh, Pete, it's good to see you!"

They embraced, holding each other tightly for a moment, and Pete said, "It's good to see *you*. I should have gotten up here before. How are you, dear?"

"More important, how are you?" She stepped back, her hands upon his shoulders, and looked up into his face anxiously. "Oh, Pete, you've lost weight. I'm so sorry, darling. Darren and I both are. The afternoon you called us about the divorce, I cried half the night. I wish there was something we could do. Isn't it funny, people always say that, but there never really is anything, is there?"

"It's all right. You're just not to worry."

"Well, I can't help but worry. I wish you could get away for a bit and come up and stay with us. Couldn't you? We'd so love to have you."

"I know," he said, his voice affectionate. "And if I could get away, you know there's nowhere I'd rather be."

"Bless you, darling."

They entered through the tall doorway, arms about each other's waists. From the large entry hall a flight of steps led down into a living room of gargantuan proportions: high-beamed ceiling, flaring walls of glass, a great stone fireplace wall, and over the polished wooden floor and the backs of chairs and divans, the vivid colors and designs of Indian blankets. Walls and tables displayed the masks, shields, and carved wooden figures of primitive African and New Guinean art.

As she led the way down the steps, Myra said, her voice suddenly altered, "He's in his room, Pete. I didn't tell him you were coming. Sometimes I think it works better if people just appear."

"But last time I was here he was so much better," Pete said.

"We ended up going out to dinner and riding around for a couple hours, remember? It was great."

"Well, there doesn't seem to be any way of predicting it. Would you like a drink, dear?"

"I don't think so, Myra. I have to get back in a bit."

"Are you sure? I'm having one. Darren won't be home till late tonight."

"All right. If you are, then I'll have one with you."

The old dog went off to lie on the hearth before the crackling fire, and Myra led the way once more to a bar that was a low wooden island before a wall of glass. Pete sat down in one of the deep upholstered chairs there, putting down his book and leaning forward on the wide bar top.

"So tell me all the news. Did Tom Orley make it into the grad school at Cornell, or didn't he?"

"Oh, Pete, isn't that funny! Do you know I was about to ask you the very same thing? What would you like, darling? I'm having a Scotch."

"Oh, anything. A beer or Fresca. Beer'd be great."

"I'm afraid I'm terribly low on news," she said as she bent down to a refrigerator concealed beneath the bar. "I feel out of touch with everyone these days. None of the old crowd ever seems to stop by anymore."

"It's just that they're pretty much all scattered by now, you know. Jobs and grad schools all over the map."

"I suppose."

She uncapped the beer bottle and set it before him with a glass. Pete watched her as she dropped ice cubes into another glass and went about making her own drink. She was very slim, dark hair pulled into a large silver barrette at the back of her head, heavy silver bracelets on her thin wrists, and a large silver and turquoise necklace at the open neck of her silk shirt. There was something youthful and resilient about her body in the well-cut jeans that was belied by her face, tense with strain and anxiety, and shockingly haggard in the gray light.

"So tell me more about this new doctor," Pete said cheerfully. "From what you said on the phone, he sounds very promising."

"Oh, I think he really is," she replied, her voice livening. "I'm very impressed with him. Did I tell you what he said to us on the first interview? He made the analogy to burned out electronic circuitry. He said in his opinion too much time had already been wasted in trying to repair fused circuits, the problem now was how to develop new bypass circuitry that would function instead. I think that's very good, don't you?"

"Yes, I do." And then Pete said, his voice casual, "And what about Bruce, does he like him?"

"Oh, I think he does. Of course he still won't keep appointments or anything like that, but—" Her voice trailed away, and suddenly her hands were motionless on the bar top. "Oh, what difference does it make anyway? None of them really knows what they're doing. There simply hasn't been enough research yet, they—"

"Myra, it doesn't work that way! There could be a breakthrough tomorrow in any one of a dozen allied fields, genetics or biochemistry, or the Dream Lab at Maimonides or—"

"I suppose. That's what Darren always used to tell me. All right, Barnaby, I hear you. Just a minute, darling. It's his kidneys, poor old thing."

She walked away, the dog at her heels. Pete sipped from his glass, then turned his chair on its swivel. He looked out over the huge, colorful room and finally to the wall of glass beside him, a glimpse of the highway far below crawling with antlike vehicles, the stretch of pale beach beyond, and the endless gray expanse of the sea tracked with long, white lines of running surf.

As she returned, Pete said, "My God, this is a great house, Myra. When you've been away awhile, you appreciate it all over again. Ever since I was so high, the best memories I have are of times spent in this house, and the trips you used to take us on."

"They were good times, weren't they, Pete?" She smiled. "I think back to them a hundred times a day. Way back to when you and Bruce were little boys; you were such marvelous boys, both of you, always exploring and learning, it kept us on our toes just to keep up with you. And then when you were older, surfing on the beach, and you'd come tearing back up the hill here and turn the kitchen upside down making submarine sandwiches and fooling with Bruce's ham radio station and calling girls on the phone and— Oh, Pete, I meant to tell you! I was cleaning out a cupboard the other day, and I came across a cylinder of color slides. I put it in the projector so I could file them away with the others and they were so marvelous. Do you remember that summer when you and Bruce worked on your Science Fair projects? The most marvelous pictures of you at work and my studio absolutely crammed full with Bruce's electronic equipment and your seawater tanks. And me with the station wagon loaded to the top with supplies, and a wonderful one of Darren staggering up the steps lugging an absolute ton of books he'd brought home to you from the office!"

Pete laughed with her. "Those crazy Science Fair projects, I remember that. That was the summer we both thought we were pushing back the frontiers of knowledge single-handed!"

"Darling, don't laugh! Both of those crazy projects just happened to finish in the top five in the National Finals, and Darren and I were so proud of you we nearly burst! Oh, do you remember, one of you stepped on a hot soldering iron that summer. It nearly scared me out of my wits. Was it you or was it Bruce?"

"It was me," Pete said, grinning. "And I've still got the scar to prove it."

They were silent for a moment, then her smile was gone and she said, "Pete, tell me something. What did we do wrong? Did we expect too much of Bruce? Did we pressure him too hard without even being aware that we were doing it? Was it—"

"Myra, stop it! You've nothing to blame yourself for. You and Darren— Well, from the time we were all little kids back in elementary school, we envied Bruce because he had you for parents."

"Darling, I'm really sorry. I don't know what's come over me today." She blew her nose determinedly and walked back to her drink on the bar top. "Here I haven't seen you in such a time and I'm really longing to hear all your news. I'm not going to ask about you and Killian because I know if there's anything you feel like telling me, you will. Tell me about your work instead. What marvelous new things are you into these days?"

Pete caught her hand. "Myra, what is it? This isn't like you at all. Tell me what it is."

She was silent for a moment, and then her face was stretched tight against weeping. "Oh, Pete, it's Darren," she said unsteadily. "He's given up. It's just happened in the last few weeks. He's simply given up. It's as though he's suddenly turned his back on Bruce and walked away from the whole thing. I'll never forgive him for this as long as I live."

"Myra, darling, don't, don't!" Pete said. "You've both hung in here for such a long time. And now the end is in sight. Bruce is getting better. You may not be as aware of it as I am, you're here with him every day, but the last time I saw him, I—"

"Pete, there's something I haven't told you. Bruce made up his mind that he wanted to go up to Berkeley early in October. I was against it from the beginning, but Darren and Dr. Dolman—we were still seeing Dr. Dolman then—thought it was a very good sign. They kept telling me that one of the dangers now was in being overprotective. But I couldn't help it, I just had this bad feeling. The night before he left I was frantic. I phoned Schumann at the Lab and everyone else I could think of, I— Pete, he went up on a Wednesday morning, and by Saturday night he was back in the drug ward there. This time he nearly died."

"Oh, Christ!" Pete said softly. "What was it?"

"I don't even remember," she said wearily. "Some sort of heavy downers and a new hallucinogen, Darren knows. Just a minute, I hear Barney."

Pete sat motionless in her absence, his eyes fixed on a mask on the wall before him: a huge face, woven of reeds and daubed with mud, at once jocular and blood chilling.

When she returned, the dog padding across the floor ahead of her, she paused beside him, reaching out to his shoulder. "I'm sorry, Pete. Perhaps I shouldn't have told you about this, I just—"

"Myra, don't you think you're making a little too much of it? It's a setback, of course, but there have been setbacks before. Hold still, Barney, you've got a burr in your chops, old boy." When he looked up at her, his face was uncannily like Tom's in its splendid assurance and self-confidence. "I think the trouble is, you're mixing up two separate problems. Problem A–Priority One is still Bruce's recovery from the brain damage he apparently suffered after one particular LSD trip, right? And he is making progress, you can't doubt that. Once he does recover, whether or not he continues to use drugs, well, that's another problem altogether, isn't it?"

"I suppose," she said dubiously. "Ah, bless you, Pete. You're the one who never gives up on him."

"Because I see no reason to," Pete said, and his smile at that moment was pure Nedith. "Look, I'd better get in there and say hello to him. I haven't all that much time."

"Stay for dinner, darling, stay the night. Darren's going to be terribly disappointed if he doesn't get at least a glimpse of you."

"I wish I could. But I'll be back up in another couple weeks and make a weekend of it, that's a promise."

Pete left the room, but when he returned to retrieve the book forgotten on the bar top she was standing once more before the glass, her figure dwarfed by the towering wall and the vast landscape beyond. She was weeping quietly.

Pete hesitated, then picked up the book and softly left the room.

As he walked along a gallery of oversize canvases, there was an increasing sound of discordant music. At the far end, a door stood ajar, and Pete rapped on it before he entered. The room was a large bedroom-study, dim in the gray afternoon. The music here was at a deafening volume, and a young man with a dark beard, dressed in jeans and a white shirt, was lying on the bed.

"Hey, Bruce! How are you, kid?" Pete raised his voice against the din.

The young man looked at him without surprise, pleasure, or even any particular interest. He did not speak, but he lifted his hand finally, reaching up to a row of knobs and switches on a shelf behind him and turning one of them to decrease the decibel level.

"So how's it going, Bruce?"

The young man spoke at last. "Pete," he said, "the man from the sea," the words slow, spaced, and even.

"That's me." Pete's voice was strong and cheerful. "How about you, Bruce? What have you been doing?" He hesitated, then finally sat down upon the edge of the bed, the only place in the room where conversation between them was possible over the sound.

After a pause, Bruce said suddenly:

> —Of his bones are coral made;
> Those are pearls that were his eyes:
> Nothing of him that doth fade—

Pete glanced at him quickly while he worried the small book in his hands. "Damn, it's good to see you," he said at last. "I should have gotten up here before. I've been busy as hell, but that's no excuse."

"What is it? a spirit?" Bruce said all at once. "Lord, how it looks about!"

"*Tempest*, Act One, Scene Two," Pete said drily. "Your stereo is sounding really good. What did you do, buy new speakers or redo the wiring?"

After another pause, Bruce said, "Old Pete! So how's everything with the United States Navy?"

"Up your mizzenmast too, bub! I haven't seen anything of them since last summer, and I've already told you about the project I did for them then."

He waited and then said, "Bruce, how'd you like to go out somewhere for dinner? How about it, drink a little wine or something?"

Pete tried again. "What's this music you're listening to? I don't think I know it."

This time after another of his long, eerie pauses, Bruce answered him. "It's Stockhausen. Do you like it?"

"Not very much." Pete remembered the book in his hands and held it out. "Here, I thought you might like this. If you haven't already read it. It's an American psychiatrist's account of his experiences with Zen meditation in Japan. I think it's very good."

Bruce took the book and turned it, examining it from all sides intently as though it were an alien artifact. "How's Killy?" he asked suddenly.

"At the moment, I wouldn't know."

"That's right," Bruce said. "I forgot. She had her chance to be a good Navy wife and flubbed it, the silly girl. What's protocol now, Pete? Marry a Nam widow, no rating below a captain?"

Pete rose from the bed and crossed the room to turn on a tall, shaded lamp on the end of the desk.

Bruce was smiling, a gleam of white teeth through the dark beard. "You'd better pay attention to such details, Pete. Otherwise you won't make admiral in time for a dolphin command at the Battle of Mindanao Deep."

"Get off my back, Bruce," Pete said shortly. "I felt the same way you did about the draft and you know it. Doing some work for them in my own field beat going to Canada, and I still believe that. So did you at the time."

There was another silence between them. Pete leafed through several pages of a magazine and returned it to the desk. "So what do you say? Want to go out somewhere and grab a bite to eat?"

When he did not answer, Pete returned to the bed. "I hear you were up in Berkeley last month. See anyone I know?"

After another of his eerie time lags, Bruce sat bolt upright on the bed and caught hold of Pete's arm, his face suddenly animated, his speech rapid and precise. "Pete, I want to tell you the damndest thing. You're going to have trouble believing this. I heard a story while I was up there that I can't put out of my mind. I met a guy in a hospital, and he told me about this holy man out in Denver. It seems this guy spent the whole early part of his life trying to find the way. He never gave up. Finally, about eight or nine years ago, he was experimenting with some kind of shellac remover and wild aster root and he landed back in a Denver hospital. But this time a pair of doctors there came to see him and interviewed him for days. They finally decided that he was the one. They decided to let him hear the sound. Now you have to understand, Pete, that this was no ordinary sound they had in mind, this was a sound such as no human being had ever heard before. Think of it, Pete! A sound that the human ear is not even remotely constructed to accommodate. When the day came, they drilled a hole for it through the bone of his skull. And then they hooked up their machines and he listened. Just once. Pete, he's never come down since! God's Truth! They kept him in the hospital for a while, and then they sent him home. There are about a hundred people now who make pilgrimages out there to see him a couple times a year. Pete, he's never come down to this day! This guy says he never speaks, he has no motor locomotion, but a face that is indescribable. A saint in ecstasy, but those are just words. This guy says you get the most incredible high just being near him. The only trouble is, that pair of doctors left Denver years ago. This whole group is still looking for them, though, among them they've been in hundreds of hospitals by this time, from one end of the country to the other. All they can do is go on looking. Isn't that a fantastic story? Think of it, Pete, the sound it must be! The gut rumble of the universe, the fart of infinity! To hear it just once and never come down again! My God, Pete, once you know of it, how can you think of anything else? You have to yearn for it every conscious moment, you'd crawl for it on your hands and knees, you'd—"

"Bruce, what are you talking about!" Pete's face was a mixture of incredulity and disgust. "That's a pretty sick story, for Christ's sake! Don't you understand what happened? That pair of doctors used that poor guy as a guinea pig for one of the early experiments with ultrasonic therapy and—"

"Don't try to tell me about ultrasonics, Pete. Not for Christ's sake, or anybody else's!" Bruce interjected fiercely. Then his anger was gone and he was smiling once more, white, even teeth gleaming through the dark beard. "You poor bastard, you," he said, his speech slowed again and entirely without expression. "You don't even know what I'm talking about."

"No, I suppose I don't," Pete said.

Bruce dropped back against the pillows, and they were both silent for a long time while the music continued to fill the room.

Pete cleared his throat. "What about it, Bruce? Want to get something to eat? I'm starving."

After a time, Bruce said serenely, "Get my mother to fix you something then. Feeding people is her raison d'être. She thinks there is no cosmic ill that can't be cured by a well-broiled steak and a bit of salad."

"Actually, I don't give a shit about dinner. I was just hoping we could rap awhile. I've got some things on my mind."

When his friend did not respond, Pete spoke again. "For God's sakes, don't shut me out, Bruce. Not tonight! I need you."

Bruce looked at him then, his eyes luminous. "Bless thee from whirlwinds, star-blasting, and taking!" he said. "Poor Tom's a-cold." He rolled over on the bed, reaching once more to the knobs on the shelf above and returning the volume of sound to its former earsplitting level.

Pete sat beside him a moment longer, staring at his own clasped hands between his knees.

"*King Lear*, Act Three, Scene Four," he said at last softly, and got up and left the room.

Fifteen minutes later, Pete made a phone call from the restaurant on the beach. With his long frame wedged uncomfortably against the wall of the booth, he jabbed at the numbered buttons. A female voice answered, instructed him to hold on, and then suddenly he was saying, his voice warming, "Hey, Sarah! It's Pete."

"Pete!" She sounded pleased. "How great! Where are you?"

"Malibu. I'm up for the weekend. How are you, Sarah? Is everything all right?"

"I'm fine. Everything's fine. What about you?"

"Fine. Working my tail off. Nothing new."

"Which reminds me," she said. "Last week I was waiting to see Dr. Staub at the university, and I was looking through a journal there in his office. I came across the most fantastic report that you'd read at some scientific get-together last summer. Terrific! What are you up to anyway, Pete? Bucking for a Nobel?"

Pete grinned. "Oh, sure. I'm in the exact right field for a Nobel. We pick one off every couple years, you may have noticed."

"Don't complain, buster! At least you're the right sex for one. Would you care to count up the number of women who've ever been awarded the Nobel Prize?"

"Well, now," he said happily, "I'm glad you asked me that. There's Marie Curie and—"

"Oh, go fuck yourself! Male chauvinist pig! Pete, can you come by? I'd love to see you."

"I wish I could. But I'll be up again in a couple weeks, maybe we can have dinner or something then. I miss you, too."

"Great. Don't forget now."

Pete shifted his position, crossing his long legs and propping himself against his hand. "Have you seen Killy?" he asked, his voice casual.

"Yes, a few times. I used to run into her at a women's lib meeting I go to every week, but she hasn't been coming lately. I gather you're separated or something. I'm really sorry, Pete."

"I know you are," Pete said. "Incidentally, I saw Bruce this afternoon."

"Oh?"

"When did you see him last?"

"It's been a long time. Months. Last spring, I guess."

The line went still, and then Pete said uncomfortably, "I'm sorry. I didn't realize. I just assumed that—"

"No, that's all right. How is he?"

"Essentially the same."

She laughed. "Oh, great! Beautiful! I still can't make any sense out of it. After all the LSD he'd taken, how could he blast out of the world on one particular trip like that and never get back? Did he will it, or what?"

"Sarah, we've talked about this a hundred times. It was either a cumulative change in brain chemistry or impurities in that batch of LSD. Nobody really knows. Myra told me today though that they're on to a new doctor who seems very promising."

"What does that make, the hundred and fiftieth new doctor who seems very promising? It's lucky Myra and Darren have the money for these kinds of games. I suppose it's a comfort to them." And then she said into the silence, "All right, I suppose you think I'm some kind of rotten human being now because I still don't traipse out there to see him every week and—"

"Oh, shit! Why would I think that? Look, Sarah, I realize how really difficult it's been for you—"

"Not anymore," she said. "I've opted out, Pete. I've had to. The last few times I went out there— Pete, I couldn't do it anymore. It's like walking into a time machine, it's a trip into the past. Like walking into a garden where everything is dead and the dry leaves blowing. That whole drug scene was years ago, it's over now, finished. Bruce doesn't seem to realize it, but the world has moved on. There are too many real problems, too many real things that—"

"Sarah, the guy is sick," Pete said mildly. "I gather from what Myra says that nobody comes anymore. I don't mean you necessarily, but how is he ever going to get better holed up in that room with his stereo? Anyway, it's Myra I'm thinking about as much as him. She seemed—I don't know, strung out today, not like herself. I think she's beginning to fall apart."

"Look, I'm sorry for Myra, I really am. She's a fantastic woman. When I used to think about getting married and having children, she's the kind of wife and mother I wanted to try to be. She didn't deserve any stupid fucked-up part of this. But there's nothing I can do for her anymore, Pete. Don't ask me!"

"I'm not asking anything of you, Sarah. I wouldn't have brought this up at all if I'd known you felt like this. I'm sorry."

"You're sorry!" she said. "Jesus Christ, I'm the one who's sorry! I loved Bruce more than I loved my life! I took LSD with him, and his stinking creepy crawlies, I followed him just as far as anyone could have on this earth, but that didn't mean anything to Bruce, did it? He was on a private trip all his own. Well, great! So now let him rot up there in Malibu. If it's up to me, he'll have to. I have my own life now."

"Sarah—"

"Oh, Pete, shut up!" She was weeping.

"I'll call you in a couple weeks. Good-bye, hon."

Drops of sweat shone on Pete's face, and he peeled off his heavy sweater as he exited the phone booth. He plunged out the door into the cool, misty darkness. For a time he stood motionless upon the hard-packed, dry earth of the parking area, the tips of his fingers shoved into the back pockets of his jeans, his face turned unseeing toward the highway, the passing pairs of yellow headlights in the fog, and the huge, black hills looming beyond.

M ICK BY THEN WAS DRIVING SLOWLY ALONG
a broad residential street in Beverly Hills, his attention
divided between the search for house numbers in the early darkness and the rising needle of the temperature gauge on the dash
in front of him. The red sports car, he was discovering, was not
adapted to prolonged driving in city traffic. The heat of the
engine was radiating uncomfortably through the firewall, and
the smell of it permeated the car interior. Even as he watched,
the temperature needle jumped again. In a sudden decision, he
shot on through an intersection in defiance of a stop sign and
swooped into the only empty parking spot, which as it happened
was on the wrong side of the street. He turned off the engine
and yanked loose the seat belt. Piling out of the car, he went
round to the front. He hunted for a hood catch, burned his fingers on the hot metal, cursed, kicked one of the wide tires, and
turned his back on the car. From the lighted number on the
house across the way he deduced that he could not be more than
a block from his destination.

As it turned out, he walked more than three blocks before he
found it. It was a large, two-story, white stucco house with a
tiled roof. With its perfect yard and drapes drawn at the windows, the house was indistinguishable from any other along the
quiet street.

For an instant Mick was beset by an overpowering tempta-
tion to walk by without stopping. As he instead turned and
started toward the door, he could not conceive of anything he
was less inclined to do than this.

He mounted a broad, shallow step at the entrance, pushed a pearly bell button set in the wall, and snapped his lighter nervously at a cigarette. There was no sound from the other side of the carved wooden door, and after a moment, verifying the number in his mind, he reluctantly rang again. He waited some more and finally clanged the ornate wrought-iron knocker. Scarcely able to believe his good fortune, he gave it a last twenty seconds before he turned away grinning. Just then the door opened.

A blond girl in a green dress peered out. "Yes?"

His first startled thought was that Linda had produced a child who was, incredibly, her exact physical replica.

"Hello. I'm—is it—Linda?"

"Oh, Micky, it is you, isn't it! It had gotten so late I was afraid you weren't going to come."

But the voice was Linda's beyond question.

"I'm sorry I'm late. I took the wrong turn off Beverly."

"I should have given you directions. You've been away so long. Oh, Micky, it's been years and years! I don't dare count them anymore, do you?"

"Yes, it's been a long time."

"I'm sorry, come in." She reached out toward his arm, then pulled her hand back nervously. "Here I'm babbling like an idiot and you're standing out in the— Please come in."

He stepped past her into the warmth of a large entrance hall. It came to him that unconsciously he had been braced for twenty years of change in her, a fat, untidy Linda perhaps, or a sharp-voiced one with dyed hair and a gaunt, overly made-up face. Instead, she appeared not to have changed at all, only the clothes were of another time and fashion, the same diminutive figure and, even more incredibly, the same pretty, childlike face and short, shining, pale hair. He was curiously relieved to find her so unchanged, and at the same time increasingly wary of her because of it.

"This silly door," she was murmuring. "Sometimes it sticks."

"Let me," he said automatically.

She moved aside, and Mick pulled the heavy door partway open, then gave it a hard shove. It slammed resoundingly, but at the last moment some part of the latch mechanism failed to retract, and with a spine-crawling screech of metal against metal, the door popped once more ajar.

"I think it's the knob part that sticks," she explained unnecessarily.

"Yes, I can see that," he answered with a prickle of irritation.

He examined the latch and then, turning the knob, attempted to ease the door into place. He was not successful.

"It's done this a couple times lately," she said in her soft, breathless voice. "I'll have to get a repairman. Or maybe it just needs oil, do you think?"

He tried several more times, holding the knob in various positions and putting his shoulder to it, but the door refused to close.

"Now this is just silly," she said as she tried to peep over his shoulder. "Leave it, Micky. It doesn't matter. I'll do it later or get someone or—"

Mick went on tussling with the door, and the sense of her hovering close behind him only added to his discomfort.

"Micky, I think if you would sort of jiggle the knob."

In a sudden fury he rattled the knob violently, then heaved at the door with all his strength.

"Oh, you've cut your finger, look, it's bleeding!" She seemed at the point of tears. "Micky, don't try anymore, please. Just leave the silly thing and come in. Please, Micky."

Perspiring, his skinned knuckle stinging, the sweet floral scent of her perfume strong in his nose, he considered at that moment tearing the door from its hinges and flinging it into the street. Instead, he said with an effort, "Linda, for God's sakes get out of the way and kindly shut up for a minute while I see how this thing works."

"I'm sorry."

She backed away and waited silently while Mick examined

the latch. He turned off the night lock and tried once more unsuccessfully to ease the door gently into place, but on a second try it suddenly closed without effort.

"Thank goodness!" she murmured. "Micky, I'm so sorry. Come in now, please."

He followed her through a doorway, discovering that his legs were stiff with tension. He had a vague impression of a large, well-furnished, and rather characterless living room, and over her shoulder Linda was saying shakily, "Micky, I really feel terrible about this. Do you think you should put something on your finger?"

"No, it's all right. It's just a skin scrape. Forget it."

She led the way across the thick-piled carpeting to a pair of large divans upholstered in gold-and-white brocade that faced each other before a fireplace.

"Please sit down, Micky."

She hesitated, then perched herself upon the edge of one of the divan cushions, her hands clasped in her lap.

Mick snuffed out his cigarette in a glass ashtray on the coffee table but remained standing before the fireplace, where a yellow gas flame danced over a cement log without warmth or smoke or crackle.

Struggling to regain his composure, he said, "Well, you always wanted a big house on a street with trees, Linda. You finally got it."

"Yes. Yes, it's—" She leapt to her feet. "Let me get you a drink. What would you like? I'm having martinis."

"I'd rather have Scotch, if you have it."

"Of course." She set off toward a bar in one corner of the room. "You used to drink Cognac. I have that, too."

"Scotch'll be fine, thanks."

"Micky, we got involved with that silly door, I haven't had a chance to tell you," she said, the words nervously slurring together. "You really look marvelous. Some men are so lucky, they just get better as they get older."

He followed her, a handkerchief surreptitiously wrapped about his skinned knuckle.

"You're the one who really looks great, Linda. You haven't changed at all."

"Oh, Micky, I have! I hate it. The years just go. Isn't it fierce?"

She added another splash of whiskey to his glass uncertainly, then reached for a martini glass and put it down on the bar top beside a tall, slender glass pitcher. The bar was not scaled to her diminutive size; when she tilted the pitcher in her small hands, the contents overflowed the stemmed glass into a puddle.

"Oh, skit!" she said softly, using the childish substitute word that he recalled. "Micky, I'm such an idiot. I made Scotch on the rocks. Would you rather have soda?"

"No, that's fine."

"Are you sure? I could dump it in another glass."

"It's all right."

"I'm terribly sorry. I don't know why I didn't think to ask."

"Look, it's fine!"

She dabbed at rivulets on the pitcher and lifted it onto a teak tray that already held, in addition to his drink, a silver dish heaped with cocktail mix and a plate of crackers and cream cheese dip.

"Want me to take that?"

"Would you? I'll bring mine, it's all drippy."

She followed an instant later, carrying her glass carefully together with a stack of small, white, monogrammed paper napkins. She put them both down on the coffee table and settled herself into a corner of the divan, stepping out of her shoes and drawing her slender legs beneath her.

"Thanks, Micky," she said as he handed her the glass. "Why don't you sit here?"

He sat down obediently beside her, finding the sofa too soft and too deep for his liking.

"Well, cheers."

"Yes, good luck." She extended her glass briefly in his direction.

"Cigarette?"

"I still don't. Do you still smoke so much? They say it isn't good for you."

"Yes, I've heard that," he said drily.

The quiet throughout the house added to his unease. There was no distant hum of a refrigerator or furnace motor, gurgle of pipes, or even rumble of traffic. Only the gas flame flickering breathily on the hearth while Linda sipped at her drink in short, hurried gulps.

"It seems so funny, doesn't it?" she said, smiling at him uncertainly. "I mean after all these years, you and me sitting here having a drink together. Tell me about yourself, Micky. Are you married?"

"No. You already asked me that on the phone."

"That's right, I forgot. Have you been married? I mean since us."

"No."

"But you don't race anymore, do you? I haven't read about it in the papers for a long time."

He brushed at his hair ferociously, uncrossed his legs, reached toward the ashtray, and floundered among the downy cushions.

"Look, I think I'll sit over here if you don't mind," he said, sliding from the couch. "Get to the ashtray and the tidbits and all that."

"Micky, you don't have to sit on the floor! Move over a chair."

"This is fine."

She rose on her knees, her face distressed. "But that's awful! If you'd like a straight chair, there are lots of them in the dining room."

"Oh, for Christ's sakes! You mean it's not allowed to sit on your floor, or what?"

"I'm sorry. I just didn't think you'd be comfortable."

"It's fine."

He reached for a napkin for beneath his glass and helped

himself to a handful of cocktail mix that he did not want, sitting on the rug beside the coffee table with his back to the fireplace.

"Micky, maybe you don't like me asking you questions like this. I didn't mean to pry. I'm really interested. I guess that's only natural."

"Of course I don't mind. Why should I?"

"Then you don't race anymore?"

"No. It's been about three years now."

"I thought you didn't. That's what made me think— I mean, I thought maybe you'd given it up to marry and settle down. Why did you stop then?"

"I didn't exactly plan to, if that's what you mean. There were a couple things. I was burned pretty badly in a crash. You may have noticed my hands. They did a great job of skin grafts on my face, but there's not so much they can do about eyes. I haven't much peripheral vision left now in my right eye."

"I'm terribly sorry. But maybe that's why you look so marvelous, Micky. They say skin grafts are much better than having your face lifted."

"Yeah, I'll bet."

"So what do you do now? Test cars or—or what?"

"Sometimes. And I still have a contract for tire tests. Actually, the last couple years I've been teamed up with a few other guys building and racing our own cars. It's been great, but it looks like we may go broke. A month or so ago, I was offered a PR type job with a parts company, and I may take it."

"I see. But it was what you always wanted to do, wasn't it? I mean racing and cars and all that. It was more important to you than anything."

"That's right. I've got no complaints at all."

She propped her chin upon her hand. "But Micky, I'm surprised you didn't marry again. There were always so many girls who— Why didn't you, Micky? It wasn't because of what happened to us, was it?"

"Hell, no. Everyone these days has at least one marriage that went sour, haven't they? As a matter of fact, I lived with a girl in Europe for quite a few years. It amounted to the same thing."

"Were you happy with her?"

"Yes, most of the time."

"But you didn't want to marry her?"

"I don't know. We were talking about it. Then one night she had a brain hemorrhage and died three hours later."

"I'm terribly sorry," Linda said. "Neither one of us seems to have had much luck. It's fierce, isn't it?"

"Depends on how you look at it actually. You get the good and the bad. It seems to be about the same for everybody."

"Do you really think that's true, Micky?" she asked. And then she said, "So it's sort of funny, isn't it? Killy's the only child you've ever had."

"Yes, I suppose." His voice was not altogether pleased, and before she had time to speak again, he said, "What about you, Linda? You always wanted a big family. Do you have other children?"

"No, me neither. Do you remember, I had that kidney thing before Killy was born? Then I had a miscarriage the first year Marv and I were married. When Killy was three I tried again, but I lost that baby too, and a few months later they did a kidney surgery. They said I couldn't have children after that."

"That's too bad."

"Yes. Marv wanted to adopt, but I'd never do that. I don't think it would be the same."

"And Marv, how is he? I take it you still see him and all that."

"Oh, yes. He's great. He's gotten to be very big in his field, you know. His books are very successful, and he lectures in Europe now and everywhere. It's marvelous."

"I'm sorry your marriage didn't work out," Mick said. "And that's the truth, Linda."

"I believe it, Micky. Marv and I are still very good friends though. His wife, Nat, is a darling girl, too. She was a student of his when he lectured up at Berkeley once."

"And how's Milly?" he said, searching his mind.

"Who?"

"Milly what's-her-name. You were always great friends, you'd been at school together."

"Oh, Milly! Oh, she's fine. She moved back east ages ago, but we always write on Christmas cards and all that."

A telephone began to ring loudly from the hallway, and Linda scrambled from the divan. "Excuse me, Micky," she said.

Mick waited, fidgeting his glass on the damp napkin. By now he was acutely uncomfortable, his spine rigid with tension. He was disturbed by the static, unlived-in quality of this room. He stared for a time at a picture on the wall opposite him, a large drawing of a female nude in charcoal, gold, and umber, with a troubling disproportion in the figure, and in the face an expression somewhere between ecstasy and terror.

A moment later Linda hurried back into the room. "I'm sorry, Micky. Some people, you tell them that you're busy and they go right on talking." When she had settled herself once more among the cushions on the divan, she held out her empty glass. "Would you mind?"

"Sure." With one hand braced against the table edge, he rose gladly to his feet. "Well, this is a switch anyway," he said in an attempt at lightness as he bent over the tray. "You always used to be a one-drink girl."

"Was I?" For an instant her face was somber as she took the glass. "Yes, I guess I was. Oh, Micky, I'm sorry! You must be ready for another drink, too."

"Not yet, thanks."

"Well, good luck then."

"Cheers. How about a cracker or something?"

"No, thanks, Micky."

Mick remained standing, hands in pockets, teetering on his heels. Linda sipped at her drink, the glass cupped childishly between her hands, her pale hair shining in the soft light. Watching her, Mick thought of the girl she had been when he first met her, fearful and inhibited but also tender and loving, and at times capable of real passion. Not that he had been all that patient or adept himself. Too bad by the time they had grown accustomed to each other they had already fallen into the bad habit of taking their quarrels and differences to bed. His memory stirred, and in a flash it was all there, a racing season long ago: the speed and color, the heat, the smells, the noise, black frustrations and disappointments, blindingly bright moments of triumph, the unrelenting sawteeth of competition, the heady awareness of first achievements and acclaim, flashbulbs and crowds and always the eyes, admiring, speculative, or merely curious, but the eyes always upon him. And away from the track, the special camaraderie of a small, closely knit world, the endless jokes, the legendary pranks, the drinking. And the nights with Linda in hot, uncomfortable hotel rooms.

What he recalled, now, was not the cold, churning fury of their angers and dissension but a young man's half-incredulous pride and joy of possession and unremitting sexual need, the potent appeal she had had for him in those days, even petulant, quarrelsome, or complaining, her soft, fluting voice, her childish gestures, her laughter, her tears, the doll-like prettiness of her face unchanged before him, the wide-spaced, hazel eyes and tilting nose and deep-cleft chin, and in his flesh the tactile memory of the perfection of her warm, curved body. Mick moved involuntarily, cracked his shin against the table edge, and yelped aloud.

"Micky! Oh, that must have hurt! Are you all right?"

"Yes. Damn clumsy, that's all."

Shaken, he snapped his lighter blindly at a cigarette.

"Micky, you've gone white! Are you sure?"

"It's all right. I have a trick knee."

"Maybe you ought to sit down. Don't you think it would help if you put your leg up?"

No, she had not changed, he thought grimly, still like her perfume—a little too sweet and a hell of a lot too persistent. And all the tensions and irritations since he first set foot in this house suddenly gathered and exploded.

"Look here, Linda," he said. "This is all very pleasant, sitting around bullshitting, but we were supposed to be discussing this idea of my meeting with Killian, weren't we? I happen to think it's pretty damn stupid. What makes you so sure she even wants to see me?"

She stared at him, startled. "Micky, I thought it was all decided. I've already told her you're in town, she's planning on dinner tonight, she's absolutely thrilled."

"I don't remember that anything was decided. All I agreed to was to come over here and discuss it with you."

The remembered stubbornness was there suddenly in her voice. "Micky, we went all over this on the phone. Killy wants to meet you, and I think it's terribly important that she should. Especially since all these years you've never once so much as—"

"Let's get one thing straight right now, Linda," he said flatly. "I don't intend to listen to any hearts-and-flowers routines from you or anybody else about how I've neglected my own child for all these years. When you were after me for permission for Marv Shapiro to adopt her, you made it perfectly clear that you'd found a man who had all the qualifications to be a good father to her, which, according to you, I didn't have any of. You also made it pretty damn plain that all you ever wanted from me again was my word that I'd stay away from her and not confuse her, just leave her alone, and you too."

The room was thunderously still. Linda put her glass down on the table, her hands shaking, her face taut against weeping.

"Micky, I didn't mean that the way it sounded. I just said the first thing that came into my head because I was scared. I can't bear for Killy to be disappointed." She paused, then continued, her eyes pleading, "Everything you said just now is true, I wouldn't ever try to deny it. But things like that are between you and me, they've nothing to do with Killy. I guess meeting her doesn't mean much to you, and maybe that's understandable under the circumstances, but it means a great deal to her. I don't know what else to say, Micky, except if you could do it I'd appreciate it more than I can tell you."

"Oh, Christ!" he said helplessly. "Did I ever say I didn't want to meet her if she wants to meet me? I'll be glad to take her to dinner or whatever damn thing she has in mind. Look, I could use that other drink now. I can fix it myself, can't I?"

"Of course. If you don't mind."

Mick fled, and she called after him, "If the ice has melted there's more in the fridge."

"Right."

He took refuge behind the bar, shaken now more with self-disgust than with anger, feeling that somehow he'd been had. Linda had changed after all, he thought bitterly, she had gotten smarter. Somewhere along the line she had learned how to give ground when it was expedient in order ultimately to get her own way. He selected a taller glass from a shelf, and while he fished ice cubes from the bucket, he noted from the corner of his eye that Linda was replenishing her own glass from the martini pitcher. He went about making his drink slowly, returning the bottle to the shelf, wiping off the bar top, and when he could delay it no longer, he carried his glass back across the room.

"Micky, I am terribly grateful to you. This really does mean so much to Killy, I wish you could believe that. She should be here soon." And then she said, looking up at him, "Micky, I'm sorry if it makes you uncomfortable waiting here with me."

"Hell, no. Why do you say that? It's good to see you, Linda."

He sat down on the edge of the divan opposite, hunching forward to lean upon his knees, and from somewhere in the silent house there came the loud chiming of a clock. His shoulders twitched.

"Micky? There's something I'd like to tell you, if you don't mind." Linda glanced up from her glass. "It's not because of anything you said a minute ago either. For years I've thought that if we should ever happen to meet again I'd like to tell you this."

She paused, and instantly on guard, he said, "Go ahead."

She smiled briefly. "Now the time's come, I don't exactly know how to put it. I guess I should just say it. Micky, if I hurt you years ago, I'd like you to know that I didn't mean to and I'm terribly sorry."

Whatever he had expected, it had not been this. "Linda, my God," he murmured, embarrassed. "That's all twenty years behind us now. You were just a kid, we both were. Forget it."

"There must be something wrong with me," she said forlornly, "but I've never understood why knowing the reasons for the things people do changes anything. It still hurts, doesn't it? Oh, Micky, why can't people communicate with each other? It's so sad. Even people like you and me, who were terribly close in one part of our lives and had a child together, and still there's no way for us to—" She stopped, tears rolling from her eyes.

"Oh, Christ!"

And then he heard with enormous relief the prosaic sound of a key rattling in a lock and the opening of the door.

Linda caught her breath and dabbed at her eyes with the back of her hand. "Killy, is that you?" she called, her voice strained. "You're home early, darling."

Mick heard the recalcitrant door close easily on the first try, and the next moment Killian appeared in the doorway.

Against all logic, Mick had expected a child. What he saw was a young woman, tall and composed, wearing jeans with wide, flapping bottoms and an extraordinary embroidered pink Chinese coat, frayed and faded, wads of gray stuffing bulging out of splits in the fabric. Her long, smooth, brown hair was held in place by a narrow scarf tied Indian fashion across her forehead, and she carried a leather shoulder bag. A beautiful girl, Mick thought incredulously, a great figure, lovely face, and rare perfection of coloring: skin, hair, and eyes. And a girl who bore no resemblance or relationship so far as he could tell to the red-faced, blanket-wrapped infant he remembered, least of all to himself.

"Hello," she said. "Am I interrupting something?"

"Oh, Killy, of course not. Come in, darling." Linda leaned forward nervously to set her glass on the coffee table and spilled the remainder of her martini over her dress. "Oh, skit!" She rubbed briefly at a damp spot on her skirt with a napkin, then looked up, her face beseeching. "I'm sorry, I can't just introduce you as though you were two strangers, it's too fierce, I—"

"Oh, Mommy-doll, what makes you think you have to!" Killian bent and touched her cheek for an instant to the top of Linda's shining head. She came on around the table then and held out her hand to Mick. "Hello. You look exactly like your pictures. Except your hair is so light. Linda, you never told me he was as blond as you are. What a black sheep I really am!"

Mick took her hand quickly, grateful for her small effort to put them all at ease. Her hand was slender and cold in his, covered with small rings, and her leaf brown eyes were nearly on a level with his own. He was astonished that she should be so totally unlike Linda. And then he thought he detected something faintly unsure in the shape of her smile and impulsively tightened his hold upon her hand, taking care not to squeeze her rings into the flesh of her fingers.

"Hey, no black sheep!" he said. "The pride of any flock, I should think. How are you?"

She withdrew her hand immediately. "I'm very well, thank you," she said primly. "How are you?"

"Fine," he murmured with the feeling that he had already done something to put her off.

"Killy, you can't go out to dinner in that crazy old coat," Linda said, her voice still stilted. "Please go change, darling."

"I was just about to." Then she added, her eyes steady upon his, "I can be ready in an hour. Or I could be ready in fifteen minutes. Which would you rather?"

"Fifteen minutes would be real great," he said with genuine gratitude. And then, embarrassed, amended it. "But I don't want to rush you."

"All right, twenty minutes." Her voice was amused. "And, Linda, don't fuss. I had absolutely no intention of going out to dinner in this coat."

She left the room quickly, her smooth hair swinging upon her shoulders. Linda dabbed at her eyes again and turned to Mick anxiously. While he searched for words, she said, "So what do you think, Micky?"

"What?"

"What do you think of her, of Killian?"

"She's great, Linda. She's beautiful."

"Isn't she marvelous? Doesn't she remind you of Daddy?"

For the first time since he had entered this house, Mick laughed, spontaneous guffaws of genuine mirth, until he leaned weakly against the fireplace wall. When he was able to speak, he said, "No, I'm sorry, but she does not remind me of your father. Your father was about five feet tall with red hair and built like a beer barrel."

"Oh, Micky," she said, wounded. "But her mouth is exactly like his, and the shape of her nose. Didn't you notice?"

"I guess I'll have to take a better look," he said, still smiling.

Linda swung her legs over the edge of the divan and reached for the martini pitcher. "And she's terribly bright too, Micky. She tests above one sixty. Her IQ, you know."

"That's good, isn't it?"

"Micky! It's very, very good!"

She curled herself back into the cushions, and reminded, Mick sat down again himself on the divan opposite.

"Now you can see why I'm so worried about her. She has so much. And to see her just drifting now, it scares me."

"It's been a rough period for her, hasn't it, her divorce and all that? She probably just needs a little time."

"I know, but I'm afraid if she waits too long she'll never go back to school. She says she won't. I can't understand it. She's always adored school. She was majoring in anthropology. Ever since junior high she's been mad about anthropology. And now she says it's just dry dead bones and it doesn't interest her any longer."

Mick was only half listening, still struggling against his mirth. "Don't you think you worry too much?"

"How can you not worry, Micky? There are other things like—well, drugs. I know she smokes pot, I guess they all do, but she's told me herself that she's taken LSD, and that's dangerous. Micky, children die these days! Pills and speed and hepatitis from needles, how can you not worry?"

Mick was silent, rigid and red-faced, and she paused to stare at him dubiously.

"And this man she's going around with now, Robbie. I mean, he really is sort of nice, he used to be a professional basketball player. Micky, believe me, it isn't that I mind because he's black. The world really has changed and—"

Mick lost his battle suddenly, collapsing against the divan arm and roaring once more with laughter.

"But it's true! What's the color of a person's skin got to do with anything? Anyway, she's on the Pill, so—"

"Oh, Christ, I'm not laughing at that! It's what you said a minute ago about her looking like your father." He rocked helplessly, seized by another spasm.

"But, Micky, she does remind you so much of Daddy, doesn't she? Why do you think that's so funny?"

"I guess it was just the way you said it. I'm sorry," he said meekly when he was able to speak. Giddy with released tension, he attempted to concentrate on what she was saying. "Micky, she's simply not motivated anymore. I don't understand it. I must have done something wrong when she was small—"

"Linda, for God's sakes. She's grown up now, you can't live her life for her."

"But there are things about her that I don't understand any-more, that's what scares me." She slid off the divan and reached again for the martini pitcher. "This hippie business and drugs, it honestly doesn't worry me that much now. You should have seen her when she was fourteen, then she was a real flower child. For one solid year I was absolutely terrified that she was going to run away and go live in the Haight. Thank goodness at least she never got into politics and demonstrations like so many of them did. But when she started at the university and met this boy she married, everything seemed to change. Of course I thought she was terribly young to marry, but Pete was a marvelous boy. From a very good family and very stable and mature. He's a marine biologist and brilliant in his field already, can you imagine? Besides that, he was so sweet and considerate and terribly loving, Killy absolutely adored him, too. Micky, they were so in love it made you ache to see them. Oh, Micky, not even one year! And I still don't know what went wrong. I'd always thought that Killy and I had such a good relationship, but she simply refused to discuss it with me. And Pete was just very sweet and polite and said it was something I'd have to discuss with her. All I know is that Pete's lawyers finally threatened to countersue for adultery and Killy never denied it. Isn't it fierce?"

She paused, looking at Mick pleadingly, but he was only half listening once more, this time with the vague feeling that she was divulging details of Killian's private affairs that were none of his business.

When he did not speak, she went on again. "But, after all, things go wrong in a marriage, and sometimes people do crazy things to hurt each other, we all know that. I mean—we certainly know that. But there's something else. Pete's still in school, but it just happens that his family is—well, terribly well off. Killy wanted money, a lot of money, a huge cash settlement and enormous alimony. Oh, Micky, that made me feel so embarrassed! Of course she didn't get it, that's when Pete's lawyers got tough and threatened to countersue and all that. But what made her do that? Believe me, she was never brought up to be so—so materialistic. That's one thing Marv and I are absolutely alike about. Of course since my divorce, Killy and I have never had very much, but she's always been so good about it, Micky. We've skimped and gotten by and she never—"

She had his undivided attention at last. He stared at her incredulously and then bounded up from the divan. "Linda, what in hell are you trying to tell me? When Shapiro adopted her, it was my understanding that he assumed full financial responsibility for her, and that's regardless of divorces or—"

"Micky, please! I'm trying to tell you something about Killy, and you're getting all mad and excited and flying off in some other direction entirely. Please!"

"Yes. Well, suppose you explain to me why Killian has had to grow up doing without, and then you can tell me anything else you like. All right?"

"Micky, I never said she did. You said that. Marv always paid child support, and he still intends to pay for the rest of her education. We've just had to be careful, that's all. Believe me, Killy's never gone without anything that was really important. Anyway, that's not the point. Micky, please sit down, would you? It's terribly hard to talk to you when you're walking around like that and jingling and twitching."

He mumbled something and alighted once more on the edge of the sofa. Her hands were trembling again, and she put her glass on the table.

"Anyway, what I was trying to say, Killy's always had a wonderful attitude about money. She's always had jobs, even after she and Pete were married. So why do you suppose she did it, asked for that huge amount of money from Pete's family? Micky, you're not really listening to me, are you?"

"Yes, I'm listening, but I don't know, Linda. How in God's name would I?"

She was silent, and at last she said, "No, I guess you wouldn't. And I don't know, either. Micky, I have to go to the powder room."

She came up from the cushions and steadied herself noticeably against the arm of the divan. "Silly foot's asleep," she murmured. "If you're ready for another drink, Micky, help yourself, won't you?"

Once she was gone, Mick leapt to his feet again, fumbling for his cigarettes. In truth it was an idea that had never before occurred to him, but he was confronted now by an unsavory glimpse of himself as he must certainly appear to Killian's steady brown eyes: the insensitive, self-centered bastard who had walked away when she was an infant, never once reappearing to see how she fared or if she were provided with even the barest necessities of life. Oh, Jesus, what had he let himself in for?

He listened to a faint sound of rock music from the floor above, and it was then, with the image of Killian's accusing face floating before him, that it suddenly came to him, the mysterious change in Linda's appearance that had been haunting him for the past half hour. It was her eyes of course, and he should have recognized it immediately.

He recalled now with perfect clarity the serene, untroubled gaze of the young Linda. It had been one of the first things he had noticed about her when they met, and it had remained one of her most enduring charms for him, the most serene and quiet eyes he had ever known. What was missing now was that most vital wellspring of her singularity, and with it her splendid, innocent, inviolate self-confidence and surety.

This realization shocked Mick profoundly, and he was seized by a helpless grieving.

Just then Linda pattered back into the room. She paused to look at him, cocking her head, and swayed just perceptibly, steadying herself against the table edge, then reaching once more for the seemingly inexhaustible martini pitcher. "Micky, let's not be gloomy anymore. It's been so many years. Come sit here and let's have a drink and be friends. Please?"

Still shaken, he came around the table obediently and seated himself beside her.

She stared into his face searchingly and suddenly giggled. "Funny Micky!" she said. "And your funny cars, vrroom, vrroom,

vrroom!" She giggled again. "Good luck." She tilted her glass in his direction, slopping liquor upon the cushions.

"Cheers."

"Let's not talk about Killy anymore," she said. "Let's talk about something else like old friends. Let's talk about you, Micky."

"No," he said through an ache in his throat, "why don't we talk about you? Tell me about you, Linda."

"Oh, Micky, there's nothing to tell. I'm just an ordinary kind of person like I've been all my life. I live along from day to day the way people do. And I've got Killy and— Well, there's just nothing to tell."

Once more he was filled with helpless, grieving anger as he looked at her small upright figure in the corner of the big sofa, her pretty girl's face with the anxious and vulnerable eyes.

"It's funny, isn't it?" she said ruefully. "I often think about it. Life doesn't turn out the way you expect it to at all. Is it the same for you, Micky? I mean, when you're very young you always think that everything's going to be all right. Everything seems so simple then. Like me. All I ever wanted was a home and a husband who would love me back and lots and lots of marvelous little fat, happy babies. Micky, I don't even know what I did that was wrong!"

"Linda, don't!" He took her hand without being aware of it.

"I'm sorry. I know I shouldn't say things like that. My analyst always used to tell me that I— I mean it's just luck, isn't it? You have it or you don't. Isn't it fierce?"

"Yeah, it's fierce." He felt tears smarting in his eyes.

"Micky, you're a very good person, do you know that? I always knew it, even when we had such terrible fights." Her face was tender, and she lifted her hand, the merest brush of her fingertips against his cheek.

"Don't cry, Micky," she said. "I'm terribly sorry. I'm sorry it didn't work out for us years ago, that I couldn't have cared enough about your silly cars and all that to be a really good wife to you. I'm sorry your girl died and you got hurt and burned and couldn't race anymore when you loved it so." There were tears shining now in her eyes. "And, Micky, I'm sorry your daughter has grown up a stranger to you and you had to meet her tonight like a stranger and I couldn't even think of anything to say to help you to—"

"Ah, baby!"

He put his arms around her without stopping to think about it, and she clung to him, burrowing her head beneath his chin. He held her for a moment, her body soft and resilient in his arms, her sweet-smelling hair against his face. The unseen clock struck again in a rapid, mellow crescendo of sound. Mick heard it at first dimly and then with a tolling like Big Ben.

He was aware of several things at once, her quick, shallow breathing, her body moving against him, small, sharp fingers clutching at the back of his neck, her other hand fumbling inside his shirt.

"Micky?" she murmured. "Sweetie, listen." She rolled her head back onto his shoulder. "Send Killy on ahead. Tell her you'll meet her at the restaurant later, she won't mind."

He did not hear what she was saying, he was staring, fascinated, into her face, seeing it with a total clarity as through a zoom lens: the tiny mole beneath the fine, pale hair at her temple, the fuzzier texture of the false eyelashes she wore mixed with her own, the pink of her mouth through the smears of her lipstick. In that instant the shy child-wife with the serene and inviolate eyes retreated forever into the realm of memory. He felt the slippery fabric of her dress beneath his hands, smelled the sickly odor of gin on her breath warm against his face, discovered that his leg was twinging where it was bent awkwardly against the edge of the divan, and that he was a thousand years old and chilled and weary, repelled not by the voraciousness he saw but by its utter and somehow dreadful impersonality.

"Sweetie, please," she murmured, eyes closed, her warm hand groping along his belly.

Mick moved then. He bent down and kissed her upon the mouth, retrieving her hand from inside the top of his trousers and moving her gently away.

"Oh, hey!" he said. "I'm sorry, hon. All this auld lang syne stuff must have got to me for a minute. Forgive me, I couldn't help myself. You're a pretty terrific armful of woman, I guess you know that."

She was silent and motionless, sitting back upon her knees where he had left her, licking at the remains of her lipstick, her eyes intent upon his face.

"Oh, Micky," she said in a soft, matter-of-fact voice. "Now I've spoiled everything, haven't I?"

"Linda, what are you talking about?"

She shook her head violently, her forehead suddenly furrowing, her mouth turned downward, and tears gushing from her eyes. "No, don't touch me!" she wailed.

He had hold of her hand as she struggled off the divan, weeping noisily.

"Linda, listen to me!"

"No, let me go! Let me go!"

She flailed at him with her other fist, and he let go of her hand at last. She darted away for a few steps, lost her balance, floundered, and fell into the coffee table. Mick was already in motion, but he was too late. For one sickening instant he thought her head would strike the edge of the heavy table, but it was her shoulder instead. Glasses tumbled, and the martini pitcher smashed. An instant later Linda was scrambling on hands and knees amid the debris on the floor, golden droplets of urine sliding down her nylon-clad legs, her weeping abruptly stilled.

"Oh, my God!" Mick said softly into the silence. "Are you all right?"

She allowed him to lift her to her feet, a slack weight in his hands.

"Oh, Micky, look what I've done!" she said in a small, wondering voice. "I was so nervous before you got here. I wanted to be so dignified and like we could be friends. I wanted everything to be so nice, and now look! It's all horrible and messy and disgusting!"

She wept again, twisting away from his hands and on around the table, her voice rising. "Keep away from me! I know what you think of me, you think I'm a drunk and a whore! Keep away from me!"

And from the doorway behind them, Killian said in a clear, composed voice, "Well, shall I go back upstairs again, or what?"

It occurred to Mick that if there were a merciful providence anywhere in the universe, he would be instantly transported from this house, never to return to it so long as he lived.

"Linda, for God's sakes, stop that!" he said. "You're barefoot and there's glass all over the damn floor." He made a sudden dive after her, scooped her up, struggling and kicking, and then turned to Killian. She stood just inside the door, combed and elegant in a smart tan pantsuit, her face entirely without expression.

"And you," he said to her in a mounting fury. "Why don't you stop standing there looking down your nose and go get a broom or something? Well, go on! I'm not going to rape her, you know, no matter what you may think!"

Killian went.

Mick strode across the room and dumped Linda unceremoniously into a large chair, where she collapsed like a doll, burying her face in her arms as she wept. He returned swiftly, picking his way through shining bits of glass, and snatched up his cigarette package from a puddle on the top of the coffee table. The remaining cigarettes were soaked, and he crumpled it all furiously and hurled it in the direction of the gas flame. He waited then, grim faced, with only the dreary sound of Linda's weeping as she huddled in the chair. Killian reappeared an instant later carrying a yellow plastic wastebasket, a roll of paper towels, and a broom. He went to meet her.

"I'll take care of this," he said shortly. "You look after her."

He set to work wiping sticky blobs of cheese dip from the

carpeting while Killian murmured over Linda. "Don't cry, poor Mommy-doll, it's all right, love—" she soothed in the crooning, consoling voice that women use to comfort other women, and finally led her from the room.

Working rapidly, Mick swept bits of glass into the waste can, threw soggy napkins after it, and wiped off the tabletop. He returned one unbroken glass and the silver bowl to the tray. When he was finished he carried everything to the bar and left the broom leaned against the wall there.

He retraced his steps, looking a last time for any sliver of glass he might have missed. The house was completely still once more. The tabletop was dry and empty, the gas flame flickered on; the room already had resumed its static, unlived-in look, only a few wet blotches remaining on the carpeting, and Linda's shoes lying abandoned beside the sofa.

Mick bent and picked up the shoes. They were very small, bright green, stub heeled and blunt toed, frivolous and entirely feminine. He looked at them for a moment, then put them on the floor beneath the table and walked out into the hallway to wait for Killian.

WHEN HALLIE ARRIVED HOME FROM WORK that evening, she found an enormous white florist's box outside her door.

"Oh, Tom!" she murmured. The box was nearly as big as she was, and while she juggled it, groping for the keyhole, the telephone began to ring inside. Hallie jabbed frantically with her key, found the lock at last, and pushed open the door with her foot. She plunged on through the doorway, forgetting in her haste the dimensions of the florist's box, which caught upon the doorjamb at either end, catapulting her back into the hall. She kept her balance but somehow spilled the contents of her open purse.

Hissing with exasperation, Hallie dropped the box to the floor and shoved it end first through the doorway, snatching, at the same time, at a rolling lipstick, as the telephone continued its imperative jangle. A few more seconds and she abandoned the entire litter and fled to the bedroom, pink faced and breathless, to scoop up the phone from the bed table.

"Hello? Oh, Tom! How are you, darling? Where are you? You sound so nearby."

"I'm at the Cape," he said cheerfully. "I just got in. How are you, Mrs. C.? Did I get you out of the shower?"

"No, I just this minute got home. I was unlocking the door when the phone rang. Tom, what have you done? The biggest florist's box I've ever seen in my life! I could barely get it through the door."

"Hallie, you sound short of breath, are you all right?"

"Darling, of course!" she said as she turned on the lamp on

the bed table. "I told you, I was just rushing to get to the phone before it stopped ringing. And I couldn't get the door open and I dropped everything. You know."

"Well, take it easy. Stop and catch your breath for a minute. Do you want to go back and close the door?"

"Tom, would you mind? I dropped my purse, and my wallet is probably out there in the hall. Could you hold on just for a second?"

"Look, don't rush. The boy's just come with some ice. I'll fix myself a drink, and you go pick up your purse. When you get back I've got something to tell you, Mrs. C."

"Oh, good! I won't be a minute, darling."

She dropped the phone upon the bed and hurried back into the living room, turning on lights as she went. From the public hallway she retrieved her wallet, an enamel compact, an address book, and an earring, and back inside in the apartment she shrugged and bent to drag the littered interior doormat away from the door so that it would close. Slipping out of her coat then, she hurried back into the bedroom, lugging the florist's box with her. She put the box on the bed and sat down beside it, lifting the phone.

"Tom?"

He had not yet returned, and relieved, Hallie pushed her fine fringe of hair away from her flushed face and with the phone snuggled on her shoulder fell to work at loosening the violet strings that secured the box lid.

"Hallie, are you there?" Tom said a minute later.

"Yes, darling. All under control now, thanks a million. So how's your trip going? How was your flight?"

"Now you sound better. Everything's fine. The flight to Houston last night was a bore, but I came over here on a plane with some NASA fellows, so that was all right."

"Do you know you got off last night just in time? I heard on the radio this morning that about an hour after you left they closed the airport because of the fog."

244 — Maritta Wolff

"That was luck. I tried to get space on a later flight, too. Look, I've got some news for you, Mrs. C."

But she was already saying, "So tell me about where you're staying, Tom. Is it beautiful? I mean beach and palms and flowers and all that?"

"Well, the town here is not exactly the garden spot of America. Actually, it's just another big, flossy motel, it could be Vegas or anywhere. And in case you're interested, it's pretty damn chilly here tonight. So much for sunny Florida!"

"Tom, I wish you'd get yourself a topcoat. Why is it that California men always think they can go east in the winter in a raincoat? Where did you have dinner, or did you eat on the plane?"

"I'm just going out to dinner now. Someone's picking me up in a couple minutes."

"Tom, what were you going to tell me? I interrupted you, you said you had something to tell me."

"First, you tell me why you were so late getting home. I'll bet you a nickel that damn Volkswagen stalled out on you again. Come on, tell me the truth."

"Oh, darling, it did not! It's really fixed this time, it's purring like a kitten. No, I stopped by Miss Runkleman's after work. Tom, you know it really is terribly interesting, people are so interesting. You remember Miss Runkleman, the one I told you about who—"

"I remember. Your ex–handbag saleslady. So what about that idea of getting her a job in the local leather repair shop?"

"That's it, Tom. It seems there were ramifications to all this we didn't think of." Working with one hand, Hallie at last began to jiggle the lid from the florist's box. "Tom, what on earth's in this box! It smells heavenly! No, I told the girls at the store about your idea over coffee this morning, and they all thought it was an absolute inspiration, too. We got so carried away that I took early lunch hour and rushed straight off to the repair shop. He really is a very sweet young man. At first I don't think he knew what to make of the whole thing, but luckily his wife was there, and she is sharp as a tack. So we finally got it sorted out, and at the end, they were both madly enthusiastic about the idea and anxious to give it a try. Then Mrs. Marks, who is Miss Runkleman's closest friend at the store, took late lunch hour and dashed over to her apartment. Oh, Tom, this is what we never thought of! Miss Runkleman was furious. Actually, she was insulted. She thought the whole thing was beneath her. The very idea of tending counter in some grubby repair shop! Five or six of us went over after work and had a drink with her, and by then she was livid. Honestly, it would be funny if it weren't so sad, she— Oh, Tom!"

"Maybe now that she's made her point she'll let herself be talked into it. Why don't you—"

"Thomas, what have you done! The most fantastic roses! They're unbelievable!"

"Are they red? They're supposed to be red."

"Ah, they are red! Not that dark American Beauty color but a perfect clear, pure red, red, red! An armload of them with stems a yard long! Tom, what on earth—"

"We're celebrating. The champagne comes later, when I get home. That's what I've been trying to tell you, Mrs. C. Hang on to your hat, we're going to get married!"

"Tom!"

"Don't sound so surprised, it's about time, isn't it? I made up my mind yesterday. Damn funny, though, I never realized it until I got to Houston last night. I wanted to phone you then, but I hated to wake you up. I'll get my lawyers started at the paperwork on Monday. Then in a few weeks, Nedith can file the divorce. I'm going ahead with the idea of selling out the business at the same time, so there are a few things in that connection I'll need to put in order before the merger can be finalized. But by May or June it should be wrapped up. Then we'll get the hell out of here, travel for a few months and—"

He talked on, his voice eager and enthusiastic, and Hallie listened, ever more silently, hunched finally over the phone on her knees, her head rested upon her hand.

"Hallie? Are you still there?"

"Yes, darling."

"Well?"

The scent rising from the box of roses was overpowering, and she got up quickly and backed away from the bed, tiny drops of perspiration shining suddenly upon her face.

"Well, as the man said, 'Say something, if it's only good-bye!' "

"Tom, I just don't know what to say. I think when you get home we ought to talk about this and—" She leaned to crank open a window behind the drapes.

"Hallie, what's the matter? Maybe I shouldn't have sprung this on you on the phone like this."

"Oh, darling, no! It's just that my head's spinning and— Well, I just don't think this is something where you ought to rush into a decision."

"Mrs. C., you're a delightful woman! After two years, would you really say we're rushing into this? Come on, Hallie, putting it off any longer is only a hell of a stupid waste of time for us both, and you know it as well as I do. So what is it, what's the matter?"

"Oh, Tom, nothing's the matter. It's marvelous. I'm sort of numb, that's all. I just don't want you rushing into something. I think when you're home we should discuss it and—and—"

"Oh, Christ!" he said. "Something tells me I've made a boo-boo. It's a bad habit I have, isn't it? I always tend to grab the ball and start running."

"Tom—"

"No, I think I've gone at this all bass-ackwards. I'm sorry as hell, Hallie. Let's start this over again. I love you, Mrs. C. I'd like to spend the rest of my life with you because without you nothing's worth a single good goddamn to me. Will you marry me?"

"Oh, Tom, you idiot!" She was suddenly between tears and laughter.

"You think about it," he said, his own voice not altogether

steady. "I sure as hell never meant for you to feel you're being rushed or pressured into anything. We'll talk about it when I get home."

"Oh, darling, don't! Now you must feel like I've thrown cold water all over you, and that's the last thing in the world I intended to do, I—"

"Oh, hell! Just a minute, Hallie, hold on, will you?"

He was gone, and an instant later there was a faint sound of voices. Hallie rubbed at her eyes determinedly.

"I'm sorry, Mrs. C.," he said a moment later. "Couple guys just arrived to pick me up for dinner. Look, why don't I call you back later on?"

"Tom, listen. You know all the important things without me having to say them, but I want to say some of them anyway. I love you, darling. I miss you every single minute you're away from me. You're the beginning and the middle and the end of every day of my life. And I'm so happy right this minute that I really think I've gone round the bend a little, so I'm probably not responsible for what I've been saying. Or not been saying."

"Bless you! I feel pretty good myself right now. So you think about what I asked you, all right? Look, I have a hunch this is going to be a late night, maybe I'd better call you tomorrow. Incidentally, there's a chance now I may not get back till Sunday. Take care of yourself, Mrs. C. I miss you."

"Tom, wear your raincoat. And good luck with your clever gadget. Good-bye, darling."

"Bye, Hallie."

"Tom? Tom, thank you for these gorgeous roses—"

But he was gone. Hallie put down the phone, and all the light and animation faded from her face. She was shivering in a draft from the window and reached behind the curtains to close it. She stood for a time, her face increasingly distressed, and at last carried the florist's box off to the kitchen. She climbed onto a stool there to rummage for her largest vase and washed and dried it before she filled it with water. When she reached into the florist's box, however, she immediately stuck her hand upon one of the rose thorns, surprisingly long and sharp. Hallie winced, murmuring under her breath, and examined her finger, where several drops of blood welled, crimson as the roses in the box. After that, she lifted each flower gingerly until the large cut-glass vase was filled, and another smaller vase as well. She carried both vases into the living room and lingered there, then returned, in sudden decision, to the telephone in the bedroom, where she dialed.

"Hello, DeDe?" she said after a moment. "How are you, dear?"

"Hallie, how good to hear you! I'm fine. How are you?"

"Oh, fine. Everything's fine. DeDe, do you know how long it's been since I've seen you? We talk on the phone and weeks go by, months—"

"I know. Sometimes I wish they'd never invented the damn telephone."

"So I was just thinking," Hallie continued. "Why don't you jump in your car right this minute and come over here and have dinner with me?"

"You mean tonight?" She hesitated. "Damn, I've already eaten. I'm getting to be a regular old lady. I eat when the sun goes down, along with the cats."

"No, I was late getting home tonight, I completely forgot. I never stopped to look at the clock."

Her voice was so unmistakably disappointed that DeDe said, "Hallie, I tell you what. Fire up your coffeepot and I'll turn mine off and come have a cup of coffee with you, how's that?"

"Oh, DeDe! But it is getting late, and it's so far for you to drive. Why don't we meet somewhere in the middle?"

"Oh, for pete's sakes, how long does it take on the freeway? I won't stop to change or anything. You're tired after working all day. Go ahead and eat your dinner, and I'll be there in forty minutes."

"Marvelous! It'll be so good to see you. Bye, dear."

* * *

Less than an hour later Hallie heard the whir of the worn-out buzzer and opened the door upon a tall, bony woman in a worn mink coat, her graying dark hair pulled back from her plain, pleasant face into a ponytail.

"DeDe, how marvelous!" Hallie cried with genuine delight. "You're an absolute love to make this long trek tonight."

"I should do it more often. It's mostly just getting started." She enveloped her friend in a bear hug. "Hallie, you look wonderful! You know, girl, every single time I see you, you look younger. I wish I knew your secret. Oh, I know your secret," she added mournfully, "but a fat lot of good it does me. I haven't had a man around the house in so long I'll bet I've forgotten what to do with one!"

"You're just the one to talk." Hallie smiled. "You haven't changed a wink in twenty years nor will you ever. Let me take your coat."

With Hallie's assistance, DeDe struggled out of the heavy coat, juggling a handbag and a small, tissue-wrapped bundle.

"Hallie, my God, look at those roses! No wonder it smells like a funeral parlor in here. They talk about long-stemmed roses, but those are ridiculous!"

"Aren't they fantastic?" Hallie said with a shade of discomfort as she hung the coat in the closet. "Don't let me forget to give you some when you go home. Where do they ever grow flowers like that, I wonder."

"They must fly them in from Hawaii," DeDe said, pushing up the sleeves of her untidy black sweater. "How is Tom anyway?"

"Are you sure they grow roses in Hawaii? Oh, Tom's fine. He's off on a business trip, he left last night."

Hallie's voice was so carefully noncommittal that DeDe glanced at her sharply. "Here, for you," she said, offering the small bundle.

"DeDe, you shouldn't!"

"It isn't anything. Just some pot holders for your kitchen. They have pictures of herbs on them, so they made me think of you."

"But I love them! Look, like old botany prints, they're beautiful. Thank you, dear. I need them, too. You know me, I'm always scorching pot holders. Now. I made a pot of coffee, or would you rather have a drink?"

"I'd love some coffee, but first I'd better use your bathroom. I must be getting too old for driving freeways at night. I just about peed myself a couple times getting over here."

Hallie laughed. "DeDe, I miss you! Why don't we get together more often? Go on to the bathroom, love, I'll pour the coffee."

When DeDe returned to the kitchen, Hallie was carefully placing a frothy dessert on a plate. "My God, Hallie, what's that!"

"Isn't it awful?" Hallie said ruefully. "But under all that meringue, it's your favorite pie, chocolate cream. The minute after I phoned you, I ran out to the little pastry shop around the corner."

"You know, that's the most sinful looking pie I ever saw in my life! Never mind, let's go to hell in a bucket. We can always skip lunch tomorrow. Hallie, don't bother with that tray. Let's have it here at the kitchen table, it's cozy."

"All right. Sit down and I'll get the forks. That package is for you, by the way."

"Hallie, honestly!" DeDe said, pleased and embarrassed, tightening the rubber band that held her ponytail.

DeDe tore open the paper and unfurled a long chiffon scarf of muted pinks and orange. "Hallie, it's gorgeous! But it must have cost a fortune!"

"Oh, it did not. My discount at the store, remember? Anyway, I had to have it for you the minute I saw it, it's your colors."

"It certainly is. I must have an orange and pink aura or something. Hallie, do you know that the prettiest things I own are things you've given me? My God, just look at that pie, it must be six inches thick! Sit down now, you look tired."

Hallie obediently pulled out a chair in the cramped space at the other side of the table. The kitchen was cluttered and small, an old-fashioned tiled counter beneath tall, narrow cupboards, a sink, stove, and refrigerator of ancient vintage. But it was a cheerful room, with pots of herbs and violets lining the windowsills and a large Victorian oil on the wall above the table: still life with pitcher, fruit, and flowers.

They attacked the thick wedges of pie then with gusto, chattering together. Actually, it was DeDe who did most of the talking: a description of her hapless adventures in selling a last litter of Himalayan kittens, an account of a vivid and apparently prophetic dream she had had the week before in which she had careened through dark streets at the wheel of a police car. And how last night a woman driver with a bug in her power steering system had grazed DeDe's car and crashed into another one. And sure enough, because of the drizzle, the police officers had loaded all parties concerned into the police car for the customary exchange of names and insurance data. Wasn't it strange and interesting, the way these things worked out?

Hallie agreed that it was indeed, but she was noticeably less than her usual self, and DeDe watched her as she rambled on between mouthfuls.

They finished their pie and, amid laughter and groans, treated themselves to second helpings. After that, DeDe carried the plates to the sink, and Hallie, eyes closed, determinedly scraped the tempting remainder of the pie directly into a garbage sack. She filled the coffee cups a second time and went to fetch her needlework. DeDe watched her go, her face openly worried now as she dabbed absently at a spot of chocolate on the front of her black sweater, which was liberally plastered with pale cat hairs. When Hallie returned she carried the smaller vase of Tom's roses, which she placed upon the tabletop before she sat down again. Hitching her chair around into the light then, she donned a pair of plastic-rimmed magnifying glasses and spread the square of needlepoint upon her knee.

For a moment there was a companionable silence between them while the toiling motor of the old refrigerator ground. DeDe leaned comfortably upon her elbow, stirring her coffee in a cloud of cigarette smoke. Hallie plied her shining needle, her face, fringed by her blond hair, somber. The peacock blue-green beads that Tom had given her glowed at the neck of her loose blue caftan, and on the table the red roses blazed, elegantly disdainful of the scarred paint, faded vinyl, and comfortable clutter about them.

DeDe said at last, her voice warm with affection and concern, "Hallie, what's the matter? I knew something was wrong the minute I heard your voice on the phone. What is it, hon?"

Hallie sighed and secured the glittering needle under a thread of stiffened gauze. "Ah, it's Tom, of course," she said miserably. "I suppose I've really known for a long time that this was going to happen. Oh, DeDe, why is it that all my life I've been so stupid about never facing up to things? Now it's finally happened and I'm just not prepared!"

"Oh, Hallie," DeDe said softly.

Hallie's eyes were upon her hands, clasped together over her needlework. "He telephoned this afternoon. He says his mind is made up, he wants to start divorce proceedings right away."

For an instant DeDe was transfixed; then she threw back her head and whooped. "Oh, Hallie, you nut! For a minute you had me scared to death, I thought that— Never mind. Oh, Hallie, that's wonderful! I'm so happy for you!"

Hallie looked at her silently, her face tragic.

"Hallie, for pete's sakes! He does want to get married, doesn't he?"

"Oh, yes. He's—full of plans. He wants me to hand in my notice at the store next week. Meanwhile, he has certain business arrangements to make that may take five or six months. He's going to sell his business, some sort of merger deal that he's been thinking about for a long time. Once that's done, he wants to travel for a while. He says the day the divorce is final, we'll be married wherever we happen to be. Or come back here, if I'd rather."

DeDe's eyes were shining. "Hallie, it all sounds perfectly wonderful. I just don't know what to say!"

Hallie was silent again, picking at the bright wool in her lap.

DeDe stared at her and skinned back her hair. "All right, spit it out, Hallie. You don't want to marry him, or what? You've found out that he's got a nasty temper and he gripes about the way you boil his eggs and the message units on the phone bill and—"

"Oh, DeDe!"

"Well, what then? I suppose you'd rather go on just the way you are now?"

"I don't know," Hallie said. "Yes. Yes, I think I would."

"Oh, that is great!" DeDe said angrily. "You mean go on forever with this—this dingy backstairs kind of arrangement, seeing him three or four nights a week if you're lucky and sitting home the other nights in case the phone might ring, and spend the rest of your life getting fallen arches back of that damn hosiery counter and skimping along from month to month trying to stay ahead of your bills and— Oh, yes! That's just a dandy way to live. Anybody'd be a fool to ever want to change it!"

"Don't, DeDe! You know what I'm thinking about just as well as I do. It's his wife. They've been married for twenty-seven years. Twenty-seven years! And now, he's going to look her in the eye and tell her that he wants a divorce."

"Hallie, you bumble-headed idiot! I could wring your neck!"

"I know. I must sound like the worst kind of hypocrite. I know it's a little late now for me to start thinking about Nedith Fallon. Well, I've thought about her before this, don't think I haven't! I've thought every hateful thought about her that there is, if you'd like to know. By now I know by heart every shabby, tricky excuse that people make to themselves. Oh, DeDe, isn't it funny? Well, isn't it, when you stop to think of it? Me, of all people! Now the shoe is finally on the other foot. And I can tell you, it pinches on this foot, too!"

"Oh, God, I knew this would happen someday!" DeDe said despairingly. "You listen to me, Hallie! Charlie Christopher and Tom Fallon are two different men, it's two different marriages and two different sets of circumstances altogether."

"Oh, DeDe, it still comes down to the exact same thing, and you know it as well as I do. Anyway, I've learned to live with that, but this is something else. I'm not trying to justify myself, but it really is one thing to—to see Tom the way I've been doing, and something else to break up her marriage."

"What kind of marriage! Or do you really think that Tom's lied to you and that—"

"No, of course not. Something obviously went terribly wrong between them years ago. Tom's had a lot of women in his life, he's never made any bones of it to me. But all the same, for better or for worse, their marriage has lasted. Until now."

"Has his wife known about it, I mean other women?"

"Yes," Hallie said reluctantly. "Tom says she never stops throwing it up to him in left-handed sorts of ways. She's just never made a direct issue of it."

"Does she go around with other men?"

Hallie shook her head. "Tom says he thinks she closed off that part of her life years ago. There are other things that are simply more important to her. She adores her children, and then—you know, possessions. Houses and automobiles and clothes, just a pleasant life, shopping and going off to the Golden Door with a girlfriend and—"

"In other words," DeDe said brutally, "she'd rather put up with Tom's affairs than risk upsetting her mink-lined applecart. Well, there are a lot of women like that. I suppose that's why you put up with Charlie all those years, too."

"DeDe, don't! Charlie needed me and I knew it. But I never stopped caring. Every time he had an affair it whittled me away a little bit more. Finally there was nothing left but a tiny nub of myself. For a long time I thought that was the indestructible part that would last forever. But it didn't, did it? You know that."

Hallie got up from her chair, the needlework falling unheeded to the floor, and walked to the small, discolored sink.

"DeDe, I know what you're trying to do. But don't you see, that's exactly the point, it is an entirely different situation. Tom is not another Charlie, nor do I pretend that Nedith Fallon feels about things the same way I did. The real point is, she and Tom have been married for twenty-seven years. She's had to accept certain things, make compromises, work out some kind of life for herself. She'd have had to do that, wouldn't she? And now when Tom tells her that he wants a divorce, it's all going to fall down around her ears."

"And about time, if you ask me," DeDe said. "The best thing you ever did in your life was divorce Charlie, and you know it."

Hallie opened and closed a faucet aimlessly, water splashing into the sink. "But my divorce was my own idea, because I couldn't stand my life the way it was another minute. And I was younger than she is now. And maybe I'm tougher. It's not easy, to have to face yourself and pick up all the bits and pieces and start your life over again. Oh, DeDe, I hate it! What kind of happy life is it going to be for Tom and me if we start it off by doing someone else in the eye?"

"Rats!" DeDe said. "You never did anyone in the eye in your whole life, Hallie Christopher! Just come back over here and sit down and listen to me for a minute. Please?"

Hallie came, looking miserable, and DeDe hitched about in her chair, shoving at her sweater sleeves. When she spoke again, her voice was moved. "Hallie, you've always been a real sister to me. Marrying you was the only good thing that louse of a brother of mine ever did for me. You and I have been through so much together. I honestly don't believe I could have made it after Bob died if it hadn't been for you. So please listen to what I'm going to say. Charlie Christopher was my brother. I watched him grow up into a spineless, shifty, spoiled, selfish man. You didn't have a thing to do with that, Hallie, he did it all by himself. With a little help from my mother. He cheated on you from the day he married you and then never had any more guts than to run home to you every single time with his thing between his legs and blubber and cry how he couldn't live without you and how it was never going to happen again. And you stuck by him all those years. If it hadn't been for you, he'd have ended up in jail or the gutter, and everybody knew it. No, let me talk!

"You stood by Charlie and were loyal and loving to him and never complained a word to anyone, not even me, and he broke every promise he ever made to you and frittered away every penny either one of you had in the world on women and dice in Las Vegas and half-assed land deals and— Oh, it still makes me furious every time I think about it! I don't know how you stood it as long as you did, any other flesh-and-blood woman would have broken down years sooner. No, let me finish this, Hallie. I don't know anything about Tom Fallon's wife, but I know you. Ten years ago I watched you fall apart and then climb all the way back from the bottom of the hole, and there isn't one woman in a thousand who could have done what you did, the way you pulled yourself together and divorced Charlie and stopped drinking and got out and found yourself a job for the first time in your life and made a whole new life for yourself and stuck with it. And the miracle is, it never soured you or made you hard. Sometimes I marvel at you, Hallie. You must be a very, very old soul. Anyway, you're the best person I've ever come across in my whole life and—"

"DeDe, don't, don't!" Hallie said helplessly. "I only wish I were one tenth of what you think I am. It was my weakness to put up with things, you never understood that. It would have been much better for poor Charlie if I'd screamed and thrown the dishes. Anyway, that's all in the past now, it has nothing whatsoever to do with this."

"But it does!" DeDe said urgently. "It's got everything to do with it. Hallie, you've been through so much misery in your life, Charlie, and the babies you lost, and— But now things have finally begun to come right for you. You've found a wonderful man who's crazy about you, and his only main fault that I can see, he's stood by a bad marriage of his own for twenty-seven years or whatever it is. Are you going to hold that against him and let it ruin everything? Darling, face it, you're not sixteen anymore and neither is Tom. And now you've got this chance to make each other happy for the last years of your lives. Hallie, you've earned this, don't you see? You deserve it. There isn't a person who knows you who wouldn't tell you the same thing!"

"DeDe, I love you!" Hallie said. "I don't think I'd be here either, if I hadn't had you standing by me through thick and thin. But none of that matters. Life doesn't hand out payment due slips to anyone, the Judgment is supposed to come later. Oh, DeDe, we can talk like this till we're blue in the face, but it doesn't change anything. I don't believe that anyone in this world deserves to be happy at the expense of someone else's grief, and neither do you."

"Hallie!" DeDe wailed. "All right, then turn it around the other way for a minute. What right has she, just because she's had a good thing going now for twenty-seven years, to—"

"That's a matter between her and her own conscience. It's really not my concern."

"Hallie Christopher, you're a fool!"

They were silent then, both their faces distraught and half angry. At last DeDe hitched about in her chair and reached for her cigarettes. "All right. That's the way you feel about it, all right," she said practically. "So what do you plan to do then? Give Tom up, I suppose?"

Hallie was still, her eyes very round and dark. "Like hell I will!" she said through her teeth.

DeDe smiled and broke into laughter, delighted, contagious peals of it, and then they were both rocking helplessly in their chairs and the roses on the table teetered.

When their giggles had subsided, Hallie said, wiping at her eyes, "Oh, DeDe, what a fraud I really am! What a phony!"

"No, you're not," DeDe said sympathetically. "I know how bad you feel about Tom's wife because you're the kindest-hearted person on earth. But there is such a thing as being too softhearted for your own good. I'll bet you a cookie that if it was the other way around, she wouldn't waste one little minute worrying about you."

"That's not fair. You don't know that. DeDe, what shall I do? I know Tom well enough to know once he's made up his mind to something, he's going through with it. Do you think it would help at all if I went and talked to her myself?"

"Oh, that's a dandy idea! What would you say to her, 'Please don't be mad but I'd like to marry your husband'?"

"No," Hallie said soberly. "I suppose I'd just try to tell her about me, how you've got to believe in life no matter what because one day when you least expect it you can walk around a corner into a miracle."

"Something tells me that would go over like a lead balloon," DeDe said. "Oh, Hallie, just don't worry about that woman. Go ahead now and be happy, for pete's sakes."

"But, DeDe, why must it be like this? I sometimes think there is something terribly wrong with the way we live, our whole idea of marriage and relationships between men and women. Here this is the happiest thing that's ever happened to me in my life, all I want is for all the bells to ring and everyone to dance in the streets right along with me."

"I know. Well, at least you can count on me. I intend to dance my shoes right off at your wedding, you better believe it."

"Bless you. And one of these days I intend to do the same at yours, you better believe that, too!"

"Sure you will!" DeDe said, grinning. "One day my doorbell is going to ring, and there'll be Mr. Right himself standing on my doorstep. 'Mrs. Hawks,' he'll say, 'I saw your ad in the paper, kittens for sale. Will you marry me?' "

"Now don't laugh! It could happen, you know."

"Ah, Hallie, I'm really going to miss you," DeDe said. "I don't care though. It'll be worth it to me to know that things have turned out for you the way they have."

"What are you talking about!" Hallie's voice was hurt. "Me marrying Tom is not going to change anything. You're the only sister I've got, for heaven's sakes!"

"Oh, Hallie, I only meant—well, you said you were going to travel. You might end up living anywhere."

"If we do then wherever it is you'll come to visit every single year."

Hallie, on hands and knees beside the table, was busily retrieving her fallen needlework and yarns, and DeDe cupped her chin upon her hand and stared down at her for a moment.

"Hallie, have you thought at all about that part of it? Marrying Tom is going to change your life a lot, you know that, don't you? It's the kind of thing you never pay any attention to, but Tom Fallon happens to be a very rich man."

Hallie laughed, and then bumped her head on the underside of the table as she reached for the scissors. "Damn it! DeDe, what money Tom has or hasn't got is the very least important thing about him." Her voice was amused and confident. "I'd marry Tom if he hadn't a penny. What difference does it make? I'd be happy to spend the rest of my life in Supp-Hose back of that stocking counter to support him if I had to. I'd jump at the chance!"

"You probably would, you nut. The point is, you're not going to have to. You're going to be living a whole different life instead, all overnight."

"Nonsense. Tom and I are very compatible in that area. He doesn't care buttons about—well, you know, the ostentatious, extravagant things you can do with money, any more than I do. Nothing's really going to change at all."

"Well, I should hope it would, for pete's sakes!" DeDe said. "And I should hope you'd have sense enough to enjoy it."

"Look at these poor roses," Hallie murmured. "They really don't seem very comfortable in this vase, do they?" And then, as she began to rearrange the flowers, she said, her tone shifting, "DeDe, of course I know there'll be certain changes. And you know I'll enjoy them, too. To travel, for instance, it would be so marvelous to really see some of those places from the *National Geographic*, and absolute heaven not to have to crawl out of bed every morning at a quarter of seven! Or to be able to buy a present for a friend without having to look at the price tag first. Imagine just being able to lose a filling out of your tooth without going into a panic wondering where the money's to come from to put it back in! Of course I'm going to enjoy it."

"Well, you're never going to have to worry about another dental bill again as long as you live, that's for sure," DeDe said. "You've always been kind of mean about letting Tom spend money on you though. I hope you don't intend to go on that way."

"That's ridiculous, Tom's always giving me things. Just because I wouldn't let him take over my bills and buy me an automobile and— I'm entitled to some pride, aren't I?"

"Sure you are. I just always thought you kind of overdid it."

"Do you honestly think so?" Hallie's hands were still for an instant among the roses, her face thoughtful. "Maybe I did. Maybe I really am oversensitive about such things. If I am I suppose it's because I am so insistent now about being my own woman. It's terribly important to me. I worked so hard to get there, and for so long it was all I had. Anyway, once we're really married, I think I'll feel differently about it. Tom loves to give me things; it'll be one of the ways to make him happy, won't it?"

Her words began tumbling together then. "Oh, DeDe, I'm going to be such a good wife to him! I'm going to make that man happy from morning till night every single day that I live!"

"Hallie, I'm so happy for you! If I was any happier right this minute, I'd just float off in my astral body!"

"I know, dear."

Embarrassed, Hallie plucked the roses, dripping, from the

vase. "I suppose it would be an absolute crime to cut these stems," she murmured, "but I'm going to do it anyway."

"Look out for those thorns, you could butcher yourself," DeDe warned as Hallie tackled the thick stems with the scissors. "Hallie? There's just one other thing that worries me. From what you've told me, Tom's always been quite a hand for women, sort of in the habit of chasing around. I guess you've thought about that."

Hallie was silent for a moment, snipping away. "Yes, of course I've thought about that," she said matter-of-factly. "Tom's a very—vital man. And I'm not exactly a glamour girl anymore, actually I never was. But Tom loves me, and there is so much I can give him. DeDe, there is such a hunger in that man for companionship, for enjoying and sharing, just doing things together, we . . ." Her voice trailed away, and when she looked up, her smile was small and frightened. "Well, it's always a gamble, isn't it?"

She returned the roses to the vase, shaking them apart gently, the crimson opening buds nodding among the dark green foliage. Shorn of their stem length, they became a fragrant, homely garden bouquet. Hallie gathered up the cut stem ends and carried them to the garbage sack.

"And what about Tom's children?" DeDe said. "You've never met them, have you? How do you suppose they'll take this?"

"I don't know. Sally is the older one; she's married, you know, and has two babies of her own. I get the idea that she and Tom aren't very close. He says she's a perfect replica of her mother, they're great friends." Hallie sat down again, brushing at straggling wisps of hair about her face. "It's the boy, Pete, that I'm most concerned about. Tom really adores him. It's so sad, he's only twenty-three and going through a divorce of his own. Tom says he's very mature, a wonderful boy, so maybe he'll adjust to this." Her voice was wistful. "I hope so. I'd like so much to know him."

"Boys are pretty apt to side with their mothers, though, aren't they?" DeDe said dubiously.

"That's what they always say."

"Well," DeDe said, looking at her watch. "Listen, I have to get home. Do you know what time it is, girl? But did somebody say something about a drink? I'd better have one before I face up to that damn freeway."

"I think by now we both need one. I'll get the ice."

BACK IN THE HOUSE IN BEVERLY HILLS, KILLIAN appeared at last at the top of the stairway and descended to where Mick waited in the silent entry hall.

"I'll get my bag," she murmured.

"Will she be all right here?"

"Of course." Killian looked surprised. "Anyway, she's already phoned a friend, and he's on his way over." She paused in the doorway. "Unless you'd rather not go out to dinner now. If you don't want to, it's perfectly all right."

"No, unless you'd rather not."

"I'll get my bag," she said again.

She retrieved her purse from a chair inside the living room; it was an ancient velvet bag fringed with cut steel beads and suspended from a long chain, which she slung over her shoulder.

He opened the door, and they stepped out together into the chill darkness. The perverse door swung effortlessly closed behind them, but Mick did not notice. He was feeling nervously through his pockets again for the cigarettes he did not have.

"The car's a couple blocks up the street. Would you rather wait while I fetch it?"

"I don't mind walking."

"Sure?"

"No, I like to walk."

He plunged off along the dark, empty sidewalk, and Killian lengthened her steps, matching his quick, uneven stride. His face in the gloom was abstracted and grim. Killian glanced at him several times, seemingly about to speak and each time thinking better of it.

It was Mick who said at last, stiffly, "I'm sorry about what happened. You probably think it was my fault."

"Of course not," she said. "It's not the sort of thing that's anybody's fault, is it?"

She hesitated, then added in a rapid rush, "You're probably thinking now that Linda's turned into some ghastly alcoholic type, but that's not true. Honestly. I think seeing you today just made her terribly nervous, it had been so many years and all that."

"Sure. I understand."

She took a quick extra step to keep up with him and leaned forward to look into his face. "I'm not trying to pretend that Linda doesn't drink a lot. It's just that today really wasn't like her. She never cries or gets messy. Usually she keeps herself right on the edge, where she stays sort of pleasantly, happily mellow. You know?"

"It's only another block now," Mick said. "I'm sorry to make you hike all this way."

"What is it? Do you think I'm lying, that Linda gets fallingdown drunk every day of her life?"

"No," he said shortly. "If you'd really like to know, I was thinking that this is a hell of a way for you to be talking about your mother."

"Fantastic! You really are terribly uptight about all this, aren't you? What's your birth sign, by the way?"

"What?"

"Your sun sign. When were you born?"

"April. Where would you like to have dinner?"

"Anywhere you like is fine with me. You mean you'd rather I had lied and tried to make you believe that Linda never drinks at all?"

"There used to be the Casa Veneto out Santa Monica. Do you like Italian food?"

"I like all kinds of food. I'm afraid the Veneto went out of business, though, several years ago."

"Here we are," he said. "No, you'll have to get in on this side. I'm parked the wrong way."

"Marvelous! Do you know I really thought this was the front end of it? Oh look, you've got a parking ticket."

She bent lithely over her left foot, her long hair falling forward, folding herself neatly into the bucket seat, and Mick closed the door after her with a solid clunk. He yanked the ticket from under the wiper blade and tossed it to the floor of the car before he entered at the other side.

"Don't you really think it's a little unfair?" Killian asked. "Why are you determined to go away thinking that Linda's turned into one of those sickening, sloppy, middle-aged woman drunks that you see in bars who—"

"Look, do you mind!" Mick said in a sudden contained fury. "If you've got this bloody marvel IQ like your mother says, I should think you might have figured this out without me having to tell you. This is something I don't feel like talking about. Just leave it, for God's sakes, be, why can't you!"

Mick sat for a moment, his hands upon the wheel, Killian silent and rigid beside him, and then he started up the engine and shot away from the curb. They rode in silence for several minutes while he zigzagged through a maze of residential streets.

"What about the Bel-Air Hotel?" he said at last with obvious effort. "It used to be a very pleasant place."

"Why not?" Killian said coolly. "I haven't been there since my wedding reception, and that doesn't seem to have turned out all that well either."

"Look, I didn't mean to—"

"Don't be silly. Anyway, I love the Bel-Air. I don't have hang-ups about places and favorite music and that whole sentimental bag."

"Somehow I'm not surprised to hear that," he said drily.

After that they were silent for a long time, until the lights of the Strip were behind them and the car was accelerating into the long, dark curves of Sunset Boulevard.

Killian turned her head at last and surveyed his face in the dim light. She reached out her hand suddenly to the black, padded dashboard.

"What a fantastic contraption!" she said. "All these crazy dials and switches as though you were going to the moon in it. I'm sorry I don't understand your thing about automobiles and racing them and all that. I suppose they make marvelous toys, but frankly, I think all automobiles ought to be legislated out of existence. Ecologically, we can't afford them any longer."

Mick remained silent, his eyes on the road.

She stole another glance at him and continued. "You know, I have a friend who was into skydiving for a while. When he was very young, naturally. He used to say that jumping was a mystical and religious experience for him. I expect driving fast may be the same for you. Do you find it so?"

She studied his impassive profile.

"Oh, shit!" she said. "Why don't you just drive me back to town."

Instantly, he swung the car off into a dark road between large trees, slamming the brakes to wheel lock, the rear end sliding a full one hundred and eighty degrees in a cloud of dust, then shot out into the street and on again, heading back in the direction from which they had just come.

"Fantastic!" Killian said, slowly relinquishing her grip on the padded bar on the dash. "It has to be Aries. When were you born in April?"

"The second."

"Then I was right. Definitely a fire sign. Me, too. I'm a Sagittarius. Linda, of course, is the perfect Cancer. Imagine her being married to an Aries like you! Poor Mommy-doll!"

"Why do you keep calling her that?"

"What? Oh, Linda. Does 'Mommy-doll' offend you? Do you think it indicates some deep-seated aggression, some uneasiness

I feel in the child-parent relationship that takes the form of role reversal and—"

"Forget it. I'm sorry I asked."

"Actually, I've called her that ever since I was in therapy when I was six. The playhouse bit, you know."

She glanced at him briefly. "Or maybe you don't know. It was a sort of dollhouse, with all the rooms open at the top. And there was a mommy doll and a daddy doll and a little girl doll and the doggy doll. You played games in it like what happens when the daddy doll comes home from the office at night. With the therapist hovering over you like God or the tooth fairy. Really divine! I wonder how many people have told their analysts by now that they have this feeling they are living their whole lives in that dollhouse with the therapist still there hovering over the chimney tops watching absolutely everything they do. Are you still in love with Linda?"

"What?" Mick said, startled. "No, of course not. It's been twenty years, for God's sakes!"

"Then why are you so uptight about her?"

"I'm not uptight about her. It's a peculiar experience, that's all, seeing someone you've been married to years later like this."

"Has she changed very much?"

"Yes. And no. Look, would you tell me something? Tell me about Marv Shapiro, what's he like?"

"Marv?" Her voice was amused. "What do you want to know about him?"

"Well, he's—your father, after all."

"What has that to do with it? Did you ever meet him?"

"Yes, once. A long time ago."

"What do you remember about him?"

He thought for an instant, his eyes upon the taillights ahead. "A talkative little guy in a three-hundred-dollar silk suit. Aside from being a bit pompous and wrapped up in himself he seemed a pretty decent sort."

"That's rather good."

She removed a slim twist of paper from a tin box in her purse and began to search along the dash for a lighter. Mick extended his own from his pocket, and she bent over the flame, the twisted paper ends flaring as they ignited.

"Thank you. So. Was he married to Linda then?"

"What?"

"When you met Marv years ago, was he married to Linda?"

"No, not yet."

"You mean Linda was still married to you."

"We'd been separated for a while. Actually, it was a meeting they'd set up to get my power of attorney so she could get a Nevada divorce."

"Had you known about Marv before then? I mean that Linda was planning to remarry."

"Yes."

"Did you mind?"

He hesitated for the barest instant before he answered matter-of-factly, "No, not very much."

"Did you and Marv get on? Do you mind talking about this?" she asked brightly. "I think it's terribly interesting."

"Look, you don't happen to have any cigarettes, do you?"

"I'm sorry, I hardly ever smoke them."

She held out her small roll of paper inquiringly, but Mick shook his head.

"I didn't punch him in the nose if that's what you mean," he said. "Though he kept being so damn bloody reasonable that I came close to it a couple times."

"Then I expect you did mind more than you thought you did," Killian said, with interest.

"Well, the whole thing had to be a little dicey, didn't it? Actually, I was relieved they wanted to get married, it let me off the hook. It was the way he'd moved in on the whole situation, he had everything so damn well organized. He sprung the adoption thing on me that day, too, apparently they'd—"

Mick stopped abruptly. Killian did not speak either, and for an instant the silence was strained. Mick turned the car into a driveway and brought it to a halt on the asphalt parking area at the side of a low stucco building.

"I need to buy some cigarettes," he said, opening his door and putting one foot on the pavement. "I'll be back in a minute. Then we can decide where to go for dinner."

He left her sitting in the car, and she took one more drag, then snuffed out the burning tip of the joint and put the unsmoked portion back in the box from her purse.

When Mick returned he slid into the driver's seat with a lit cigarette in hand and threw the pack on the dashboard. He did not start the car.

Killian looked at him and said, "I expect what you really wanted to know about Marv is why he and Linda divorced, isn't it? What went wrong with their marriage and all that?"

He turned his head to her, his eyes very intent behind his glasses. "Yes, it is," he said, baldly. "Do you know?"

"I was there, after all," she said. "I was fourteen. They didn't want to wait for a California decree because Natalie was pregnant, so Linda went to Reno. It was all perfectly friendly. I was in school, naturally, so Natalie moved into the house and looked after things while Linda was away."

And then she added quickly, "But if you're thinking it was all some ghastly trauma for Linda, it wasn't. The marriage had fizzled quite a while before that, and she and Marv were both—you know. Going around with other people."

"Why did the marriage fizzle?"

Killian shrugged. "It wasn't any one huge or dramatic thing. Maybe it would have helped if they could have had children together. Linda couldn't, you know. Marv wanted to adopt, but Linda wouldn't. He said it was her way of refusing to accept the fact that she couldn't have more children herself. He wanted her to see a psychiatrist, but Linda wouldn't do that either. Poor Mommy-doll! She can be terribly stubborn once she makes up her mind to something."

"Yes, I know," Mick said.

"Fantastic! I keep forgetting. Yes, I expect you do." She sat quiet for a moment. "If they had adopted, at least it would have given Linda something to do. You really can't make a whole life out of polishing the silver and driving one child to ballet lessons and the orthodontist. The trouble was, Marv was always so busy, patients all day and then lectures and meetings and whichever book he happened to be writing at the time. His idea of relaxation was to go to parties and spend evenings knee-deep in women. Linda began to complain that she never saw him anymore. I don't think Marv took her complaints seriously in the beginning, or he pretended not to. The really infuriating thing about him, he'll never argue. By the time Linda got to the point of screaming at him, he just kept on being terribly reasonable and insisting that she see an analyst."

Killian looked at Mick through the smoke in the car and then continued. "Really I think Linda simply lost her confidence in herself and gave up on the marriage. To this day she'll say things about how she expected too much of marriage and demanded too much of marriage partners all because of her rotten, rejected childhood."

She shrugged and snuck a glance at Mick.

"Linda's always told me that you and she divorced because you preferred racing automobiles and partying to being married and raising a family."

"I'd say that was a reasonably accurate statement," he said tersely. He threw the butt of his cigarette out the window with a snap of his arm. "Let's go, shall we?" he asked, and turned the ignition key.

Mick's attention was upon the traffic as he guided the car out of the parking lot. He was silent after that, appearing to have lost all interest in the subject.

Killian watched his hands on the wheel and finally said, her voice cool, "I hope you haven't gotten a wrong impression from what I've been telling you. Linda was perfectly happy with the way things worked out, you know. And she could certainly have married again if she'd cared to. She still could, obviously."

"Sure. I realize that."

"But it's true! She knows quantities of people, she's—"

"Look, I believe you. Why are you getting sore about it, all of a sudden?"

"I'm not getting sore, it's your attitude in general. You walk in this afternoon after all these years and spend an hour or so with Linda, who happens to be at her absolute worst, and on the basis of that, apparently you feel competent to sit back and pass judgment on her!"

"Now you're back to that again. You're wrong, you know. I don't make a habit of passing judgment, as you put it, on anyone. Christ, Linda least of all!"

"That's exactly the attitude I mean! Don't think you have to feel so sorry for her, please. It's sickeningly patronizing and self-righteous of you, if you'd like to know. It's also totally unnecessary."

"I'm not going to try to argue with you about this. You're the one who's got an idea in your head and—"

"Would you mind turning right up here at Sunset? I'm meeting some people at a place on the Strip. You could drop me off if you don't mind."

"What about dinner?"

"I'm really not hungry."

"Look, why don't you just simmer down? The deal was, I was to take you to dinner, wasn't it, and you've got yourself all prettied up for it, so let's go. How about Scandia?"

"I honestly can't think of anything duller than going to a ghastly expensive place like Scandia and sitting down now to some huge, elaborate meal that neither of us wants to eat simply to satisfy a stupid social ritual! I'm late as it is, I'd rather you just dropped me off."

"If you're sure that's what you want. This is your show."

"There, it's that orange-colored front up ahead where all the bulbs are blinking. Why do you say it's my show? I was perfectly willing to go along with all this, except now I really feel I've done all the talking about Linda behind her back that I care to do for one night."

"Oh, Christ, so that's it," Mick said. "Look, I'm sorry. I really am. I can see why you've gotten your feelings hurt. I didn't mean for us to spend all this time talking about your mother."

"Didn't you? That's odd, because I have the impression now that that's the only reason you asked to see me in the first place. I can get out right here."

Mick stopped the car opposite two other vehicles parked at the curb in front of the blindingly bright facade and turned to look at her, his expression baffled and half angry. "I told you I was sorry. Why do you want to say a thing like that? You're the one who wanted to meet me and get acquainted, or that's what Linda told me, so—"

For one unguarded instant her face was stricken. "Is that what Linda told you? Beautiful! She told me this morning that you were the one who phoned up last night out of the blue and said you wanted to see me!"

It was very still inside the car.

"Oh, Christ!" Mick said softly.

"It's perfectly all right," Killian said, staring straight ahead of her. "Linda ripped us both off. Actually, it's my fault, I should have known."

From somewhere in the street behind them, a car horn honked impatiently.

"Look," he said awkwardly, "I really did phone your mother last night, of course I—"

"Please don't feel you have to lie now to spare my feelings or something stupid. Lately Linda's been hatching up all sorts of plots for the good of my psyche. With a little help from Marv. I should have guessed that this was her idea the moment she brought it up."

The imperative horn behind them had been joined by others.

Mick stared at his hands upon the wheel, and Killian picked at a loose bead on her purse.

"And so it goes," she said suddenly and laughed.

She turned to Mick then, chin lifted, her face grave and composed in the illumination of the flickering coffeehouse sign.

"Thank you for the drive," she said with quiet dignity. "I don't know what else to say except that I'm truly sorry you've been put to all this inconvenience."

"Oh, for God's sakes! Look, I'm the one who's sorry, I—"

She laughed again, a little shakily. "Don't! The world is full of sorry. Let's not be sorry, either of us, not for any of it. I'll promise not to be sorry if you'll promise not to be sorry. All right?"

She reached out her hand to his upon the steering wheel and, before he realized her intention, leaned over in the seat and kissed him on the mouth. The next instant she had the door open and was alighting from the car. Mick grabbed at her coat-tails, yanking her unceremoniously back inside, and jammed the car into motion. At the corner he turned away from the clogging traffic and down a steep hill into a warren of residential streets.

He drove aimlessly for several minutes, then cleared his throat and spoke. "Okay. I'll admit it was a jolt for me, seeing Linda tonight. I didn't expect it was going to be, but it was. Somehow I couldn't just walk out the door and put it all out of my head. I didn't mean to be rude to you or make you feel I was pumping you about things that are none of my business. You were somebody who could fill in the picture for me, and that's all I had on my mind for a while. It was damn nice of you to be so patient with me, and I owe you an apology. All right?"

He glanced at her briefly in the gloom and saw only her long, smooth hair, her face turned away to the window.

"Hey, you're not crying, are you?"

"Of course not," she said scornfully.

He continued to drive, shuttling back and forth through the dark, winding streets. After a time he said, "About the rest of it, if I've never thought much about meeting you, it's because it never occurred to me that you'd be interested in meeting me. I suppose you must have felt the same. Now here we are, and what difference does it make who told what to whom to set it up? If you really want to go back to that joint on the Strip, you've only to say the word, but since we're here, why don't we start all over again and have a go at it? It doesn't have to be any big deal, does it? Maybe we'll find out inside of an hour that we bore the hell out of each other."

She remained silent, and Mick snapped his lighter at a new cigarette.

"I've been meaning to tell you, you look real great, by the way. I like you a lot better in these clothes than that getup you were wearing this afternoon."

She turned her head at last. "Those others were just my ethnic clothes," she said neutrally. "I was visiting friends in Venice."

"Hey, does this mean you're going to forgive me for acting like such a shit?"

"Don't be silly. I was just as uptight about Linda as you were, you know. I've been behaving in a pretty shitty way, too."

They smiled at each other then with a tentative and cautious approval.

"So where do we start?" Killian said. "Hello, progenitor! Or at least I'm told that's who you are."

"I know what you mean. Seems damn peculiar, doesn't it? All I remember is a baby in a basket with a lot of ruffles, and that's not much help either. Apparently we both have to take Linda's word for quite a bit at this point."

She laughed. "I know. Fantastic! At least you remember a baby in a basket. I didn't even know you existed until I was eight. Marv was all for telling me from the beginning, but Linda wouldn't hear of it. Not until Marv convinced her one night that I'd overheard part of an argument they'd been having. Poor Mommy-doll! She still funked the whole thing, so it was Marv who had to tell me."

"That must have come as a shock. It must have been really rough for you."

"It wasn't like that at all. I think I was more relieved than anything. Practically everyone I knew at school had divorced fathers, I'd often wondered why I didn't. I didn't tell that to Marv, though, he was trying so hard to make the adoption seem like such a cozy, loving thing so I wouldn't feel deprived."

Mick turned again briefly to look into her face. "Most divorced fathers come to visit kids. Didn't you think I was a son of a bitch for walking out of your life completely?"

"Never," she said promptly. "Children are very clever about emotional things. My best friend in those days was a girl named Chris, and I used to make up marvelous stories to tell her about how much you wanted to come to see me but Linda wouldn't let you. I must have had a terribly healthy ego, mustn't I? I really believed it. I used to feel really sorry for you, off somewhere pining away, wanting to see me and not being allowed to. Fantastic! Actually, you never pined the least bit, did you?"

And then she added quickly, "I mean, under the circumstances, how could you possibly have? How could you possibly have fantasized any meaningful relationship with a baby in a ruffled basket!"

"I went to Europe the year of the divorce," Mick said evasively. "Even before that I was pretty uninvolved. Linda was probably dead right about all this, you know. Shapiro was a better father to you than I ever would have been."

Killian shrugged. "Now that is something we're never likely to find out, isn't it?" she said cheerfully. "Anyway you were always a marvelous fantasy figure for me. When I was twelve—puberty, you know—and spending most of my time being pissed off at my parents, I used to steal pictures of you from car magazines in drugstores and sleep with them under my pillow. I made up the most beautiful stories about how I would run away and come live with you and you would love me madly and understand me completely and we'd be divinely happy ever after. It was really marvelous; it carried me right through to real boys and sex. I was the lucky one, you were stuck with that baby in the basket."

"Serves me right. I should have had enough imagination to think of you growing up. Actually, I never did. I suppose part of the trouble is, I've never known many kids. Except for the car freaks, and they're usually boys."

"Well, so much for archaeology. At least now we've gotten all that out of the way."

"Archaeology, that's your thing, isn't it? Or so your mother told me."

"It was anthropology, and someday I may go back to it. At the moment I'm rethinking what I want to do with my life."

"Goddamn it!" Mick hissed suddenly, slamming his hand hard against the dash.

"What is it?"

"Just one time," he said, "you'd think if someone was going to insist on loaning me a car, at least they'd loan me one that was halfway useful for driving around in a city."

He cut sharply to the right side of the street and up over the curb, entering the driveway of a restaurant covered with neon.

"Come on," he said as he flung open the door. "We're stuck for a while, so we may as well have a drink or something while we're waiting for this thing to cool off."

He was around the back of the car in time to take her hand as she alighted.

"You're a funny man," she said. "Can you really imagine anyone daring to loan you a Volkswagen? Cars are your thing, after all."

She was smiling as they walked together toward the front of the restaurant.

"Hello, offspring," Mick said, grinning at her. "You know, it strikes me that I'm the lucky one after all. I'll never live up to the guy in the picture under your pillow years ago. But from my point of view, I can tell you already you're one hell of an improvement over that baby in the basket."

"I should hope so!" Killian said. "And don't go jumping to any conclusions for a while yet. I can tell you that there always comes a time when pictures under pillows make very poor company."

"I'm relieved to hear you say that. My God, what have we here!" he added as he pulled open the door. "Fake Italian greasy spoon from the look of it. At least they have a liquor license. How about an antipasto to tide you over till we get to a place to eat?"

"And minestrone and bread and a glass of wine. Perfect! Why don't we eat right here?"

"I'm game if you are. Maybe it's better than it looks."

They were seated at a table covered with a spotted red-and-white-checked cloth beneath a flimsy wooden trellis festooned with huge clusters of plastic leaves and grapes. After an animated conversation in Italian with the waiter, punctuated by an effusive handshake, Mick said, "I'm told the specialty of the house is cannelloni. Want to try?"

"Marvelous."

When the food and drinks were ordered and the waiter had departed, they surveyed each other unabashedly in the candlelight: a compact, muscular man in a tweed jacket and dark turtleneck, unruly blond hair, weathered, youthful face, eyes bright blue behind the tinted lenses of his glasses; a tall girl in a modish, buttery colored pantsuit, a string of turquoise beads at her throat, long, smooth hair and strikingly rich, dark coloring. And common to them only a similar air of energy and vitality.

"You know, I'm really enjoying this," Mick said. "I didn't expect to, but I am."

"I thought I'd feel strange and uncomfortable," Killian replied. "But I don't at all. May I have one of your cigarettes?"

"Have one of your own if you like."

"I don't really want to. I only did it in the car because I thought it might bug you."

They both smiled openly.

"So. Your mother tells me you were in court yesterday filing for a divorce. Or is that something you'd rather not talk about?"

"Of course not. Except it's really all so dull. Just a run-of-the-mill mistake. I married a fish."

"That's hard to believe. Looking at you, I'd say he must have been a pretty stupid character then."

"I didn't mean it that way. Sexually, we were very suited. But water is Pete's true element. I happen to be fire. Earth and fire."

"Meaning what exactly?"

"Meaning we didn't get on. Actually, I don't think I really want to be married. Not to anyone, ever. Though someday I will want to have a child."

"Why not? Girls seem to have all the options these days. You sound like women's lib, are you?"

"I'm not an activist of any kind. That's part of my problem. I think it's a holdover from growing up in the sixties. Fundamentally, I'm just a leftover flower child, a genuine love and peacenik. Sometimes it makes me feel very old."

"I shouldn't worry about that if I were you. Tell me about this Pete guy, though, how long were you—"

But she was already saying, "How do you happen to speak Italian so fluently? I thought it was England where you'd mostly lived."

"Occupational. And then I lived with an Italian girl for a long time. How about you, are you good at languages?"

"I have an ear for rhythms, but I'm very poor at grammar. The one I'd love to learn is Chinese."

"Damn good! Take you a few years though from what I hear. So tell me more, what do you do for fun? Ski, surf, anything like that?"

"I've never been very into sports. Just the usual things you learn when you're a child. Pete taught me to scuba dive, but I always get a very claustrophobic feeling under the water. My real one thing is t'ai chi ch'uan."

"What's t'ai chi ch'uan? Is that the kung fu thing with the poles?"

"That's very good! Actually, it isn't, but you're close—"

An hour later, as they were lingering over espresso cups, Mick was saying, "So that's about it. To make a go of car building you have to be super at engineering. And/or at business. I found out that I'm not all that good at either. Between you and me, I also found out that it bores the hell out of me. So what now? Like you, I'm at a place where I have to do some rethinking about my life."

"It's very difficult, isn't it?" she said. "It always comes back to this same thing, the only dependable and unchanging thing about life is that it's forever changing."

"I'll buy that. The trick is being able to recognize it when you've finally reached the end of something. You're very serious about this yin-yang business, aren't you?"

"Of course."

"Well, it certainly fits everything I've ever been able to learn about human life. I like the part about inner balance and the energies and all that, too. Maybe I haven't exactly followed all you've been saying, so don't get mad at me if I say it sounds a bit more like sitting back and letting things happen than going out and living your life. I'm not so sure I approve of that at your stage of things."

Killian laughed. "That's not exactly true," she said. "Anyway, you needn't worry. All my life I've had a terrible tendency to roar off and do things without stopping to think them through. That's why the *I Ching* is so good for me."

"What does your book say that you should do with yourself now, incidentally?"

"So far I've been afraid to ask. I only throw the coins for unimportant things, it's a way to learn the hexagrams. For a really important thing, I'd never ask unless I was desperate. I mean like real survival."

"I see," Mick said, amused. "Or, actually, I don't. What the hell kind of oracle is that then?" He looked at her across the tabletop. "You know, I get the idea that your marriage is still a pretty tender spot with you. According to your philosophy, it would be just as bad a mistake to walk away from something too soon as it would be to hold on to it too long, right?"

"Naturally." She was silent then, drawing small indentations upon the checked tablecloth with her fingernail. "Actually there was more involved than just run-of-the-mill differences between Pete and me, though."

"I'd guessed that. Look, you needn't talk about it unless you want to, you know."

"No, it's just that I haven't talked about it very much to anyone." She hesitated again, and at last she said, painfully, "You see, Pete and I had this very special relationship. I know people always say that, but we really did. Then something came up, a sort of crisis thing, that involved me spending a day or so with an old friend of mine, a man who— Well, it was Rob, the man I told you about. The first real loving sex I ever had in my life, years before I even met Pete. Anyway, when Pete found out I'd spent this time with Rob, he—" There was a tremor in her voice. "Well, Pete just assumed that I was making love with Rob again. I mean it never once seemed to cross his mind that it could be anything else."

Mick waited for her to continue, but when she did not, he said gently, "I realize your generation is supposed to be more relaxed about these things, but from my point of view, there are worse crimes in this world than a guy being jealous about a wife he's a lot in love with. Especially when it's an old boyfriend. You mean Pete wouldn't believe you when you told him the truth?"

She was still silent, absorbed in her pattern of scratch marks on the tablecloth.

"Hey, you did tell Pete the truth, didn't you, and give him a chance to say that he was sorry and all that?"

She looked up reluctantly at last. "Not exactly," she said.

"The day after it all came up, I phoned Rob and told him the marriage was over. By the time Pete got home that night, we were in bed together for real."

"Hoo boy!" Mick said incredulously. "I'll bet you never stopped to look that one up in your old Chinese book, did you!"

"What was there to look up?" Her voice cracked. "Special relationships between people are terribly fragile along with being terribly rare. They can't ever be put back together again, can they? Like poor Humpty Dumpty, not by all the king's horses nor all the king's men! And once you've had this very special thing with a person, how can you settle for a second-rate relationship with him later on?"

Mick looked at her, searching for words, but at last he merely said, offhandedly, "Well, there are relationships and relationships. You know, I think what we need right now is a drink."

"Anyway, tell me now about you," she said. "Tell me about the most special relationship you've ever had in your life and what happened to it."

Five minutes later he was saying, "So when Gina died, it left a pretty big blank in that part of my life, obviously. Oh, the last year I went racing, there was a German girl. Not exactly what I think you mean by 'loving sex,' but very pleasant. As a matter of fact, I ran into her again last year and we spent a great holiday together. At that favorite spot of mine in Austria I told you about. I'd like to take you there one day. But nothing really important or all that satisfying either. It's funny, though, just this afternoon I ran into a woman out here, the first time since Gina that I've met a woman I'd really like to know better."

"Marvelous! Tell me about her."

"Uh-uh. I'm superstitious. Anyway, it's too soon. And I gather that she's married."

They fell silent, and Mick teetered back in his chair against the trellis-covered wall.

"Damn," he said. "This is great. Why didn't we get around to it years ago? Think of all the time we've wasted."

"I know, it's the same for me," she said. "How many people in this world can you feel really close to? What is it they say, 'I feel like I've known you all my life.' But then, in a funny way, perhaps I have."

He dropped the chair legs onto the floor abruptly. "Come on, let's get out of here. There's something I want to show you, a place I want you to see."

They walked hand-in-hand back to the car. Once they were driving again, their conversation dwindled into companionable silence, Killian leaned close to him in the bucket seat.

"Hey," he said suddenly. "You said you were meeting some people. Maybe you have other things to do tonight."

"Strange," she said. "At this moment I can't think of one other thing I'd rather."

"Good."

"What about you?"

"Can't remember a thing I'd rather," he said, grinning.

"Good. What is it that you want to show me?"

"You'll see in about one minute. It's an old house that belonged to my aunt."

"Linda once told me that you were raised by an aunt. Is this the house where you lived when you were a child?"

"I suppose you'd say Theo raised me. I spent most school holidays here. My father died in a plane crash when I was thirteen."

"Your aunt doesn't live here anymore?"

"She died this summer. She was my great-aunt, actually, my grandfather's sister. I'm sorry as hell now that you two never got to know each other. She'd have liked you very much."

"That's something you can never really be sure about with people, isn't it?"

"I'm sure. She would have said you had spirit. Theo was always very high on girls with spirit."

"Do you mean spiritually developed?"

"No, it's an old-fashioned expression. She meant full of fire, spit in your eye, and all that."

"Oh, yes. Beautiful! But I thought it was horses that had spirit."

"As I remember, horses, according to Theo, were either cranky or willing. Girls had spirit."

"She sounds divine. You were very fond of her, weren't you?"

"She was great. I'll show you a picture of her in a minute. Here we are now."

He parked the car under the low-hanging tree limbs, and a moment later they climbed the steps at the front of the house.

"Fantastic!" Killian said when they were inside. "What a really marvelous, funky old house! Did you slide down that banister when you were a little boy?"

"Sure," he said, grinning. "Try it, if you like. Very tame though. What I used to like better was climbing to the roof of the gazebo in the garden. I'll show you that, too, in a minute."

"It's an incredible house. Like a movie set. Is that a room under the stairway?"

"Yes." He reached for the light switch. "Theo called this the telephone room. Originally it must have been for storage."

They moved on, drifting slowly from room to room, Mick turning on and off lights as they went.

In the library he said apologetically, "The appraisers have raised hell in here. It used to be a nice room. Theo had a great collection of books on early California."

"Are those pictures of you?" Killian said. "Wait, let me look."

"It really is a damn shame you couldn't have seen this place while Theo was still living here," he said a moment later as they walked on toward the rear of the house. "You can't get much of an idea of it now."

"You love this house, don't you?"

"Well, I've spent most of my life living out of suitcases. It's about the only home base I've ever had."

"Will you keep it?"

"I wish I could. My brother wants to sell it. I suppose they'll tear it down and build a damn condominium or something."

She reached out to his hand. "How sad! You'll be losing a link to your past. Oh, what a marvelous room, absolute Art Nouveau!"

"Theo used it for a breakfast room. There was always sun here in the morning and the garden outside."

He moved to the great bow of window glass and reached for a light switch. "There's the gazebo I told you about. Can you see it, it's pretty dark."

"Beautiful! It is all like something in a movie, *Death in Venice*, or one of those. Did you really climb to the top of that when you were small?"

"And got a couple proper whackings from Theo when I did it, too!"

They stood silently together for a moment, Mick looking out into the old garden and her eyes upon his face.

"What a marvelous little boy you must have been. All fantastic energy and skinned elbows and knees. What did you like most then?"

"Different things. Cars, mostly. I bugged Theo until she taught me to drive when I was nine or ten. What about you? Something tells me it wasn't dolls."

She laughed. "Too right! Kittens and guinea pigs and books. And pretending things. When I was nine and started guitar lessons, there was almost one whole year that I was a famous folk singer. That was right after I was a prima ballerina with the Bolshoi and just before I was a terribly dedicated Peace Corps worker in Africa!"

He laughed as he switched off the garden light. "Come on, there's something I especially want you to see."

They walked back through the house, hand-in-hand again, and ascended the winding staircase. On the second floor, he turned on a lamp in Theo's sitting room and then stopped short, confronting a vacant section of wall.

"Oh, hell, it's gone! My brother said he was packing up stuff to put into storage."

"What was it?"

"Theo had a lot of old family photographs on this wall. There was one of my mother I wanted you to see."

"Linda told me that your mother died before you could remember her, the same as hers did."

"Yes. There was this one great picture of her, though, that I've always especially liked. It was taken when she was sixteen. That was back in the twenties, so she had short hair and one of those loose-topped dresses with the straps, but you still remind me of it a lot. Her coloring was like yours and an expression you get sometimes when you laugh. A sort of— Never mind, you'll see the picture one day. I'll get Trav to hunt it up."

"I'd like that very much," Killian said. "This is a good room, you know? It has good vibes. Now show me the room where you slept when you were a little boy."

"It's nothing much like it was in those days," he said as they continued along the corridor. "Theo redecorated it a few years back."

"I want to see it anyway."

He reached inside the door to a light switch, and several shaded table lamps came on. It was a large room, neat and impersonal, the wide bed covered with a dark blue velour spread, the long double chest of drawers filmed with dust. But the tops of the low bookshelves were crowded with trophies, and there were more of them with photographs in open shelves to the ceiling; one wall was covered by a huge and vivid racing mural.

"Fantastic!" she murmured.

"That was Theo's idea," he said apologetically, his eyes upon the photo-mural. "It was the first race I won in Europe."

Killian walked to the open shelves. "I never saw so many thingamabobs. Did you really win them all?"

"Well, it's mostly here. Theo enjoyed the hardware. They're actually not all that interesting."

He was already reaching for the light switch, but she said, "No, wait, I want to see them. They're all symbols, aren't they, of something you were very good at doing and you loved very much."

"I suppose."

He wandered to a desk across the room while he waited, opening one of the drawers to poke dubiously into its contents and closing it again. He sat down upon the edge of the desktop then and lighted a cigarette, watching her as she examined the trophies and photographs, bending to read titles along the rows of books. She came to rest at last at the bed beside him and sat down on the edge of it, looking up at him candidly.

"This is a very impressive room, John Miguel Luis!"

"My God, don't tell me you know about that!"

"Of course. It was in an article once in a car magazine. John Miguel Luis Alvarado y Francisco Sanford. Fantastic!"

"Yeah, it's fantastic all right."

"The magazine said it was a family name."

"I suppose, if you want to go back umpteen years on my mother's side. Apparently she was very large on her ancestor, though. The story goes that when my brother was born, it cost my father a pair of diamond earrings to talk her out of it. When I was born his luck ran out."

She tipped back her head to laugh, her thick, shining hair sliding on her shoulders. "From all that, how could you possibly get to be called Mick? I asked Linda, but she didn't know."

"Just one of those nicknames you get stuck with. It never mattered to me, one way or the other. We are what we are, aren't we, and all names are just the tags people hang on us. Or maybe I only feel that way about it because I started off life with such a damn silly one. You know, the color of that spread is really great for you, you should wear that shade of blue."

"I often do. And I think it's sad, too, you should feel that way about your name. Now that I know you, I can see it suits you very well. A beautiful, extraordinary name for a beautiful, extraordinary man!"

"Why, thank you, ma'am!"

He bent down over the bed, and she lifted her face for his kiss, reaching her arms about his shoulders. He lingered for a moment, his cheek against hers, then stood up again.

There was suddenly a silence between them.

Mick turned away to the desk and opened and closed several of the drawers aimlessly. "Damn, I suppose I ought to sort through this junk. Old letters and papers have never been my specialty." And then he said, his voice light, "Hey, do you know what time it's getting to be! I never meant to monopolize your whole evening. Do you think your friends are still waiting for you back at that joint on the Strip?"

Killian giggled. "I doubt it very much," she said, her eyes upon him warm and faintly challenging. "Especially since I made them up. Actually, I didn't have a date to meet anybody anywhere tonight."

"For some reason I had a suspicion about that," Mick said, grinning. "All the same, I think I'd better be getting you back to town. Your mother will be worrying, won't she?"

"Not in the least. I hadn't planned on going back to Beverly Hills tonight anyway. But I'm afraid I'm the one who's been monopolizing your whole evening."

"Oh, hey!" he said, his face genuinely concerned. "That's not true. It's been great. It's been really great for me, you know that, don't you?"

"I thought it was," she said, "because it's been so great for me. Ordinarily you don't feel like this unless it's a two-way thing."

"I'm glad you feel that way," Mick said. "I really mean that."

"Well, perhaps there'll be other times," Killian said, her voice suddenly colorless.

"Damn right!" he said a little too quickly. And then amended it. "Or at least if it's up to me, I hope there'll be a lot more other times."

"I'd like that, too."

But a mood was broken, a strain and awkwardness between them as they turned out lights and left the house.

Back in the car, Killian gave him directions to the apartment in Westwood, and after that their conversation dwindled.

At last she said, "I expect it was a disappointment to you in some way, wasn't it, showing me your aunt's house in Santa Monica?"

"What? No, of course not. Why do you say that?"

She hesitated, then spoke slowly, choosing her words carefully. "Well, sometimes there are places that have very special and personal meaning to us. We hope to share that with somebody else, and it has to be a disappointment to us if the other person doesn't pick up on our exact feelings and—"

"Oh, hell, no," he said. "I spent a lot of time in that house, obviously I remember a lot of things about it. For you, seeing it like that, empty and for the first time, it has to be entirely different, just a house. How could it be anything else? I just wanted you to see it, that's all. By the time I get back out here again, it may be gone."

"All the same, I have an impression that—"

"No, you couldn't be more wrong. Look, there's something I've been wanting to say to you before this evening was over. I wouldn't presume to try to give you advice or anything like that. It's just how I happen to feel about something. All right?"

"Of course."

"It's about what you told me back there in the restaurant. About your divorce and all that. If I were you, I'd forget the whole thing and go back to Pete. The sooner the better."

Whatever Killian had been expecting, it was not this. She raised her eyebrows. "Why do you say that?"

"Do I turn right here?"

"Yes, it's about five more blocks, almost to the top of the hill. Why do you say that?"

"Well, I don't mean to come on as though I were trying to interfere in your life or some damn thing. It's just my reaction for whatever it's worth. Go back to Pete. Tell him the whole story now and take your chances."

"But I explained to you what happened. Why do you say that?"

He was silent for a moment, his eyes upon the dark road. "Maybe because I've been this whole route before you. That's as good a why as any, isn't it? It's mostly ego or pride, or whatever you want to call it, you know. You're in love with the guy, so bend a little, give a little. It's something I had to learn to do. It'll be worth it to you, that I can promise. At least give him a chance. If you don't, it may be something you'll regret for the rest of your life."

She was very still beside him, and then she said, "There. It's just ahead on the right, those steps with the lights."

He pulled over and stopped before a steep flight of concrete steps leading up to a multi-tiered white stucco apartment building built into the hillside.

"You're not sore at me, are you?" he asked, attempting lightness. "That's the best thing about unsolicited advice, you know, you can always tell me to fuck off with it."

"No, it's perfectly all right. As a matter of fact, I've been thinking about the same thing myself."

"Hey, I'm glad!" He turned to her then and took her hand. "I don't know how to tell you how really bloody marvelous this has been for me, I—" He leaned forward and kissed her lightly instead.

For an instant, Killian clung to him fiercely, then she whirled away and out of the car, plunging up the steep steps without a backward look.

Mick jammed the car into motion, shooting away along the narrow road and on over the crest of the hill.

PETE SPENT THAT FRIDAY EVENING AT THE RESTAU-
rant on the beach just as he had done the previous night. As
the evening wore on, he had the dining room to himself, seated
in a booth in a corner, books spread out before him beneath a
small Tensor lamp, his wide shoulders, fair, unruly hair, and keen
face illumined by that one spot of light in the shadowy room.
Sometime after midnight he looked up, scribbling something in
a notebook beside him, and then, frowning, turned to stare out
the window at the dark water, the tide rising and retreating over
the shining sand.

And so it happened that when Killian arrived he first saw her
as a blurred reflection in the dark window glass. He turned,
stared, his face impassive, then rose so abruptly that he knocked
hard against the table, slopping coffee from a mug over the open
pages of the notebook. For a moment neither of them said a
word.

"I knew you'd come," he said at last, then added in a sudden,
awkward rush, "Scratch that. I hoped you'd come."

She began to speak, stopped to clear her throat, and said, her
eyes large and dark, "I hoped that you'd be here."

"Let's get out of here."

He scrabbled up books and notebook, grabbed his sweater,
and they walked back along the corridor to the front of the
building. Pete reached over her shoulder to the wooden door,
pushing it open, and they stepped out together into the cool,
damp night, moving on to the old convertible parked at one side
of the lot. Pete tossed the books into the rear seat while he

opened the door for her, and Killian clambered in with unchar-
acteristic awkwardness.

"I'm staying at the house out here."

"Charlie told me."

He was pulling on his sweater as he came around the back
of the car and hunting for keys in the pocket of his jeans as he
slid onto the seat. They did not speak again in the several minutes that it took to drive to the beach house, a half mile up the
highway.

The garage door closed automatically behind the car, and
Pete piled out, hurrying in the darkness to help her to alight. He
touched her for the first time then, her hand briefly cold upon
his, then hastily withdrawn. They moved together into the
kitchen, where Pete pushed a light switch. In the sudden overhead illumination they stood awkwardly apart.

"Would you like something to eat?" he said. "There's eggs
and stuff."

"No, I've eaten."

"Hey, you're shivering. Let's go in by the fire."

They walked on into the shadowy living room, lighted only
by a table lamp in a corner and filled with the faint smell of
woodsmoke. Pete went ahead to the fireplace, pushing aside the
screen to poke at the smoldering logs. Behind him, Killian fumbled with the ends of a long crocheted scarf she wore about her
throat.

The fire leapt up suddenly, and Pete returned the poker to
the brass tool holder. "Here, let me help you."

An instant later her scarf and bag had fallen to the floor and
they were holding each other tightly, her head beneath his chin.
For several minutes they stood so, then suddenly they moved
apart, shedding their clothing with hasty, fumbling hands until,
naked, they embraced once more. They made love where they
were, on the heavy rug strewn with shoes and clothes, in the
flickering firelight. They lay for a long time, arms and legs inter-
twined, with no speech beyond murmured endearments. Killian

wept suddenly, and Pete kissed her tears away, drying her cheeks tenderly with his lips and tongue.

When the fire died down at last, they parted reluctantly. Pete pulled on his jeans and went to the garage for more firewood, and Killian, swathed in a dustcover borrowed from a chair nearby, padded barefoot to the bathroom. When she returned, Pete was sitting on his heels on the hearth, a new pile of logs beside him, and she came to stand behind him, resting her hands upon his bare, tanned shoulders.

"I found you some cigarettes in the kitchen," he said. "They're probably stale though."

"Marvelous! But I've given up smoking."

"Great. We'll use them for kindling."

He reached for the package and she caught his arm, laughing, a rich, contented purr in her throat. "Don't you dare!"

"Faker!"

She sat down on the edge of the rug. Pete struck the match for her and then stretched out beside her, head propped upon his hand. The fire flamed up, and Killian loosened a knot at her shoulder, letting the sheet fall away. She smoked in silence while Pete watched her contentedly, reaching out now and then to move his hand lovingly over the curve of her breast or the length of her leg.

"You'd missed me," he said all at once, his voice soft and exultant. "You'd really missed me!"

"Yes, I missed you," she said. "And you'd missed me."

"Goddamn right!" he said fondly.

She threw the cigarette suddenly into the hissing logs of the fire. "Pete—" she began.

"Sssh!" He reached out quickly, touching her lips with his fingers. "Not tonight. We did too much talking altogether, you and me. Tomorrow is soon enough."

She looked at him searchingly for a moment longer and then leaned over to kiss him, her smooth hair falling over his chest. He pulled her down beside him, and she settled her head comfortably upon his shoulder, stretching out her legs, fitting her body to his, rubbing at the top of his bare foot with the tips of her toes. After that they were still, at rest in the warm, rosy firelight, while outside the sea rumbled against the sand and rocks.

Ten minutes later, Pete said softly, "Asleep?"

"Uh-uh," she murmured. "It's a waste of time. I may never sleep again."

He laughed and rolled over to face her, hands caressing, tongue moving delicately through the spiraling convolutions of her ear.

Killian trembled against him and then wriggled suddenly, freeing a hand to unsnap the waistband of his jeans. "We'd better let Peterescu out of here," she said. "Before he busts this zipper wide open!"

Pete lifted his hips from the rug, reaching to help her peel off the jeans while their soft laughs intermingled.

"Good old Peterescu!" he said. "This is an occasion he may never stop rising to. He's no fool, he knows when he's found the way home!"

3
Saturday

MICK AWAKENED SATURDAY MORNING TO THE buzz of the telephone beside his bed. He groped for it sleepily, found it at last, and heard the impersonal voice of the hotel switchboard operator announce that it was eight o'clock. He muttered something, coughed, and clattered the receiver back onto its cradle. The room was dim and cheerless, drapes closed over the windows, clothing strewn across furniture and the top of the opened suitcase. Mick lay still for a moment in the warmth and comfort of the bed, his eyes open and unblinking, then sat up abruptly and flung back the covers. He sat at the edge of the bed, hunched naked and shivering in the chill air, rubbing at his hair. Then he picked up the phone once more to order coffee and rolls, and went off to the bathroom.

Twenty minutes later, when the tray was delivered, he was showered and shaven, answering the knock barefoot in a pair of trousers. He deposited the tray upon the top of a chest of drawers and turned on a light to hunt for change. Once the boy was gone, he pulled a plug of coffee-stained paper from the spout of the pot, poured steaming coffee into a cup, and continued to dress while it cooled.

Ten minutes after that he poured a second cup of coffee and lighted his first cigarette of the day. Fully clothed now, his tinted glasses in place, he sat down on the bed with the small, dusty address book he had retrieved from Theo's the previous night.

At first the name eluded him, and he set the pointer at the letter C and pushed the bar at the bottom experimentally. Given

Theo's orderly turn of mind, he really did not expect to find the name he sought there, and he did not. He closed the lid again, frowning, and concentrated upon it. Holstead, Holliman? It seemed to be an H, in any case, and he set the pointer once more and pushed the bar. This time he found it immediately, recorded in Theo's precise black lettering, "Cynthia Holman," and the number.

Mick hesitated, glancing at his watch, and finally dialed.

The voice answered after the third ring. "Hello?"

"Mrs. Holman, please."

"This is Mrs. Holman speaking."

"I'm sorry to call so early, but I'm just on my way out to an appointment. Did I wake you?"

"No, you didn't. Who's calling, please?"

"This is Mick Sanford. We met yesterday in the garden over at Theo's."

"Of course. How are you?"

Her voice warmed slightly, but it was still more remote and colorless in his ear than he had remembered it.

"How are you? You know, I still feel bad about upsetting you like that, there at the end. I should have insisted on driving you home."

"No, really, it was perfectly all right. And it wasn't your fault, honestly."

"Just the same, I—"

"But I think it's terribly nice of you to think of me like this. I've thought about you, too. Did you take your daughter to dinner last night, and how did it turn out?"

Mick hesitated, squinting against the cigarette smoke. "Actually, I didn't. I chickened out at the last minute."

"Ah! But perhaps it's all for the best. We have to trust our own instincts."

"I suppose."

And then out of a silence, he said, "One reason I called, I've been thinking about this. My brother tells me that Theo had scrapped her will and was in the middle of thinking out a new one when she died. You two were great friends. There must have been things that she wanted you to have. Or that you'd like to have now as a remembrance. I'd like to see that you get them."

"I'm so glad you brought this up. As a matter of fact, I'd been wishing I knew where to get in touch with you. I have some books that belonged to Theodora, and I'm very anxious to return them. It was stupid of me not to think of it yesterday."

"Well, I'm not much of a book collector. If you enjoy them, keep them. But there must be other things. Anything of hers you'd like, I know Theo would want you to have it. If you'd like to think about it, I could call you late this afternoon." He paused. "Or if you happen to be free, maybe we could get together for that drink you didn't have time for yesterday."

"Well, I— Yes, why don't you stop by for a drink then? I'd really feel much more comfortable about the books if you'd at least take a look at them."

"Great. What time would you like me?"

"Whenever's good for you. I imagine you're the one who has a full schedule. My whole family happens to be away today, so it doesn't matter to me."

"Hey, then maybe you're free to have dinner with me. That would be even better."

"That's very kind of you. But I don't think—"

"That's all right. But I would like to stop by for a drink if you're sure I'm not intruding."

"Oh, no. I just meant— Well, you really don't have to take me to dinner, you know."

"I do know," he said. "But I'd like to have dinner with you very much."

She hesitated perceptibly before she answered. "All right. I'd like that, too."

"Great! Is seven-thirty all right?"

"Fine. Do you have the address?"

"No, I'd better take it down." He scribbled briefly on a pad of paper. "Seven-thirty then. I'll be looking forward to it."

"Thank you. I'll see you then."

Mick put down the phone and sat a moment longer, turning the little address book in his hands. And then, glancing at his watch, he rose from the bed.

FOR HALLIE, THAT SATURDAY WAS AN INTER-
minable day. She rose at her accustomed early hour, dressed,
ate a hurried breakfast, and headed out into the dark morning for
the drive to the store where she worked. She went, smiling, about
her duties but was increasingly nagged by the memory of last
night's phone conversation with Tom, when she had met his marriage plans with what she was now certain must have seemed a
particularly wounding lack of enthusiasm. Now that she had rec-
onciled herself in some measure to the idea of his divorce, she
longed to make it up to him. She could not feel at peace with herself until she had. And so the hours dragged by.

Before his departure on Thursday, Tom had left her a pair of
previously purchased tickets for a travel film that evening. It had
been her first thought to give them away, but at the last minute
she decided to use them herself on the theory that Tom would
expect her to and therefore would be certain to phone before she
left for the theater. Hallie hastened home from work at last, still
rehearsing in a corner of her mind exactly what she wanted to
say to Tom when he called. In growing anticipation, she quickly
showered in a trickle of water with the bathroom door left open
to hear the phone and continued to listen for its ring while she
prepared and ate her sketchy dinner.

But the phone remained perversely silent. Hallie's spirits fell
steadily as she watched the clock, and she lingered over her lipstick until the last possible moment before heading reluctantly
to her car. By then she would infinitely have preferred to forgo
the film, but she had invited Mary Marks, a co-worker, to use the

extra ticket with her, and it was too late now to cancel their plan to meet.

It was not a fortuitous beginning to her evening. Since she was late, she had to drive faster than she felt comfortable, hunched nervously over the wheel of her old Volkswagen, swallowing the childish lump of disappointment in her throat. It was past time for the film to begin before she reached the theater, and she was forced to hunt for a parking space in the most remote corner of the parking lot. When she did find a spot, she pulled in too close to the adjoining car and was able to open her door only partway. She slipped out through the constricted space, sidled hurriedly between the automobiles, caught her heel in some small declivity in the asphalt, and fell sprawling to her hands and knees.

For an instant she remained there, stunned, the rough asphalt stinging against her palms. Hallie was not prone to accidents, major or minor; as a matter of fact she could not recall that she had ever before fallen in such a fashion. More shaken by the unaccustomed indignity and sense of helplessness than by any actual physical effect of the fall, she scrambled to her feet, grateful at least that there had been no one to witness her ignominy. She limped off between the rows of parked cars then, straightening and brushing at her coat, her right knee scraped and smarting. A moment later she was waving reassuringly to Mary, who waited outside the entrance, and they rushed together into the theater. Miraculously, the film had not yet started; the lights were just dimming as they hurried down the aisle behind the usher. Hallie slid into her seat, breathless and perspiring, her right knee still stinging, her left ankle twinging, and made up her mind to enjoy the film at least, since she was here.

And she did try. After the first ten minutes, however, her attention began to wander. The vistas of pale beaches, palm trees, bright flowers, and wide, bicycle-clogged streets between pastel-painted buildings all began to seem alike to her and frankly tedious. She wriggled in her seat, felt her scraped knee gingerly, only to discover a hole in her stocking over a scab of coagulating blood, and wished fervently that she had never come. She imagined the telephone at that very moment ringing in her empty apartment. Oh, damn, damn, damn, she wailed to herself.

Then Hallie forgot about the film and even about Tom's phone call. There was a painful throbbing in her ankle that she could no longer ignore, and her foot felt numb and clumsy. She bent down finally on the pretext of retrieving her fallen program and discovered that her ankle was swollen to nearly twice its normal size. Now this is just ridiculous, she told herself. What on earth is happening to me?

A moment later, the film mercifully came to an end. The lights came on, and she and her friend began to make their way up the crowded aisle. Hallie hobbled along as inconspicuously as she was able and dangled her scarf by its corner in an attempt to conceal her unsightly knee. Yes, it was an interesting film, wasn't it, she lied brightly, her morale then plunging to a new low as she glimpsed herself with a sudden savage clarity: a limping old woman with a hole in her stocking, fat, double-chinned, dowdy, and ready to cry.

"Hallie, you're limping," Mary said over her shoulder. "Did your foot go to sleep?"

"No, I turned my ankle a little getting out of the car. It's nothing really," Hallie said gamely. "Shall we have coffee and a bite, or a drink?"

"Oh, Hallie, would you hate me if we didn't have a drink tonight?" Mary explained with a certain gloomy satisfaction that she was still suffering from whiplash from a recent minor traffic accident. Drinks would definitely be on her on some future occasion if Hallie would let her get home to her heating pad.

But of course, Hallie said, squeezing her arm sympathetically and with enormous relief.

By the time they reached the parking lot, however, Hallie was limping so noticeably that Mary broke off in the middle of her description of her physical therapy treatments and demanded a closer look at her friend's ankle. Oh, heavens, yes, she said, her eyes rolling up in sympathetic horror, a bad sprain at the very least. And she should know better than most just what Hallie was suffering since she had become afflicted with weak ankles these past few years. Hallie could only murmur that nothing like this had ever happened to her before. Well, as we get older we all have to expect these things, you know, Mary assured her with relish.

They reached her yellow Mustang, and Mary produced a neatly rolled elastic bandage from the glove compartment, carried against just such emergencies. She presented it to Hallie, together with lengthy and detailed instructions for the care of her ankle until she could see her doctor for X-rays and professional treatment. Hallie listened reluctantly, teetering on her good foot and taking care to keep her skinned knee well hidden.

Mary drove off finally amid waves and chorused good nights, and Hallie hobbled away in the direction of her own car. Thank goodness; now with luck she would be home in fifteen minutes. Even if Tom had forgotten about the theater tickets, it was still early and he would be certain to phone again.

The parking lot had emptied out by then. Hallie paused to wipe away a heavy film of moisture from the rear window with a wad of tissue from her purse, then collapsed into the seat. Inside of a minute, however, it was apparent that her misfortunes were not over. The Volkswagen refused to start. Hallie tried again. She had bought a new battery only several months before; her heart sank. She switched the lights on and off, then tried repeatedly to start the engine. She gave up finally and slumped back in the seat, faced with the dismal prospect of a trek on her painful ankle to find a telephone followed by the long wait in the deserted parking lot for the auto club emergency truck.

She saw the headlights just then, swinging in at the entrance to the lot, and with immediate relief grabbed for the door handle. It was five or six motorcycles, swinging wide into a rapid pattern of crisscross figure eights, motors roaring, polished chrome twinkling in the light. Hallie stopped. Some quality in the anonymity of the riders in the darkness brought her up short, and with a prickle of unease she pushed down the door lock instead. For several minutes she sat rigid, listening to her heartbeats and watching in the rearview mirror the intersecting beams of the headlights like a collection of baleful comets flashing in a night sky.

They were gone as suddenly as they had come, falling into a sedate line at the parking lot exit and disappearing into the distant street. In the deafening silence Hallie breathed again and unclasped her perspiring hands from the steering wheel.

Now this is just ridiculous, she told herself, a bunch of perfectly nice boys on motorcycles who probably would have been happy to help! What is happening to you anyway? And in that instant, by some trick of body memory, she relived the moment of her fall, the frightening helplessness and loss of dignity.

Stop that right now, Hallie snapped at herself. You are making drama out of something perfectly ordinary. You stepped in a hole in the darkness, twisted your ankle, and fell, the sort of thing that people do all the time.

Ah, but not you, some other corner of her mind jibed slyly, not you, Hallie. What is it? Are you trying to punish yourself already for Tom's divorce?

Absolute rot, she flashed back in mounting fury. I don't care what the psychologists say, I don't believe it, not a word of it. And now you, she finished to the hapless Volkswagen, you wicked, untrustworthy old collection of nuts and bolts, I won't have this either!

She tried again, and the engine caught, coughed, coughed again, then began to run unevenly. Hallie coaxed it, feeding gas with the utmost care. The engine continued to run ragged, but at last she shifted gears and backed out. When she shifted the second time, it nearly stalled, but somehow she kept it running and crept toward the lighted exit.

KILLIAN AWAKENED THAT SATURDAY MORNING to the sound of the sea crashing upon the beach. Instantly tensed and aware, she lay still beneath the blankets. She was alone, she discovered, on the mattress that Pete had carried down from the floor above the previous night, and there was an aroma of brewing coffee mixed with the woodsmoke from the embers on the hearth beside her. She rolled over, lifting her arms above her head to stretch, but the air was chill against her skin and she retreated beneath the covers, pulling them back up to her chin. She remained there for several minutes, staring out the wide window into the gray morning, the colorless merger of sand, sea, and sky.

Then there was a careful, muted rattle of pans from the kitchen, and Killian gathered herself up. She retrieved blue under- pants from the floor and donned them and her jeans, moving on, shivering, to rummage in Pete's canvas bag at the foot of the stair- way. When she arrived at the door to the kitchen, she was wear- ing a gray, long-sleeved sweatshirt that came nearly to her knees. The shining kitchen was warm and bright, and Pete, his fair hair uncombed, stood before the stove tending sizzling strips of bacon.

"Hey, you're up!" he said. "I was going to bring you breakfast in bed."

"It smelled too good. I couldn't wait."

There was something guarded between them this morning, and Pete's eyes upon her were appraising. But he held out his arm to her as he turned back to the smoking pan, and she came to lean against him for a moment, her cheek against his shoulder.

306

"Shall I make some eggs?"

"They're ready to go. You can make some toast if you like. Bread's in the fridge."

Killian went to the refrigerator and explored the contents of the large grocery bag. She found the loaf of wheat bread and fruit as well, dumping the oranges, apples, and bananas into a bowl from the cupboard while Pete spread the crisped bacon on a paper towel.

"Shall we eat on the deck?"

"Too cold, I'd think," he said. "But I haven't been out."

"I'll see." She padded off.

She was gone for several minutes while Pete rinsed the steaming pan at the sink and searched for butter in which to cook the eggs. When she returned, her hair was windblown and she carried several stubby, dried weed stalks in her hand.

"Beautiful!" she said. "The air is unbelievable. It's warmer than it was but still too cold for sitting out. We'd better eat in here."

She dropped bread slices into the toaster and carried silverware and paper napkins to a white Formica table.

"So tell me all the news," Pete said, a shade too bright and casual. "How are Mark and Chris? Are they still in Oregon? Their baby must have been born by now."

"No, they came back down here last month. They're fine. The baby's three months old now, a boy. He's so tiny and marvelous."

"Great. What did they name him, Krishna?"

"Gautam, actually." She grinned.

"Hey, your milk's about to boil over." He reached quickly for a knob on the front of the stove. "I think there are some mugs in that cupboard over there."

They were silent for a time, Killian engaged in combining the proper mixture of hot milk and coffee in an oversize yellow mug while Pete divided eggs and bacon between two plates.

"Anyway, they're going to another commune in New Mexico the first of the year," she said suddenly.

"Mark's a very talented guy. Too bad he can't seem to get it all together."

"Is that really what you think?" Killian asked coolly. She was already seated at the table, her feet hooked behind the chrome chair legs and the steaming mug cupped between her hands. "I've always thought that Mark had his head together better than almost anyone I know."

"If you mean his religion, I'd agree," Pete said mildly. "And communal living is great, if that happens to be the kind of life he wants for himself and his family. I just don't think tilling the soil is really his thing, do you?"

Killian shrugged, frowning over her coffee, and Pete carried the plates to the table, sliding out the chair across from her. Otherwise the room was silent but for the muted roar of the sea.

Pete lifted his coffee cup awkwardly. "Well, here's looking at you," he said.

"Yes."

They touched the cups together, gazing at each other with eyes direct and steady. And then Pete reached out and circled her slim wrist with his fingers.

"You're not wearing your wedding bracelet!"

"No." Killian's face was impassive, but her eyes slid away and she bent down to retrieve the paper napkin that had fallen from her knees. "Have you seen Bruce? I meant to ask you."

His eyes were still intent upon her, but he released her wrist. "Yes, I was there yesterday afternoon."

"I haven't been out. I knew Myra would—you know, want to ask a lot of questions and all that. But I phone him every few days. I didn't think you'd mind."

"Mind! Why would I mind? I appreciate you doing it. Bruce needs all the human contact he can get at this point. How do you think he is?"

"I don't know. Sometimes we talk, it's marvelous, he really communicates. Other times, he simply isn't there. Eerie! I honestly don't know. What do you think?"

"I don't know, either," Pete said. "Except I felt like a jerk yesterday. After I saw Bruce, I phoned Sarah."

"You mean no one had told you? Did it upset her, I mean that you thought she was still—"

"Yes. I felt pretty stupid about the whole thing."

"Why should you have? You didn't know." Killian nibbled at a strip of bacon. "Actually, it's fantastic. Sarah's put a whole new life together for herself, apparently just in the last six months. Even her personality has changed. She's very into women's lib. And she's living with this girl now. They seem very close and very loving."

"Oh, my God!" Pete said softly.

"I'd think you'd be happy for her. Sarah was terribly in love with Bruce."

"I know Sarah was in love with Bruce! I walked enough hospital corridors with her, for God's sakes, to know that. I also happen to be the one who sat in the drug ward with her for twelve hours the night she OD'd."

"All right, so what is she supposed to do now? Even in India, suttee went out a hundred years ago!"

"Look, I'm not blaming Sarah for anything. But I can be sorry for the way it's worked out for them both, can't I? I'm not blaming her. Situations change. Obviously people change, too, don't they!"

Pete sucked air in an effort to control his rising voice and anger. Killian, spine rigid, stuck her bits of weed stalks around the edges of the fruit bowl.

"Would you like some more coffee?" she said at last.

"No, thanks."

After another pause, she murmured, "I think I'd better call Linda."

"The phone is disconnected. We can go down to Charlie's in a minute."

"There's no hurry."

"How is she?"

"What? Oh, Linda. She's fine. The same. And your parents?"

"Fine. The same."

"By the way, guess who I had dinner with last night. My father."

"Marv the Knife! How is he?"

"Not Marv. The absolute real thing. In the beginning, there was! Mick Sanford."

"Amazing! How did that happen?"

"Linda arranged it. I expect it was something she and Marv decided would be good for my psyche."

"Oh, shit! Aren't they about ten or twelve years too late?"

"Of course."

"So what did you think of him? Did you like him?"

Killian removed a dried and shredding cigarette from the pocket of her jeans and straightened it carefully for a moment. "Very much. I mean as a human being. It was funny, I didn't get the least feeling of him as a parent."

Pete rummaged for matches in a drawer behind his chair and then leaned across the table to strike one for her cigarette. "Under the circumstances, I don't suppose there's any reason actually why you should. Will you see him again?"

"I don't know. Somehow I doubt it. I think it ended up making him feel uncomfortable."

"I suppose that's understandable, too. He must be an interesting man, though. Everything I've ever read about him, he was one hell of a competitor. That has to take a special kind of ego, hubris, whatever. You've a touch of that yourself, you know."

"I doubt it's an inherited characteristic. Are you implying that I'm some kind of ego freak?"

"I'm not implying anything," Pete said. "I've always loved your ego just the way it is, and you know it." He shoved back his chair abruptly and held out his hand. "Come on, let's go make your phone call. I'd like to get some air."

Five minutes later they were on the beach, jogging along the ruffling edge of the smooth, gray water. The wide strip of sand

was deserted except for a shaggy brown dog who sniffed inquis-
itively at a strand of rotting kelp and, further on, two small children bundled in bright jackets running back and forth under the
watchful gaze of a chilled young woman in a raincoat.

When they reached the restaurant, Pete took Killian's hand,
leading the way up the precipitous dirt path. He gave her coins
from his pocket then and waited, leaned against the weathered
undertimbers of the building, his eyes upon the sea. She
reappeared several minutes later.

"Everything all right?"

She nodded. "The air feels warmer. You know? I think it's
going to burn off."

Pete squinted briefly up at the overcast sky. "Not today.
Maybe tomorrow. Let's go up to the cove, want to? I'd like to
take a look at what's happening out on that little rock reef."

"You're mad! It's been chilly up here for a month. The water's
already freezing cold."

"I have a wet suit at the house. We can stop off."

"All right. Then we'll take some food and have a picnic."

They jogged once more along the water's edge, matching
strides with practiced ease and pleasure, and arrived back at the
house red cheeked, windblown, and breathless. Pete poked up
the fire on the grate and went off to the garage for another armload of logs while Killian cleared away the breakfast table.

A few minutes later they set forth once more, Pete, clad in
the sleek black rubber wet suit, carrying fins and mask, and Killian with a blanket slung over her shoulder and a brown paper
sack of fruit and cheese and bread. They turned this time in the
opposite direction and walked for nearly a mile as the beach
became narrower and the cliffs steeper.

Their destination was less a cove than a small semicircular
indentation in the rocky face of the cliffs. This section of beach
appeared entirely deserted; even the highway was no longer visible. They deposited Killian's blanket and bag at the base of the
cliffs and crossed the rocky strip of sand to the water's edge,

where dun-colored sandpipers skittered away, leaving trails of tiny star-shaped tracks behind them. Killian watched while Pete slipped on the fins and doused the mask briefly in the water.

She shivered suddenly, hugging herself against the wind. "It's so desolate today! As though there was no one anywhere for miles. Pete, be careful, won't you?"

Pete spit upon the faceplate and spread saliva evenly over the glass with his finger. "Why, Mrs. Fallon," he said lightly, "I didn't think you cared!"

Killian was abruptly still, her face rigid as he adjusted the mask. He walked into the water, waddling splayfooted in the rubber fins. The bottom fell away sharply, and an instant later he was swimming with powerful strokes in the direction of the submerged rocks, the tops of several of them just visible above the surface of the water. Killian wept then, tears streaming from her eyes and the forlorn sound of her crying mixing with the sibilant churn of the surf.

She searched at last in the pocket of her jeans for tissue and, finding none, wiped her nose and eyes upon her sleeve. The promise of sun was gone now, the colorless cloud layer was lower overhead, and the wind was cold. She sat down with her back against a rock and covered her bare feet with the blanket, pulling her knees up to her chin. She hunted an apple from the sack beside her and began to munch at it disconsolately, tears still shining on her cheeks. For a long time she sat so, her eyes fixed upon the spot of water around the offshore rocks where Pete surfaced and dove, time after time, as completely in his element as a seal.

After she had returned the apple core to the sack, she rose, walked onto the narrow strip of sand, and turned her back on the ocean. She stood motionless for several minutes, feet apart, spine straight, eyes turned unseeingly to the massive cliffs as if marshaling some calming inner force. When she began to move at last, it was with slow control, lifting her arms out before her to shoulder height, palms turning outward, arms slowly falling back until her hands were at the level of her waist. She turned to the left and back to the right again with a sensuous rotation of her torso, pivoted on her right heel, weight smoothly shifting, stepped out wide upon her left foot, following through after her lifted forearm, knees deeply bent, in perfect balance, the ageless, classic, and beautiful posture of warding off the unseen adversary.

Twenty minutes later Pete swam in, rising from the water like some dark sea creature once his feet touched shallow bottom. He paused to strip away his rubber headgear and caught sight of Killian upon the sand. He stopped to watch, his face contained beneath his wet hair, legs braced against the surging waves.

Completely engrossed, hair blowing in the wind, she moved slowly on through the flowing shadowboxing postures of the Chinese t'ai chi ch'uan: repulse, retreat, ebb and flow, forever turning and returning, as ancient and timeless and a part of nature as the movements of the waves themselves. When she was finished, facing once more toward the cliffs, she took up a meditation posture, arms raised in a still, embracing circle, enfolding some private universe, her face serene. Pete waded ashore then and removed the fins from his feet. Detouring around her, he walked to the blanket and began to rummage inside the food sack. Aware of him suddenly, she focused her eyes again and lowered her arms.

"Oh, hi! I didn't hear you come."

"I missed your t'ai chi, too," Pete said. "It's strange, it's like burning incense, it leaves a fragrance in the house. I missed it."

"I always wanted to teach you."

"Apparently I should have learned."

"So what did you find out on the rocks?" she asked quickly. "Are there lots of funny little sea people living there?"

"Actually not so many as I'd hoped to find." He turned to offer her a slice of bread and cheese. "There's one group you'd like though—"

He caught sight of her reddened eyelids then and the tear tracks on her cheeks and fell silent, his face suddenly grim.

"Let's go back to the house, should we?" she said.

"What about your picnic?"

"It's too cold. I'd rather have a hot shower and sit by the fire."

"All right."

They gathered up their belongings silently and set off down the beach. Pete took her hand once on a rocky stretch where the footing was slippery and uncertain, and after that they walked hand-in-hand. They did not speak again, each apparently enveloped in solitary thoughts.

Once they reached the house, Killian went to turn on an electric heater in a bathroom while Pete poked up the fire. They showered together, soaping each other's backs companionably, lingering to luxuriate in the spraying needles of hot water until the bathroom billowed with steam. They returned to the fire in the living room then, Killian sitting on the hearth to dry the ends of her hair, wrapped in a striped terry-cloth bathrobe she had found in a closet, Pete stretched out on his back beside her. Their lovemaking this time was less urgent, gentler and infinitely tender. After that they were quiet for a time, Killian lying relaxed, hands clasped above her head, Pete propped upon an elbow, his hand moving caressingly upon her body.

"Hungry?" he murmured.

"A bit."

"We'll go down to Charlie's after a while. Have a steak or something."

Killian reached out. "You've gotten thinner, I can nearly count your ribs. You've lost weight even if I was a lousy cook."

"You were a great cook. I was too fat." He tweaked gently at the tuft of dark hair in her armpit. "And you've gotten shaggier."

Killian laughed softly. "You always made me shave."

She paused for a moment, her eyes steady upon him, then said very deliberately, "But some men like it this way, you know. They find it sexy."

Pete froze, his hand falling away from her. After several still, unbreathing seconds, he said, "So. I hear Rob went to court with you."

"It was marvelous. You can't imagine what that court is like, such a ghastly, empty, nothing kind of place. And there was Rob, real as rain, six foot eight in a wild African shirt. That jive judge nearly fell off the bench. Beautiful!"

"I'm sure," Pete said. "You've had a lot of fun and games out of this altogether, haven't you? What was it you'd asked for, nine hundred dollars a month alimony and a two-hundred-thousand-dollar settlement?"

Killian laughed again. "I've been absolutely dying to hear. Did that really bug your mama?"

"Yeah, it bugged her quite a bit." Pete's voice was dry and without expression. "I realized that's why you did it."

"I honestly couldn't resist," Killian said. "Just a going-away present from me to her. Your mama is so marvelous when she gets off on a really good 'I told you so.' It must have been very nearly her finest hour."

"Undoubtedly. It made it particularly pleasant for me, of course." Pete rolled over suddenly and onto his feet.

"All right," he said icily. "Now I have some news for you. The fun and games are all over. You and I are going to talk this out, right here and right now."

Killian sat up quickly, pulling the blanket under her armpits, and for an instant her face looked small and white and frightened.

"What's the use?" she said. "We talked last summer in La Jolla, didn't we? You said yourself we did altogether too much of it."

"Oh, yes, we talked last summer! About everything on God's earth except apparently what's actually involved here. We were both too chicken to take a chance on that."

"It's not a question of being chicken. There are some things that talking doesn't help."

"At least we'll try. Look, why did you come out to Charlie's last night anyway? Because, as I remember it, we made a promise to each other once, sitting there in the back room at Charlie's at three in the morning full of wine and love. We promised each other that if we ever ran into real trouble, if it ever went to smash for us for any reason, we'd meet one last time there at Charlie's no matter what, and we'd try one last time, for the sake of everything we'd had together, to talk it out. I assume you remember that."

"Yes, I remember," Killian said. "It's funny, isn't it? At the time we promised that I honestly didn't believe there was a single chance in the entire universe that that could happen to us."

"My God, do you think I did!" He closed the zipper on his jeans and snapped the waistband. "But come out of the clouds for a minute and consider the facts. You were in court day before yesterday getting a divorce. Don't tell me that we don't have anything to talk about!"

"Pete, it's no use. Nothing has changed at all. I think I'd better just go home now."

He laughed, the sound muffled as he yanked the shirt over his head. "That's wonderful! You mean all this was just a friendly gesture or something, just for fucking old times' sake? And now it's over and you're ready to go home! What do you think I am? I'm flesh and blood, you stick a knife in me and I bleed! Look, I asked you a question, if you didn't want to try to salvage this, then why did you come out to Charlie's last night anyway?"

She stared at him mutely, shivering in the warmth of the roaring fire.

"Come on, be honest," he said brutally. "It couldn't have been because you wanted to get laid."

"All right." Her voice was soft and wretched. "If you really want to know, I came because I thought you would, and I couldn't bear to think of you sitting there waiting for me. Now does that answer your fucking question!"

He stared down at her silently, and for a brief moment his face looked gaunt and years older.

"In other words, you only came because you felt sorry for me. Am I expected to appreciate that?"

"Why do you say things like that! You know it's not true.

Why did you come? You were there when I got there, weren't you? Why did you come to Charlie's last night?"

"Unfortunately you know why I came," he said, his voice suddenly tired. "That's why you knew I'd be there. I came because I happen to be in love with you."

Her eyes were suddenly enormous, dark and blazing. Naked on all fours, she scrabbled for the bathrobe and bounded to her feet. "You sanctimonious son of a bitch!" she hissed. "What do you think gives you the right to talk down to me like that, as though you were a—a little tin Jesus all crucified and bleeding on a cross! We're both here for the same reason or no reason at all."

"Forgive me. Considering what's been happening lately, I have a little trouble buying that. I think you're trying to say that you still love me. Shall we count the ways?"

"You count, you fucker!" She yanked the knot in the belt of the bathrobe, her angry face inches from his. "What is it that you want from me? Shall I put my hand in the fire for you, or would you rather I drowned myself off the end of the Malibu pier?"

"Look, that was a cheap shot, I'm sorry. All right, I'll accept that. We're both here, and for now at least that's enough."

"You'll accept! I don't give a fuck what you'll accept! It's no use, for Christ's sakes, can't you see that? Pete, this is you and me talking to each other like this! When you and I have to try to explain and justify how we feel about each other, there isn't very much left to talk about, is there, or fight for or anything else."

"I said all right. It's a lot of semantic garbage anyway. We're both here. So what happens next?"

"What do you mean, what happens next?"

"The divorce, for instance. Are you going to drop it?"

"No."

"Will you come back to La Jolla with me right now?"

"No."

Pete laughed. "That's letting it all hang out! It doesn't leave us much to discuss, does it?"

"I told you that five minutes ago."

He turned away blindly, bracing his arms against the rough sandstone bricks of the fireplace chimney.

"Go ahead and hit me," Killian said scornfully. "That's what you feel like doing, isn't it? I saw it in your face."

"Damn right!" he said. "I could beat you with my fists. I'm trying not to, but if I did, it might make more sense than anything else that's happened around here in the past twelve hours. Are you going to marry Rob?"

Killian laughed. "You know, you've developed some kind of fantastic tunnel vision. Our minds don't even work in the same way anymore. Divorces and marriages are just words and pieces of paper. What do they have to do with what really goes on between two people!"

He turned his head to look at her briefly. "At least be fair. I'm no more hung up on the formalities than you are and you know it."

"Marvelous! Then why did we marry in the first place? It was your idea, wasn't it?"

"My God, what difference does that make now! In our case, there seemed to be some practical reasons for it."

"Such as?"

"What are you trying to get at? You know what I'm talking about. Family reasons, for one thing."

"Family reasons," she said gleefully. "Aha!"

"Why are you trying to make a big deal out of this all of a sudden? You know what I'm talking about as well as I do. I'm fond of my mother, but I don't have to defend her. She's a pretty frustrated woman, and one form it takes is being overpossessive with me sometimes. I had some sort of dim-witted notion that if I married you, I could keep her claws out of you. Why should I mind admitting that?"

"In other words, we married because of your mama."

"Don't talk shit! We married because we loved each other and wanted to make a life together, and because of the children we were going to have one day. What the hell difference did it make if we went through some kind of a ritual, we'd already made the commitment, hadn't we? Or are you trying to tell me now that I talked you into that, too!"

"Don't be ridiculous! But a commitment that two people make to each other is alive and growing and organic. Marriage is something imposed from the outside, completely rigid and static, it's an absolutely bankrupt institution anyway, it's—"

"You know, I think I'm losing my mind," Pete said conversationally, leaning against the fireplace wall as he stared at her in disbelief. "You and I are standing here having some kind of stupid, illogical argument over whether or not we should have gotten married in the first place! All right, I'll concede I talked you into marrying me. Now you tell me something. The place we are right now, what did some mumbo-jumbo marriage ceremony have to do with anything?"

"Not one single thing. That's exactly the point. And neither does a divorce. That never seems to have occurred to you, but for a while I was actually childish enough to think that if we cleared away all of this—this outside, social-conventional crud— there might be a way for us to get back to basic things. I mean the way it was with us in the beginning, two people who loved and respected and trusted each other. You never seem to have thought of that!"

"You're right, I never thought of your divorce exactly like that," Pete said. "But I'm glad you've brought this up. Let's do talk about some basic things for a minute. Let's talk about one very basic thing, like mutual trust. How do two people live and love together, married or not, without at least a rudimentary system of mutual trust? Jesus, if you had some irresistible urge to spend a weekend shacked up with Rob Wilson in Mexico, why couldn't you have told me about it? We always agreed that sexual fidelity for the rest of our lives wasn't a requisite of our idea of a relationship. Why didn't you tell me? I might not have liked it, but I sure as hell could have lived with it a lot more easily than the idea of you sneaking off to do it behind my back!"

Killian looked at him. The fire popped and crackled cheerfully upon the grate, and the waves outside rumbled over the sand. "Fantastic!" she said softly. "I was right, nothing has changed. We're still exactly where we left off in La Jolla last summer. A divorce hasn't changed anything, and neither has time, or being apart. Nothing has changed at all."

"It's changed this much," Pete said. "Tell me why. Make me understand why sleeping with Rob again was so necessary to you that you could lie and sneak to do it. I was so goddamn happy with you every minute twenty-four hours a day that you were everything I wanted or needed on earth. It never even occurred to me that it was possible for you not to feel the same way. Explain it to me, how I could have been so stupid and so wrong and, if that's what you want, we'll wipe the whole thing out, it never happened."

"You know, you make me sick," Killian said. "I mean ill, like vomit on the floor! It must be a kind of masturbation for you, you must get some kind of high standing there talking to me about love and trust as though you had invented them. I don't think you even know the meaning of the words. You're right, I was too chicken to face up to that before, but now I have to!"

"Don't you think that under the circumstances you're being a little unrealistic? Come on, tell me. Make me understand why it was so important to you and where it was that I failed and we'll work out the semantics for all this later."

She stared at him for a moment, and then she said quietly, with a tremulous dignity, "If you find it so interesting, you can spend the rest of your life working out the semantics for all this. I honestly don't care anymore and I'll tell you why. It just happens that I hadn't made love with Rob Wilson for three years or even thought of it, not until you found out about that weekend in Mexico and blew the roof off. And then, if you'll kindly remember, I didn't sneak. I did it in our own house, in our own bed!"

The room was suddenly thunderously still.

"Somehow I find that hard to believe," Pete said at last, his voice colorless.

Killian was rummaging once more in the canvas bag at the foot of the stairway. "It's true. Whether you believe it or not is not my problem, not any longer."

"But it doesn't make any kind of sense! If you wanted to spend some time with Rob, or if he was in trouble and needed you, whatever, I wouldn't have thought about it twice, and you know it. Rob was one of your oldest, closest friends, when did I ever object to that? But you went to a lot of trouble over that weekend, sneaking around on buses and telling me a string of lies. Why? Why all that shit just for a couple of days in Mexico unless you—"

"You know, it's terribly interesting. Do you realize this is the very first time you've ever asked me that? All you ever had to do was ask."

"All right, I'm asking now."

"All right, I'm telling you!" She pulled a faded yellow shirt over her head and then reached inside the collar to gather up her mane of hair, pulling it free to fall once more over her shoulders. "I went to Mexico that weekend to get an abortion. Isn't that a riot? Some romantic rendezvous!"

"I don't believe it! How could you have been pregnant?"

"I know. I couldn't believe it either. It must have happened when I went off the Pill. Remember when Jenny and I both decided that the Pill was making our hair fall out and we went in together and got the loops? It must have happened then."

"An abortion!" Pete said softly. He sat down in a chair as though his legs suddenly would no longer hold him and stared at her dumbly.

Finally he said, his lips stiff, "Whose child?" And then, an agony in his voice, "No, please! I didn't mean that. You know I didn't mean it. Please!"

Her back was to him, her hands fumbling with the snaps on the waistband of her jeans. "I had to borrow the money from Rob. He went with me to hold my hand. And that's all."

For thirty seconds after that neither of them spoke or moved. Pete laughed. "It's like a resurrection," he said, a tremor in his voice. "For months now, whatever I was doing, in the back of my mind somewhere I was going over every day we ever lived together looking for the reasons. It never did any good, I always ended up back in the bedroom. What else could I think?"

Then the room was very still for a long time, except for the omnipresent roar of the sea.

"Oh, my God, what do I do now?" Pete said in a soft, wondering voice. "Tell you that I'm sorry?"

She made a small sound between weeping and laughter. "Love means never having to say you're sorry!"

"Yeah, I know. The trouble with Erich Segal, he lacked imagination."

Once more the room was still. Her head was drooping, her hair fallen forward to hide her face. But her hands were trembling so badly that she thrust them into the pockets of her jeans.

And then Pete said it at last. "But why didn't you tell me? Why wasn't I there? Jesus, why was it some other man holding my wife's hand when she had an abortion!"

"Why does that matter now? It's all past history, isn't it?"

He was up and across the room in one bound, seizing her roughly by the shoulders, his fingers digging into her flesh. "What are you talking about! Look, I'm not trying to minimize or justify the way I behaved. But you! You were willing to let me believe you were shacked up with Rob rather than tell me the truth. You were willing to put us both through this kind of hell for months. Why?"

Her face was pale and rigid as she struggled not to weep. "I would have told you. You never asked me. The instant you found out I'd been in Mexico with Rob, you took it for granted that I'd sneaked away to make love with him. After that, I didn't care what you believed anymore."

"I realize all that, but that's not what I mean. Let's go back to the beginning for a minute. You never even told me when you found out that you were pregnant. Why?"

"Because I never meant for you to know, that's why. If that— that nasty-minded Bohner woman hadn't happened to catch a glimpse of Rob and me in Mexico while she was down there buying her fucking cheap flowerpots, none of this ever would have happened, would it!"

Pete stared at her. He appeared not far from tears. "I'm trying to understand this. Believe me! Why was I never supposed to know?"

"Because it didn't concern you in the way it concerned me. We were so happy, our life was so absolutely perfect. If I was stupid enough to get myself pregnant, that was my problem."

"I want to understand this," he said. "More than anything in my life. What made it your problem instead of our problem? It was our baby, wasn't it, that ended up dead in a slop pail in Tijuana?"

Killian winced, her face chalk white. "That's exactly the point. If we'd started talking about it, it would have been a baby. As long as I didn't tell you, it was just a—a condition of mine and I could handle it."

"That's pure fantasy and double talk. There may be girls who have the capacity for that kind of rationalization, but you don't happen to be one of them."

"All right. Maybe that is only partially true, I'm trying to be absolutely honest. It would be terribly easy for me, wouldn't it, just to say now that I didn't dare tell you because I was afraid you'd talk me into having it, the same as you talked me into getting married. But that's not the whole truth either. What I really was afraid of was that I might talk myself into having it. I couldn't take the risk."

"Why couldn't you?" Pete said. "I don't get any of this. This is something I thought we had all sorted out from the beginning. We agreed that we both wanted kids, one of our own and adopt a couple more, ideally six or eight years from now. And you were the one who always said that you had conflicts about abortion, so I thought we also agreed that we weren't going to live with nature holding some kind of shotgun at our heads. If you accidentally got pregnant, at least the first time around we'd have the baby and the hell with it. No problems, no hang-ups. Isn't that the way we decided it?"

"I know that's what we decided. I changed my mind."

"Obviously. But you didn't care to tell me about it."

"Don't say that! I wanted to tell you about it!"

"Sure you did! Except you thought it didn't concern me or some damn thing. Or you didn't trust me."

"I never said that. I said I didn't trust myself."

"That's more double talk. It amounts to the same thing, doesn't it?"

He turned away, bracing himself against the wrought-iron balustrade, his shoulders hunched and rigid as though he struggled to endure some fierce physical pain.

She reached out toward him, her face anguished. "Pete, will you listen to me for a minute? Pete?"

"Yes."

"Try to understand this. Please." Her voice was trembling, and she stumbled over words in her earnestness. "It's terribly important that you understand exactly how I felt. From the time I first fell in love with you and started living with you, well, it was really traumatic for me. I felt like I was absolutely merging with you. I felt like I was losing my own identity completely. In a way it was marvelous and I wouldn't have changed it, but it scared me, too. It wasn't your fault, and I realize you didn't feel the same way. Maybe that's because you're more mature than I am, or because you're already deep into the work you want to do and all that. Or maybe women really do submerge themselves more completely in relationships than men do because of— Are you listening?"

"Yes, I'm listening."

"Please listen, because I'm trying to explain to you the best

I'm able. It was nothing you did, even unconsciously. It was me. I expect it was just a matter of me getting used to how it felt to be in love. You know, getting it all together again. But before I had a chance to, I found out that I was pregnant and I went into a panic. I could see myself just sinking out of sight into marriage and child rearing and adoring every minute of it until it was too late, until I'd discover in a few years that I'd lost myself completely and had ended up as an absolute nothing, just some sort of ghastly—appendage fastened onto you and sucking all my life and sustenance from you, and— Do you understand what I'm trying to say?"

"Maybe. Unless this is your elaborate way of telling me that you weren't sure you wanted to stay married to me any longer, let alone have a baby with me."

"Don't be so fucking single-minded! All I'm telling you is, I didn't want to have a baby yet. Not until I'd worked out these feelings and gotten back to being more sure of myself, exactly who I am and what I am. Pete, it wasn't just something that was terribly important to me, it was important to our whole life together. I had to feel that I was my own separate person with my own separate identity again, making a voluntary commitment to you because I loved you and another kind of commitment to raising our children. It was for your sake, too, don't you see? I mean what kind of a relationship would it have been for you if I'd just given up and let it happen, until I was absolutely dependent on you and living my whole life through you? Then it's not even a relationship any longer, it's a trap!"

She paused, watching him, and when he did not speak, she said, "What's the use? I don't think you even understand what I'm talking about."

He turned his head. "Hell, yes, I understand. You didn't feel that you were ready to have a baby when you weren't even adjusted yet to being married. What's so hard to understand? All you had to do was tell me. What makes you think I'd have been any more anxious than you were just then to make such a big change in our life together? Our life suited me just fine the way it was! Why couldn't you have sat down at the beginning and told me exactly what you've been telling me just now? Jesus, why couldn't you do that! Well?"

Killian was silent. She licked at her lips, but her eyes did not flinch from his. "Because I was afraid," she said. "Because I was afraid that in some part of your mind you would think it meant that I didn't love you enough, or in the right way. And then I was afraid that, out of guilt, I'd insist on having the baby just to prove to you that I did."

"Oh, Christ!" He turned away blindly, slamming down his fist upon the flimsy metal balustrade so that it shook up the entire flight of steps. "It always comes back to the same thing, doesn't it? You couldn't trust me!"

"Trust!" Killian said. "I'm sick of that word! Do you know what I think? I think you're the one. I think you are absolutely totally unable to really trust anybody ever!"

"You may be right," Pete said. "I've just had a crash course in what it's all about from you. You sneaked off to Mexico behind my back and had a baby of ours killed and then when some of your lies caught up with you, you let me spend the next four months believing that our marriage had been so highly satisfying to you that you had to fuck around with Rob Wilson on the side!"

"I killed our baby, as you seem to like to put it, because I loved you more than I loved it! You believed exactly what you wanted to believe about me. Apparently you didn't know me any better than that or have any more respect for me as a human being!"

They stared at each other for a moment mutely, with identically anguished and bewildered faces.

"How could you!" Killian said. "How could you think our marriage meant so little to me? I thought you knew me better than I knew myself!"

"I begin to think I don't know you at all. What's more simple and human and loving: you make a baby together, you abort it or you have it together. What made you think you had the right to go off and do that by yourself?"

There was another pain-filled silence between them until Killian said, "You know, I really think you have some kind of hang-up. It's probably because of your parents' marriage. It's not my fault that you grew up listening to your father tell lies to your mother while he was off having affairs."

Pete sat down on one of the lower steps. "Now that's about as pertinent as me telling you that you have this exaggerated fear of a marriage relationship destroying your identity because of the way your mother's life has turned out. Unfortunately, neither of us is in a position to argue it. It won't hold up, though. You're not your mother by a million miles and, God knows, I'm not mine. Nor my father either. If we've fucked up our marriage, it's our own responsibility."

Killian walked away to the fire. She stood for a time with her back to him, rubbing at her arms as though she were cold.

"What shall we do?" she said finally, her voice soft.

"I don't know."

"Does knowing about the abortion make you feel different about me?"

"I'm not sure. I never thought I'd be sentimental about an abortion. Maybe it's finding out about it, fait accompli. Now I keep thinking of a dead baby."

Killian was very still for an instant, and then she nodded. She turned and began to gather up her belongings briskly, scrambling into her denim jacket, slinging her purse strap over her shoulder, and wrapping the crocheted muffler several times about her throat.

Pete did not speak or move.

When she was ready, she paused to light a cigarette from the crumpled pack.

"Do you want me to drive you back to town?" he said then.

"No, I'll hitch, or phone from Charlie's."

"If you'd rather."

"I'm wearing one of your shirts," she said. "I'll mail it. Or maybe I'll bring it down to La Jolla myself. In a few weeks. Shall I?"

He looked up at her, and all at once the puckered line of white appeared across his upper lip and slowly lengthened, livid as a scar slashed across his tanned face. "That's not good enough," he said harshly. "Either you come home with me now and we find out if we're able to heal each other, or we leave it the way it is."

She did not even hesitate. "Fine," she said, nodding again. "If that's the way you want it. By all means. I'll mail the fucking shirt."

She turned away and walked quickly to the glass door onto the deck. With the door open, however, she paused once more.

"Pete?"

And then she said, her back to him, "I should have asked the *I Ching* before I went to Mexico, you know. I wish now that I had."

She waited, but he made no sign or answer. She went out the door and closed it softly behind her. And then she ran, head ducked in the drab, misty twilight, clutching at her bag and floundering in the soft sand.

AN HOUR OR TWO LATER MICK PARKED THE RED sports car in front of the house in Brentwood and trod up a cement walk strewn with fallen sycamore leaves. Cynny answered the door promptly, greeting him with her smile.

"How nice," she said, holding out her hand. "Come in out of the chill. I'm so glad you're a native, it's a bore always having to apologize for this kind of weather to out-of-towners."

"Actually, after London, this seems pretty balmy anyway. You know, it's damn nice of you to have dinner with me on such short notice."

"It was nice of you to ask me. You're rescuing me from a TV dinner or worse. Let me take your coat, we've time for a drink, haven't we?"

He glanced at his watch. "I'll leave it to you. I made a reservation for about now at that Chinese place on Wilshire. Do you think we should get on over and have a drink there?"

"Maybe we should. It's a Saturday night, so they'll be crowded. We can have a nightcap here later. I'll get my coat."

She disappeared through a doorway, and Mick, jiggling keys and coins in a trousers pocket, glanced about briefly while he waited: a wide hallway with a tall bouquet of chrysanthemums on a gleaming tabletop at the foot of the stairs, a glimpse of a large, uncluttered living room with a wide fireplace, comfortable, cheerful, and unpretentious.

Cynny reappeared carrying a black shoulder bag and a white leather coat with a shaggy sheepskin lining.

"If there's someplace else you'd rather have dinner, I'm open to suggestions," he said as he held her coat. "Half the places I remember seem to be out of business. A friend of mine recommended Madame What's-her-name's."

"No, I think you'll like it. It's very pleasant, and the food is marvelous." She checked her purse briefly for keys and then reached out to several light switches on the wall. "I'd better turn these on," she murmured. "Even Putzi, our dog, is away tonight. It's ridiculous, isn't it? If I were a burglar I'd make a beeline for the most brightly lighted house on the block, wouldn't you?"

"Don't apologize. I've been visiting a friend who's just built a new house. The first thing he showed me was the burglar alarm system. He's got the damn place wired up like the Louvre!"

"Isn't it awful? We really are all paranoid."

She checked the door latch after her, and as they started down the steps into the misty darkness, he stopped short. "Oh my God!" he said. "What in hell is that!"

They stood silent for a moment, looking through the bare tree limbs to a gargantuan vapor trail glowing orange-red against the dark western sky, terminating at one end in a tear-shaped, iridescent cloud, all of it like some giant, malignant tulip flowering suddenly in the sky upon an implausibly twisted stem.

"It's a missile shoot from Vandenberg," Cynny said. "Or Mugu. It's beautiful, isn't it? That pearly, pale-colored patch of vapor is from the second-stage firing, I believe."

"What do you mean, missile? What sort of missile?"

"I've no idea. It's always terribly classified."

"You mean this sort of thing happens often?"

"Now and then. We do have the Pacific Missile Range right at our doorsteps, you know. Oh, look, it begins to look like a bear! See, a bear sitting up on its haunches!"

"Some bear!"

As they continued to watch, the vapor cloud spread and diffused like a giant oil slick in the sky, rainbow spectrums glittering at the edges.

"You know, that's one hell of an ominous sight," Mick said.

"I suppose it is. Nancy, a friend of mine, says these rocket trails are the hieroglyphics of our time. She always says that someone had better damn well learn to decipher them and soon, before the time runs out."

They watched for a moment longer, then he took her arm as they descended the shallow steps. "I must have been away too long," he said. "Lady, I begin to think you live in a pretty spooky world out here!"

Cynny laughed and said, "Ah, what a gorgeous automobile! It really is the most beautiful one I've ever seen. I'm dying to ride in it."

Fifteen minutes later they were touching glasses across a tabletop in the crowded, dimly lighted restaurant.

"Cheers," Mick said. "So tell me. Have you made up that list of things you'd like to have from Theo's?"

"No, I haven't," she said. "I'm sorry."

"Maybe it would be easier just to go over and browse around a bit."

"Oh, Lord!" She put down her glass, her face faintly troubled, and stared for a moment at her fingers, interlaced before her. "I hope you'll understand this. It's really so nice of you, and I do appreciate your thoughtfulness and your generosity. I loved Theodora, and I'll always have marvelous memories of her and of that house. But to go and—and scavenge among her possessions now, I—"

He reached out his hand to hers. "It's all right. I feel the same myself."

"But you shouldn't! It's so sad it turned out like this. Theodora always meant for you to have that house, and everything in it. I'm sure you know that."

Mick shrugged. "It's just as well it turned out like this. I'd probably have felt I ought to divvy up with Trav anyway."

They were both silent for a moment, then Mick said, "At least you have some of her books. Are you sure there isn't something else? I really feel badly about this."

"Please don't," she said, her face distressed. "All right, one thing then. If you're sure it isn't something you want, or your brother. Theodora had an old paisley shawl that she loved very much. She always kept it on the little sofa upstairs. I'd love to have that. It would remind me of her."

"Hey, great! I'll see that you get it before I leave."

"Marvelous. There's truly nothing I'd rather have."

Mick watched her across the table, admiring the poise of her dark head above the white silk shirt she was wearing, the contrast of her pale eyes behind her dark lashes. She was smiling, but it suddenly occurred to him that recently she had been weeping. Her eyes were carefully made up with a touch of pearly eye shadow, but even in the soft light of the restaurant he could see a telltale puffiness about her eyelids and a hint of moisture in her eyes as though she were not far from tears once more.

"Look here," he said abruptly. "I'm afraid I've depressed you with all of this. I didn't mean to. Let's talk about something else, shall we? Tell me about you. Thanks to Theo, I have a feeling there isn't a great deal about me you don't know by this time. You'll have to admit that you have me at a disadvantage."

"It isn't as bad as all that, honestly. And Theodora only talked about you because you were her absolutely favorite relative. She adored you. And admired you very much."

"I think that last is putting it a bit strong. The going opinion of me around the family has always been somewhere between ne'er-do-well and oddball. At least Theo was always loyal."

"She was considerably more than that," Cynny replied. "I always remember something she said about you once. She said she admired you with all her heart because you were the complete man of your century. Because, she said, when the history of the twentieth century was written, it would be the story of man's relationship to his machines. And no mechanical contrivance that man has yet come up with, she said, involves his total being more completely, body, mind, and spirit, than a racing machine."

"Oh my God!" Mick said incredulously.

"Have I embarrassed you?"

"I'm not sure. You're very good at changing the subject, by the way. It's all right, if you really don't feel like talking about yourself, I'll let you off the hook."

"Of course I don't mind. If you're really that interested." She hesitated. "Let's see. Well, start at the beginning, I suppose. Born in a small town in Connecticut, only child. My father was a lawyer, my mother grew prize dahlias. Terribly nice people, no complaints about my childhood whatsoever. Married my first year in college, just at the end of World War Two. To one of those glamorous Air Corps characters with the bashed-in cap, regular Army, West Point, the whole bit. Once the war was over and we had a chance to get acquainted, it came as a great surprise to us both that we really didn't like each other all that much. Divorced, finished school, lived in New York for several years working for a fashion magazine. Came out to the Coast on an assignment and met Jim. Married him two months later. He's an engineer, electronics. Computers and all that with an aerospace kind of firm. Two children, you know about that. The usual suburban housewife thing. And that's about it. All terribly ordinary."

"Somehow I doubt that," Mick said. "What I'm really interested in are the things you left out of that story, but I suppose it will have to do for openers."

"It's all you're going to get," she said. "Do you really think I intend to squander an opportunity like this? There are dozens of questions about racing I'm absolutely dying to ask you. If you wouldn't find it a complete bore, that is."

An hour later, Mick fell silent over the teacups. "My God, I've been talking your ear off," he said apologetically. "You're either the world's best listener or a bona fide racing freak. Which is it?"

"But I've loved every minute of it," Cynny said. "I think I'm what you'd call a Johnny-come-lately racing freak." She hesitated, loosening a loop of blue lapis beads at her throat. "I suppose I may as well confess. It was Theodora who turned me on to it in the beginning, Theodora and her books."

He watched her glowing face with pleasure, then said, "Are you sure you wouldn't like dessert or more tea or something?"

"No, thank you. It was a marvelous dinner. I've really enjoyed every minute of this, but we should give someone else a chance at the table, do you think?"

"I see what you mean," he said, glancing toward the crowded foyer as he reached for the check.

"I'd like to go to the powder room before we leave. Shall I meet you in the lobby?"

He rose to pull out the table for her.

"Good deal. I'll see you in the lobby then."

When Mick reached the foyer several minutes later, there was no sign of her. He picked his way through the crowd to stand against the wall, fumbling for his cigarettes while he waited. She appeared just then from a side hallway, wearing her white leather coat once more. She paused, looking about her, and when she caught sight of him, she smiled, her face lighting.

Mick went to meet her. "All set?"

"All set. Did I keep you waiting long?"

"No, I just got here."

"Good."

He pushed open the door ahead of her and struggled with it for a moment in an unexpected gust of wind. Outside, while they waited for the attendant to bring the car, the wind continued to blow, whipping at Cynny's long tweed skirt and sending dust and papers flying along the street.

"Oh, hey!" Mick said. "Do you feel that? Now I know I'm back in California."

"What?"

The wind rose again just then in a hard gust, blowing eerily warm against their faces in the night chill.

"Oh, damn," she said. "It's a Santa Ana! All these years in California and I still hate them. Especially this year, when I've been hoping for a rainy November. It's been so long, and we need the rain so badly."

Her voice was suddenly so forlorn, her face so somber, that Mick took her arm again.

The car arrived, and he handed her into the bucket seat. Several blocks down the street, she was still silent beside him, and Mick finally turned his head to look. He found her staring straight ahead, all the vivacity drained from her face.

He waited a moment and then said lightly, "You know, while you were off powdering your nose I was thinking we ought to go see a race. The sprints are running at Ascot tonight, and we've still time to get out there before the hundred-lap main event. I'll admit they're not as glamorous as the sporty cars at Riverside or the big machines at Ontario, but on the other hand, sprint cars on a half-mile dirt oval are not a bad way to begin. Would you like to go?"

"I'm sorry," she said, her voice colorless. "Ordinarily, I'd love to, but tonight I don't think I'm up to it." Then she amended it. "I've been fighting off a headache all day, and it finally seems to have caught up with me."

"I'm sorry. You should have told me back at the restaurant. We needn't have sat around there so long."

"No, that's all right. And I do still want you to come in for a minute and take a look at those books."

"Look, the books are yours. I've made a nuisance of myself long enough."

After another silence she turned to him, reaching out to his arm. "Oh, hell," she said. "Now I've been rude and I didn't mean to be. It's not a headache, I—well, it sounds so stupid and self-involved, but I—have several personal problems on my mind tonight. I really shouldn't have come out to dinner with you at all. I was afraid I wasn't going to be very good company."

"You were great company, and I'm damn glad you did come. Obviously, I realized yesterday that you were troubled about something, and I'm really sorry. Is there anything I can do?"

"You've already done it. You've helped me keep my mind off my tiresome self for a couple hours, and I'm very grateful."

"Sure you won't change your mind about Ascot then?"

"Honestly, I'd rather not, if you'll promise to give me a raincheck." She smiled at him, but her eyes weren't in it, and he nodded to let her off the hook.

"Look here," Mick said after a pause. "I don't mean to intrude, but I gather your family are all off somewhere tonight, and I don't much like the idea of leaving you alone in an empty house when you're feeling bad. Wouldn't you like to round up a friend or something?"

"No, I'm all right," she said quickly. "Actually, I suppose I've been avoiding friends. You must know the feeling. Not that our demons aren't perfectly real while they're still swirling around inside our heads, but when we begin to talk about them, it's like Pandora's box, isn't it? Once you've let them out, you've got to deal with them, and then nothing is ever the same again."

"True," he said. "But then it's been my experience that it sometimes works the other way, too. Those demons can seem pretty damn real while they're churning around in our heads or guts or wherever it is they like to congregate, but once we let them out, sometimes they just dissolve and disappear. Poof, nothing left to deal with, and then we wonder what all the fuss was about."

He was rewarded with a wisp of a true smile. "I'm afraid this particular crew is here to stay." Then she added, "Please, let's not talk about it anymore. I'm sure I've made it sound much more important than it is. I just didn't want you to think I hadn't really enjoyed meeting you and dinner tonight and—"

"I understand."

A moment later he said, "Oh, hey, I've just had another idea. I promised Bob I'd take this car out for a run while I was here, and tonight is my last chance. Why don't you come along? Bring your demons with you, be my guest. If you don't feel like talking, you needn't. It beats sitting alone in an empty house, doesn't it?"

When she hesitated, he added quickly, "I'd take it very kindly if you would come. Now that you've brought up the subject of demons, I can admit I have a small-size crew of them working me over tonight, too, and I don't much feel like being alone."

She hesitated an instant longer and then laughed. "Oh, dear! Demons do like company. Besides, you know how much I love riding in this divine little car. All right, I'll come. If you really mean it about not expecting floods of sprightly conversation."

"Great! Of course I mean it. No social chitchat whatsoever. We'll just drive. Let's go up the coast. Maybe we can find an empty canyon road somewhere and really find out how well this little bomb's been put together."

HALLIE MANAGED TO REACH HOME IN HER AIL-
ing Volkswagen, arriving nervous and exhausted. The
engine had continued to run ragged, there was almost no accel-
eration, and at every red light along Wilshire it nearly stalled.
Reminding herself of Tom's oft-repeated warning never to
entrust a mechanical difficulty to attendants at an unknown gas
station, she nursed the car along, praying only that she might
reach the haven of her own garage.

Safely parked there in her own stall, she turned off the labor-
ing engine with enormous relief and clambered out upon her
swollen ankle. She lingered for a moment beside the fickle,
downtrodden vehicle, and finally she sighed and patted one of its
fenders forgivingly. Doubtless Tom was right, the car was just
too old. And as he had warned her, it likely had been foolish to
spend the money recently on repairs. For what on earth was she
to do now? Certainly she could not manage another major
repair bill so soon. She did not remember that her impending
marriage to Tom was likely to take care of this.

She was just unlocking her apartment door when she heard
the long-awaited ringing of the telephone. She got in as quickly
as she was able and eagerly scooped up the phone. But it was
merely a lonely and talkative woman friend. Hallie explained
apologetically that she was expecting an important call and put
down the phone again with a promise to call back in the morning.

Sitting in the dim, empty apartment for the second time that
evening, Hallie was on the verge of tears. She hoisted herself up
from the chair and limped off to the radio in the kitchen, switch-

ing on every light in her path, and resolutely turned on an FM music station. She undressed then and cleaned her skinned knee, swabbing it gingerly with antiseptic. Trying not to listen for the telephone, she donned a cheerful crimson robe and returned to the kitchen to tidy up the remains of her dinner.

A moment later, however, when a cherished china cup slipped from her hand beneath the tap and broke into a dozen pieces, Hallie gave up and sobbed out loud, tears rushing from her eyes as she rocked disconsolately over the edge of the sink. She wept for several minutes while the radio played on and then wiped her face with a bit of paper towel. It occurred to her that she need not wait for Tom's call any longer. She could simply phone him herself.

She dried her hands and limped back into the living room, her spirits rising at the thought. She rarely had the occasion to phone Tom—or the opportunity, for that matter—so it was with some excitement that she now rummaged in her desk for the copy of his itinerary. She dialed the number of the motel in Florida carefully, reminding herself that even with the time difference he might not yet have returned for the night. When she reached the motel, however, she was told that he had checked out just after dinner. Puzzled, Hallie hung up and consulted the itinerary once more. She recalled his remark that there was a man he might have to see in Huntsville. Or he might already be on his way back to California. In either case, she reasoned, he likely would still be in transit. She returned the paper to her desk and turned off the light.

It was too late to begin one of a half dozen housekeeping chores that she had slated for this weekend, and still too early for bed. She turned on the educational television channel to a symposium of foreign news correspondents and settled herself in a corner of the divan with her needlework, her swollen ankle elevated on the cushions. But after ten minutes, she found the newsmen depressing and switched from channel to channel, finally shutting off the TV altogether in the middle of a deodorant commercial. She wistfully considered a gin rummy game with her invalid neighbor, but she disliked leaving the apartment in case Tom might still call, and she hesitated to use her telephone for the same reason.

Finally she went to bed and read for an hour, but neither the world of spies and counterspies nor a singularly dull account of an archaeological dig in Iran succeeded in lulling her to sleep, and she eventually gave up and simply turned out the light. A faucet dripped audibly in the bathroom, and there were faint sounds of music and laughter from the apartment building next door. Hallie stared at the shadowy ceiling. She tried to remember whether Mary had advised an ice bag for her throbbing ankle or a heating pad. She longed for Tom, his presence, his voice, his laughter, his touch. And she thought of Nedith finally, and of the impending divorce.

Ten minutes later she sat up angrily, turned on the light, and hobbled off to the bathroom. At the back of a crowded cabinet shelf she found the small bottle of sleeping pills, untouched for two or three years. She examined the bright-colored capsules dubiously, wondering if they were still safe to use, but at last she swallowed one of them, washing it down with a mouthful of tepid tap water, and returned to bed. She read once more, felt a relaxing drowsiness at last, turned out the light gratefully, and this time fell immediately asleep.

The party next door broke up an hour later. There were loud voices from the sidewalk below and a roar of automobile engines. But Hallie slept on.

She dreamed that she was meeting Tom in some vast, beautiful parkland. While she waited she strolled contentedly in bright summer sun along a path between trees and exotic flowers and foliage. Suddenly she came upon a large, gray metal mailbox mounted on a post overgrown with vines. From out of the leaves just beneath the mailbox, she noticed the small, flat, brown head of a snake, forked tongue flickering. In her waking life, Hallie shared the common terror of all snakes and reptiles, but in her dream she found this snake merely charming. She paused to watch, wishing Tom might arrive so she could share with him this spectacle. And as though in answer to her thought, she caught sight of him at that very moment approaching along the path in front of her, carrying his attaché case, his raincoat flung over his shoulder. He hailed her, smiling, and to her disappointment at that instant the snake disappeared. The vine leaves stirred and rustled, and in the omniscience of her dream, she realized with horror that the small snake had been devoured by a larger one, whose gleaming black-and-white-splotched coils she glimpsed moving amid the foliage. Tom, oblivious, came on up the hill to join her, passing the mailbox, and suddenly Hallie saw the black-and-white snake emerge from the vegetation; it was enormous, larger than both her arms together. The snake came straight after Tom, coiled high and swaying, and while Hallie watched, frozen in terror, the snake changed itself into a huge, pale lynx with tufted ears and a cruel muzzle, padding on great deadly paws just behind Tom's back. In a small, strangled voice, she heard herself cry out to Tom, "Don't look, don't run, be careful, oh, be careful, there's a tiger just behind you!" Tom smiled at her tolerantly, the cat prepared to spring, and in her small dark bedroom smelling of roses, Hallie turned, moaning, upon her pillow.

Nedith went to a dinner party that night and returned home late in an uncommonly good mood. She met the private patrol car just as she was slowing her heavy, shining Cadillac for the turn into the driveway and exchanged reassuring waves with the uniformed man at the wheel. She let herself into the house and went directly to the bedroom and the radio before she hung her sable jacket away in the dressing room closet.

A good evening, she reflected as she removed the heavy jade and pearl clip earrings she was wearing, a nice party, a lot of fun. She lingered before the mirror for a moment, admiring her reflection in a sleeveless, low-cut green-and-white jersey pantsuit as she massaged her earlobes.

Oh, damn, she thought irrelevantly for the hundredth time, how maddening about that telephone at the beach. She would like to phone Pete right now, for instance, just cheer him up a little, make sure that he was all right. At least he had remembered to phone her tonight before she went out, although he had sounded a little strange. Remote and not quite like himself. He said he'd been shut up in the house reading all day, so perhaps that was it. He had always had a fantastic capacity for concentration, but he also had the ability to turn it off like a faucet when he was through. Pete normally was such a good-humored boy, talkative and full of fun, a really marvelous sense of humor. She hoped this stupid marriage and divorce thing was not going to change him. There was something Tom had said about him being bitter. Oh, she could wring Killian's neck. If only Pete had never laid eyes on that rotten little hippie.

But, as a matter of fact, Nedith was in too good spirits just then to work up a proper degree of venom, even toward her ex-daughter-in-law. She was humming softly as she hung her suit in the closet, and her thoughts slid away. Nell and Don, that whole crowd for that matter, were always such fun. And you could always count on Nell to serve a divine dinner and then top it off with some marvy low-cal dessert so you needn't feel too guilty about the drinks you'd had earlier. And what's his name, the Ferguson man, her dinner partner, had been a lot of fun, too. He had certainly been attentive enough, he'd acted as though he was quite taken with her, but being just divorced, he was naturally on the make for any reasonably attractive woman. She supposed she had been a bit naughty, flirting with him as she had, he had seemed absolutely taken aback and verging on surly when she told him he couldn't come home with her for a nightcap. Well, what did he really expect? Nell must have warned him that Nedith didn't play around. Of course men never really believed that about any woman, did they? They were all such egotists, they assumed themselves irresistible.

Nedith giggled out loud and pirouetted back before the mirror in her bra and sheer panty hose. Fantastic, she told herself, patting her sucked-in belly approvingly, not a single bulge in the wrong place, if she did say so. Really too marvelous, the way that Ferguson man had practically fallen out of his chair when Don showed the color films from Acapulco last spring and he got the first look at Nedith in that crazy black, three-ring bikini.

Nedith spun away to the bathroom, clad now in a brief, lace-trimmed green nightgown. Before the mirror there she began carefully removing her silky eyelashes and wiping off mascara and eye shadow with moisturized cotton pads. Funny about men, she reflected, that term *cocksure* really fitted every one of them. Oh, not that two thirds of them weren't loaded down with secret doubts about their capabilities, but they were all convinced women were put on this earth to flop down on their backs for them at a moment's notice. It really upset them when a woman wouldn't do it; it was one more example of the stupid ideas men had about what women were really like. It came as a shock to a man to find that there were women who not only had control of themselves sexually but actually put higher value on things besides sex.

Nedith moved faster, deftly rolling locks of her bleached hair around pink plastic curlers, rubbing moisturizing cream into her face and throat, and then her hands, forearms, and elbows.

After all, she was the perfect example, wasn't she, a normal, healthy woman with all the normal, healthy desires, and no one on earth would dream how difficult it had been for her to learn to discipline herself. It had been worth it, though, even though she realized that most of her friends thought she was the most fantastic square in the world. Early on, she had simply made up her mind that she would never give Tom the satisfaction, not if they both lived to be a hundred. Let him go right ahead and make a fool of himself, screwing every woman in sight, that was no reason for her to sink to his level. Every day of her life was proof that it was possible to live by your marriage vows, regardless of what sacrifices you were called upon to make. Besides, she'd have to be insane, wouldn't she, to jeopardize her position legally, financially, and every other way just for some stupid roll in the hay.

"Oh, April showers, they bring May flowers—" she caroled softly. The cream jar lid jammed crooked on the threads, but she did not take the time to straighten it. Leaving the jar uncapped and a comb fallen to the floor, she turned off the dressing table lights and whirled back into the huge bedroom. She yanked down the covers on one of the twin beds without stopping to remove the spread and crammed a wad of tissues under the pillows. She snapped off the radio and then the lights, one after another. When the room was in darkness, only the soft glow of the outdoor lights through the thin curtains, all of her haste abruptly ended. In her nightgown, she drifted across the room, sliding her bare feet through the silky pile of the heavy carpeting. At the chest against the wall, she opened a drawer and groped beneath piles of lingerie until she found it, a long, ridged hard-rubber nozzle, once an attachment of an electric massage machine long since discarded. When her hand closed upon the nozzle, her breathing became rapid and shallow as she closed the drawer again.

"—Isn't raining rain you know, it's raining violets—" she sang in a toneless murmur back to the bed. Beneath the sheet and blanket, she rolled onto her back, shoving one of the pillows beneath her buttocks. She was very still, not even the sound of breathing, as she spread her legs voluptuously apart. She moved the tip of the rubber nozzle slowly and deliberately upward along the soft skin of her inner thigh, across her bristling patch of pubic hair, and gasped out loud at the instant painful and delightful swelling and contraction.

Outside, the wind rose in a hard gust, rattling dry palm fronds and sending a pattern of leaf shadows dancing across the curtains. Nedith did not hear or notice.

MICK AND CYNNY DROVE NORTH ALONG THE Coast Highway, speaking only occasionally above the roar of the powerful engine, absorbed in their own thoughts and the motion of the car. The highway was dark and traffic sparse, and countless stars blazed overhead. Mick drove fast through narrow drifts of swirling sand in the headlight beams, the wind buffeting at the small automobile.

Somewhere above Malibu, Cynny broke the silence and said suddenly, "So tell me about your demons. Unless you'd rather not."

"Mine aren't very pretty, I warn you." He hesitated, frowning. "I—lied to you on the phone this morning. I did take Killian to dinner last night. I didn't expect it would be, but it turned out to be a pretty big experience for me. She was really great. I was the one who blew it. It's no good telling myself now that it doesn't matter to me, because it does."

"I'm sorry," Cynny said, looking at him. "But perhaps it isn't as bad as you think, perhaps you only imagined that—"

"No, I blew it," he said. "You can take my word for it. Care to tell me about yours?"

"All right." She, too, hesitated before she spoke again. "You remember I mentioned that my son had gone off on a surfing trip this weekend. After he left yesterday, I was tidying up his room, and I found a shaving bag that he had forgotten to pack. In it was his marijuana stash. I wasn't all that surprised of course, he's seventeen. But in the sack with the pot was a handful of nasty-looking pills and capsules. I did find that—pretty shattering."

"Oh, hey," Mick said quickly. "But you still can't be sure. Maybe they were just—"

"No. The moment I saw the damn things, it was like the missing piece to the jigsaw puzzle, everything fell into place. The whole change in his attitude and behavior this past year, his weird ups and downs of mood, a lot of things. He's been using them for a long time. I should have realized."

"Oh, Christ, that is a rough one," Mick said. "But look here, I get the idea it isn't exactly an uncommon problem with kids his age. By now there must be a number of ways all set up for working on it and—"

"Oh, yes. It's funny, you read all the articles and go to the meetings, and I've sat on a half dozen committees, but still you don't expect it ever to happen to one of your own children."

"I know." He reached out to her hand comfortingly. "Oh, Kee-rist!" he finished in a roar of disgust.

"What?"

Before he had a chance to answer her it became all too apparent. The engine was winding down, a loss of power that was rapidly slowing the car's momentum.

Mick, grim faced, snapped toggle switches along the dashboard. "It's been off a bit the last couple miles. Now I think we may have a problem."

"Ah, the poor thing!" Cynny said. "It's such a marvelous little car. I hope it hasn't broken itself."

"Marvelous bloody little nuisance! Serve it right if it's chewed up its own valves! They stuck the engine back in it in a hurry yesterday morning because Bob was determined to have me drive it. Great crew of mechanics we have here!"

The car was moving ever more slowly, rocking momentarily in the wake of a huge trailer truck that thundered past to disappear in a galaxy of colored taillights.

"Never mind," Mick said comfortingly. "We'll make it to the

top of this hill anyway, and then we'll take it from there. I haven't driven along here in a good many years. You don't happen to be familiar with this stretch of highway, do you?"

"Not well enough to know what's over this hill, I'm afraid. I drive it often enough, too, going up to Santa Barbara."

The car was moving now at a crawl.

"How about that!" Mick said an instant later. "We're in luck. See those lights about a quarter of a mile ahead over on the sea side? And a nice, long hill to coast down. By the time we get to the bottom, we should even have enough steam to get this sick cow over there and off the highway."

And they nearly did. At some point down the long grade, as their speed increased, Mick swung the car into the center lane. He delayed until the last instant, allowing an oncoming car to pass, then turned the wheels to the left, aiming on a long angle at a narrow dirt driveway. The driveway inclined upward; the red sports car made it nearly to the top, its front wheels onto the hard-packed dirt of a small parking area, and there it came to a complete halt.

"Oh, shit!" Mick said. "Sorry about that. I'd better push the damn thing out of the drive."

"I'll help."

"No, you won't!"

"Of course I will!"

She opened the door quickly and clambered out into the sudden force of the wind. For an instant, she nearly lost her footing, clinging to the side of the car for support. Then she ducked her head into the collar of her coat and braced her arms against the doorframe as Mick was doing on the other side.

"Now!" he shouted to her, his voice nearly lost in the wind. They tussled with the small car together, Mick reaching inside to wrench at the wheel, and a moment later they had pushed it off to the side of the lot.

Cynny climbed back into the car, and Mick slammed the door after her. By the time he entered on the other side, she was leaned back in the seat, breathless and rubbing at her eyes.

"Are you all right?" he said quickly.

"Of course. Just dust in my eyes. Fantastic! I had no idea it was blowing like this."

"It's a real Santa Ana now. It's beginning to crank up out of the canyons. Look, it was damn nice of you to lend me a hand. I'm sorry as hell about all this."

"Don't be silly."

Mick turned off the lights and clicked a row of switches across the dash. In the silence, the wind was very audible, spirals of dirt and sand and scraps of paper dancing across the parking area. There were only two or three other cars parked there and on the other side of the lot a double row of small, drab motel cabins badly in need of paint, arranged in an L shape, and at the end of the longer row a glimpse of the sea, dark and churning, flecked with whitecaps and plumes of spray.

"Oh my God!" Mick said. "What a cheery spot to be marooned! Look, I don't know what to say except that I feel pretty dumb about now."

Cynny laughed. "Oh, honestly!" she said, her face amused. "Now why should you? It isn't your fault."

"Well, at least there must be a telephone in there. I'll ring up Bob and tell him to get his tail out here with another car."

"I have an auto club card, would that help?"

Mick grinned. "Not really. Though it would serve Bob right if we did let them hook his baby onto a tow truck. Want to come in with me, or stay here?"

"I'll stay." She was scrambling out of her heavy coat. "I haven't gotten my breath yet from this crazy wind."

"I don't think there are any locks on these doors. It looks a bit unsavory around here. Sure you won't come?"

"It's all right. Look, it's absolutely deserted."

"Well, I'll only be a minute."

He opened the door, letting in a gust of wind, and paused to peel off his raincoat and toss it over the back of the seat.

"Take care. I'll be right back."

He set off at an awkward trot, his head lowered against a cloud of flying sand, moving toward what appeared to be an office where several naked lightbulbs across the facade were swinging in the wind.

In the dim car, Cynny found a piece of tissue in her purse and dabbed at her face and eyes with it. There was no sign of life around the forlorn little cabins or any sound except for the wind chuffing and whistling about the car. Cynny exchanged the tissue for a comb and leaned forward to the rearview mirror in an attempt to make some order of her blown hair. The wind died down suddenly, and she paused, hearing the muffled booming of the sea.

Mick returned just then. "All I got was Bob's stupid answering machine. The old character in there loaned me a flashlight, though, so I'll take a look. If it's nothing I can fix in a hurry, we'll shove the damn thing over the side into the ocean and call a taxi."

"Would you like me to hold the flashlight?"

"No, stay in here out of the wind."

Several minutes later he closed the shining hood and returned to the car, rubbing at several smears of grease on his hands.

"Any luck?"

He shook his head. "I'm really sorry about this. I'll go back in now and call a cab."

"If it's just on my account, don't," Cynny said. "Why don't we wait a bit longer? It would take a cab ages to get out here anyway. And I can't imagine that your friend would be very happy at the idea of us just going off and leaving this little jewel sitting here, would he?"

"That's putting it mildly," Mick said. "Not that I give much of a damn about that at this point. All right, if you don't mind, let's give Bob another half hour or so. I have an idea. It's warmer now, would you like to walk down to the beach? Maybe we can find a spot out of the wind and look at the ocean for a while."

"Marvelous. The sea is so beautiful tonight."

When they left the car it seemed that the wind might have abated, but by the time they reached the end of the row of cabins, it blew again full force, whipping at Cynny's skirt and the coat she wore draped about her shoulders. An instant later they were afforded a full view of the beach, empty and windswept, the sea all but obscured behind a veil of blowing sand.

"Not a good idea," Mick shouted into her ear. "We'd better go back."

They turned, leaning into the wind, which was by now hot against their faces, Mick's arm about her shoulders as they stumbled along.

Once they were back within the shelter of the car, Mick laughed. "I don't know," he said. "I'm beginning to feel positively snakebitten. Every idea I come up with turns into a disaster. Here," he added, presenting her with a handkerchief from his pocket. "Maybe this will help a little. Your eyes must be full of sand."

"Thanks."

She dabbed at her eyes and then said abruptly, "It's not just Joby and the pills. Of course I'm sick about Joby, but as you said, it's a problem that a lot of families have had to face these days. When something like this happens, a family simply has to close ranks and face it together with love and patience and understanding. But *that's* what I've had to face these last twenty-four hours. We're not a family. We're not even a marriage any longer. We haven't been for the last five or six years, but I wouldn't admit it to myself until now." Her voice wavered. "There, I've finally said it out loud," she said with a shaky smile. "Now all the demons are out and multiplying and I'm going to have to deal with them and nothing really is ever going to be the same again."

"Oh, Christ!" Mick reached out to her shoulder. Then he said, his voice rough and angry, "You know, I really think we can do a little better than this. Give me one minute, I'll be right back."

Once he was gone, Cynny struggled against tears. Then she

sat quietly, her eyes fixed upon an empty beer can that rolled across the parking lot with a seeming life and purpose of its own.

When Mick returned he opened the door on her side of the car. He carried a paper sack, his pale hair windblown and a streak of grease across his cheek. "Come on," he said cheerfully, extending his hand. "That old gentleman in there is a friend indeed. He's come up with a half bottle of Scotch, two splits of soda, and a sack of ice cubes."

"Fantastic!" she said. "Absolute heaven!"

He led the way, her hand still in his. "Number seven," he said into her ear. "It's a good number at least, but if it turns out to be too dismal, we can always bring our drinks back to the car."

"If it has a bathroom with warm water where I can wash away some of this grit, it will seem like a perfect paradise."

Ten minutes later they were saluting each other with lifted glasses across the corner of a small, rickety desk, the top liberally dotted with cigarette burns. It was a singularly unattractive little room, dominated by the large bed covered with a garish, woven spread: grimy walls, stained and threadbare carpeting, limp, sleazy curtains stirring over the windows in drafts around the loose frames, dismal brown lampshades splitting at their seams. The chair in which Cynny was seated, her legs curled up beneath her skirt, was upholstered in a soiled and faded chintz, and Mick had carried over the only other chair in the room, a creaky wooden one with arms tufted in a particularly lurid coral-colored vinyl.

"Well, they don't come much worse than this, do they?" he said. "But I suppose, like they say, any port in a storm. Cheers."

"Cheers. Anyway it's not that bad. I've washed off layers of sand, and I think it was monstrously clever of you to scare up this Scotch. A drink was a marvelous idea. Thank you very much."

He leaned forward to hold the lighter to her cigarette. "My God! Thank you for being so nice about me stranding you out here in the middle of a sandstorm! If I hadn't known it already, I'd know it now, you're a very special lady."

"Thank you. But I don't feel very special at the moment."

A minute later, out of a drift of smoke, she said, "Since I said as much as I did out there in the car, I think it's only fair to say the rest of it. It's not Jim's fault our marriage quietly disintegrated years ago. No, that's not exactly right. What I really mean is, it's at least as much my fault as it is his, and probably a great deal more."

"It never matters that much whose fault it is, does it?" Mick said cautiously. "Anyway, it may not be as bad as you think right now. All marriages hit these low spots. Maybe this will turn out all for the best. It may give you a chance to talk things out and—"

"No. That's something else that got lost a long time ago, communication. Anyway, it's too late now, there's really nothing left to salvage. It sounds so dreadful to say it, but I don't even have that much emotion about it. Just a sort of nostalgic sadness over something that really ended a long, long time ago. Somehow that doesn't seem fitting."

" 'Not with a bang but a whimper,' " Mick said.

"Yes, but it seems so sad. There ought to be at least enough feeling left for a few tears and recriminations. I do blame myself. I'm the one who set up a pattern without even realizing what I was doing. Jim worked so hard at his job, it engrossed him so completely, it demanded so much of him. I understood that. I thought I was being such a good wife when I kept him insulated from all the everyday domestic ups and downs. But that was such a deadly pattern, why couldn't I have seen it? Eventually, I was permitting him not to be a husband any longer, or a father. I suppose finally I was prohibiting him from being either one of them, even if he'd wanted to try. It's so awful when you think of it. Barriers, even loving, protective ones, turn into prisons. What a lonely man he must really be!"

"I wouldn't be too hard on myself. When two people settle into a way of life, it's only because it suits them both, you know."

"I suppose," Cynny said. "Ah, did you feel that? The tide must be coming in. When the waves hit the beach, this whole little building shudders."

An hour later, Mick was folding precise creases in an empty cigarette package. "This is the part I'm ashamed to tell you about," he said. "Because it makes me feel like—I don't know, a particularly dirty old man, I suppose. After we got over that first hurdle, when I was behaving like such a shit, pumping her about her mother and her mother's divorce and all that, it all went so great. She's a terrific girl, bright and funny and not uptight about anything. We hit it off so well, we had such a good time getting acquainted, trading off bits and pieces of our lives the way—well, I may as well say it, the way lovers do at the beginning when—"

"But look here—"

"No, let me finish this. Then I got the idea of taking her out to Theo's. I knew it wouldn't mean anything special to her, just a funky old house, but I thought I'd like her to see it at least, before it was torn down and gone. She was great about it, she liked it and she was really interested in how it was for me when I was a kid. We wandered around a bit, and all at once it hit me." He paused, frowning over the pleated paper in his hands, and when he spoke again his voice was lower, the words uncertain and slowly spaced. "What hit me was that everything I was feeling about her by then was about as goddamn unfatherly as you can get. What I wanted to do was put my arms around her. Christ, I suppose in the back of my head somewhere what I really would have liked to do was make love to her! I was so rattled when I realized, all I could think to do was what I did: get her the hell out of there, load her into the car, and dump her off at her boyfriend's without any explanations. Well, I warned you it wasn't very pretty. I'm not exactly proud of myself."

"Oh, Lord!" Cynny said and laughed. "But that's all so terribly normal, you know."

"What?"

She leaned forward in her chair. "Dear John Miguel, listen to me for a minute. Fathers who have lived with their daughters every day of their lives and watched them grow up into beautiful young women have flashes of that very same feeling. So think how much more likely you were to feel that way about a daughter you hadn't laid eyes on since she was a baby."

"Is that true? You're not just saying it to—"

"Of course it's true. If it weren't so utterly natural and commonplace, why do you suppose taboos against incest are among the oldest and strongest ones we have? What you felt was completely natural. You handled it in the only decent way you could think of, you've nothing to be ashamed of whatsoever!"

"Oh my God!" he said. He leaned back in the teetery chair, rumpling his pale cowlick. "Oh my God!" he said again. "But I botched it all the same. She didn't understand why I turned off on her all of a sudden, dumping her without any explanation. I could tell her feelings were hurt, she thought that it was something she'd done, that I was disappointed in her or some damn thing."

"You can make it up to her next time you see her," Cynny said. "If she's as honest and direct as you say she is, you can simply tell her the truth. That all this came as a shock to you and you didn't know how else to handle it. She'll understand. I expect she may have been having feelings about you in the very same area, whether she was conscious of it or not."

Mick reached for the Scotch bottle. "Well, you've just sent most of my demons packing, you realize that. Damn! You are being honest with me, aren't you? You're not just telling me all this to—"

"Absolutely honest. And if you think about it for a minute, your own common sense will tell you it's true."

"I suppose." He frowned over it, and then said suddenly, "Hey, you know I liked hearing you call me John Miguel a minute ago. Nobody except Theo has called me that in a good many years. I hope you'll do it often from now on, will you?"

"I'm so used to hearing Theodora—" she murmured, self-conscious all at once. She turned away from his gaze, snuffing out a cigarette carefully in the heaped glass ashtray. And then she looked up, her face crinkling with humor. "Could I ask you something? This has been bugging me for the past hour. I begin to think I've led a terribly sheltered life or something, but, for pity's sake, why is there a coin box attached to the side of this bed?"

Mick leaned forward to look across the expanse of gaudy bedspread and laughed. "I can't be a hundred percent sure, but I think it's some sort of vibrating machine in the springs."

"Really?" She laughed in pure delight.

"I think so." He fumbled in his pocket. "Would you like to try?"

"Thank you, no. It seems a bit seasick-making. I'll take your word for it."

Sometime later, with the Scotch low in the bottle and the small room filled with drifting cigarette smoke, Cynny was saying, "I wonder how we come by it, this fantastic capacity we have to fool ourselves? I suppose it's because our image of ourselves is so terribly important to us. Once we have one we like, there doesn't seem to be any length we won't go to, to maintain it. I don't have to look back any further than three or four days ago, and I want to gag on my own self-righteousness. I must have been so damned pleased with myself. The noble, enduring little woman, playing out the pretty unsatisfactory hand that had been dealt me with what I flattered myself was style and grace. Really! The last of the bloody Victorians, keeping up the perfect facade by being dishonest with myself, and dishonest with Jim, and with the children, and everybody else around me for that matter. I'd have more respect for myself now if I'd at least been honest and admitted to myself that I was such a coward I'd rather put up with it all than face up to making such a drastic change in all our lives. Instead of that I just drifted along in my own private fantasy. Then one breath of reality and the whole house of cards collapsed. If it hadn't been Joby and his wretched pills, it would have been something else."

"Well, I think there are worse things than trying to play out a bum hand with a little style and grace." Mick had pulled his chair around to lean against the wall, his feet propped upon the edge of the bed. "I sometimes think we put too much value on honesty altogether these days. Anyway, we all resist change, maybe because nothing is ever simple and clear-cut, black or white, this or that. The hell of it is, of course, things change in spite of us. Nothing ever stays the same; either we move along with it a little at a time or one day we have to accept it and make a hell of a big change all at once. I was talking about all this with Killian just last night. She's very into Taoism, the yin and yang and all that."

"She must be a very wise little girl."

"A hell of a lot wiser than I was at her age, I can tell you. Although it doesn't seem to have prevented her from having her own marital problems. As I told you, she's in the middle of a divorce."

"Oh dear, wisdom doesn't seem to have all that much to do with it, does it? I've listened to myself talk tonight, all the ins and outs and ifs and maybes, and it's ridiculous. I have an awful feeling that beneath all the rationalization, probably way down beneath all the layers of culture and civilization too, it comes down to one terribly simple basic thing: that years ago, perhaps without even being particularly aware of it, Jim delivered me a mortal wound in my sense of myself as a woman and I'll never forgive him for that so long as I live! My God, we're all such bundles of ego, how do any of us ever manage to get married in the first place, let alone stay married!"

"Beats me," Mick said. "Except it seems to be a pretty basic need we all have. The worst of it is, we don't even seem to learn all that much from our mistakes. When Linda and I fell in love, we were just kids. I'd have taken a shot at getting the moon down out of the sky for her if she'd wanted it. But she didn't. I couldn't get over it. All she seemed to want was just to be with me, twenty-four hours a day. A kind of total merger, two people into one. I thought it was a miracle. I felt like a whole person for the first time in my life, a part of myself found and miraculously rejoined. I thought we had it made.

"And then all of a sudden she split off like an amoeba. She hated racing, it turned out. It took up too much of my time, and hanging around racetracks was not her thing. As a matter of fact, it was everything she hated most rolled up into one package: heat and noise and dirt and cars that could hurt people. She was sick of living out of suitcases, she said. She wanted a house on a street with trees, she wanted a baby. Once I got over the shock that we weren't just one person after all, what she wanted didn't seem all that unreasonable to me either. It left me pretty wary of the whole marriage proposition though, especially in my situation. It left me especially wary of those illusions I'd had about total mergers.

"So you can be damn sure it was different with Gina. Of course, we were older, for one thing, but we each had lives of our own and respected that. Gina had this job at a publisher in London and it meant a lot to her and I was damn glad of it. Actually, we never made that many demands on each other. As I say, I was wary of marriage by then, and though Gina had drifted away from the church, I think she still had qualms about actually divorcing the bloke back in Italy. Gina liked racing, well no, she didn't like it, she'd had a brother who racked himself up in a race car. But at least she understood it. She flew out weekends during season. We had a lot going for us, a lot of feeling between us. Now shall I tell you something pretty damn illogical? Sometimes, in the back of my head somewhere, I used to miss that closeness I'd had with Linda at the beginning. Gina and I never had that. She was a great girl, I hurt like hell for a year or two after she died, but I still missed that one thing sometimes when I was with her. How's that for illogic?"

"We're illogical beasts, apparently," Cynny said. "I suppose I really fell in love with my first husband, Terry, because he was so beautiful in that bashed-down Air Corps cap. There was a war on, and he was the epitome to me of what it was all about, our beautiful brave boys off to do battle for us. We were very young, too. When we had a chance to get acquainted later on, it was a disaster for both of us. He was an absolute bundle of emotion; he was either suicidally down or fantastically paint-the-town up, or furiously kick-the-chairs angry, or so bored he couldn't bear it. He had no sense of humor whatsoever, about himself or anything else. For me it was like trying to live in a volcano. He told me once that he found me as flat and two-dimensional as a paper doll. It was a relief to us both when we called it a day. So naturally, guess what first attracted me to Jim? He was so controlled and cool and self-contained. Now this is where the illogic comes in. I hadn't been married to Jim more than two or three years when I began to feel as though I were wandering alone through some perpetual arctic waste. It's hopeless, isn't it?"

"You don't really believe that, do you?"

"No, of course I don't. Of course there are good marriages. My father and mother had one. I suppose I grew up expecting that everyone did."

"I assume my parents did too. Although my mother died before I was old enough to remember much. The little I do remember is great."

"What on earth does it take, I wonder."

"Damned if I know. It's probably as individual a thing as can be. Needs that mesh. A real desire to make a go of it. Being well suited in the bed. Sharing. And enough maturity or whatever it takes to give each other a little leeway at the same time. Who really knows?"

"I suppose it would help if we could be a bit more logical in our choice of partners."

"I wonder. Because it sure as hell takes love, and that's the exact point where all the logic first seems to break down."

Then he said deliberately, "For instance, like me meeting you yesterday afternoon. Sure, I wanted to get better acquainted with you, but by then something pretty overwhelming had already happened to me. What is it? Why is it that ten or fifteen minutes after I met you, I began to realize it was more important to me than anything else in my life? What has logic got to do with this? I just like to look at you. I like the color of your eyes and the way you move and the way you laugh. We sit and talk, and the more I find out about the way your mind works, the more it pleases me. I like—"

"Oh, don't!" she said, her voice soft and anguished. "Please!"

"I realize this couldn't have happened at a much worse time for you. We don't get to pick our times either, do we? It would probably be a hell of a lot better if I was telling you this a month or two from now, but I have to get on a plane in a few hours. I don't have the choice."

"Oh, no, it's not the time. Honestly. It's just that—well, we don't even know each other. Emotionally, or any other way. We—"

"I realize that. Would a couple months make that much difference? Look, maybe I've got my wires crossed because I'm hoping so damn hard it's true, but a few times tonight, the way you've looked at me and smiled, I've gotten the idea that—"

"I'm not denying it. Why did I come out to dinner with you tonight when all I really felt like doing was staying home and pulling the covers over my head? Why am I here right now, for that matter? That's not the point."

"If it's not the point, then tell me what the hell is."

"Look, I've never been able to be—casual in this area. I don't think you are able to be, either. If we were talking about a—a one-night stand, it would be different." The last cigarettes in her pack tumbled out over her skirt to the floor. "We're—it's not right, it's—inappropriate."

"Inappropriate! What makes it inappropriate? You mean because you're still married to that joker?"

"Of course not!" She had retrieved one of the cigarettes and was striking matches futilely with trembling hands. "It's— Well, I have two children. And I must be older than you are, and—"

"Oh my God!" Mick said incredulously. "That is the most idiotic statement I've ever heard come out of the mouth of an adult woman! You are not my aunt Theodora, stop coming on as though you were." And then he said, mock-tragically, "Oh,

Christ, I know what it is! It must be that stupid thing I said to you in Theo's garden five minutes after I first met you. I was afraid right then that I'd blown it. The Friday afternoon sherry parties, and that stupid crack I made about old dowager types tottering around on canes! What can I say to you? Forgive me, sue me, shoot me! I'd be down on both knees, but I can't, I have a bum leg!"

"Oh, idiot, get up from there! Oh, my dear!" And then they were both laughing, holding each other fiercely, her cheek against his as he crouched on the floor before her chair.

Forty minutes later, with the thin curtains billowing at the opened windows as they aired smoke from the room, they were still laughing, lying face-to-face on the creaking, quaking bed.

"Fantastic! All this for a quarter, it's never going to stop!" Cynny gasped through tears of mirth.

"Good old bed! It may not be able to make it past two point two on the Richter scale any longer, but at least it's giving us its all!"

"Ah, it's so silly, for years I've heard about X-rated motels, but this is just ridiculous—"

And then he was saying angrily, "Goddamn it, this is not the way I want it! I don't want you to have to remember a dingy, broken-down motel room off the highway somewhere. I want the Bel-Air Hotel at the least with the swan and—"

"I don't give a damn about the silly swan, but I'm not going to have this anyway! You were right, the time is all wrong. It's so stupid and unfair. Any other weekend of my life, but not this one. Do you really suppose I'm going to have you think that twenty-four hours after I finally faced up to the fact that my marriage was over, I—"

"What? Hopped into bed with the first man who came along? No, come back here. All right, go ahead and cry if that's what you feel like doing." He held her tightly for a moment or two, then propped on his elbow to lean over her, held her face tenderly between his hands. "You listen to me for a minute.

Maybe I'm flattering myself, but I don't think it's anywhere near as simple as that. If it were, you'd have hopped into bed with some lucky guy years ago. I gather that's the way it happens for most women. Then about twenty-four hours after that they have their big revelation that their marriage is a flop. You had other things on your mind this weekend. What I'm going to remember is that if I got you here at all on this particular weekend of your life, there must be something about me you really like."

A half hour later, out of arguments and with clothing tossed away onto the floor, they were making love with the ecstatic simplicity of a first encounter. They talked some more and slept, finally, entwined in each other's arms, then awakened with the morning light to make love once more.

Then with bursting physical energy, Mick was out of the bed and, barefoot in trousers and shirt, off to the telephone in the motel office. When he returned ten minutes later, Cynny was in the bathroom. "In here, darling," she called out as he entered the room.

"Hey, guess what, it's really hot out there already. The wind's died down, and the sea is smooth as a lake."

"Eerie! I don't care what anyone says, Santa Anas are eerie. Did you reach your friend?"

"Yes, he'll have a car out here in a half hour. And the van to pick up his baby out there in the parking lot."

He leaned against the doorjamb, watching her contentedly. She was wrapped in a white bath towel, busy with comb and lipstick before the small, splotchy mirror.

"How do you feel?" he asked after a time.

She turned her head to smile at him. "Fantastic! I'm floating somewhere out past Venus and Mars. And you?"

"Fantastic! I'm in free fall doing cartwheels somewhere out around Jupiter. Are you hungry?"

"Starving."

"We'll have wheels in a few minutes, where would you like to go for breakfast? Hey, we could check in at the Bel-Air!"

She dropped her lipstick on the edge of the washbowl and came to him, reaching up to his crisp, windblown hair.

"Hang those swans," she said. "I'd rather stay right here. Forever, I think."

He bent to kiss her bare shoulder. "That might just be arranged. We'll talk about it at breakfast."

"Good."

They held hands, surveying each other with unabashed pleasure for a long time.

"But you have a plane to catch," she said at last.

"You must be out of your beautiful little skull! There'll be other days and other planes, for God's sakes."

"Marvelous."

Then after another moment, she said, "But if you were to catch that plane today, how soon could you be back here? The absolute very first possible moment that you could possibly manage."

He thought about it. "A month, I'd think. It might be cutting it pretty fine, but I could be back here in a month."

"Sure?"

"Positive."

"A month. That's four weeks. Twenty-eight days."

"Hey, do you want me to catch that plane today?"

"Oh, my love! What do you think!"

They embraced, and after a time, still holding her, he said, "I think I see what you're driving at. It would give you a little clear, uninterrupted time to sort out some things that need sorting. I can't say I like it, but I see the logic in it for you."

"I don't like it either. But what I do like is the idea of a time when I'd be able to put my mind to you, relatively clear and undivided."

"Hey, I think I'd like that, too. Of course I'd also like it if you'd put some other parts of yourself to me besides your—"

"I'm delighted to hear that. I was rather thinking along those same lines myself."

They kissed again, and then he said, "What it really comes down to is which would be easiest for you. If you'd rather have me standing by—"

"You will be standing by. You've already given me the courage of lions and the strength of armies. Here or wherever, for me you're standing by."

"All right, then I'll catch the plane."

"Oh, damn! I'm having second thoughts already. Will you phone me?"

"Every day."

"Four weeks is a long time."

"Twenty-eight days."

"My God, I'm taking the most fearful risk! It's a chancy world. Suppose you didn't come back. You will come back, won't you?"

"What do you think! Anyway, the risk is all on my side. What if you should decide while I'm away to patch up your marriage and muddle through, stout fellow, and—"

"Darling, you don't believe that!"

"No, I don't. All right, I'll go, but I won't like it."

"No, now I think I've changed my mind completely. A month is too long. We'll have to talk about this at breakfast."

"Hey, breakfast! I'd better get my shoes on, those guys will be here any second."

When he returned to the room fifteen minutes later, she was combed and dressed, gazing out the window at the little strip of ocean visible between the cabins, the water pale in the morning light and placid as a pond.

"All squared away," he said, car keys jingling in his hand. "The van just pulled out with Bob's little trinket aboard. Now I'm going to get you something to eat."

"That marvelous little car! Imagine it being clever enough to break down at this exact spot of highway!"

"Damn right! Its instinct was perfect. I don't know that I can say the same for its taste, but—"

"Oh, bah!"

"What were you thinking about? You looked very sober."

"What? Oh, when you came in. Actually, I was thinking about Nancy. She just popped into my head for some reason."

"Who's Nancy? Oh, I remember, the rocket trail girl."

"Fantastic! How do you happen to remember that?"

"I must have been listening to every word you said. Do you suppose that's it?"

"I think it must be. Anyway, I was feeling a bit guilty about Nancy. We had a long talk the other morning. She's been sowing the same seeds of disaster in her marriage that I did long ago. With one large difference. She's in love with her husband, so all of her alarm bells have started ringing. Naturally I was counseling her to grin and bear it. Now I can't wait to tell her how wrong I was."

"You can call her when we get to breakfast."

"Of course not, silly. Tomorrow will be time enough."

"All set?"

"I think so."

She picked up her purse, and he carried her coat along with his jacket.

At the door, she paused, her hand upon his arm, her eyes suddenly bright with tears. "Wait, I have to take a last look. This is the most beautiful room in the world. I want to remember every least little thing about it forever."

"Including that calendar nude over there on the wall?"

"Especially that calendar nude. And those ghastly lampshades."

"You know, I have an ominous feeling that you're the kind of girl who keeps anniversaries, too."

"Damn right. And this is going to be a very special anniversary, I warn you."

"Oh my God!" he said. "Then we are doomed! I can see us coming back here every year from now till the end of time. Till we're old and gray and the bed is down to one jiggle per minute, at fifty cents a shot, allowing for inflation. And the paint will be peeling off the walls by then and—"

"I know. Now we're fated."

They were laughing as they left the cabin, arms about each other's waists.

4
Sunday

NEDITH AWAKENED EARLY THAT SUNDAY MORNing. For a moment she lay motionless, suspended between sleep and waking, staring at the long expanse of curtains, gold with sunlight. She was minded suddenly of awakenings in the bedroom of her childhood: toy shelves, teddy bears, and flowered wallpaper, starched white, ruffled curtains, rustle of leaves and the leisurely whir of lawn sprinklers through the window, bicycle wheels and the thud of the Sunday paper on the porch boards below. And the child who waited in her narrow bed listening for the first sound of the father's voice to set the emotional climate for the day. Not the mother's voice, eternally whining and placating, but the heavy man's voice: the terse grunts of hangover, the dreaded bellow of quarrel and complaint, or most infrequent but always to be longed for, the blessed, teasing lilt of good humor.

The memory was not a pleasant one. Nedith flung back the covers and got out of the bed. Thrusting her feet into slippers, she looked at the clock on the shelf of the headboard and regretted that she had not been able to sleep for another hour or two. But now it was too late, she was alert and already teeming with energy. Briskly belting her short quilted silk robe about her, she went into the bathroom, avoiding more than a glimpse in the mirror as she passed. Nedith hated to look at her face without cosmetics. From the bathroom, she walked on to the kitchen, where she removed a large coffee mug from a cupboard, filled it from the tap, set it inside a shining glass-and-chrome microwave oven, adjusted the knobs, and set off for the front of the house.

Loosening bolts and chains, she stepped at last outside the door, where the wind immediately fluttered her robe against her bare legs. A hard, gusty wind, dry and hot as the breath of a furnace.

Why, the Santa Ana is blowing, Nedith thought, how divine! She looked up for confirmation and found indeed a pale blue, cloudless sky. It was going to be one of those hot Santa Ana days that sometimes came early in November, a perfect day for being in the sun. Elated, she walked along the pebbled path to the circular drive, where the Sunday *Los Angeles Times* lay waiting, neatly tied with string. As she walked back, the wind came again, whipping at the ginger and tree fern among the rocks and sending dry leaves scudding across the concrete. Nedith was already reorganizing her day. A perfect day for brunch by the pool. She'd gotten a halfway promise from Pete that he would stop by on his way back to San Diego, she'd phone Jean of course, and then, if they had not had too late a night last night, perhaps Sally and Jack would come and bring the children. While she was about it, she might phone the Herberts, too. God knows they were the dullest people on earth, the Herberts, but Pete had dated Judy quite a bit one summer several years ago; she'd ask the Herberts to come and bring Judy. Quiche Lorraines from the freezer, green salad with shrimp, and Bloody Marys and all that.

Highly pleased with herself and the prospect of the day ahead, Nedith switched off the oven and removed her mug of boiling water. She stirred in several spoonfuls of freeze-dried coffee crystals and carried it back to the bedroom. There she opened one of the glass doors behind the gold draperies, elevated the head of the bed, arranged pillows, turned off the electric blanket, fetched a tray from the dressing room closet, and a moment later was settled cozily back in bed with her coffee and the Sunday paper. While she searched through the bulk of newsprint for the Home Magazine section, the telephone rang on the table beside her, and Nedith answered it through a cloud of cigarette smoke.

"Yes?"

"Hi, Mum. Is this too early, are you still asleep?"

"Pete, I'm so glad you called! No, of course not, darling, I'm just having coffee and the paper. Pete, isn't this weather divine? The Santa Ana's blowing."

"You're telling me! It's blowing a gale up here out of the canyons. It's hot as hell already, and the sea's glassed over like a lake."

"Marvelous! I get so sick of gray, cruddy weather. Pete—"

"So how was your party last night?"

"Oh, it was a lot of fun. Some crazy drink called Skip and Go Naked, did you ever hear of Skip and Go Nakeds? And a marvelous dinner, and Don showed the movies he took when we all went to Acapulco last spring. Darling, what time are you coming in? I'm planning a brunch for around one, but I thought if you could get here a bit early, we'd—"

"That's the thing, Mum. I don't think I'll be able to make it today. I really have to be back by afternoon, so I thought I'd get out early now, ahead of the beach traffic, just get on the freeway and keep rolling."

"Oh, Pete, you promised! And it's such a perfect day for brunch by the pool. Sally and Jack are bringing the children, and the Herberts are coming and Judy. You haven't seen Judy in ages, have you?"

"I'm sorry, Mum. I really have to get back. Give everybody my love, all right? Tell them I'll see them next time."

"Pete, I don't think it's fair. I hardly got to see you at all this trip, you went chasing off to Malibu and—"

"I'll tell you what, suppose I come up again next weekend? I'll come up on Saturday, that's a promise."

"But it's such a marvelous day today, a perfect day for sun and people and brunch by the pool. It would be such fun. Judy'll be terribly disappointed, darling. I told her you were here. I can't think what I'm going to tell her now."

"I know," he said lightly. "I'm just a party poop. By the way, Judy Herbert's at Radcliffe this year, I forgot to tell you. I had a letter from her a couple weeks ago. She's living with some guy in Cambridge and says she's never been so happy in her life."

"Oh, hell!" Nedith said ruefully. And then she laughed and Pete laughed with her.

"Oh, all right," she said. "Don't come. But you're sure about next weekend, you promise."

"I'll be up on Saturday. It's a date."

"Why don't you come Friday night? You could just as well, couldn't you?"

"Actually, no. Look, Mum, I'm in an outdoor booth at the market, it's a hundred and twenty degrees in here, and there's somebody waiting for the phone. So I'll see you Saturday. By the way, will Dad be home?"

"Darling, I wouldn't have the least idea. Why?"

"Well, since I'm coming up, I'd like to see you both. I'm liable to get pretty tied up after that, winding up things." He hesitated. "Incidentally, I've decided about the fellowship. I mailed the letter this morning. I'll be leaving for Europe in about a month."

"Oh, Pete!"

"I know you've gotten turned off on the whole idea for some reason. But I had a chance to think about it while I was up here, and I feel now that it's something I can't afford to pass up."

"Pete, don't do it! You know what I told you the other day, you can't just keep on going to school forever, darling, you—"

"Look, I'd better run. This guy's having a fit waiting for the phone. Tell Dad I'll be up Saturday. I'll tell you more about my plans when I see you."

"Pete, I think it would be a terrible mistake. Think about it some more, darling. You don't have to make up your mind in such a hurry, do you?"

He laughed. "Mum, it's already been two months! Cheer up, a year's not a very long time. Besides, you and Dad can always come over in the spring for a visit. April in Paris, you'd like that, wouldn't you?"

"No, I'll tell you what I'd like," Nedith said, her cheeks suddenly pink. "I'd just like to see you your old self again. Up until the last year or so, you've always had ambitions and—and drive and goals. Now you seem perfectly satisfied just to drift along or something. It's really sad. And if you want to know what I think, I think it's all her fault, I really do!"

"Look, I realize you're disappointed," he said, his voice stiffening. "But I also think you're overreacting a bit."

"Well, you can't deny it, can you? From the minute that Killian got her hooks into you, you began to change, you—"

"Mother, I have to go. I'll see you Saturday."

"Pete? Well, if you're going to Europe, you could at least wait till after Christmas, couldn't you? I don't see what difference it would make if—"

But he was already gone.

Nedith slammed down the phone. "Oh, shit!" she said.

She snuffed out her cigarette furiously in the small china ashtray and reached for her mug. But the coffee was now lukewarm and brackish, and she pushed the whole tray away impatiently, rolling over onto her side beneath a layer of scattered newspaper.

Her first coherent thought, once her anger began to subside, was that, thank God, at least now she would not have to invite the Herberts to brunch, they were truly the dullest people on earth. It came to her then that she really did not care if anyone came to brunch, for that matter. Her enthusiasm for the idea was gone. Now it had turned into just another day with absolutely nothing to look forward to. Nedith lay still in the bed, tears of self-pity swimming in her eyes, and stared at the picture on the opposite wall, a large collage of abstract flowers in a narrow gold frame. She hated that picture, she was thinking, she really hated it, even though it had cost a small fortune.

The hot wind gusted about the house, rattling leaves and billowing the curtains. It occurred to Nedith then that it was not just a single day that had gone flat and stale and empty for her, this was what her whole life had long since become: waking, sleeping, yesterday, tomorrow, and the next day and the next. And it filled her with a sudden terror.

She came out of the bed, legs flashing, pink curlers bobbing. Well, I won't have it, she told herself furiously. I won't live like this any longer, I won't! I'm alive, I'm me, I exist!

She hesitated for only a fraction of a second, then headed to the desk against the wall. The key was in a tooled leather box containing photographs and old letters. She unlocked the lower drawer quickly and yanked out the fat folder, marked with the name of her legal firm. She spread it open on the desktop, leafing through papers impatiently until she found the one for which she searched, the copy of the detective's report with the name, Mrs. Hallie Christopher, and the address on one of those tacky old streets somewhere off Vermont. And in the margin, the telephone number in ink, in Nedith's small, precise numerals, jotted there after she had looked it up out of curiosity.

She left the file open on the desk and returned to the bed. Sitting bolt upright there amid a sea of newspaper, she blew her nose briskly and lighted a cigarette. She set the telephone on the bedtray in front of her and without the least hesitation began to dial.

TOM HAD ARRIVED AT INTERNATIONAL AIRPORT even earlier that Sunday morning, his body still stiff from hours of cramped sleep aboard the jet. He crossed the street from the terminal building and trudged on into the vast parking area, lugging his bag, coat, and attaché case, jostled by the wind that swirled corkscrews of dust and paper about his feet. The sun was already surprisingly hot, and by the time he reached the dusty blue sports car amid the sea of empty automobiles, his face shone with perspiration. He stowed his luggage in the trunk, unlocked and opened the car door, then peeled off his jacket and necktie.

The interior of the car was cooler than outside, he discovered, and he dropped into the leather bucket seat gratefully. In spite of the small breakfast aboard the flight, his mouth was dry and stale from the whiskey and cigarettes of the previous evening, and his body was sluggish with fatigue. He was glad to be back all the same, though, and did not regret the impulse that had led him to take this early morning flight instead of spending another night in Florida. He could always grab a couple hours' sleep at Hallie's later on.

Leaving the airport, he got on the freeway and drove fast, cutting back and forth through the scattered Sunday morning traffic, peripherally watchful for the black-and-white of a highway patrol vehicle. He drove with pleasure, finding rest and relaxation in concentrating on the mechanics of it. But in some compartment of his mind, he was also aware of the knowledge he had received the previous afternoon, the knowledge that he had failed to win the contract of which he had been so confident. He did not think of it now, he was merely aware of it, that this knowledge awaited his exploration and assessment at the appropriate future time.

At Hallie's apartment building, he found a parking spot along the curb and stepped out into sunlight filtering through sycamore limbs. The foyer was cool and shadowy. He made the slow, creaking ascent in the elevator, and at the apartment door let himself in.

He tiptoed across the dim living room to the bedroom and saw that Hallie still slept, curled in the middle of the bed. Smiling, Tom pulled the door shut without a sound and went off to the kitchen, swinging that door closed behind him as well. He turned on lights there and, with a pleasant sense of homecoming, went about making a pot of coffee. While he waited for the kettle to heat, he prowled about the room, exploring the contents of a bread box on the shelf, testing flowerpots on the windowsill for dampness and adding water to one of them. Finally, leaned against the sink, legs crossed, he sipped at cold tomato juice until the kettle boiled, then measured water into the top of the pot. With the aroma of freshly brewing coffee beginning to fill the kitchen, he returned to the front hall in search of the Sunday paper. He was just coming back to the kitchen when the telephone rang, and he rushed to scoop it up, cutting off the sound. He carried the receiver back into the kitchen, letting the door swing closed again over the cord before he spoke.

"Yes?"

"What a coincidence," Nedith said. "You're just the one I want to talk to."

For an instant, Tom was stunned. "Nedith! What's happened? Is it Pete?"

She laughed. "That's very funny. It's pretty obvious just who in your family rates first with you."

"Nedith, for the love of God! What's the matter, what do you want?"

"I'll give you a half hour to get home and find out," she said and slammed down the phone.

Tom dropped the receiver back onto the cradle, picked it up again, and began to dial furiously, then stopped mid-number. He returned the phone to its place in the living room and went to listen at the bedroom door, but there was still no sound from within, so he moved on to the apartment's front door. With his hand on the knob, he hesitated, then returned to scribble a note on the back of an envelope that lay on the kitchen table: "Something's come up, back as soon as I can, love you." He left it propped against the coffeepot and left.

Twenty minutes later, with a squeal of tires, he brought the blue sports car to a rocking halt on the loop in front of his house. He was out of the car, door left swinging, almost before it stopped. It was hotter here in the hills and very quiet, only the dry wind blowing hard. Tom unlocked the massive door and pushed into the silent foyer.

"Nedith?"

"In here," she answered from down the hall, and Tom headed quickly in the direction of the bedroom.

"Well, that was quick, I must say," she said as he appeared in the doorway of the huge blue-and-gold room. She was sitting upright in the bed, her hair still wound in pink curlers, spooning leisurely at a half grapefruit on the bedtray in front of her.

"All right, now suppose you tell me what in hell's going on around here," Tom said, his voice shaking with fury.

She studied him for a moment, spoon poised. "Don't you think it would make a lot more sense if I were the one to ask you that?"

"Where did you get Hallie's number?"

"The phone book, where else? You look terrible, by the way. Aren't you getting a little long in the tooth for these kinds of weekends?"

Tom wadded up his jacket, threw it at a chair, and came into the middle of the room.

"Come on, Nedith, get to the point. I'm not in the mood to play games with you. What is it that you want?"

"All right, let's do get to the point. The point is, I've had enough. I'm fed up to here, if you'd like to know."

"Meaning exactly what?" Tom said.

"Meaning exactly this." Nedith paused to take another deliberate bite from the grapefruit. "I'm giving you two choices, right now. Either you leave with me on the Cunard round-the-world cruise on the twenty-eighth of November, or I'm filing for a divorce."

Tom stared at her. Outside, the wind blew hard, rattling dry leaves and palm fronds together, and the thin drapes over the open patio doors billowed. He began to laugh, hard, head flung back, short, powerful legs braced apart.

Nedith put down her spoon and watched him, her dark eyes alert.

When he was able to speak, he wiped at his eyes and began to grope for his cigarette package. "I'm sorry. Private joke, I'm afraid."

"Well, I'm glad you find it so funny. You keep saying get to the point, so why don't you? Which is it going to be?"

Tom snapped his lighter, and out of a puff of cigarette smoke he said, "File the divorce, Nedith. God knows it's about time, don't you agree?"

She was still for several seconds, then she shrugged her shoulders. "All right, then I will. If you're sure that's what you want."

"Yes," Tom said. "It's what I want."

She was silent again for a time, studying her fingers clasped before her on the bedtray. "Naturally I'll want this house," she said at last. "And under the circumstances, I mean your ladies' lingerie girlfriend and all that, I don't see that it should be considered community property."

"No problem," he said, a suggestion of amusement still left in his face. "Have this house by all means, Nedith. Free and clear, with my compliments."

"Good. I'm glad you intend to be fair and reasonable about all this. I wasn't sure you would be."

"Where would you get an idea like that?" he said, his face sobering. "You must know me better than that by now. Why would I be anything less than fair and reasonable with you? Married or divorced, I see no reason for your life to change in any way. You have my assurance on that."

"How generous and thoughtful!" she said with delicate irony. "But then you've always been such a considerate husband, haven't you?"

"Look, I don't see that there is anything else we need to discuss at the moment," Tom said brusquely. "So, if you'll excuse me, I have a lot of things to do today and—"

"Well, there is one other thing—"

She paused, a cigarette in her fingers, searching for matches in the side compartments of the bedtray. Tom hesitated, then crossed the stretch of carpet to hold out his lighter.

"Thanks," she murmured. "I hope you're going to understand this, Tom, but I'll want to sell out my half of the stock in the company."

"That'll be up to you, certainly. As a matter of fact, I'm thinking of selling out the whole shebang myself. I've been considering an offer for a merger for some time now. Actually, I'd hoped to finalize the deal in the next five or six months, but I just lost out on a series of contracts I'd been counting on, so it may take another year now, or a year and a half."

"Oh, really? I'm not sure I'd want to wait that long."

"Why do you want to worry your head over all this now?" he said impatiently, picking up his coat. "This is what's better left to the lawyers. I'll have mine get started on it first thing tomorrow if you like."

"Yes, I think you should do that," she said. "My lawyers have already done most of the preliminary work, of course, but now naturally they'll want to—"

Tom had reached the doorway, and he stopped abruptly.

"What lawyers?"

"What?"

"I said, 'What lawyers?' "

"When you mumble like that, I can't understand a word you're saying. It's Barton and Lewis. Barry Lewis is the one who's actually handling it for me."

"Son of a bitch!" Tom said through his teeth.

"Well, you certainly didn't think I'd jump into something like this without legal advice, did you? And you've always said yourself that if you're going to spend a fortune on lawyers, you might as well have the very best."

Tom laughed shortly. "You needn't worry on that score, Nedith. You seem to have already gotten yourself the most notorious pair of divorce settlement sharpies in town. How long has all this been going on, by the way?"

"I'm so glad that you approve," Nedith said. "Then you may be interested to hear that Barry advises me—"

"No, first I'd be interested to hear how long you've been conniving with lawyers behind my back."

"That is so ridiculous! How can you call getting a little legal advice to protect my interests 'conniving with lawyers'? Anyway, considering all the things you've been up to behind my back for all these years, I don't see that—"

"What I don't see is any point to continuing this discussion, frankly. Since you have counsel, let's leave it to the lawyers, shall we?"

"But I would like you to understand my position. About the stock, I mean. Barry advises me to sell out my half immediately. Regardless. He says there is always an element of risk in any company that is essentially a one-man operation, so he wouldn't consider it in my best interests to hold that stock a single day longer than is necessary. You see the position this puts me in, you pay an absolute fortune for this kind of advice, and—"

"You know, I think I'm beginning to get the picture," Tom

said softly. "Just what have you got up your sleeve anyway, Nedith, some notion of scuttling my business for me?"

She laughed. "Now that is so absolutely typical of you! Why should I want to scuttle your business? That would be like cutting off my own nose to spite my face, wouldn't it? Anyway, you'd have the first chance to buy out my stock yourself, so how can you possibly say a thing like that!"

"It would strip me just now to buy out your stock, and what should be more important from your point of view, it would strip the company besides. Something tells me that your sharpie lawyer may already have intimated as much to you. Did he?"

"Well, he does tell me that with the slump in aerospace spending, your company isn't in the healthiest condition just now. I really don't see why you're trying to make such an issue out of all this. Just a second ago you yourself were telling me that you intended to sell out."

"I'm not talking merger with anyone until I'm in a position to deal from strength, Nedith. If that escapes you for some reason, I'm sure Barry Lewis would be happy to explain that it's only simple business procedure. When I have some good quarterly earnings figures behind me, I'll be ready to talk merger and not before."

"Isn't that a little risky? There simply aren't that many aerospace contracts around anymore, are there? It seems to me in another year the company could be in a much worse condition than it is right now. But naturally I wouldn't presume to try to tell you how to run your business. All I'm telling you is that, upon the advice of my attorneys, I'll be selling off my half of the stock immediately."

"Oh, come off it, Nedith! Barry Lewis and company have a reputation around this town for being very shrewd characters. They are not advising you that it is in your best interest to cripple my business. This has to be your own idea. It smells of vendetta or blackmail—which? I asked you this before. What is it you really have up your sleeve anyway?"

"Why do you keep asking me that? It was your own idea, wasn't it, that I file for a divorce. I gave you a choice."

Tom stared at her incredulously. "What in hell are you talking about?"

"I suppose you weren't listening. You never listen to me. All I said was that either you sailed with me on the Cunard round-the-world cruise on the twenty-eighth or I'd file a divorce. You're the one who said to file the divorce."

"My God, you can't mean to tell me that this whole ploy is just an attempt to pressure me into taking a two-month cruise with you!"

"You're the one who's talking about ploys and pressures and blackmail. I gave you a perfectly fair choice. You know very well you promised me that trip, and you've been stalling on it now for two years."

"I can't believe it!" Tom said. "I think you're actually serious about this!"

He turned away and moved into the dressing room, where he tossed his cigarette butt sizzling into the toilet. When he returned, he sat down upon the edge of the other twin bed. He was silent for a moment, leaned forward over his knees, contemplating his interlocked fingers.

"Well?" Nedith said.

"Look, I haven't been entirely candid with you," he said slowly, choosing his words. "I think the time has come when I should be. I was laughing a minute ago because it's quite a coincidence. If you hadn't brought up the subject of a divorce today, I intended to. The fact is, Nedith, I'm in love with Hallie Christopher and I want to marry her."

Nedith sat bolt upright, pink curlers bobbing and two spots of color appearing in her cheeks. "I don't care to hear this, you know. I'm sure there have been a dozen women in the past twenty years, and if this had come up during your affair with any one of them you'd have said exactly the same thing. It disgusts me, and I don't want to hear it!"

"Not true, Nedith," he said gently. "All things considered, I never expected I'd want to marry anyone again as long as I lived until I met Hallie. I assume you've had a full report on all this, courtesy of your attorneys and their snoops, so you probably are aware that I've known her for a couple years now, and that's exclusively, you might say. It no longer comes under the heading of a temporary fling, which, God knows, I've had enough of to be able to tell the difference. I'm in love with Hallie, and I intend to marry her."

"I told you I didn't want to hear this! It really doesn't interest me. And I'm sick of you accusing me of pressuring you and blackmailing you. You promised me this trip. All you have to do is keep your promise, and then as far as I'm concerned you can go right on fiddling with your contracts and mergers and your precious company for the rest of your life! Why is that so much for me to ask?"

Tom looked at her for a long time before he answered. "You know, I don't understand you. That's putting it mildly; actually I find you incomprehensible. If it's a trip you want, you could take a girlfriend and leave tomorrow. Why me? Just tell me why, in God's name, you are determined to spend two months bottled up with me on a cruise ship considering what our life together has become these past few years, and particularly in the light of what I've just told you about Hallie. Can you possibly explain that to me?"

"Because you promised me this trip," she said doggedly, her dark eyes flaring with anger.

"No, there has to be more to it than that," he said flatly. "Come on, Nedith, be honest for once in your life. What's really going on in that devious mind of yours? You couldn't possibly be thinking that this trip might turn into a second honeymoon, could you?"

In a flash, Nedith leaned out over the edge of the bed, spat in his face not entirely successfully, then dove headlong back into the pillows and burst into tears.

"What do you think I am!" she wailed, while Tom, grim faced, wiped spittle from his shirt collar with a handkerchief. "You don't know the first thing about me or the way I feel about anything. I'm sick of my life! How could you understand that? You have women and fun and everything you want. I don't have anything. I just sit here in this damn house. You don't even pay attention to me. It's like I didn't exist. I'm sick of it! I'm sick of never having anything to look forward to. I'm sick of my friends calling me 'poor Nedith' and laughing at me behind my back. Other women's husbands go on trips with them, why can't you? Pretty soon I'll be old like my mother and they'll lock me up in some creepy place with a lot of creepy, senile things in wheelchairs and my life will be over. I just want to go on this trip and have a little fun. You owe me that much, after all these years, you owe me!"

She sobbed hard into the pillows, and Tom rose and walked to the opened glass doors. The wind was blowing harder now, hot as a furnace against his face, leaves rasping together. From somewhere in the direction of the pool a piece of furniture overturned, clattering upon the flagstones, and from beyond the ridge of the hills, there was an ululating wail of sirens.

After a time her weeping quieted, and he walked back to the bed. Her face was hidden in the pillows, only two or three of the big hair curlers and the vulnerable nape of her neck visible. He did not touch her, but he sat down finally beside her.

"Nedith, I understand more than you know," he said. "No matter what you think, my life hasn't exactly been all beer and skittles either. What's the point for either one of us to go on like this? It's a pretty thin and dismal prospect, isn't it? Apparently you've finally found out that it takes more than sable coats and new houses. Well, it takes more than boat trips, too. It's not too late, you know. What is it the kids say, 'Today is the first day of the rest of your life.' Let's pack it up, Nedith. Go on from here and make a new life for yourself while there's time. Get some new interests, meet some new people, get married again. Start living the way human beings were meant to live, for God's sakes! I think that's something we both owe to ourselves."

She rolled over suddenly and sat upright, scrubbing tears from her face.

"That's very funny! Me marry again. You must be mad! I learned everything about men I ever need to know from you, Tom Fallon. Starting way back when Sally was a baby in a crib and I was all swelled up, pregnant with Pete. All I had in the world back then was my marriage to you, and you spit on it. I'll never forgive you for that as long as I live. You have the nerve to sit there and tell me I don't know how to live like a human being, as if I were some kind of monster or something. Well, if you think I'm such a monster, kindly remember that it was you who turned me into one. I married you with all the good faith in the world, the rest of it is your doing."

"It won't wash, Nedith," Tom said. "A couple years ago if you'd told me that, I might have believed you. I spent a lot of years feeling guilty about you. But no more. That's one thing Hallie has taught me at least. You are today exactly what you've made of yourself, Nedith. I refuse to take any responsibility for that!"

"Marvelous! How convenient for you! Apparently your lingerie saleslady is quite a philosopher."

"Yes, and a lot of other things besides that I doubt you could even begin to understand. But let's not go into that. Just remember there are a number of things I could tell you, too, about yourself as a wife, but it seems to me that most of them have already been said a few hundred times in the past. I don't see much point anymore in trading recriminations."

"Absolutely. I couldn't agree with you more." She swiped at her remaining tears, and then a smile broke through, her unabashed and utterly charming smile. "So. Which is it going to be then? Are you coming on the cruise with me, or aren't you?"

Tom looked at her, then laughed. "Nedith, you are a piss-cutter," he said. "I'm sorry, but that's the only expression for it that comes readily to mind. You have all the propensities of an armored tank, along with a frightening faculty for tuning out everything in the world you don't care to hear. Well, you had better hear this one thing and remember it. Either we divorce now with your cooperation, or we divorce a year or so from now at my convenience. Either way, I'm going to marry Hallie Christopher."

Nedith leaned back against the pillows and stretched leisurely, arms lifted above her head. "Nonsense," she said briskly. "I know you too well for that. After all these years, who should know you better than I do, for heaven's sakes! One of these days you'll meet somebody else, and you'll forget your lingerie saleslady even exists. Two months is a long time, you know. A lot can happen in two months."

"I wouldn't count on that if I were you," Tom said. He rose from the bed, his eyes upon his wristwatch. "Now if you'll excuse me. This is the time of day when I should be able to track down Sam Fiedelman somewhere around the twelfth hole over at Hillcrest. You'll hear from me as soon as I've had a little chat with him about community property stock sales and related matters."

"Go right ahead, but it won't do you the slightest bit of good," Nedith said. "Barry went into all of this very thoroughly." She reached beneath scattered sections of newspaper and fished out the file folder. "I have all his figures right here. You're welcome to look them over if you like and save yourself a trip to Hillcrest."

"Thanks all the same." He paused in the doorway and looked back at her. "Let me give you one last piece of friendly advice," he said. "You're not going to get away with this, Nedith. You've used up the last of my tolerance for you this morning. Don't think you can trade on my generosity or gentlemanly instincts any longer. If it's a fight you want, it's a fight you're going to get. No holds barred."

"Marvelous, why not?" she said. "It should give us a lot to talk about aboard ship, don't you think?"

He disappeared, and Nedith lay back, smiling, against the pillows. She heard the slam of the front door behind him and, a moment after that, the snarl of the car engine.

Nedith was humming to herself, and suddenly she sang at the top of her voice, "—isn't raining rain you know, it's raining violets!"

Ah, she felt good, she discovered, thrumming and vibrating with energy, more alive actually than she had felt in years. I am, I am, I am, she exulted. I really do exist. Even Tom knows that now!

The hot wind blew hard around the house, and from closer by now, though still beyond the ridge, sirens continued to wail.

NANCY FRIEDMAN WAS ANOTHER EARLY RISER that morning. She and Dave had attended a party the previous evening, and for the first time she could recall since her college days, Nancy had had more drinks than were good for her. Consequently she'd spent the first part of the night between fits of dizziness and repeated trips to the bathroom. When she did fall into a deep, stunned slumber, it was only to awaken again with the morning light. Her first awareness was of being suffocatingly hot, and she threw back covers, stretching her bare feet out into the air while she groped for the control box on her side of the king-size electric blanket. Her nose and throat were painfully dry, she discovered, her head pounding dully, and her stomach still queasy. Then she noticed the sun strong against the drawn drapes and, with a guilty sense of having overslept, slid from the bed, taking care not to awaken Dave.

In the bathroom she leaned against the washbasin gulping tepid tap water, which neither slaked her thirst nor settled her stomach. There were already sounds of activity from the children's rooms and the noise of a television set, the shrill voices of the Sunday morning cartoons. Sam, her four-year-old, arrived just then through a connecting door, barefoot in pajamas, to announce that they were all hungry and ask could they have waffles for breakfast.

Yes, she supposed they could, Nancy said, meanwhile please go turn down that TV set before they woke Daddy. She dressed hurriedly in the adjoining dressing room, pulling on woolen slacks and a long-sleeved shirt, and thrusting her bare feet into thonged sandals. It was not until she arrived in the kitchen that she realized it was only the unaccustomed sunlight after several weeks of overcast that had persuaded her she had overslept. Actually, it was just seven-thirty.

Nancy swore softly and opened the kitchen door to take further stock of the unusual weather. Walking to the end of the large flagstone terrace, she felt the first breath of the dry, hot wind and the promised heat of the day ahead. Beyond the terrace was a large backyard, grass neatly mown but littered with children's toys, and enjoying the novelty of the sunshine now, Nancy wandered off to one of the half-planted flower beds and began to yank at its weeds.

The children converged upon her several minutes later, three small, pajama-clad figures bounding over the grass. They were hungry, they chorused. When was she going to make their breakfast?

Had they noticed the weather, Nancy countered. Wasn't the sunshine marvelous?

Yeah, it was neat, they agreed without enthusiasm. Could they have waffles for breakfast?

But waffles were such gooey, indigestible things. How about a nice omelette instead, and bacon?

Her suggestion was met by immediate moans and cries.

All right, Nancy capitulated, she had some wheat flour, she would make them some very special and different waffles, how was that?

Yech, they announced in one voice as they disappeared once more in the direction of the television set.

Nancy returned to the kitchen, where she swallowed two aspirin and a handful of vitamin tablets with a glass of Clamato juice from the refrigerator. Her improvised wheat flour waffle batter was not a success. When the children thundered in during the next commercial break, they found her scraping stuck and burning bits of dough from a smoking waffle iron.

Just don't yell like that, Nancy pleaded desperately. Mommy

390 — Maritta Wolff

has a headache this morning. How about some nice French toast?

She was immediately confronted by three small, angry faces. No, waffles. You promised!

"Mommy, you are so dumb," her nine-year-old daughter informed her. "All you have to do is get frozen waffles with blueberries from the supermarket. Then you just toast them in the toaster like on TV."

"Frozen waffles are loaded with preservatives and chemicals," Nancy announced through her teeth. "Preservatives and chemicals make you sick. They don't tell you that on TV, do they?"

"Other kids get to have nice frozen waffles with blueberries that you toast in the toaster," Sam wailed. "Why don't we ever get to have nice frozen waffles with blueberries that you—"

"Oh, shut up!" Nancy snapped. "Get out of this kitchen and leave me alone. You'll get your waffles. And why don't you shut off that stupid TV and go outside and enjoy this heavenly weather for a change?"

"Yech!" they chorused.

"Mommy, you are so dumb," Sam added patronizingly from the doorway. "If you've got a headache, you're supposed to take Anacin tablets. It says so on TV."

"Out!" Nancy screeched.

Twenty minutes later, peace was restored. The children had carried off plates of waffles swimming in syrup to the television set, and Nancy sank down in a kitchen chair. The phone rang, and she picked it up quickly, hoping that Dave would not awaken and require his breakfast before she had restored some degree of order.

"Nan, are you still asleep?" asked Mary Barnum, her hostess of the previous evening.

"No such luck," Nancy said. "I've just finished making waffles for the kids for breakfast."

"How do you feel?" Mary asked sympathetically.

"As well as can be expected, thank you. Did I make a proper fool of myself last night? I can't remember a thing that happened after about the middle of the evening. Did I break the dishes and insult the guests? Tell me the absolute truth."

"Of course not. You were fine."

"Come on, Mary. What did I do?"

"Well—" Mary said. "You were very talkative for a while. You had quite a fight with that movie critic man who came with the Sneiders about violence in the movies. And then at some point Dolly started quoting *Jonathan Livingston Seagull* the way she always does, and you told her that it was nothing but piffle and nonsense—"

"Oh, great! Poor Dolly! What else?"

"Well, let's see. After that I think you got another drink and went off and sat in a corner and sort of glowered at everybody for a while. Then right in the middle of everyone talking, you started saying, 'Bobby Johnson'—no, 'Watson.' You just kept saying 'Bobby Watson, Bobby Watson, Bobby Watson' over and over again. Dave said it had something to do with a play you were in when you were in college."

Nancy groaned. "I can't think what got into me, I haven't thrown down a flock of drinks like that since I can remember. I'm terribly sorry, Mary. It was a lovely party, too, what I can remember of it."

"Don't give it a thought, everybody's entitled to get smashed once in a while. Nan, the reason I called, it's so warm my kids are planning to spend the day in the pool. I thought when Dave comes over to pick up Alan for tennis, why don't you send your kids along? Give you a chance to get your head together or go back to bed or something."

"Mary, that would be marvelous," Nancy said gratefully. "Are you sure it's all right?"

"Don't be silly."

They talked on for several minutes, and in one corner of her mind, Nancy was already exploring the possibilities of an unexpected free Sunday, a bit of time entirely for herself. When she put down the phone, she had decided that this might be the exact warm and pleasant day she and Cynny had hoped for, for their rock-hunting expedition up the coast. Unless Cynny had other plans. She quickly dialed the number and heard the answering machine. She left a message and puzzled over it after she hung up. Odd that Cynny should be away so early in the morning. Probably she was just out in the garden enjoying the heavenly weather. In which case she would be certain to phone back before Nancy was ready to leave the house.

In a sudden flurry of energy, Nancy packed dishes in the dishwasher, put brioche for Dave's breakfast into the oven to warm, swept on to the bedroom wing to stuff her three progeny into their clothing, and bathing suits and towels into a beach bag. In the dressing room then, she peeled off the heavy trousers and shirt in favor of a cotton top and slacks. Dave by then was shaving, and Nancy brought him up to date on domestic developments.

Fine, he agreed absently over the whir of the electric shaver. And, by the way, how was she feeling?

She was feeling perfectly all right, Nancy announced a little stiffly. As a matter of fact, she was just off to meet Cynny. They were going to look for rocks for the garden.

She paused before the mirror, running a comb hastily through her bright hair and putting lipstick on. She scooped up her leather shoulder bag and called last instructions through the door. The English jam he liked with the little strawberries was on the table next to his plate, and try not to forget the beach bag.

Not to worry, he assured her. Have a good time.

She doubled back to the children's rooms, stopping briefly to assist Jenny with her braids. They were all to mind their manners, she instructed, and it would be nice if Jenny would offer to help Mary serve the lunch. Also try to see that Sam didn't pick on Benji Barnum, would she remember that?

Yech, Jenny said disdainfully through her braces.

With hugs and kisses all around, Nancy was gone. On her way out she grabbed a battered straw hat of Dave's, and a moment later she was backing the large red station wagon out the driveway. She was actually in the street before she remembered that Cynny had not phoned her after all.

Oh, bother, Nancy told herself. She had to buy gasoline anyway. She would phone again from the gas station.

She pulled in at a service station a mile or two from the house. While the attendant filled the tank, she went off to a phone booth but once again got the recorded message.

Oh, hell!

Nancy hung up the phone and lingered for a moment in the hot, stuffy booth. It did seem odd, Cynny hadn't mentioned any plans for the weekend. With Jim away she was not likely to have gone out of town. But perhaps something had come up at the last minute. In any case, she obviously was not at home.

Nancy plodded back to the station wagon. And it was such a perfect day for rock hunting, she mourned. While she lingered indecisively, the wind came in another hard gust, snapping the bright tricornered plastic pennants strung overhead and overturning a rack of oil tins. Nancy climbed back into the car, blinking against the dust. Oh, well, she decided as she rummaged for the credit card, why not drive up the coast herself? It was too heavenly a day just to sit at home. There was one particular canyon that she had in mind; they had driven out there last summer to take a look at a day camp for Davey. At least she could locate it today, then she and Cynny could return another time.

When she reached the Coast Highway, however, she discovered that the entire population of Los Angeles had decided to take similar advantage of the good weather. She fell into line behind strings of campers, the smaller motorcycles and Volkswagens with surfboard racks darting in and out through the turgid flow of vehicles. It was already hot, and along with the engine noise and exhaust fumes, she felt a twinge of her earlier headache.

She was tempted to abandon the whole idea, thinking wistfully of a quiet, peaceful day alone at home instead, with the hi-fi and a book. But she crawled on, caught in the hypnotic traffic flow, squinting at the sun reflecting off shining paint and chrome, shivering in the blast of the air-conditioning, rewarded by occasional vistas of the open sea.

By the time she passed Malibu the traffic had sped up some, and she maneuvered the station wagon into the right lane to watch for intersecting canyon roads. She couldn't remember the name of the canyon she had in mind and passed by several because they didn't look familiar. It occurred to her finally that she had already driven too far, and once more she was minded to turn back. Then she caught a glimpse of one more intersecting road and impulsively swung the station wagon into it. This was certainly not the canyon she remembered either, she decided, but since she had come this far, why not take a look?

Thirty seconds later she had an eerie feeling that she had strayed into another world entirely, a thousand miles removed from the crowded beaches, streaming traffic, gas stations, and lunch stands back behind her. The road was narrow, winding tunnellike between hills that towered into the clear, empty sky. She met no other cars, there were no signs of habitation, only the great hills close on either side, golden with dry wild oats and dotted with the gray-green of sage, tall, dead spikes of yucca, huge boulders, and craggy outcroppings. Who would believe it, a whole other world, rugged and unspoiled, and only a stone's throw from the urban sprawl and congestion. She would not have missed this drive for anything, she exulted, and she could not wait to show all this to Cynny. What luck that she had chosen this particular turnoff.

She drove on for several miles, meeting no other car, seeing no sign of life, winding between the huge hills. The wind blew harder here, twitching the wheel in her hands and sending sudden clouds of dust across the narrow blacktop road. She noted that the space between the hills had widened somewhat, and up

on the left she caught glimpses of a broad, dry streambed running parallel to but well below the road. To her delight, it was
liberally strewn with rocks of every size, shape, and color. How
divine! The perfect canyon after all.

The road was rising gently now, and she drove more slowly,
searching for a pull-off. She found one of sorts, just where the
road began to rise, a pair of tracks angling to the left into a dense
tangle of shrubbery. She nosed the car into it cautiously and
stopped. The tracks descended at a steep angle from the road to
the streambed below. They were narrow, barely wide enough for
the station wagon, she deduced, but they did end at a relatively
level spot suitable for parking, and the surface appeared firm,
dry, baked earth and rock. With a mild sense of adventure,
Nancy trod on the accelerator, and the big red station wagon
descended obediently, bushes scraping hard against its sides. As
it turned out, the level space at the bottom was smaller than it
had appeared, and she was forced to park at a steep angle. She set
the hand brake carefully, shut off the engine, and eagerly opened
the door.

Unprepared for the temperature outside, she stepped into
heat so sudden and intense it was a physical blow to the body.
For an instant she recoiled, grabbing for the battered straw hat
on the car seat and jamming it on her head. She closed the door
and stood for a moment uncertainly, enveloped in the breathless
heat and stillness. Then, tempting herself with the thought of
the array of rocks below, she began to descend the bank toward
the streambed, dry grass and weeds crackling beneath her feet.

By the time she reached the bottom, she was bathed in perspiration and her freckled skin was livid over her bare arms and
face. There came a gust of wind just then so strong that it nearly
knocked her from her feet. She scrambled for balance, clutching
at her hat and at the bank behind her, her eyes smarting with
dust. The wind stopped as abruptly as it had begun, and the stillness descended once more, no sound anywhere, no motion of
twig or leaf. Nancy discovered that her knees were rubbery, her

heart beating in loud, dull thumps. She moved into a patch of shade beneath an overhang of scrub oak and sat down upon a boulder. Just too damn hot to be out here, she decided crossly, her sense of adventure dwindling. Once she caught her breath, she would return to the car and give up the entire project.

She sat on the rock for a time, hunched over her knees, poking idly at the caked earth with a stick, staring at the ridge of the hills. She thought once more of the party the night before and whatever had possessed her to have all those rotten drinks and tee off on everybody. Thank God, at least she couldn't remember all the things she'd said. But there was one thing she remembered only too clearly, something that had happened once they were home and in bed. Dave had been very sweet and sympathetic, and after one of her trips to the bathroom, when he had offered her his shoulder again and a cool, wet cloth for her head, she had clutched at him suddenly and said, "Dave, tell me something. Could we possibly leave Los Angeles? I mean, could you get a job someplace else?"

"Oh, I suppose," he had answered. "Nothing quite as interesting as what I'm into now maybe, but there's that firm in Baltimore that's been after me for quite a while. Why? Would you like to move back east?"

"Baltimore's not far enough," she had said. "I was wishing that we could really move. Like to Woomera, Australia. Don't they have aerospace in Australia?"

Dave had laughed. "That's a pretty tall order!" And then he had said, his voice gentle and concerned, "Nan, I think we ought to talk about this. I know you've been going through a bad period lately. As a matter of fact, I was talking about it to Al at lunch just yesterday and—"

"Oh, Dave!" she had said tremulously. "You don't know how bad! Sometimes I feel like I can't bear it another day. I've hated to bother you with it, you work so hard and such long hours. But honestly, I don't think it's just me. It's the quality of our life, it's not good enough, not good enough for the kids, not good enough for you and me. I think we've got to make a change, I think that—"

"I know," he'd said soothingly. "It's been rough for you. You feel at loose ends. You don't have enough to do. So what I was thinking, we both feel the same about overpopulation and all that, but what the hell, we can adopt, can't we? We always said we wanted a houseful of kids, so why not? There are plenty of B-priority kids up for adoption and no waiting, so why don't we get on the ball and—"

And out of a fury of frustration, Nancy had said spitefully, "Oh, lovely! And whose idea was that anyway, yours or Alan Barnum's?"

"Hey, honey, take it easy! Didn't we always say we'd love to have six or eight kids around the house? Al agreed with me, that's all. As a matter of fact, he said Mary went through a period pretty much like yours just before she got pregnant with Karen, and—"

"We'll talk about it tomorrow," Nancy had said. "My head is absolutely splitting. We'll talk about it later, okay?"

As she remembered it now, sitting disconsolately upon her rock in the midst of this empty landscape, her throat swelled with tears. The wind blew again, and Nancy clung to her hat and the rock, dry leaves threshing together above her head. When the wind stopped, her attention was caught by the stillness. It suddenly occurred to her that there was something uncanny about such a total silence, not the cry of a bird or the scurry of a rabbit, no sound of any living creature, not even an insect. Nancy stared about her uneasily. It was as though the very hills had drawn in upon themselves against the savage onslaught of the heat, lying motionless like crouched giant beasts in wait. Waiting for what? She grinned weakly at her own fantasy and felt a sudden prickle of apprehension across the back of her neck. There was some positive menace of nature here that she was not able to identify.

Nancy rose to her feet. Now she wanted only to be away

from here. She began to clamber up the bank toward her car, her feet sliding in the dried, strawlike grasses.

The sound, when it came, was as startling as rifle shots. A deafening roar of motors, ripping apart the stillness of the canyon and engulfing her in earsplitting sound. Nancy jumped, grabbing at dry limbs to keep her balance, her heart pounding again. Just a motorcycle on the road, she told herself, no, several motorcycles, coming fast from the direction of the coast. But the sound did not recede, rather it ceased abruptly, motors close by cutting off, one after another, into silence, the ominous stillness of the canyon settling in once more.

Nancy remained motionless for a moment, straining her eyes in the dazzling sun for some glimpse through the heavy brush that lined the road above. Thank God at least for the presence of other human beings close at hand, she thought. All the same, when she set off again, she moved quickly, climbing on up the bank toward the security of her car, listening intently, her eyes still fixed upon the thicket that marked the edge of the roadway. But she saw nothing, and heard nothing more after that, only her own heartbeats and her breathing, labored from her exertions.

Actually, sound played strange tricks in these canyons, she reassured herself uneasily. Those motorcycles had certainly stopped, but that did not necessarily mean they were that close by, they might well have passed over the hill and continued on another mile along the road, for instance. In any case, what did it matter? In another minute, she'd be back in her car and on her way out of this spooky canyon forever.

But just as her hand closed upon the hot door handle of the station wagon, she heard another sound that all but stood her hair on end: a hoarse cry, unmistakably human, a despairing scream of pain and terror. Nancy stood transfixed, straining her ears to hear more. And once again there was no further sound.

Nancy was not a particularly timid woman, and suddenly she felt a steadying wave of anger as well. Now this is just ridiculous, she snapped at herself. Whatever is going on here is no concern of mine. All I've wanted to do for the past five minutes is get into my car and get out of this godforsaken place! But some alarm bell in a corner of her mind warned her that although so far her presence might have been undetected, once she started up the engine, that certainly would no longer be the case. There had been something so unsettlingly wrong about that outcry that, in truth, her nerve failed her at the thought of backing her car slowly out of this concealing underbrush into the middle of whatever or whomever had produced such a sound.

There had to be a vantage point from which she could see what was happening out there. She had already caught sight of an outcropping just beyond the ledge where she had parked. She judged that it must afford a view of the road on either side. Suiting action to thought, she was already scrambling for hand- and footholds among the rocks. She climbed with furious energy, scraped the skin of her knee and tore her trousers, lost her hat in another gust of wind, but at last she reached the top. She ducked down cautiously and inched around to a cracked cleft that promised her a view.

She peeped out, and there, sure enough, was the blacktop road at the crest of the hill. Back down the slope on her side, the road was empty, shimmering in the sun. In the other direction, however, it dipped abruptly and widened out into pull-off areas on either side. And there they were, ten or twelve motorcycles leaned on their parking stands, a dazzle of polished chrome. The riders were mostly young and all male, some of them bearded and long haired, clad in jeans and boots, leather jackets and colored T-shirts. They were drawn up in a rough circle, grouped in twos and threes before their silent machines, and in the middle of the circle, sprawled upon the roadway, was a boy, half-sitting, half-lying, yellow haired and slight of build, blood streaming down his white face.

What Nancy first felt was a wave of pure relief; the road on her side of the hill was open and clear, five minutes back to the coast and out of this place. Meanwhile, winded and dizzied in

the heat, she teetered on the rocks, peeping in fascinated disbelief as the scene below unfolded like a picture on a TV screen.
The young riders appeared to be conferring quietly, but the
menace was as real as bayonets, as inescapable as the stark animal terror exuding from the bleeding boy crouched at its center.

It came to Nancy then that her hour had struck, her moment
of truth was unexpectedly at hand. Was she to get into her car
then and sneak away, joining the faceless hordes of the uncar-
ing, the alienated, and the uninvolved, that segment of modern
society which she most deplored, those knitters beside bloody
guillotines?

No, never, Nancy vowed. I won't, I can't!

She was already shinnying down the rock spill, heedless of
torn clothing, skinned knuckles, and broken fingernails, her
mind racing. How many miles back to the coast, what chance of
flagging down a car, or how much farther after that to a telephone or the Malibu Sheriff's Station? Too far, in any case,
involving too much time. Because what that pathetic, terrified,
bleeding boy obviously no longer had was time. Whatever was
to be done must be done now, she reasoned, and therefore
entirely by herself.

She had one bad moment when her sandal wedged between
two rocks, but she managed to yank her foot free and leapt the
rest of the way to the ground. Kicking off her other sandal, she
ran fleetly to her car. She slid onto the seat, turned the ignition
key, and slammed the shift lever into reverse gear. Clutching the
steering wheel, she accelerated hard in reverse, struggling to
hold the wheels within the narrow tracks.

Once the car was in the road and the wheels straight, Nancy
shifted into drive and trod down hard on the accelerator, the big
wagon roaring up the hill with all the starting speed of which it
was capable. She hurtled over the crest, already braking hard,
tires squealing. The motorcycle riders were in motion, scattering to clear the road in front of her. As she brought the car to a
rocking halt, she noted that the yellow-haired boy was at the

back of the crowd, struggling silently between two larger men, who held him by the arms.

Nancy lowered the window beside her several inches, and over the soft idle of the motor shouted sternly, "What's going on here!"

No one answered, no one moved. No one appeared alarmed or in any way apprehensive, only a row of staring faces on either side of the road ahead of her.

It seemed to Nancy that an eternity crept past while she sat there, shivering in the breathy whoosh of the air-conditioning, perspiration drying on her flushed and grimy face.

From the corner of her eye she saw, beneath a coloring book on the seat beside her, the shiny tip of a toy she had confiscated from a member of Sam's car pool on Friday. She snatched it up now, the large, shiny, six-shooter revolver, held it up above the window level in the most convincing fashion she was able to muster, and lowered the glass a few more inches.

"This gun is loaded, and I know how to use it," she called out. "Don't any of you come near this car!"

The dispassionate spectator part of herself heard this, her voice cracking with strain, and nearly giggled at the idiocy of the remark, since not one of them had made the slightest gesture toward her car.

Nothing changed, no one moved, the sun beat down into the silent canyon.

Caught in an impasse of her own making, Nancy brandished her toy gun like a TV heroine and saw everything before her with crystal clarity: the embroidered patch on the knee of one boy's jeans, the heavy silver concha belt that another of them was wearing, a bearded man with two fingers missing from his hand, a large turquoise Navajo bracelet on a wrist, one boy with a particularly appealing and sensitive face.

Now this is just ridiculous, Nancy told herself wildly. Even in a nightmare your adversaries pay attention to you!

She took a deep breath, hoping that her voice would remain

steady, and snapped, "You there, with the blood on your face, come over here. Let him go right now!"

She was so alert for any sign of a threatening motion that she noticed the burly, bearded man nod his head just perceptibly, and suddenly the boy was free and racing toward her car, crouched like an animal. Nancy fumbled at a battery of buttons, finding the one that released the door locks. The boy yanked the door open and dove into the car. He slammed the door after him, Nancy pushed buttons to relock it as she trod on the accelerator, and the big station wagon leapt forward and away. Over the sound of her own motor, she heard the loud splutter and pop of starting engines behind her, saw dust rising in the rearview mirror, and in one moment of pure terror, screeched, "Are they coming after us? Are they coming?"

The boy beside her was twisted on the seat to look back, but his voice when he spoke was strangely calm, almost bored. "No," he said. "They won't come."

The big wagon bounced forward along the narrow road, Nancy clutching at the wheel, but the sound of motorcycle engines vanished with the dust. She brought the car to a jerky stop and turned off the motor. She opened the car door, the better to hear, but once again there was no sound from anywhere, no sign of life between the towering hills, only the stunning heat and sinister silence.

"They must have gone back the other way," she said unsteadily. She was shaking, bathed in perspiration. "Oh, my Lord! I think we're all right now. Isn't it fantastic?"

The boy beside her did not speak, and when she looked at him she discovered that he was staring fixedly at the toy gun still jammed between her knees, the barrel rammed against her stomach.

Nancy laughed. "Oh, that," she said giddily. "Don't worry, it's not really a gun at all. I mean it's just a toy. I took it away from a little boy in my car pool and forgot to give it back. Isn't that fantastic!"

She picked it up by the barrel and tossed it over her shoulder into a welter of children's sweaters, Coke cans, and toys in the rear of the wagon, chattering on out of an intoxicating sense of relief and triumph. "This child's father brought it to him from a business trip to Texas, can you imagine? I don't approve of guns or any kind of war toy for children, though I suppose we have to be grateful that I had the thing." She laughed again. "Wasn't it crazy? I never thought they'd just let us drive off like this, did you?"

The boy did not speak, sitting motionless beside her.

Nancy stopped herself with an effort. "I'm sorry," she said. "I guess I'm a little hysterical. Things like this don't happen to me every day. Are you all right? I mean, did they hurt you very much?"

"No, I'm all right," he said in the same calm and detached voice.

She looked at him and thought, Why, this boy looks like an angel in a painting, those delicate, beautiful features and that curling, yellow hair. And then she felt a wave of indignation, noting the large bruise on his cheekbone and the blood that still dripped from his nose and from a split in his upper lip.

"Ah, they really beat you, it's sickening! I'll get you to a doctor right away."

"I'm all right," he said again.

"No, you're going to need stitches in your lip, and your nose may be broken. Look, if it's money you're worrying about, don't. I think the Malibu Emergency would be the best place, and it's near the Sheriff's Station. The sooner you report this, the better."

At some quality in the boy's silence, Nancy quickly amended her suggestion. "Of course, that part of it is up to you. I think it's awful though to let them get away with doing things like this to people. But you think about it and do whichever you think is best. We'll get you to a doctor anyway."

By then she had noticed several other things about him, an unpleasant gamy odor beyond any ordinary smell of sweat and dirt, and his eyes upon her, uncommonly still, pale blue, shallow and unblinking.

"I think there's room to turn around just up ahead, don't you?" she said uncomfortably. She slammed the car door and reached for the ignition key.

He moved so suddenly that he took her completely by surprise. She never saw where the knife came from, only the shine of the steel blade in his hand. He had caught her neck in his doubled arm, cutting off her wind, and in that split second before Nancy prepared to fight for her life, she did not even try to scream. She was only thinking, I must remember to tell Cynny. It's such a commentary on our culture. These days you can't even tell anymore who the true victims are!

It was over in a minute. The boy backed out of the car, the knife still in his hand. He attempted to retract the switchblade, but the mechanism was bent or his hand was too unsteady, and he threw it away instead into the bushes. He peeled off his blood-soaked T-shirt and tossed it back onto the car seat. He crouched upon his heels for a time then, his thin chest still heaving from his exertions, rubbing dirt aimlessly into the blood on his hands, his forehead wrinkled in a frown, his eyes fixed unseeingly upon the towering ridge.

When he stood up at last, there was no longer any sound from inside the car, and he fell to work with casual, quick efficiency. He examined the contents of Nancy's leather bag until he found her wallet, transferred the bills and coins from it to a pocket of his jeans and, after an instant's hesitation, a gasoline credit card as well. When he was through, he slung the bag around several times by the shoulder strap and let it sail over the bushes into the streambed below. He slammed the car door then, the sound loud in the breathless silence. Before he entered the car on the other side, he wiped blood from the vinyl seat with one of the children's sweaters from the rear. He started up the car, drove forward to a place where he was able to execute a tight turn, and headed the wagon back in the direction of the coast. He drove fast for several miles, tires squealing in the curves of the winding road. As he drove, he watched the sides of the road alertly, slowing once or twice before he finally stopped and backed up for twenty-five or thirty feet.

At the place he had chosen, the land fell away precipitously into a gulley grown up with chaparral and scrub oak. He surveyed it critically, standing beside the opened car door, his yellow hair gleaming in the sun. He turned back then, leaned in, and grasped her beneath the arms. He pulled with all his strength, chest heaving once more, face shining with sweat, his breath coming in hoarse gasps. After a short and desperately fierce struggle, she fell from the car to the edge of the road. He paused, gulping air, then heaved again with all his slender strength. She slid down the steep bank over the slippery golden grass, slid faster, rolled, and disappeared crashing into the dense, tinder-dry foliage at the bottom of the gulley. Once the leaves and branches were still, all that remained visible was one bare foot, a scrap of blue-and-white-checked trouser leg, and the dark smears of blood upon the dried grass of the bank.

The boy scrubbed off the vinyl seat again with another sweater, moving now with frenetic haste, then made a bundle out of both sweaters and his own bloodied T-shirt, wrapping them around a couple of blood-soaked children's books and tossing it all into the gulley. He paused briefly, his forehead wrinkling, and finally, kneeling on the seat, began to rummage through the welter of toys and cans in the rear. He came up at last with a pool toy, a little figure of a helmeted diver attached to a long plastic tube. He ripped the small figure away from the end of the tube and, out of the car again, opened the gas tank and jammed lengths of tubing into the aperture.

Kneeling then beside the rear wheel of the car, he began to suck frantically at the other end of the plastic. His face reddened with his efforts, and blood spurted from his cut and swollen lip. Several times he moaned aloud in pain, small, forlorn sounds lost in the vast stillness. Several times he was forced to stop to regain his breath, hastily plugging his finger against the end of the tube each time and watching despairingly as the liquid slowly sank. It was nearly five minutes before he spat a mouthful of gasoline and the thin stream ran free. He dribbled the gas back and forth over the dry grass along the roadside and then, letting the tube hang over the bank, he returned to the back of the wagon to snatch up several empty soft drink cans and a glass Coke bottle. He ran gasoline into each of them and tossed the cans into the underbrush of the gulley. When he had finished, he yanked the tube out of the tank and tossed it after them.

He found the rag in the glove compartment along with several packets of paper matches. He scrubbed hard at his hands with the rag before he tore it and crammed part of it into the neck of the Coke bottle. Holding the bottle carefully between his knees, he drove the car forward another fifty feet. The wind blew once more, extinguishing matches as fast as he struck them, but at last he had a protruding edge of the rag charred and smoldering. He jumped, a sudden nervous fear in his face, and hurled the bottle toward the gasoline-soaked grass of the bank behind him. The car leapt forward while he watched the rearview mirror.

Nothing happened. Nothing at all. There was only the glass bottle shining in the sun beside the road.

The boy cursed under his breath. He opened a second book of matches, ignited a corner of the folder, tossed it out the window, and roared off.

For an instant, the flame all but flickered out, then the matches ignited in a sudden tiny burst. Grass caught, a flame grew, twirled in a lazy spiral, pale in the bright sun, grew again, and divided, lingered, danced. A small blackened splotch of char and ash appeared and spread along the road with incredible speed. Shrubs caught, and greasy yellow smoke plumed upward. The flames turned bright orange and leapt ten feet into the air, spinning upon themselves in a brief search for further fuel. The wind came again just then, and all at once the entire hillside was engulfed in flame. Across the road and beyond the streambed, an opposite massive hill, lying still and somnolent in the heat, inexplicably spurted bright answering jets of fire. Flames combined, soared fifty feet into the empty sky, and thundered on. The sun suddenly dimmed beneath a roiling pall of smoke and fire into an eerie, lurid red twilight.

In the canyon, the waiting was finally over.

The boy at the wheel of Nancy's car, white faced and trembling, barreled down the last remaining half mile to the coast and barely made it, paint blistering along the sides of the station wagon. Sirens were already wailing as he shot out onto the Coast Highway and turned north.

KILLIAN AWAKENED THAT MORNING ALONE IN Rob's apartment in the hills above Westwood. She drowsed and slept again fitfully before she finally crept from the bed, her eyes still red and swollen from weeping. Pale and silent as a ghost, she drifted off to the kitchen and prepared herself a small breakfast. After she had eaten, she returned to the dim, airless living room, still clad in her nightshirt. She began the slow, rhythmic patterns of her t'ai chi, but today her concentration was less than perfect. The fierce energy that had been underlying her movements the day before was now absent.

When she finished, she returned to the kitchen and put a kettle on to boil. Rob's note was still attached to the refrigerator door with an orange, daisy-shaped magnet, two short lines in his round, schoolboy handwriting: "Back in a couple days, hon. Don't worry," the last two words heavily underscored, and then in a scrawled afterthought, "P.S. I paid the phone bill."

Killian read it again and this time removed it, allowing the scrap of paper to flutter from her hand toward an overflowing trash can. She waited for the water to boil and slumped miserably against a countertop, burying her face in her arms finally, her body bent in despair. The kettle steamed and bubbled noisily for a long time before she pulled herself erect and went to rinse a white mug. She dropped a careless pinch of tea leaves into the mug and filled it with boiling water, carrying it with her then as she drifted back into the living room. The mug grew hot; she juggled it from hand to hand until suddenly the wet handle slipped from her fingers and the mug fell, striking a leg of the divan and shattering.

Killian jumped as hot tea spattered her bare feet, then surveyed the mess before her. She felt so listless she was tempted to leave it, but she fetched a rag from the kitchen and, dropping to her knees, began to dab at the splotch on the carpet. Most of the pieces of broken china had flown beneath the divan, and she bent lower to retrieve them, her long hair fanning out over the floor. Killian jumped again, startled this time by an unexpected sight in the dim light, a long, blanket-wrapped bundle under the divan. She stared at it for several seconds and then scrambled to her feet, switching on a brass pole lamp. Flopping down again upon her belly, she stretched her arms beneath the low divan, caught hold of one end of the bundle, and began to tug. The bundle was surprisingly heavy. Killian hauled with all her strength until she had one end out in the light. It was wrapped in a soiled pink blanket, worn thin with age.

The bundle was rolled up so securely that it took her another minute to free a section of the ragged blanket hem. The cool, polished, blue-black steel gun barrels gleamed in the light, and Killian recoiled as though she had unearthed a nest of rattlesnakes. Bounding to her feet, she walked blindly to the windows, her eyes squeezed closed.

A moment later the phone began to ring, and Killian did not move or open her eyes; her quick, shallow breathing did not alter. The telephone jangled noisily six or eight times, then fell silent again. There were tiny drops of perspiration upon her forehead and across her upper lip. Finally she moved to push the window open on its track and leaned out over the sill.

The hot, dry wind gusted about the corners of the building, whipping at her hair, threshing the limbs of trees below. It was the light that she first noticed, some unnatural quality of the sunlight, and then the white, powdery ash sticking to her sleeves. There was more ash on the flagstones below, and a scum of it floating upon the clear water of the small swimming pool. And the air was still filled with it, irregular bits and pieces, sifting down as silent as a snowfall. She looked out toward the sea then, over a shimmering purple-yellow layer of smog, and saw the great ominous pall of smoke streaming across the empty sky to the west like some extraordinary, indigenous cloud formation.

Killian stared and laughed. She turned away from the window, gathering up handfuls of hair from her neck and gulping air through her opened mouth. Without hesitation, she walked to the bookshelves and snatched up her worn copy of the *I Ching* with trembling hands. She searched along the shelf edge until she found the coins and a pad and pencil, and sank down upon the floor. She sat cross-legged, spine pulled erect, and took hold of herself with conscious effort, deepening and lowering her breathing to her belly, forcing her body, muscle by muscle, to relax. She held the coins tightly cupped between her hands for a long time, her face strained. At last she tossed the coins out upon the carpet.

She threw them six times with enormous solemnity, studying the pattern of heads and tails, each time carefully adding a line to the hexagram on the pad beside her. After she had drawn the final broken line at the top, she closed her eyes, sitting until her hands stopped shaking. Picking up the pad then, she studied the hexagram intently, verifying it finally from the chart at the back of the book: Chen, the hexagram of shock, the Arousing, thunder in the spring, the symbol of beginning.

Killian caught her breath and thumbed rapidly through the pages.

"Thunder repeated: the Image of Shock. Thus in fear and trembling the superior man sets his life in order and examines himself."

She meditated upon the commentary for a long time: the frightened tiger, the terrified lizard that skitters upon the wall, the sound of shock repeated that becomes the sound of laughter: out of terror, caution, and hence good fortune, the symbol of inner calm in the midst of a storm of outer movement, the reawakening of the life force.

Enthralled, trembling with earnestness, she carefully transposed the changing lines into the new and final hexagram, and discovered it to be the symbol of the Corners of the Mouth, the holding fast to provide nourishment for what is right.

"Perseverance brings good fortune," she read. "Pay heed to the providing of nourishment and to what a man seeks to fill his own mouth with."

She brooded over the commentary, fascinated by the image of the magic tortoise who can nourish itself on air. One line she marked with her finger and thought about intently: "This hexagram contains three ideas, nourishing oneself, nourishing others, and being nourished by others."

At last, soberly, she closed the book, one line catching her eye a final time. "It furthers one," she read, "to cross the great water."

Killian stretched out her cramped legs, then drew them up and clasped them, resting her chin upon her knees, a quietness about her now.

The room was breathlessly hot, and after a time she peeled off her yellow shirt. She rose with purpose and walked to the kitchen, naked except for the string of turquoise beads at her throat. She searched in a drawer for a pair of scissors and carried them back to the cramped, untidy bathroom. Turning on the light, she began to brush her hair vigorously into a long, dark curtain that obscured her face. She seized a handful of hair from in front of her nose, slid the blades of the scissors up along it to the level of her eyebrows, and snipped. After that she worked rapidly, dropping long tendrils into a wastebasket. Ten minutes later, she studied her reflection curiously, a shorn Killian with a cap of curling, dark hair fringing her neck and cheeks, and an uneven bang above her eyes. She stared at herself with no particular pleasure and cut a bit more at either temple before she put down the scissors and mopped snippets of hair from the washbowl with a wad of toilet paper.

In the bedroom she turned on a small television set on top of a chest of drawers, switching channels until she found a report of the fire. She listened long enough to ascertain the section of hills that was involved and then, grim faced, turned up the sound and set about her packing, cramming clothing into a large canvas duffel bag, throwing in necklaces and earrings, paperback books and cosmetics.

She worked with one eye upon the TV screen, and suddenly she caught a glimpse of Pete. A TV remote unit van had turned its cameras upon a group of terrified children evacuated from a camp in the hills just ahead of the fire. In the background, she recognized Pete's lean height and blond head as he lifted frightened small boys from the back of a truck. Killian flew to the television to adjust the fuzzy picture. But Pete was already gone from the screen. A moment later, however, the cameras and a reporter picked him out once more, and this time she noted the gauze bandaging wrapped about one of his hands. He politely answered several questions concerning fire conditions in the hills, then backed determinedly out of camera range. Killian reached out to the glass screen, then switched off the TV set and turned away.

When her packing was completed, she made the bed neatly and went to the shower. She washed her newly shorn hair and toweled it into a mop of dark ringlets before she set to work with a comb, straightening and shaping it about her face as she dried it with a hand dryer. She dressed in jeans then and a thin, sleeveless shirt, and lugged the duffel bag out into the living room.

She made the phone call to Linda next, listening to the small, agitated voice for a time as her face became more exasperated. "Linda, just stop flapping," she said at last. "I do know there's a fire, but I'm not in Topanga, I've told you that. I'm in Westwood. Anyway, I'll be home in an hour, all right?" Then she put down the phone.

She turned off the lights on the lamp pole and, on her knees, shoved the pink blanket–wrapped bundle back out of sight beneath the divan. She carried broken bits of china to the trash can in the kitchen and washed dishes hurriedly, leaving them to drain beside the sink.

When she was done with her housekeeping, she sat down at the table in the living room with paper and a pencil. She made three or four attempts, crumpling the paper each time and starting over. Her last version she carried to the kitchen and attached to the refrigerator door with the flower-shaped magnet. She paused to read what she had written a final time.

Dearest Rob,

If you have to do this then maybe it is right for you. All I know is, it is wrong for me.

I guess loving each other is not enough. If we had been in love I might have known the way to make you stop this.

I didn't forget my Indian pectoral shell necklace, I'd like you to have it.

I am taking the Moody Blues records, but you may borrow them back any time you like.

P.S. You are the Mwene Mutapa.

Always.

She gathered up the stack of record albums and the *I Ching*, and slung the heavy duffel bag over her back. She left the latchkey on the bare tabletop and closed the door quietly behind her.

THE HOT AFTERNOON WORE ON. THE VAST COASTAL low-pressure area held steady, continuing to suck dry desert air through the canyons at gale force and ever-increasing temperatures. Throughout the Los Angeles basin air-conditioning units hummed, pool parties proliferated, and the smoke from backyard barbecues rose into the unusually clear air. The smog had moved out to Santa Monica and the South Bay beaches, which were packed in spite of it as the inland population sought to escape the heat. Access streets and freeways jammed with traffic. Tempers wore thin. Police department switchboards and hospital emergency rooms quickened with an activity rare for a Sunday afternoon, reflecting the increase in family quarrels and assorted violence that always accompanied this weather condition.

In the hills, the fire roared on, leaving blackened slopes in its wake, twirling and circling erratically to devour new acres of watershed in the blink of an eye, leaping firebreaks and backfires with ferocious abandon, taking on a monstrous life of its own, even creating its own temperatures and winds. World War II bombers droned through the skies to make borate drops on strategic hot spots, TV news helicopters darted mosquitolike about the fire's perimeters. In adjacent populated areas, nervous homeowners clambered to their rooftops with hoses, staring helpless at the boiling smoke as they wet down ash-covered shingles. The hot wind dried out the shingles again almost immediately. In residential areas on the immediate outskirts of the fire, hundreds of sooty, sweating firemen waged a house-by-house battle against the racing flames, winning countless numbers but losing occasional others.

New blazes broke out in Griffith Park and along Mulholland Drive and were quickly contained. In the Valley, however, another major fire burned out of control in the Thousand Oaks area, and fire officials grimly conceded that the two fires might well converge within the next several hours. Still other fires were reported in Ventura and Orange Counties. A million television sets throughout the area were turned to channels that featured live fire coverage, and a middle-aged Echo Park bank clerk with an unsuspected predilection for arson found the TV reports so gripping that he was gleefully en route to the upper reaches of Benedict Canyon with a can of gasoline.

Tom and Hallie were among the TV viewers that afternoon, but unlike Killian, they had tuned in too late to catch the glimpse of Pete. Tom, as it turned out, had eaten an early lunch for which he had no particular appetite while he and his attorney held a lengthy and unrewarding discussion of his marital problems as they affected his business interests. It was his attorney's best advice that under no circumstance should Tom permit Nedith to file a divorce within the next two months. After the first of the year, California's no-fault divorce laws would be in effect, and it was current legal opinion that these new laws might allow a more lenient attitude toward men in the courts. If Nedith could be forestalled by so simple an expediency as sailing with her around the world until February, what was the matter with that, his lawyer asked. These cruise ships were continually putting in to ports along the way, Tom could avail himself of airlines to leave and rejoin the cruise whenever it became necessary to attend to business matters. Besides, a little vacation never hurt anyone, the lawyer concluded unfeelingly. At his age, Tom would live a hell of a lot longer if he would learn not to push himself so hard.

Through all of this, Tom had kept in touch with Hallie by phone, but in her concern for him she had not found it important to mention her small misadventure of the previous evening. Consequently, when he reached the apartment at last in a seething temper, he was not prepared for the sight of Hallie hobbling about on her badly swollen ankle, her face drawn with pain. All of his frustrations came to a head at his first glimpse of her. Over her protests, he stormed to the telephone and refused to be put off by the answering service until his personal physician had been located. At Tom's insistence, the doctor consented to meet them at a hospital emergency center. Still protesting, Hallie was borne off in her dressing gown and only by dint of prodigious willpower avoided vomiting in the car from the combination of emotion, nerves, heat, and pain.

The X-rays revealed that she was suffering nothing worse than a severe sprain, and an hour and a half later she was once more ensconced on her own divan, giddy with pain pills, her ankle tightly bandaged, and a pair of crutches propped against the wall nearby. Tom, stripped down to his undershorts, turned on the TV to the fire coverage and plugged in a large electric fan.

"There, how's that?" he asked as he tipped the face of the fan in her direction.

"Absolutely heavenly," she said, pushing a fringe of damp hair from her face. "Tom, darling, now will you please sit down? You've been running in circles for hours looking after me, and I know you're hotter than I am."

"Let me get a beer and I'll be right with you."

Tom disappeared into the kitchen, and Hallie gave her attention to the TV screen.

"Oh, Tom, come look! The most fantastic pictures, it's terrifying!"

He returned obediently and stood silent for a time while they both watched a hillside wrapped in flame, a row of houses in the foreground.

"This looks like a bad one," he said at last. "And if this weather doesn't break, it'll get worse. I wonder if Pete really did leave for La Jolla yesterday or whether he's still up there."

"Oh, Tom!"

"Oh, he'd be all right, in any case, he's an old fire hand. Anyway, he's probably back in La Jolla by now. How about a cold beer?"

"No, darling. Not this minute. Please sit down."

Tom pulled a chair around to share the air from the fan and propped his bare feet against a corner of the coffee table. "How do you feel?" he asked, eyeing her.

"Much, much better. Just pleasantly woozy now from the pills. Honestly, I feel so stupid about this whole thing. I'll be fine in a day or two."

"Day or two, my eye! You heard what the doctor said. You're spending the next two or three weeks right there on that couch, Mrs. C.!"

"Oh, Tom, I'd go absolutely crackers! One week, maybe. They'll have fits at the store as it is. We're coming into our busiest time of the whole year, you know."

"What in hell are you talking about!" Tom said, juggling his frosty beer can.

"What do you mean?"

"We settled all this on the phone a couple days ago, didn't we? You were going to hand in your notice tomorrow anyway. I have news for you, my girl! You're never going to set foot behind that damn stocking counter again."

"Tom, don't be silly! Oh, look at that aerial shot! The whole mountains are going! Think of all the poor little animals and the birds. And the ants and the bees and the spiders. After all, people choose to build houses with shingle roofs in those hills. The birds and animals have no choice whatsoever."

"From that point of view, I think you have to consider these fires as a natural phenomenon then, just as they are in Africa or Australia. Never pays to take the short view in nature, Mrs. C. I believe the theory is that in the long run they renew more life than they destroy. Look, you are going to hand in your resignation tomorrow, aren't you?"

"I can't bear to think of it all the same. They must be so terrified, poor things, and no place to run to. To coin a phrase, nature sometimes is just too damn cruel."

"Come on, Hallie, quit stalling. You are quitting tomorrow?"

"Oh, Tom, honestly! I can't afford just to— I like my job. I'd be lost without it."

"Nonsense! All right, answer me just one question. After we're married, did you actually think you'd be going to that store every day and selling stockings?"

Hallie pushed at her hair. "Well, I don't suppose I've really ever given it that much thought, I—" She readjusted herself against the pillows.

"Come on, be honest."

"Oh, Tom, I don't know. No. I suppose not. Not if you didn't want me to."

"Fine," he said. "That's all I wanted to hear. Now you get on the horn first thing tomorrow morning and tell your boss lady at that plush-lined clip joint to go jump in the ocean. All right?"

"Tom, be reasonable. It's a perfectly good job. I can't just—"

Tom bounded from his chair. "For God's sakes, Hallie, what's the matter?"

"Tom, please don't bedevil me! My head's fuzzy with pills, and I suppose I'm not expressing myself very well. You asked me a hypothetical question about something I would or would not do after we're married, that's all. But under the circumstances— I mean, we can't be married for a while yet, can we, and you're going away and—"

He stared at her for a moment, and with hurt in his voice said, "I don't believe this! You know, if I didn't know you so well, Hallie, I'd think you'd chosen this particular way to get back at me because I didn't spit in Nedith's eye and tell her to go ahead and file her damn divorce the first thing tomorrow morning."

"Darling, how can you say such a thing! How can you even think it!"

"Look, do you actually believe for one minute that I like this idea of stalling on the divorce any better than you do?"

"Thomas, that's not fair. You're attributing motives to me that simply don't exist. Have I ever once pressured you about getting a divorce? You know I've never liked the idea of you breaking up your marriage. I don't like it now."

Tom laughed shortly. "That's an extraordinary statement. What marriage can you be referring to! I promise you, Hallie, the first moment I am able I am divorcing Nedith, and that may be the only thing in my entire life at this moment that happens to have nothing to do with you! Meanwhile, can you possibly think that I enjoy the idea of being trapped with her on some goddamn idiotic cruise ship for two months? It's a matter of expediency, pure and simple. I thought you understood that."

"Now that you mention it, perhaps I don't," Hallie said wildly. "Perhaps I'm not terribly good at grasping expediencies. It seems to me that under the circumstances, and feeling as you do, to go off now on this cruise with your wife is unnecessarily callous and cruel. Not just to her but to yourself and—"

"You mean it would be preferable for me to sit back and allow Nedith to dump half the stock in my company out of sheer malice? Speaking of callous and cruel behavior, I'd think that—"

"Yes, I think I do mean exactly that," Hallie said with shaky determination. "I don't pretend to understand a great deal about the ins and outs of business, but it was my understanding that you intended to sell out your company anyway. What real difference can it make if you do it now or do it later?"

"It happens to make a very considerable difference. Take my word for it."

"Exactly what difference, Tom? I think you're talking about the difference between a lot of money and a great deal of money. Isn't that it?"

"Yes, I am," he said bluntly. "As a matter of fact, that's putting it entirely correctly, and in a nutshell."

"Then let it go," Hallie said. "Darling, let it go. How could it be worth it? Money is a very relative thing. If you really wanted more of it, you could always make it later. You told me yourself you'd want to do consulting jobs, didn't you?"

Tom's face was suddenly tired and gray. "You know," he said softly, "I think in all the time we've been together, this is the first thing you've ever asked of me, Hallie. I hope like hell I can make you understand why I have to say no to you. My company represents thirty years of my life, but let's leave that out of it, it's not the most important thing anyway. What I'm primarily thinking about now is you and our future. We have to face it, Hallie, I'm not a young man any longer."

"Oh, Thomas, how can you say that! It's fantastic! You're the youngest man I know, you're—"

"Come off it, Hallie. I'm fifty-nine years old."

"Tom! Darling! You're exactly two days older than you were on the phone the other night when—"

"That's true," Tom said. "I am also thirty-six hours older than I was when I lost a contract it never occurred to me I wouldn't get. And lost it to a man who came up with a better gadget than mine based on a set of premises that I can't even begin to grasp, and applied in my own field. No wonder your instinct tells you to hold on to your job at this point."

"Darling, stop it," she said. "I won't have this. This isn't you at all. Everything that has happened today came at you too fast after what happened yesterday. All you need is time to get a second wind, my darling. I won't hear another word. Of course I'll give up the job! If that's what you want, of course I will. What does some silly job matter?"

He came around the coffee table and scooped her into his arms. They clutched at each other tenderly, murmuring promises and words of consolation. When he released her, Tom remained seated beside her, her face cupped in his fingers, his face sobered and moved.

"If you have a notion anywhere in your funny little head that I'm being unreasonable about your stocking counter, try to bear with me, will you?" he said. "You're very precious to me, Mrs. C.

I don't need any reminders of it, but I had one today anyway when I walked in here and found you hobbling about in pain. It's my intention to take very, very good care of you from here on in. Is that wrong?"

"Of course not," Hallie said. "If it pleases you, my darling, you have my permission to take very good care of me from now till the end of time."

"Good," Tom said. "Then I may as well start by feeding you ... is due about now. Anything else you'd like? Care to be lugged to the bathroom?"

"Not yet. I'll let you know when, love."

"Changed your mind about a beer? This place is beginning to heat up like an oven."

"You know, a cold beer does sound marvelous. Do you think on top of the pills, it will buzz me out of my skull?"

"Not one beer. I'll have one with you."

Tom bounced to his feet with all his former energy and headed for the kitchen.

"You know, this is ridiculous," he called back to her. "It really is like a damn oven in here. I think before I take off on any ill-begotten cruise ships, I'm going to have to find you a comfortable apartment somewhere."

Hallie laughed. "Darling, don't be silly! Besides, I can't stay on this couch for weeks the way you want me to and move at the same time now, can I?"

"The hell you can't," Tom called back cheerfully. "We'll turn the whole project over to Batesey. You don't know Batesey, she's a marvel. How would you like to live at the Marina, Mrs. C., and wake up every morning looking at the ocean?"

"Oh, Tom," she said miserably, her voice soft. "But I love this old place. It's my home. I did it all myself, and it's the only real home I've ever had."

"What were you saying?"

She was silent for an instant, and then she said, "I was just saying I expect I'd miss this dear old place."

"Balls! This dear old place also happens to be a firetrap, among other things. Seriously, what about the Marina? There are some great sea view apartments out there and only ten minutes from my office. What do you think?"

"It sounds heavenly. Why not? Oh, Tom, quick! They have a map. It's incredible the way this fire has spread in just the past hour. It's absolutely raging. Do you realize they're already beginning to talk about how to keep it out of Topanga? Oh, I— ten! Now they're saying something about a new fire. Oh, I—"

Tom appeared with two beer cans and a glass, carrying one of them to Hallie along with her capsule. He paused momentarily then beside the divan to give his attention to the television screen.

"You know, this could turn into a pretty damn bad situation," he said at last. "Apparently, there's no indication of this weather letting up, either. Fairly soon now they may have to start worrying about Beverly Glen, and that's a hell of a lot more populated than Topanga."

"I know. Isn't it dreadful?"

Tom's face was thoughtful, and then suddenly crinkling with laughter. Chuckles grew into guffaws.

"Tom! For heaven's sakes, what?"

"I've just had a very entertaining thought," he said, tears of amusement shining in his eyes. "If this weather should hold, God forbid, and if this new fire keeps moving southeast, perish the thought—"

He was off again, shaking his head in merriment, thumping his leg.

"What on earth! Tell me!"

"Why, then the goddamn fire's liable to burn up—Nedith's house!"

He danced a small jig of delight.

Hallie wept.

MICK WAS THE LAST PASSENGER ABOARD HIS flight that morning. In fact, he barely made it. He was no sooner in his seat and fastening his belt than the plane taxied away toward its runway. Mick leaned back and sat motionless for several minutes, hands folded over the buckle of the seat belt, eyes closed behind the tinted lenses of his glasses.

Once the plane was airborne, however, he sat up quickly, leaning close to the window for a final glimpse of the city below. The jet climbed rapidly, leveled off, and began its turn. Mick still looked out, his eyes fixed now upon the great stretch of bright ocean and the range of coastal foothills, sharply defined in the crystal clear air. For an instant, he fancied that he saw a smudge of smoke streaming out of one of the steep canyons and leaned closer to the glass, watching intently in that final second before the plane straightened out, climbing once more.

Five minutes later, over a cigarette and coffee, he spread several sheets of hotel stationery on the small tray before him. He wrote the first note in a rapid scrawl without hesitation and folded it directly into an envelope without bothering to reread it.

Dear Trav,

Sorry I didn't have time to get out to your place. It was great to see you, buddy. We'll be in touch, and I'll call you as soon as I get back. I've been thinking about what you said, if there was anything of Theo's I wanted to keep. I'd like a friend of hers to have Great-Grandmother's emerald ring, if you have no

*objections. I think Theo would like the idea. Mrs. Holman was
very close to Theo and did a lot for her the last couple years,
you've probably met her. Also, among the jewelry, I believe
there's some Chinese stuff, beads, jade etc. Naturally I'll buy
all this from the estate or whatever. Come to think of it, why
don't you hold on to all the jewelry till I get back to L.A.? I've
decided to come out here for Christmas this year, so I'll see you
in December.*

Mick

*P.S. That old Tiffany lamp in the hallway, put it in storage
for me, okay?*

The second note he found more difficult. He lighted another
cigarette and stared out the window for a long time before he
picked up the pen again. He wrote slowly, crumpling several
sheets and starting over until finally he was satisfied. Then he
removed a checkbook from the pocket of his jacket, brooded
briefly over its balance, and at last wrote the check. Once he had
removed it from the folder, he swore under his breath, tore it
impatiently into tiny pieces, and wrote another for a larger
amount. He reread the note then, only a few scrawled lines,
without salutation and unsigned.

*If things worked out and I hope like hell they did, consider this
a wedding present. If they didn't, you'll be at about the same
place in your life that I was when I first went racing in Europe.
I didn't expect to, but I got a pretty big bang out of being in all
those places. It helps for some reason. Of course you might
rather go to China—why not? Anyway, in case you need it,
here's an airline ticket and some traveler's checks. I'll be back in
L.A. in December. I'll phone you and hope to see you then.*

He folded check and note into an envelope and addressed it
to Killian at Linda's house in Beverly Hills. With both letters put

away in his jacket pocket, he returned the tray to the seat back with an air of chores accomplished. He tilted back his seat then, closed his eyes, and gave himself up to his thoughts, his face softened and half-smiling.

Six hours later Cynny was back at the airport. Jim's plane was late, and she was forced to make a second circuit past the terminal buildings in the thick traffic before she found him waiting at the curb with his bags, carrying his suitcoat as well as his raincoat over his arm.

She paused in the flow of traffic, and he plunged out between two cars to open the door on the passenger side.

"My God, what's happened to the weather out here!" he said as he climbed in.

"Isn't it awful? It started last night. And now there's a ghastly fire going up near Malibu."

"You're telling me! There's fire all over the place, we saw it coming in."

They kissed briefly and she drove on, inserting the big car neatly back into the traffic stream.

"So how was your trip?"

"Oh, fine. Well, actually, lousy. These trips are always the same, too little sleep and too much liquor and rich food, a real bore."

"I know. You look tired. Are you sure you're up to the McClures?"

"Hell, I forgot about the McClures," he said, yawning widely. "Oh, sure, why not? We can make it an early evening, can't we?"

"Of course. Nap a bit if you like, it'll be a half hour before we get there."

"I think I will." He leaned forward to adjust the air-conditioning vents and then settled back, his head against the headrest. "Everything all right while I was away?"

"Fine. Susan's at Laurie's. Joby went up north surfing with some other boys in a camper. They had to come home the inland route because of the fire, but they made it all right."

"Oh, Christ, why do you let him get away with this stuff! He'd have been a hell of a lot better off at home doing some algebra for a change."

"Jim, we are going to have to have a talk about Joby. And about several other things."

"All right! Just give me a couple days to clear my head, for God's sakes! It's going to be a tough week at the office."

And then, out of a silence, he said, "Did you go to the ballet last night?"

"No, I didn't," she said, her eyes upon the road.

After that the car was still except for the purr of the engine and the air-conditioning. He did not open his eyes again until they were off the freeway, drifting through the curves of Sunset Boulevard toward the sea.

"Hey, we're nearly there," he said suddenly, pulling himself upright in the seat. "I must have been asleep."

"Good. Do you feel better?"

"Not terribly." He bent down to peer at the sky ahead and then reached for the radio buttons. "My God, look at that smoke pouring out over the ocean! Are you sure the McClures are still there?"

"I hope so. At least they'll have plenty of help tonight if they have to evacuate later on. Incidentally, I'm rather worried about Nancy Friedman."

"Not her again! Now what's her problem?"

"No problem that I know of. But Dave phoned just before I left. She went out this morning saying she was going to hunt for rocks for the garden, and she isn't home yet. It really isn't like her. Actually, we'd planned to go together, but I missed her call. I suppose it's possible that she drove to Malibu and got caught up there when they closed the highway."

"Don't worry about it. If she's in Malibu, she's so busy running the whole firefighting operation that she's just forgotten to phone home."

"Jim, honestly! Sometimes you really are very unkind about poor Nan."

"Yeah, sure. Too brainy by far, that one, and no sense of humor that I ever noticed." He yawned once more, stretched, and turned to look at her: her smooth, dark head beside him, her face pale but glowing, small hands upon the wheel, silky white jersey sleeves falling away from her arms.

"My God, you look super tonight! Is that a new dress?"

"It's a pantsuit actually, and you've seen it a dozen times. It was too bloody hot to dress."

He pushed radio buttons idly, searching for another news report. "You look great anyway. Incidentally, how would you like to go out and buy yourself a diamond bracelet or something?"

"Wait, aren't they talking about another fire?"

"Well, there's one over near Benedict, you know. Besides the big one in the Valley."

"Fantastic, it's all going! Here's to Nathanael West!"

"What do you mean?"

"*The Burning of Los Angeles*, remember? Tonight looks like the night."

"You're in a strange mood, I must say. I mean it, by the way, about the diamond bracelet. We're celebrating."

"Absolutely!" She glanced at him briefly and then looked back to the road, the heavy car swinging through another curve. "What are you celebrating?"

"Well, I got the NASA contract, for one thing."

"Very good. You said it was important."

"It has ramifications. I'll spare you all the ins and outs, but in about a month now, I imagine, I'll finally be moving into the old man's office."

"Jim! Are you sure?"

"Yeah."

"Darling! How absolutely marvelous! And about time. You've worked so damn hard for it for so long, and there's no one on earth who's more competent to sit at that desk." She reached out to touch his hand quickly. "Congratulations, with all my heart. Are you happy about it?"

"I don't know. I suppose."

"You must be. I think this calls for a bathtub full of champagne or something really extravagant. I suppose it's between you and me though until it's official."

"Yes."

"Don't you really want to make an occasion of this? We could chuck the McClures and fly up to San Francisco to dinner, paint the town a little. Would you like to?"

"Yeah, I'm in great shape tonight to paint the town! Thanks anyway. I'll settle for the McClures and an early evening."

"It seems a shame for you."

"By the way, I meant what I said a minute ago. I was kidding about diamonds, I know you don't like them. But I would like you to go out and get yourself something you'd really like to have." He leaned forward and shut off the radio. "I suppose I don't tell you often enough. You're my right arm, I don't know how I'd function without you. I can't imagine being married to any other woman in the world. You— Well, I appreciate everything you are, Cyn."

Her mouth twitched, and she struggled to control it, tears shining in her eyes. "Jim, don't! I'll be slamming into a tree in a minute."

He laughed and leaned over to kiss her lightly on the cheek. "Not you," he said. "You're the reliable type. I trust my life with you completely. Now I'm serious about this. Tell me what you want for a present."

She was dabbing at her eyes with a finger, taking care not to smear her mascara.

"Let's see," she said. "What would I most like to have. A divorce."

He laughed again. "Funny lady!" he said, vastly amused. "Oh my God, look! The whole street is full of cars! You didn't tell me this was going to be a super bash. I thought it was just a dinner party."

He leaned over the seat, reaching for his suitcoat in the back.

5

Pete

BONE TIRED, TOWARD THE END OF THAT NIGHT-mare day, Pete went for a brief swim. After cooling off he would volunteer once more, wherever his services might be needed. He swam the beach between the house and the cove, finding rest and renewal in the cold water. He came in at last reluctantly, pausing at the water's edge to remove his rubber flippers.

The air was stunningly hot still, filled with the sifting ash and the unique stench of the fire. The entire sky was covered over with smoke, and a lurid reddish brown light lay over the land and upon the glassy sea. Ridge after ridge of flames were visible upon the hills, as well as the flashing red lights of countless fire and emergency vehicles. The highway nearby was closed, eerily devoid of traffic; there were only the ululating wail of sirens, near and far, a distant howling of dogs, and the faint chatter from hundreds of transistor radios turned to the same news station. The uncanny wind still blew from the land, gusting hot against his face and stirring his wet hair.

Pete had not eaten since breakfast early that morning. His mind was still and empty as a cup. He fumbled at a rubber fin and suddenly froze, transfixed at the water's edge with a shock of recognition. He had the sudden sense that the land to which he must return was in fact an environment unnatural and alien to his needs.

It was there for only a flash, a revelation, an emotion. Pete's eyes were fixed upon the burning hills, and out of some well-spring of fierce emotion, he pronounced the wordless threat:

You've had your chance, now watch out! Watch out! He glimpsed in that blink of time a nebulous vision of a new society, one that lived more simply and honestly and in harmony with nature and the sea.

Then it was gone and consciously forgotten, sinking away into some deep chasm of his mind. It would stay with him, however, through the remainder of his life, and shade all the decisions he would make.

Pete left the sea and strode up onto the land.

ABOUT THE AUTHOR

MARITTA WOLFF was born on December 25, 1918, in Grass Lake, Michigan, where she grew up on her grandparents' farm and attended a one-room country school. At the age of twenty-two, after graduating the University of Michigan as a Phi Beta Kappa with a bachelor's degree in English composition, her Hopwood Award–winning novel *Whistle Stop* was published by Random House in 1941, going through five printings and earning glowing reviews for her raw, vital characters. A special Armed Forces edition of *Whistle Stop* brought a flood of letters from servicemen and began her lifelong practice of writing to her fans.

Wolff moved to Los Angeles in the late 1940s. A year after her first husband, author Hubert Skidmore, died in a house fire she married Leonard Stegman. They had one son, Hugh. Between 1941 and 1962 Wolff wrote and published five more novels. After a disagreement with her publisher, her seventh novel was not published and languished in a refrigerator until after her death on July 1, 2002.

POCKET
BOOKS

Pocket Books is proud to announce a new publication of Maritta Wolff's bestselling masterwork, *Whistle Stop*. Originally published in 1941, this unforgettable story of passion, crime and family provides a gripping portrait of post-Depression America.

'*Whistle Stop* has a kind of raw, flaming vitality which it was impossible to resist, plus and uncanny, ironic knowledge of human motives . . . It was obvious that Miss Wolff possessed that unquenchable interest in people which is part of the born novelist's equipment and that her vein of rich invention was unlikely to run dry'   *The New York Times Book Review*, 1942

ISBN 1 4165 1157 1